"Shields," I said into the helmet's communicator. "Call in."

Electricity buzzed. Force fields flared. Before us, the leeward port to the satellite Khramya swelled like a steel eyeball, crisscrossed with strips of shiny red explosive.

"Shields in north and east wings, Ana," said a crackling voice in my ear. "We're a go."

"South is a go, too," said another voice. "We've got *Surpresan* at our backs, Admiral."

"West is a go," I said. "*Videiran*, that's a five on detonation."

"Thank you, sir," said the voice of *Videiran*'s comms officer. "Four." I nodded at my lieutenant Ludon to my left, who nodded back and bent his knees. "Three," said the ship. "Two—"

Back in Alectelo, my lady Szayet liked to ask me about the conquest of Madinabia, about my battles with barbarian chiefs. I liked to tell her a story worth the telling, whether or not it was true—substituting a duel for a long afternoon's treaty negotiation, a siege for three weeks counting supplies. She always knew, and she always laughed. *You have no talent for lies*, she'd say. *I'm sure that's what you would have done, if you'd been your own master. What's the truth?*

Well, now I was my own master, and so now there was no one to stop me and my men from applying explosives to every locked door. *Not everything needs to be brute-forced*, said a dry voice out of my memories, and, *You'll hurt yourself, Captain, one of these days*. It was such a pleasure to hear that voice.

"One," said the ship. "Go."

The door roared.

By Emery Robin

Empire Without End
The Stars Undying
The Sea Eternal

THE
SEA
ETERNAL

EMPIRE WITHOUT END:
BOOK TWO

EMERY ROBIN

orbit-books.co.uk

ORBIT

First published in Great Britain in 2025 by Orbit

13 5 7 9 10 8 6 4 2

A CIP catalogue record for this book
is available from the British Library.

ISBN 978-0-356-51940-1

Printed and bound in Great Britain by Clays Ltd, Elcograf, S.p.A.

Papers used by Orbit are from well-managed forests
and other responsible sources.

Orbit
An imprint of
Little, Brown Book Group
Carmelite House
50 Victoria Embankment
London, EC4Y 0DZ

The authorised representative
in the EEA is
Hachette Ireland
8 Castlecourt Centre
Dublin 15, D15 XTP3, Ireland
(email: info@hbgi.ie)

An Hachette UK Company
www.hachette.co.uk

orbit-books.co.uk

To my great-grandmother, who I used to be named after

THE GALAXY AND ITS PEOPLES

(Or at least the ones A. thought were important.)

THE CROSSBAR: A galactic spiral arm. Celestial bodies include:

CEIAO: The greatest planet in the galaxy. *(According to some.)* Capital is the city of Ceiao, language is Ceian (except among the wealthy, who speak Sintian). Homeworld of the Ceian Empire. After a revolution against its tyrannical priest caste, Ceiao banned religion for one hundred and fifty years. The ban has recently been relaxed.

- **Ana "Anita" Decretan.** Part-time admiral, Demipotestate, and lady of the Swordbelt Arm and the Crossbar. *(Full-time drunk.)* Former right hand to deceased commander Matheus Ceirran. At his funeral, delivered a speech that sparked a citywide riot and drove his assassins into exile. Lover to Altagracia Caviro Patramata, Oracle of Szayet. On Szayet, she is referred to as Ceirran's "disciple." *(She allows this for reasons best known to herself.)*
- **Lieutenant Cardean, Lieutenant Ludon, Crewman Ruzhaya.** Ana's sworn men.
- **Galvão Orcadan.** Former captain to Matheus Ceirran, now captain to Ana Decretan.

- **Otávio Julhan.** Full-time admiral, Demipotestate, and lord of Arqueiran and the Shieldmirror. *(Part-time human being.)* Matheus Ceirran's cousin. Heir to his fortune, and to his name. *(Don't forget to change this name to "Otávio Julhan Ceirran" once my spider-litter crosses into the city of Ceiao proper.)*
- **Captain Águeda Vipsânian, Captain Cecílio Maicenan.** Otávio's childhood friends, now his sworn men.
- **Flavia Decretan.** Ana's sister. Excellent party hostess. Patron of organized crime.
- **Teo Pulcron.** Flavia's former husband. Patron of organized crime, and later rebel against the Merchants' Council. Died by execution after his rebellion failed.
- **Sonia Couron.** Ana's childhood friend and former lover. Died in battle.
- **Mara Decretan.** Ana and Flavia's mother. Died of illness.
- **Túlio Cachoeiran.** Rhetorician, philosopher, politician, lawyer, patriot, master of the Ceian tongue. Enemy of Matheus Ceirran. Died after betraying Ceirran to his assassins.
- **Quinha Semfontan.** Former friend and mentor to Matheus Ceirran, later his enemy. Killed on Arcelia Caviro's orders after losing a civil war against Ceirran.
- **Jonata Barran.** Assassin of Matheus Ceirran. Died after losing the Battle of Micavalli to Ana.
- **Cátia Lançan.** Assassin of Matheus Ceirran. Died after losing the Battle of Micavalli to Ana.
- **Patrícia Laubian.** Assassin of Matheus Ceirran. *(Not dead yet.)*

- **Matheus Ceirran.** Commander of Ceiao. Friend to the Ceian poor and savior of the Ceian Empire; a bloody tyrant. Died by assassination. *(If he's really dead at all.)*

SINTIA: The birthplace of civilization. *(According to some.)* Capital is Sintielo, where most wealthy Ceians attend school. Language is Sintian. The Sintian language's ancestor is Malisintian, which is still used for religious purposes among worshippers of Alekso of Sintia.

- **Alekso of Sintia.** A tyrant. Three hundred years ago, conquered most of the Crossbar and the Swordbelt Arm. In the process, he knocked Ceiao several degrees off its axis, exploded Szayet's moon, caused assorted environmental and human rights disasters, etc. Across his former empire, except in Ceiao, he is worshipped as a god. Known on Szayet as Alekso Undying and known on Kutayet as the Holy Flame of the Swordbelt. *(And the way the Ceians talk, you'd think he's the only one who's ever destroyed a world.)* His body now rests on Szayet, in a tomb on the Isle of the Dead.
- **Caviro Orakolo.** Alekso's lover and disciple. Settled on Szayet after his death. Ancestor of *Dom* Caviro, the Szayeti royal house, and first Oracle of Szayet.

MICAVALLI: A planet near Sintia. Site of the last battle against Ceirran's assassins.

CEIAO 20M3: A dead planet. One of the Vigesimal Colonies of Ceiao (the name given to colonies orbiting the stars Ceiao 20 through Ceiao 29). Once it had a forest, and once it had mountains, and once it had a great and saltless sea. *(And once it had a name, and the name was Tenessa.)*

- **V.'s father.** A refugee. Died of radiation sickness.
- **V.** A poet.

THE SWORDBELT ARM: A galactic spiral arm, bordering the Crossbar. Celestial bodies include:

KUTAYET: Homeworld of the Kutayeti Empire. Language is Kutayeti. Alekso's greatest and most difficult conquest. It is ruled by an emperor, and its royal house is *Dom* Harsaky.
- **Sasha Vualo.** An ambassador.
- **Carmela Lukhaya.** A scholar.
- **Polina Harsakaya.** A prince.

SANCTA MIRTALO: A planet in the Kutayeti Empire. Home to the emperor's winter palace, Roof-without-Rain, located in a vast desert.

KHRAMYA: A satellite in the Kutayeti Empire. The emperor's rose garden.
- **Maral os-Margad.** A teenage girl.

THE FORTUNATAS: A set of rings around a planet deep in the Kutayeti Empire, near the Black Maw. Legendary and possibly nonexistent.

SZAYET: Ceian client world. An ocean planet, dotted with a few islands. Capital is Alectelo, languages are Sintian and Szayeti. The resting place of Alekso of Sintia's body. Home to the Library of Alectelo, the greatest archive and research facility in the galaxy.
- **Altagracia "Gracia" Caviro Patramata.** Oracle and queen of Szayet. Caviro's ten-times-great-granddaughter. Twin sister to Arcelia. Bearer of the Pearl of

THE GALAXY AND ITS PEOPLES

the Dead, a tiny quicksilver pearl computer said to contain Alekso's soul. Like all Oracles before her, she rules *(or claims to rule)* the planet exactly as he commands her to. As of Matheus Ceirran's death, she now bears *(or claims to bear)* a second Pearl of the Dead, which holds Ceirran's living soul. Recently dredged the Szayeti oceans of their treasure, making herself and Szayet fabulously wealthy. Lover to Ana Decretan. *(And how.)*

- **Zorione.** Altagracia's maid. Raised Altagracia and her sister from childhood.
- **Delio.** Altagracia's minister of war.
- **Sister Constanza.** A priestess and librarian.

OSTRAYET: Szayet's moon. The Ostrayeti people enslaved the Szayeti people. Alekso of Sintia shattered the moon into three pieces, flooding Szayet and sinking almost all its wealth and resources beneath the ocean. After the shattering, the Szayeti people worshipped Alekso as liberator and god.

ITSARYET: Ceian colony. Conquered by Quinha Semfontan. A planet near the border of the Kutayeti Empire. Home to an ancient temple to Alekso Undying, now a prison ruled by jailer-priestesses.

- **Arcelia "Celia" Caviro Diomata.** Former oracle and queen of Szayet. Twin sister to Altagracia. Bearer of the Pearl of the Dead after her father's death; ruled until Altagracia launched a civil war against her. With the help of Matheus Ceirran, Altagracia seized the Pearl of the Dead and the throne.
- **Sister Božena.** A young priestess.

MEDVEYET: Ceian colony. Its prince is rumored to have had an affair with Matheus Ceirran in his youth.

BELKAYET: Ceian colony. Former Szayeti colony, hundreds of years ago.

CHEREKKU: Ceian colony. Conquered by Quinha Semfontan. A secretive planet ruled by a king and a council of priests.

PLYUSNA: A satellite. The Oracle of Szayet met Ana Decretan here in an enormous barge, declared Ana the Disciple of Matheus Ceirran, and *(somehow or other)* won her heart.

THE SHIELDMIRROR: A galactic spiral arm, bordering the Crossbar on its other side. Celestial bodies include:

MADINABIA: A gas giant surrounded by a series of moons. Matheus Ceirran made himself famous by conquering these, with Ana Decretan's help. In the process of being settled by Ceiao.

FAR MADINABIA: A neighbor to Madinabia. Otávio Julhan and Ceirran met here shortly before Ceirran's death. In the process of being settled by Ceiao.

THE BLACK MAW: Also called the Great Maw, the Well of Souls. The center of the galaxy. A darkness.

I'll have to remember to cross out all these little notes before I reach Ceiao, in case someone—a doctor, or an attendant, or (God forbid) C. himself—catches sight of this notebook. Hell, perhaps it would be better to rid myself of this whole list of names. I wish I didn't have to keep these kinds of notes at all. Only my mind wanders, and I'm tired…

—V.

Goddess, tell me the story.

PART I

IN THE MIDDLE OF THINGS—

One fine summer day, when the birds were singing and the lindens had flowered and the sun had come to rest on the ripples in the river, a woman bashed her sister's skull in with a rock. So the city of Ceiao was born.

Don't like it? Well, it's only one story. Here's another: Long ago, so long ago that the days were too new to be counted, a great ship landed on a fine and fertile planet. Out streamed the people, men and women, noble and brave. They had come from a faraway city by the sea, these brave and noble people, a city where a war had been lost and all their fine towers had burned. They had fled a long way. And their leader was the noblest and bravest of them all, because building Ceiao was his destiny, and because he was the son of a god, and because he always did as he was told.

When I was young, my neighbors would tell me that the people of the second story made Ceians in their image, strong and disciplined, upright and hardworking, uncorrupted and chaste and dutiful, enlightened and enlighteners and explorers and leaders of men. For all I know, it may have even been true. That was beside the point. It was for children, and so it wasn't the truth but the lesson that mattered: Home is wherever you can take it. This is the beginning of empires.

You asked for a story. Before I begin, let me tell you the truth: I think now that the woman of the first story made Ceians in her image, too.

At the highest point of heaven there was a spark, and the spark danced, and as it danced it grew and licked with a red tongue out at the dark and at the jagged half-moons, and it spat out light and shouted, and the seagulls cried and hurled themselves off the ships and the harbor-gate and beat frantically toward the west. Through the light shot one—two—three dozen steel dots, flashing through smoke, weaving, screaming toward the town below.

"A message for you, Disciple," said a servant into my ear. "Urgent news from Ceiao."

"Go away," I said, and emptied my gun at the sky.

The drones burst. Where they'd hung in the sky, scraps fluttered, ashes falling—then, as they drifted toward the torches and strings of lanterns and flashing violet lamps, the light caught them, and the crowd that had gathered before the royal palace shrieked and leapt up, hands scrabbling in the air, snatching the flakes of gold to their chests, turning up their faces to let them fall into their open mouths.

A palace official threw her hands up. "Twenty-one confirmed hits to Admiral Decretan!" she bellowed. "The Honored Disciple wins again!"

The noblemen around me burst into applause. So did the crowd, hooting and whistling, waving cups and tankards in my direction. I let my gun fall, and so did the Szayeti next to me, a long-haired young man in the palace guard. The official stomped her feet for attention. "The prize!" she shouted, gesturing. Around the side of the steps, puffing and panting, came two of my soldiers, carrying an enormous silver platter stacked with bottles of wine.

Fire streaked across the sky again, green this time, then blue.

Behind it, an eye opened up in the black, and resolved itself into a glittering golden falcon, which spread its wings and became two leaping cats, four silver crocodiles, eight asps winding down the sky toward the horizon, a holo-forest of shining kelp curling back up from the sea and bursting into sunflowers.

I thrust my fist in the air. "Give them to the people!" I bellowed.

The Alectelans roared, surging up. The platter tumbled immediately and vanished. A dozen hands reached out and bore me up onto the people's shoulders, a riot of hot flesh and drunken voices, the river of stars rolling and swaying above me, the buildings of the Bolvardo del Tombo bobbing along the corner of my eye. Women smacked kisses onto my cheeks. Wine spilled over my mouth and down my shirt collar. I whooped, shouted, stuck my tongue out for people to drop sweets onto it, and somewhere around the third street corner fell out of their arms and into a circle dance. The dancers were screaming the words to a song I didn't know, something Sintian, and when I howled nonsense syllables in time they shrieked with laughter, tugged me back toward the palace, and shoved me toward the woman waiting at the base of the steps.

"My lady," I called, swaying, and held out a hand.

Fireworks burst again. Szayet's smile flared gold. She seized me and spun into my arms.

When we had come down to the streets of Alectelo this morning to begin the festival day, her hair had been braided tightly back, her kohl in neat wings beneath the jade on her eyelids, her crown straight and gleaming on her brow. Now that we'd paraded up and down the Bolvardo del Tombo, cheered on the footraces, feasted on fish and beer and fresh cherries with the crowd at the Summer Market, and rowed out into the harbor to light the first fireworks, the kohl had smeared across her temple and the pads of my fingers, the crown sat askew, the hair hung loose and sweet-smelling over her bare brown shoulders. I'd been dragging my fingers through that hair not half an hour ago, when we'd ducked into an alleyway near the Summer Market, and she'd walked me up against the wall and pushed her thigh between my legs and her hands under my shirt.

"What is this," she said into my ear now, "the fifteenth time you've won an athletics contest against the Alectelans this week? The sixteenth?"

I tilted my neck invitingly. She laughed and kissed me there, lingering to dig her teeth briefly into my pulse. "Fortune loves me," I said.

"Someone certainly loves you," she said, took my chin in two fingers, and caught my mouth in a long, slow, hungry kiss, her hand sliding round my waist and drifting down with interest.

Her mouth was bittersweet with wine and magnificently warm, and the rain spattering my neck was a nasty shock of cold. I shivered and pulled away. Deep clouds were collecting over the palace, blurring the poppies and monkey flowers still sketching themselves in light across the sky. Weather always came on so damn quick in this town, I thought—you couldn't trust its sky any more than its queen. At the palace door stood the messenger who'd said *Ceiao* to me before I'd shot at the drones. She'd been waiting; now she grimaced at the sky, pulled her hood over her head, and turned to duck into the dry hall.

Szayet caught the direction of my gaze. Her hand stopped moving, to my great annoyance. "The courtiers will want to celebrate your victory," she said into my ear. "Your officers will want to celebrate, too."

"We don't have to go in," I said to her dark eyelashes, her half-open lips, the wink of quicksilver pearl in her ear. "We could just stay here, you and I, until it all goes dark."

"You always say that," she murmured.

"It's always true," I murmured back.

We were drunk with sun as much as we were with wine, and with laughter more than either. When I blinked, I could still feel flecks of gold on my lashes. The shadows of the great sand-stone statues leaned over the palace steps, peering thoughtfully at Szayet's crown. To my left, smooth-faced and pale-eyed, its mouth hooked up in a sneer: Alekso of Sintia, called here the Undying. I had never seen that face outside of statues and paintings. Only two living people ever had, and one was locked in a cell on Itsaryet, and the other was striding ahead of me toward the palace's double doors.

To my right, though—older than Alekso but no less hand-some, a long scar curving along his jaw, his smile faint and unreadable—a face that I knew as well as I knew my own. Sometimes I thought I'd known it better. It was five hundred and fifty-one days since I had found my friend Matheus Ceirran's hacked-apart corpse, and three hundred and forty days since I had last touched Ceian soil, and twenty-nine days since I had last gone to bed sober. Nothing in the world was wrong with me, and I was spectacularly happy.

There were two guards at the door, one Szayeti and one Ceian. The Szayeti fell to their knees. "Holiest Oracle," they shouted over the noise of the flutes. "A blessed Feast of the Ship Boka-palo to you," and when Szayet gestured them up, they scrambled to their feet and bowed deeply to me. "Beloved Disciple."

The Ceian guard was rolling a sílfion cigarette. She caught my eye and smirked. I grinned back. "You keep telling me so," I said.

Almost a year of breathing her air meant that Szayet no lon-ger had to glare at me. It was just as good a thrill, anyway, to know that she wanted to. I grinned at her, too, and slipped my hand around her waist.

"We've received an urgent message from Ceiao, Disciple," said the Ceian. "It says—"

"Not now, it doesn't. Like hell Ceiao is seeing me before I've had a bath," I said. "We'll eat at the dice tables, I think. Does that suit my lady?"

"Well enough," said Szayet, though her expression had grown still flatter. "Tell the kitchen to bring up whichever boar has finished roasting."

They bowed again to her and pulled the doors open. Noise tumbled down the steps, into the night.

A dozen Szayeti nobles burst toward us in a cloud of thick perfume, laughing and shouting tuneless love songs, clinging to one another's arms. They paused to sweep deep and elegant bows— first to Szayet, then to me—and went swaying toward the street, calling out to strangers, waving bejeweled hands. From within the hall two dozen more arms reached out to us, encrusted with rings and bracelets—a jungle of bright eyes, pipes shrieking, incense billowing out into the dusk, blue and red light, *Holiest, Anita, Oracle, Anita, Queen, Anita—*

Szayet caught an outstretched hand and was gone. I struck a match on the doorframe, lit the Ceian soldier's cigarette, and paused briefly at the Szayeti guard's side—*how's your latest lover, that's a crying shame, cards tomorrow night in the cellars, I won't forget*—and went without haste into the throng.

Once I had charged through this hall in the middle of a gunfight, and pockmarked the granite pillars with fire, and torn the tapestries, and smashed the mosaics on the floor. Now the pillars were green marble, the ceiling was new curved glass, the walls were scattered with lanterns winking in every color, and the floor was scuffed with five hundred moving feet. Bodies pressed close on each side of me, hands on my shoulders, hands on my thighs. One of my soldiers pressed a wine cup into my hand. I tossed it back at once and reached out blindly for another.

Here were drummers, here were timbrel players. Here were dancers on the balconies, dressed in gauze and necklaces of lilies.

Here were basins of ice carved in the shapes of women, their bellies stacked high with black grapes and white melon and their arms and feet already melting onto the floor, dancers splashing barefoot in the puddles. I snatched an infant squid from a platter spilling over with shellfish, stumbled, fell into a platinum tree stretching its arms up to the ceiling—here were leaves made of gold and fruit of diamonds, here were living ivy and bougainvillea hanging down from their branches between twisting silk ribbons. Four dozen hummingbirds fluttered round the ceiling and darted down to light on the branches.

Up the stairs, to the landing where mechanical ostrich-feathered fans waved clouds of perfume down across the crowd—from this height I could see the whole curving shore of Alectelo: a handful of Ceian ships with wings folded up in the harbor, the crowd on the boulevard still dancing as the sky flashed from bronze to honey and the rain shimmered down, horses galloping round the new racetrack, noblemen diving in the marble-lined hot springs in the courtyard, a pair of tigers pacing through our rooftop garden. Around the side of the balcony, a three-headed stone serpent spouted wine, frankincense-scented water, honey. I dunked my cup in the foaming mixture at its base and threw it back. Down the stairs again, and here were more fireworks, little ones, green and violet sparks spitting up from the floor, stinging the bare thigh of a Sintian girl who shrieked with laughter and fell into the arms of a palace guard. Here a circle dance, tripping left toward the musicians—here two more of my soldiers and a Szayeti girl, pressed up against the wall together, hands moving over one another's hips—and here my lady again, sandwiched between two wide-eyed noblewomen, rolling her dice in her hand.

I slipped my arms around her waist. She startled and threw: two ones, two fours.

"Your luck's run out," I whispered into her ear.

She twisted in my arms and cupped my jaw with her free hand and kissed me slow, slow, until I shivered and gave in and opened up for her, and then she pulled back and said, "What did you mean, *You keep telling me so*?"

"What? Nothing," I said, and went to catch her mouth with mine again, but she laid her hand over my lips and I had to settle for flicking my tongue over the pad of her finger. "If you mean to begin whipping me when I blaspheme, you're a little late," I said against her palm. "There's a few years' worth of it to catch up on by now."

"I don't believe in too late," she said.

The swift and unwanted thought came to me of the scarred sandstone face outside. "That's where I part from you, I'm afraid," I said. At that her face tightened, and I grinned an easy grin and said swiftly, "Well, it's too late for you to strip me down and have your way with me back in that alley by the Summer Market, isn't it?"

"Hm," she said. The girl beside her had thrown four threes, and was pulling gleaming stacks of dekar into her bust while her friend laughed. Szayet scooped up the dice without looking and threw again: three sixes. The dealer burst into applause, but Szayet slipped out of my arms.

"Let's go upstairs," she said.

The noise of the party did not fade when we were in her rooms. The noise of the party never did. It drifted sometimes, to the shore or to outlying taverns, or it dimmed to the faint murmur of laughter and one flute—that was usually when I would muster up defiance against my hangover and descend again, dressed in a pink feather coat and bearing three bottles of Ceiao's best in my fists, roaring for all my best soldiers to come and see. But to my knowledge, whether we were there or no, whether it was market day or a holiday or a day when any decent person would have been working, whether it rained or shone or blew hurricanes from the west, the party had never yet died.

Now, while the kitharas thrummed under our feet and muffled whoops echoed over the sea, my lady held her hair away from the nape of her neck. I untied the fastening on her dress, pausing occasionally to kiss the curve of her shoulder, the high knob of her spine. Ordinarily, she would even let me leave marks on her here—one, fading purple, stained the nape of her neck like wine—but now, when my mouth lingered too long on her jaw, Szayet pushed away from me and let the loose fabric unfold itself down from her breasts to her hips to her legs.

She stepped out of the pooled cotton and went to the mirror by her window. I allowed myself to sit still and look at her, which I had not yet had my fill of today: her dark red mouth, her wide soft thighs, the long and nimble fingers of her hands. She was looking at me, too, but if what was in her face was hunger, I didn't recognize it. I could think of no reason for her to be hungry, in any case. My hair was stiff with salt wind from the harbor, my arms and legs the usual mess of old scars and muscle gone soft. My clothes were fleet clothes—a blue tunic, a soldier's belt, well-worn boots. I looked, I thought, exactly as I had looked every single day since she'd met me on the Ceian docks when we'd both been young. From the tablet I'd left on the bedside table, a red seal blinked urgently: a message from my sister, Flavia. I stepped casually to the left, so that her shoulder obscured it from me.

"Disciple," said Szayet.

"Yes?" I said.

"You answer to it when it suits you, then," she said.

"Oh, I do everything if it suits me," I said, coming toward her. "I eat and drink, if it suits me, and I come when I'm called, if it suits me. And if it suits me—" I took her hand, ducking my head to press my open mouth to her palm, but she pulled away.

"I told you I bought a new dress, didn't I?" she said. "From that new weavers' studio down by the Winter Market."

Bewildered at the change of subject, I retreated to her bed. "You told me," I said. She had a thousand pet businesses springing up around Alectelo and all the southern islands: tailors here, painters there, pearlsmiths and vintners and glassmakers and starfighter racers. Szayet, as the letters piling up in my tablet from the Merchants' Council informed me in tones of increasing irritation, needed less from Ceiao than Szayet ever had. That was well enough, to my mind. Why was I meant to give a damn whether there was Ceian steel hanging in the skies, or whether I spoke Ceian with my men at the harbor, or whether I treated with Ceian merchants at the Summer Market? It wasn't life-and-death, this place. It was only Alectelo.

Szayet went to her wardrobe, bare feet silent on the carpet, and lifted the dress carefully out. It was a liquid silky red thing, a low-cut collar and ribbons floating out at its back. Around its hem and up the skirt, gold and black crossed and crisscrossed: Sintian shape and Szayeti pattern, a mixture unmistakably of this place.

She held it out and looked at me. It took me a moment to understand what she meant. When I did, I grinned, uncertain.

She didn't smile back. My humor died. I swallowed. "It won't fit," I said.

"Perhaps not," she said, face unreadable. "Still. You'll do as you're told, won't you?"

Fortune help me, I thought, and I shed my clothes and stepped into the skirt of the dress. She smoothed the fabric up my sides, over my chest—it was too big, I'd thought, and I had been right, but she pulled the ribbons sharply at my back, and I gasped, and then the dress was tight against me, as tight as binding rope.

"Sit," she said, turning to the wardrobe without looking to see whether I would obey her.

I sat. On my knees, over my thighs, the silk ran as smooth as water. When I looked down at myself, it was like seeing two sheets of glass laid over each other: from my knees downward, my own familiar legs and feet, and then up, my belly and my breasts, Szayet, Szayet as she must appear to her own eyes.

She turned back, now holding a terra-cotta pot in her hand, and she came toward me and settled herself on my thighs, a warm weight. "Be still," she said, "and don't blink."

The kohl stick trailed over one eyelid, then the other. When she leaned back and I blinked at last, I could feel the heaviness, faint and wet.

"Open," she said.

I opened my mouth. Her right thumb pressed into my lip. Her left took my chin, holding it steady. In her eyes was a look of focus I rarely saw. Now I was not breathing.

She slid off my lap, went to the table again, and returned with two strings of pink pearls. "Bow your head," she said, and when I did, she looped one around my throat and lifted my wrist to fasten the other. At last she stood back.

"Come to the mirror," she said.

When she had begun, I had thought I would laugh. I would look grotesque, I thought, like a costume party, a theater clown. The reflection in the mirror was not ugly. It was unrecognizable. The mouth that twitched redly in its face, the hips and waist under the delicate silk, were not a soldier's, they were not a Ceian's. The black eyes within the black kohl were hardly human. They were the eyes of an insect—of a creature I did not know.

"Now I am Ana Decretan," she said, just behind my shoulder, "and you are Patramata."

"I'm not," I said, turning.

"You are," she said, and laid her cool hand on my cheek and kissed me and bit hard at my lip. Her mouth came away red. "You are my client queen, and I am the lady of the Swordbelt Arm. Lie back on the bed."

I stepped back and fell onto the pillows. She took the hem of the skirt and lifted it, and then her hand was on me, fingers working, and I swallowed and swallowed and could not speak. "Do you like this, Madam Oracle?" she said. "Do you like it, Altagracia?"

"Szayet, please," I managed to gasp.

"But you are Szayet," she said. "Open your legs, dear heart."

I threw my hand over my eyes. The pearls moved coldly and roughly over my skin. I could feel the kohl smear against them. My legs were open, and her hand was between them, and her naked animal's body clambered over mine and held it down, and I opened my red mouth and said nothing at all.

When I woke, my head was pounding. Grey morning slanted in through the window, prickling warm air. I'd slept through the storm.

In the palace wing that Szayet had rebuilt after her civil war, a solarium jutted out precipitously over a maze of priests' quarters and palace gardens. Its roof and three of its walls were clear glass, tessellated with golden wire into hexagons, so that when I came through the door I felt I was walking into a wasp's nest. A dozen cages dangled from the ceiling. Hoopoes cooed inside, sidling along their perches in flutters of orange and black.

Szayet was sitting cross-legged on one of her silk cushions, wearing a loose blue robe embroidered with peonies and eating a peach. Cushions had to be replaced rather more often than not in an aviary, but she'd told me she judged it a worthwhile expense. "Sit down," she said. "There's bread and honey left for you."

I approached carefully, eyeing her to see if she intended any sudden moves, and sat. She bent over my hands and began to apply honeycomb carefully to a brown slice of bread.

"An ambassador from your colony Cherekku came to court the day before last," she said. "You remember, of course, the war brewing between the puppet king Ceiao installed on Cherekku ten years ago and the priests' council there."

"Mmph," I said in knowledgeable tones around the honeycomb.

"Well, the ambassador was from the priests," said Szayet. "They're very low on funds, as are their enemies, and they've come to me for help. The ambassador says, if the priests are victorious in convincing Ceiao to install a different puppet king, Cherekku can offer very favorable trade deals to Szayet. But my foreign minister suggests we can do better than trade deals. He says that we could convince the priests to permanently accept a Szayeti into the council."

About one-fifth of this speech I understood. I blinked politely at her. "Mmmmph."

"Two hundred years ago, Szayet had colonies," said Szayet. "We lost them when we were poor. We became Ceiao's client state in those days, and we fell into Ceiao's debt. Now we are still Ceiao's client, but we are wealthy beyond imagination. Our neighbors beg us for favors, and we may force them into whatever terms we find favorable. Of course, now our neighbors are all Ceiao's colonies—" She paused for me to interject. I did not. Her mouth flattened. "Should I do it, then?" she said. "Arrange to install a representative of Alekso and Ceirran Undying in one of Ceiao's possessions?"

My eyes went involuntarily to her ear. A silver pearl sat in it, gold wires curling around her helix and into her temple. In the pearl's center shone a deep black fingerprint.

I'd seen her dip her finger in ink and press it to the pearl herself. I'd seen her proclaim to her people and to my gathered soldiers that this pearl held the soul of Matheus Ceirran, the immortal and undying—that Ceirran had chosen her as his Oracle, so that for the rest of her days she would be the bearer of not one god, but two. I'd seen her show the priests a smooth, unmarked pearl in her ear, and tell them that this was Alekso's soul, and the marked one was Ceirran's, and the mark would tell them which of her two Pearls she bore that day, and which of Szayet's two gods spoke through her now.

I was the only person in the world besides her who knew that there was only one Pearl of the Dead. The one that should have been Ceirran's immortal soul had been dissolved in a cup of wine by Cátia Lançan, one of Ceirran's assassins. Alekso had helped her build that Pearl in exchange for a promise that she would abdicate the throne and proclaim her sister his Oracle. She had broken that promise, and she and her god had not spoken in over a year.

Honey dripped onto her first knuckle. She put it absently to her mouth and sucked, and I saw a black streak on the calloused pad of her finger. The memory of my own eyes in the mirror, kohl-stained and unrecognizable, floated back to me. "Fine," I said.

"That's all?" said Szayet. "Fine?"

"Put whoever you like in whatever government you like," I said through a mouthful of bread. "Don't raise troops against me, I suppose. Why should it matter to me?"

"I have no interest in raising troops against you," she said with strained patience. "I thought it might matter to you whether or not we have a man loyal to Ceirran Undying in the government of one of Ceiao's colonies. Loyal to *Ceirran Undying*, Anita. Not to Ceiao." I still said nothing, and she said, "Does Ceirran's disciple think Ceirran wants Cherekku to liberalize its sex laws? Does Ceirran's disciple think Ceirran wants Cherekku to buy six thousand imperial tons of pearl from Szayet at outrageous rates?"

"What do *you* think he wants, Oracle?" I said.

"For Alectelo to be the crossroads of trade across three galactic spiral arms," said Szayet. "For a Library overflowing with books, and a sea overflowing with pearl, and land overflowing with green. For Sintian officials to speak both the Sintian and Szayeti tongues in official business—and for the Szayeti tongue to come to Cherekku, too, and even the court of the Kutayeti emperor, and Itsaryet, and all the rest of the neighboring worlds.

For new philosophy, and new theater, and new poetry, to suit a strange new future. For the Szayeti people to have power they haven't known for some five hundred years—for them to come out of the shadow of not only dead, broken Ostrayet, but out of the shadow of Alekso's Sintia, and Ceiao's shadow, too."

I shrugged, reaching for the honey pot. "You talk like you expect me to object."

She slid the pot away, and my hand closed on empty air. I grunted, outraged. She hissed through her teeth. "I speak in the hopes that you'll tell me what you want our god to say!" she said. "Greater financial support to the poor? Relaxation of immigration control? Hymns sung to his name at every morning and evening?"

Ceirran would have very much liked that last, I thought, and found myself suddenly in an ill temper. "Szayet, you and I are acting out a bad play. Write the lines for your god that you like best. Why should I care?" I said.

She'd let go of the honey pot. I snatched it up, dipped two fingers in it, and stuck them between my teeth. Szayet looked as though she wanted to smack the pot out of my hand. "Why should you *care*?" she said. "Anita, the people ask you to bring me their blessings at the docks. They bow to you in the gaming halls. They call you Honored and Beloved when they buy you drinks. They let you win sixteen athletics contests in the space of a week."

I wiped my mouth with the back of my hand. "More fools they," I said.

"More reverent," said Szayet warningly. "I have spent a good deal of gold and pearl, and risked a good deal of their love, asking them to be reverent toward Matheus Ceirran. Will you try to tell me that *you* don't understand how they feel?"

My first urge was to stand, call her one of the words I'd learned in the Szayeti bars, and stalk out of the room. I did not move. The air was too warm and thick, and my belly felt too full and sour, and my legs and my head too hot with last night's drink. Sweetness was suddenly cloying. I put down the honey and hunched over myself.

"Whenever you can't find a weakness in me, Szayet, you never hesitate to make one," I said.

At that her face went flat, and I knew that she, too, was thinking of last night. "What is *that* meant to signify?" she said.

"I'm not a clown from Diajunda," I said, "or one of these caged birds. I make a fool of myself on my own terms. So they call me Honored, so they call me Beloved—well, let them. Let them believe that Ceirran's turned from flesh and blood into some invisible magic. They can believe that I'll speak to him again. I've only ever called myself lady of the Swordbelt Arm."

"Who's calling you a fool?" Szayet said. "Who has called you a fool to your face in the last year? Ceirran's bones, Anita, you've slept near three hundred nights now in my bed, and you've slept a dozen more on the Alectelan streets to boot. How long do you mean to fear Ceian mockery? How long do you mean to laugh at my people behind their backs for naming you part of my cult and my court? How long do you mean to keep your wine and your laughter here, and your life somewhere else?"

"What's the difference?" I said, stung.

Her eyes grew cold. She opened her mouth, but before she could call me whatever name she meant to, there was a knock on the door. "Admiral Decretan," said a voice. "The morning's reports from Ceiao are in. You have an urgent message."

"Love and mercy," I muttered, wiped my sticky hand crudely on the cushion, and went to the door. "Galvão," I said, "I swear if Fortune herself tied her blindfold round your eyes, you wouldn't notice it was dark. Tell my sister this: She can take her message and—"

"It's from Admiral Otávio Julhan, sir. It's Patrícia Laubian," said Captain Galvão without ceremony. "An informer reported

from an asteroid not three thousand light-years from here—
Khramya, he says it's called. She's dug herself in there under a
false name."

My hand fell to my side. "You're certain?" I said.

He nodded. "Disguised, but it's her," he said. "The informer's
sure of it."

Councillor Patrícia Laubian. I could see her without having
to think: a pigeon-chested frame, a dozen chestnut braids, a face
under a dozen layers of bad cheap powder and worse expensive
paint. I had used to mock her behind her back for that, after
meetings ended, when he and I had been going down the stairs.

A year and a half ago, I had sat down with a boy called Julhan and made a list of two thousand names. A thousand chases
across the Swordbelt Arm, a thousand across the Crossbar; a
battle, a raid; a slit throat, a gut wound, a severed head. One by
one, the names on the list had dwindled, some by others' hands,
many by mine. Only one remained.

The last time I had seen Patrícia Laubian, there had been two
fat fingerprints of blood just below her temple, pressed into the
cheap powdered red. I had thought: She must have touched her
face, after she let go of the knife.

"Anita," said Szayet's voice behind me, sounding as if it were
coming from the far shore of the sea.

"Find four ships," I said to Galvão. "The fastest we have on the
beach. *Videiran* for a flagship, and then—*Irene*? Too vulnerable,
maybe, her engines are unarmored—no, that little snake won't
bring any guns. A hundred men for each crew."

His perpetual stiff expression cracked, and he grinned a soldier's kind of grin, wolfish and without teeth. "Sir," he said,
saluting.

"I want them ready to break atmosphere in ninety minutes," I
said. "I'll meet you at the civilian harbor. Three thousand light-
years toward the Black Maw, you said? That's nearly—"

"Anita, look at me," said Szayet sharply.

"Make haste," I said to Galvão, returning his salute, and shut the door. I heard his footsteps down the corridor, and waited for him to break into a run before I turned back to the glass walls, the golden cages.

"Make it quick, Szayet," I said. "As soon as she knows we're coming, she'll run like a rat."

She was very still in the pale sunlight. "You tell me where you're going when it suits you, then," she said. "Though you don't ask."

"If I'd stopped to speak with you last time, we'd have lost Thiago Veguion behind an asteroid storm," I said. "Would you rather have had my farewell kisses than his head? Fortune bleeding, I'll let you have your fun with Cherekku, but I'm the lady of the Swordbelt Arm, not your vassal to be ordered about! Only let me know, and I'll give Szayet a thousand apologies for presuming to do as I please in my own damned spiral arm."

"Farewell kisses!" she said. "As if I ever *saw* his head! Where did Flavia bury it, Anita, in his flower farms in the outer Ceian system? No, don't answer. Undying Lord, as if I cared. What about Councillor Cipon?—Councillor Branquon?—Sévero Selon? What haste did you need to find *them*? When you left from Szayet's harbor to kill Ceirran's killers, when you returned to Szayet's harbor to wash Ceirran's killers' blood from your hands, what did you tell the Oracle of Matheus Ceirran, except *hello* and *kiss me* and *give me more wine*?"

"It wasn't the Oracle of Matheus Ceirran that I swore an oath to when I was eighteen," I said.

Her nostrils flared. "Indeed it wasn't," she said, getting up. "Excuse me."

I went down to the beach in a bewildered rage. There I shouted murder at the hull-scrubbers and engine repairmen and weary hungover crew, was sorry for it less than a minute later, promised them each an extra portion from Laubian's loot out of my own share, and was immediately sorry for that, too. At last I managed to wrangle the ships *Videiran*, *Estrelan Polar*, *Irene*, and *Surpresan* into a lean bright column along the civilian harbor dock. Alectelans urgently offered me bread and salt. I batted them away, climbed into *Videiran*'s guts, and gave the order for takeoff.

The Szayeti atmosphere was one thing that hadn't much changed since I'd first come to this world: It still buzzed with swarms of Ceian ships. My men were flung out over the Swordbelt Arm and the Crossbar—fanatical Cherekku, old Sintia with her academies and abandoned temples, Itsaryet, Belkayet, Medveyet where Ceirran had once been a prince's lover—but the bulk of them patrolled the planet where their admiral spent her days. Nearly all the soldiers here were veterans. To Szayet, I'd made out that this was in deference to Szayeti sensibilities—the Swordbelt worlds thought it was grotesque for citizens to join the army as soon as they grew strong enough to fight, and they liked to delay that day until the poor soldier was nearly twenty. I privately felt that if I'd had to be sixteen on this world, I would've gone mad. The truth had nothing to do with respect. I wanted the older veterans near me because they were Ceirran's men, and had been Ceirran's men in Madinabia and Far Madinabia and in the streets of Ceiao. I loved them for that, and they loved me because I was one of them. Now their ships parted before us with admirable haste—Galvão must have told them our purpose. Hastily, as if it, too, knew my ends, the sky faded: first the paleness of worlds, then night blue, and at long last that deep sweet cracked-open black that meant what it had meant since I'd been a little girl: I was nowhere again, and I was in motion, besides.

Videiran was a spirited ship but a finicky one, riding high on the accretion-tide and nosing in unexpected directions when she caught her fellows' wakes. In the changes I'd made to her bridge in the last year—ceilings carved with Szayeti birds, consoles speckled with cheap bright gemstones and gold—she was a joy to give point. I ordered the navigators to set her prow toward the Black Maw and let myself devote nearly ninety minutes to the little pleasures: sitting with the crewmen at their breakfast, giving them advice on their love affairs, revisiting in painstaking detail every last maneuver, ambush, and bloody triumph of the Battle of Micavalli, and quietly promising to loan five or six of them money. Then, at last, I gritted my teeth, shut myself in the captain's quarters of the ship *Videiran*, and called my sister.

"I tried to warn you," she said, before I had so much as said hello. "Will you ever bother to answer your messages again?"

"Warn me, hell," I said. "Give me a present, more like. Uncharacteristic of Julhan to be the bearer of good news, isn't it? Maybe the boy's got an ounce of humor in him after all."

"Wishful thinking," she said. "He's only given you half the story, hasn't he? He sent you off in the direction of Khramya without telling you how far you'd be going." I raised an eyebrow, and she shook her head. "It's across the Kutayeti border, Anita," she said. "It's the Kutayeti emperor's rose garden."

I drew back in shock. The Empire of Kutayet's fingers reached throughout the Swordbelt Arm—even, if you believed the wailing from the council, toward unknown and uncharted kingdoms in Arqueiran. More and more thickly their patrollers stalked the border with our empire every year, and more and more thickly our own ships came to meet them, squadron after squadron stretching out through clustered stars, noses pressed to an invisible window.

Four different clippers had crept into the orbits of our colony planets in the last year. Merchant vessels, by their markings. Small things, gunless things, barely a few dozen civilians aboard.

What responsibility can we take for the lost and the unwise? the messenger from the Kutayeti imperial house had said in the holo that Julhan had sent me, spreading her hands wide. *What responsibility for those who unlawfully flee our orbits? Admiral Julhan, in your youthful enthusiasm, you insult the King of Kings. Why would he want to put warships on your side of the border?—how could he possibly place intelligence towers? By the Eternal Flame of Alekso of Sintia, the imperial family desires only rule of law at the border, order in the galaxy, peace for the spiral arm.* Of course, she had added with wide eyes, if we wanted to allow these trespassing vessels to return home, and face the emperor's justice—

I'd swept the holo away, then. "Justice!" I'd said. "A slow death, rather than a quick one, at the end of a different model of gun? I can tell why the poets write about it! So principled, your neighbors, I'd nearly think they were Ceian themselves—" and I'd waited for Szayet's answering silvery laugh.

But the shock at Flavia's news only lasted for a moment. "So it's a quick-change job, then," I said. "No matter. We'll run over the border, catch her, and be back on the beaches before the emperor can blink."

"You're missing the point," said Flavia. "Anita, the reason he didn't tell you is because he wants to set you up for humiliation at the hands of Kutayet's fleet. The only part of your reputation that's still sterling on Ceiao is your military record—he wants to land you in trouble, then come and rescue you. He wants to make you a laughingstock."

"Doesn't add up," I said. "If there's any piece of the Kutayeti fleet capable of thrashing me, they'll be twice as capable of thrashing him. Besides, since when do I care if I'm a laughingstock on Ceiao?"

"You didn't care when you could tell yourself there was only one Ceian who mattered," she said. "Back then, maybe it was even true. But when you spend all your days at plays or games or just plain drunk on a foreign shore, Anita, it matters to the people in the Inner City. You used to have friends in this part of the city. It wouldn't matter so much if you were *here*—if you'd bother to charm them, or call them, or act as though you want to hear a word from them—"

"I don't," I said. "Chicken-tongued paint-caked hypocrites, the whole Avenuan Libeirguitan. Who gives a damn about the Inner City? It was the Outer City who were Ceirran's friends. They don't care if I'm a laughingstock to the Merchants' Council. They burned the Libeiracópolan in Ceirran's name. Now you're asking me to love the people who barricaded their doors and prayed they'd stop?"

"Of course not. I only wish you'd pretend to," she said. "Yes, Ceiao's poor are your friends now. We're all very grateful to Matheus for that, I'm sure. But will they stay your friends if you don't do something to keep them? You don't have a commander anymore, Anita. You live and die by your own name now."

Before I could think how to answer that, the glass beneath her began blinking: a new holo coming in. I laughed under my breath. "My apologies," I said. "The infant wants to talk." Her brows furrowed, but I said over her reply, "Don't worry about me, Flavia. When have you ever had to worry about me? I'll call you when I have Laubian's head."

I flicked at the tablet. Her lovely face crumbled into light and resolved into a different one: a thin, angular, shaven-headed man with very dark skin and shadows under his eyes. "The schoolboy!" I said. "What a pleasure."

"Must you speak Sintian?" said Otávio Julhan.

I shrugged. "Nice bit of sabotage, not warning me there was a border in between me and my prey," I said in Ceian. "Did you think of it all on your own?"

He gave me a long look, but by now I was too well accustomed to his long looks to be fazed by them, and only grinned back. "How would it benefit me to sabotage you?" he said.

"It'd give you a laugh, I'd say, if I thought you knew what the word meant," I said, mainly so I could enjoy watching him try not to roll his eyes. "What is it you want?"

He frowned, peering over my shoulder. His end of the holo would be showing him the star-stained portholes of my quarters—from his expression, he hadn't expected to see them. "You've already left for Khramya?" he said.

"Where else would I be leaving for, the Black Maw?" I said.

"I called to ask you to come back to Ceiao," said Julhan.

I laughed at him for a while. He waited until I was done, hands folded in front of him as primly as a matron, which both entertained and irritated me enough that I went on laughing for another few seconds to spite him. "Tell me," he said once I'd run out of breath, "what does the Oracle of Szayet claim my cousin has ordered you to do today? Does she say he wants you to cross the Kutayeti border? Does her god claim you should wage war?"

I sat back and folded my arms behind my head. "This is about your little shrines, isn't it."

"They're the people's shrines, Admiral," said Julhan.

They were huddled collections of cairns, roughly carved statues, and painted icons of Ceirran's face. They had sprung up in empty lots and markets around the city as soon as we'd abolished the laws against religion, back in the heady days just after the proscriptions had ended, when every councillor had been gratifyingly terrified and still more gratifyingly pliable.

Flavia said, in no uncertain terms, that Julhan had paid for the shrines to be built. Julhan denied this categorically. In the end, they seemed to have come to an uncomfortable truce on the subject: When a few brave members of the Merchants' Council had tried to tear them down, they'd soon found that their dinner invitations had dried up, their creditors had come calling, and their friends in the Outer City gangs, who had been Flavia's friends since before her husband's death, had very much ceased to be friendly. "They have a purpose, Anita," Flavia had said tiredly when I'd protested. "It settles the people to worship Matheus. It makes them feel that being ruled by Ceirran's captain and Ceirran's heir rather than the Merchants' Council is no bad thing. Isn't the Oracle doing exactly the same thing in her own kingdom?"

She didn't know that there was no Ceirran in the Pearl—Szayet had persuaded me not to tell a single Ceian, with great difficulty—but to her it would not have mattered. She didn't feel that Alekso of Sintia was alive, either. A computer program could imitate a dead person as precisely as it liked, in her view, but that did not mean Flavia had any obligation to pretend the person was living in any real sense. In many ways my sister had the last truly Ceian mind left in the galaxy.

"Ceiao *knew* Ceirran," I'd said to her. "They cheered for him. They cared for him. The Alectelans are only—" The Alectelans saw me passed out on the street, the Alectelans saw me accept prizes for athletic contests I didn't deserve, the Alectelans saw every side of me that I had not bothered to make nice or neat or worth seeing. Szayet could spit and curse and weep about it if she liked, but the fact was that her world was a Ceian client kingdom in a half-colonized spiral arm, and the fact was that the spiral arm was mine to do with as I liked, and what I liked was to do nothing at all. "They're only Szayeti," I finished. "But how can Ceians—Ceians, who should know better—how can they not tell the difference between kissing a painted picture and, and—"

"And the person you knelt to at his triumph?" Flavia had said. "Anita, do you dislike the shrines because you're angry that Matheus isn't really a god, or because you're afraid that if you come home to Ceiao, you'll find out he is?"

"There's no such things as gods," I said sharply.

"Keep telling yourself that, please," she had said. "For one thing, it's true. For another, I've seen you brokenhearted over

Matheus twice now. Three times would be a little much for your poor sister to bear."

"Admiral," said Julhan now, startling me back to *Videiran*'s cabin, "a barbarian Oracle may demand what ceremonies she likes from a barbaric Swordbelt court, but what compels a decent Ceian like you to indulge her fantasy that she speaks with my cousin's voice? I bear Ceirran's name. You were his officer by oath. Among civilized people, it is our voices that should say what my cousin would want."

"What would my friend want? Enlighten me," I said.

"Come to Ceiao," said Julhan. "Open negotiations with the emperor of Kutayet. We can bargain for Laubian's peaceful transfer to Ceian custody."

I tapped my fingers on the table. Through his half-transparent head stars ran like dust toward the top of the porthole. "Zero marks for the schoolboy," I said. "I saw Ceirran's plans for invading Kutayet. Spoke about them with him not long before he died, as a matter of fact."

"Indeed?" said Julhan tightly. He hated when I called him a child. He'd turned twenty a week or so ago, but as long as I'd known him, he'd behaved as though he were forty-five. I had only six years on him—but they'd been a long six years, in my opinion. "It wouldn't be possible for me to see those plans, I suppose."

I had all of Ceirran's plans, and all of his unfulfilled orders, in my own personal papers. In the first few weeks after his death, I'd loudly taken on the burden of fulfilling them. A few unpleasant-minded councillors had mentioned that they would very much like to have independent confirmation that those orders said what I proclaimed they said, and had found themselves promptly added to the proscription lists. "Afraid not," I said.

Julhan sighed through his nose. "Kutayet will still be where it is in a month, or a year," he said. "Invade it then. Be my guest.

But, Admiral, if you tell me Ceirran intended to launch his invasion from Szayet, I'll call you a liar. Medveyet is less than a day's journey away. Itsaryet is hardly farther. These and Ceiao's other colonies are governed by reliable, loyal Ceian troops, clean, law-abiding, frugal, sensible, sober, rather than—"

"Careful there," I said.

"Rather than an independent sovereign queen," said Julhan coolly.

I stretched and began to pick at my nails with my combat knife. "I have your measure," I said. "The emperor sends Laubian home in a prison transport, and then you take half the credit for executing her, is that it?"

"I'm not interested in *credit*," he said. "My cousin, as far as I can tell, attempted to destroy his enemies by sheer force of personality—"

"And cannons," I said, blowing on my blade.

"I am trying to destroy our enemies with treaty and law," said Julhan. "What I'm *interested* in, Admiral, is a little peace. A little rationality—a little duty, self-restraint, a little Ceian virtue, the same things that those shrines are meant to instill in the people. You wouldn't need to take the lead on negotiations, if the idea horrifies you so deeply. Even your presence, the threat of your troops, would show the emperor—"

I had stopped listening. Julhan was only talking the way his elders and betters had taught him to—hell, he'd been friends with Túlio Cachoeiran, once upon a time—but it filled my mouth with bitterness to hear those words: *virtue, duty, peace.*

I was, I thought—not for the first time—missing some essential thing within me: that thing that Flavia had had many years ago, when she'd stood before a mob with her husband's body behind her, and turned the great blazing force of her mind to the desires for which he had died; the thing that this boy had had not so long ago at all, when he had sworn to hunt down the enemies of a cousin he scarcely knew; the thing that Jonata Barran had

had, when they had put aside their love for Ceirran, and called on the name of Liberty, and put their knife between his ribs. There was a scratch in my mind where something should have been. I was missing that thing that let people say, and believe, *duty*, rather than obedience, or *freedom*, rather than self-interest, or *peace*, rather than exhaustion. Or *justice*, rather than revenge.

When Ceirran was alive, I hadn't needed to think about *peace*. I hadn't needed to think at all.

"Admiral," said Julhan, sounding tired, "will you explain to me why this isn't holding your interest?"

"My deepest apologies," I said, flicking the combat knife shut. "I shouldn't have called you a schoolboy. You're a schoolteacher, is that it?"

"Will you explain to me why my cousin's cult on Ceiao doesn't interest you," said Julhan, less patiently now. "Certainly a cult of Ceirran interests you on Szayet, when it comes with night after night of—" He visibly bit his tongue. "I say again," he said, "it's one thing for the Szayeti to worship a dead pearl. As long as they remain loyal to Ceiao, they may name a seagull Ceirran and praise the heavens when it steals their bread, for all I care. But you—you are not a barbarian. You are Ceian, you are educated, you are a councillor's daughter, you fought for justice against Barran and Lançan. You knew Ceirran. You spoke to Ceirran. Have you forgotten his voice so soon, that you can really mistake that Szayeti computer for him?"

That was far too close to my own thought about how the Ceian people acted at his shrines, and it stung. "Of course not," I said, feeling my ears grow hot.

"Then why won't you give your own people—decent, hard-working people—the same kind of attention and care that you give to foreign drunks?" said Julhan. "Why don't you want to help me, Admiral? What is it that you want?"

I hesitated a long while before I replied. *Interest* was entirely the wrong word. Julhan was right: Watching the Szayeti wor-shipping Ceirran was like watching children play with dolls. I playacted along with them, but when my men and I were in pri-vate and they laughed at Szayeti ceremony, I made no protest. I had told Szayet her people's foolishness was on their own heads, and I meant it. But Ceiao mattered. I had mocked Ceiao to the ends of the earth, I had fled from Ceiao and I had hated Ceiao, but I could not laugh at Ceiao, not in my heart.

What did I want? What I wanted was to return to the days when I had never had to decide what I wanted. What I wanted was to stop waking up every day in a world where I did not have him. In lieu of that world, I had love, when Szayet would give it; blood, when I could spill it; and drink, which was abundant. And one day I would learn how to stop waking up.

"I want Laubian's head," I said at last. "And I'll have it very soon."

"Admiral—" said Julhan.

"Laubian will flee before *Videiran* puts one wing over the bor-der," I said. "If she doesn't, well, I'm grown, Julhan. I can handle myself. I'll run back to Szayet if I get myself into trouble, how's that?"

"You can't live forever with a foot in two worlds, Admiral," said Julhan.

"Nobody can live forever," I said, and ended the call there for the petty satisfaction of having the last word.

My men had gathered on the bridge, those who could be spared standing at attention, those who could not working bus-ily at navigation displays. A few of the navigators had pinched expressions—they'd looked carefully at the maps, then. "Hello, boys," I said. "Some of you might have heard we're due to cross the border today."

The officers murmured. I stretched and ambled down the bridge steps toward the captain's chair, making my gait delib-erately loose, deliberately unhurried. "Spineless little flea, is

Laubian," I said, "burrowing under Kutayet's skin when she sees trouble. Or perhaps it's that she thinks we're the cowards. That we're all milksop children here in the Ceian fleet, eh? We'll see an emperor's rose garden and we'll go whining and weeping home without so much as wetting a knife?"

"No, sir!" said one of my flight lieutenants, when I caught her eye, and officers behind her chorused, haphazard but hearty: *No, sir; no, sir; no,* sir.

"Well, then," I said. "We're on the hunt. If any one of you hears some soft-handed Kutayeti desk pilot complain about our crossing, tell 'em I made all of you do it at gunpoint."

Those shoulders that had still been hunched relaxed, those brows that had been furrowed smoothed. Not a one of my men would ever consider saying anything of the sort, under threat of death or torture. I'd eaten with them, thrown dice with them, smeared unguents on their scars. They were obligated by oath to follow me, but they were willing to do it, too—or, at least, I would have been willing to do the same for any of them, and that amounted to the same thing. They were the last real thing left in the world.

Julhan meant well, but he was a child. Negotiate with the Kutayeti? Go back to Ceiao? Beg the emperor, his children, his sisters, his grandchildren, the whole of *Dom* Harsaky to condescend to give me a woman who'd had Matheus Ceirran's blood on her hands?

Before us, bright through the wide viewscreen, hung endless, depthless stars, which no one but computers had numbered and no one but gods could name. When I stared out into the black, I fancied I could see a mote of burning green.

"Open a diplomatic communication with Szayet," I said.

"What will we tell the planet, sir?" said my flight lieutenant.

"Tell her I'm sending her flowers." I turned. "More fuel to the engines. I want to be at that garden in the morning."

To the usurper Altagracia Caviro, the wicked and bestial, the thrice-cursed heretic, the she-dog of Alectelo, she upon whom the heavens spit, she upon whom the heavens pile misfortunes, she upon whom the heavens visit pestilence, the enemy to the throne, born of the foulness of the earth, doomed into dust and wickedness, unbeloved before the face of God, self-styled Patramata:

Happy birthday!

You'd be surprised how accommodating these priests are when it comes to arranging parties. Ours were always such ascetics! Though I must be misremembering: If that were true, how could you have ever won them over?

Let me see: pink-salted trout, flat fragrant sesame cakes with fig syrup, venison liver in a date sauce so thick you would choke to death on it, quail's eggs boiled in honey and piled in dripping heaps, buttered young cattails and walnuts and goat's cheese, rows of plump crispy ducks on silver dishes, wild boar stewed in beer and gone so soft that the bones showed white, olives and fennel and little cured mackerels and oil and garlic over fat white slices of bread, and wine, wine, wine, wine. Wine, and then wine, and then, for a change, wine. I didn't know it was possible to drink so much wine. The women crush herbs into it, and powdered bone treated with yams in some secretive little factory at the foot of the mountain, and they pray to be made fit in mind and body for the spirit of the god. How they pray! You could never pray like these women—not if you tried for a thousand years.

I thought of asking for some of the herbs and powder. But we both know they would tell me I didn't need it, and the moment they did tell me, you'd know, and if you knew, you wouldn't be happy. You see how sweet I've become, these last fourteen months? You see how good? Imagine if it were *you* in prison, instead. (I do.) Would you think of me, and all my unhappinesses, these long empty light-years away?

Then again, if there was any real trouble in this prison, you would have to write to me.

You did care for me, once. I'm sure that's true, I am, I am. Even when you hated me, you heard me, and when you heard me, you hurt me. Even when you imprisoned me beneath Alectelo, and your traitorous guards patrolled my door, and I heard the footsteps of the captain who would become—perhaps who already was—your lover, scraping on the stone above my head: Even then, I knew I had hold of you. Even then, I knew that every morning and every evening, you were thinking of my voice. Alone you kept me, and alone you meant me to stay. But I was never alone in Alectelo, sister, because I knew that someday you would break.

Perhaps one day, after you've crumbled and you've come for me and I've clawed myself back onto my throne at last, I'll keep you in this prison for a while. Don't fret—it won't be for long. I'm kinder than you. And you won't mind the wait. It isn't bad wine, this. You might even like it here. More and more lately, from all I hear. And I hear more than you think.

Of course, the Ceian soldiers don't like to speak to me. (Did you mean me to think they were priests? You don't know much about fighting men.) But all soldiers are sometimes drunk, or tired. Or lonely. I'm very, very sure you know that last.

(Then again: Did *you* know there were soldiers here? Or has some Ceian—I won't name names—pulled the wool over your eyes?)

Don't fear. They don't say much. Only that they would rather be out in the black, chasing down the proscribed with their brothers-in-arms. Or that they would rather be in their homes—there's a stuttering, sickly, soft-handed girl, not a proper soldier but a radio operator or translator or sort of maid-of-all-work, who once told me that every night she dreamed she was talking with her father by a river. Or that they would rather be in Alectelo, drinking twice the wine, and making the nights run even later than they do in these halls, and serving under a commanding officer who for the last fourteen months—but didn't I say I wouldn't name names?

Besides, why should you be afraid of me? *I* don't have a habit of seducing any Ceian officer who crosses my path. All I want is to know something about the world—anything—besides this endless drudgery, this weeding the temple gardens, this scrubbing the temple pillars, this dredging the temple rivers, this drinking and drinking and drinking of wine. Even this tablet can only read books and write journals, and when the power runs down in the evenings, it can't even manage that. You've made a beggar queen of me, Gracia—or these priests have, as priests always seem to, one way or another. Perhaps those barbarians who crowned you really knew something I didn't. Perhaps I'll learn what.

The priests tell me you've told the Szayeti that even in those months of war, even when you came to that dungeon, you had Commander Ceirran's soul in your pocket.

So I know a secret: Even though you had your lover to call upon, even though you had a god to put in your ear, when you came to the dungeons, it meant that you still wanted me. It meant you broke. It meant you wanted my help, not his. It means you think of me just as I think of you. So it means you'll come back for me again someday. All I need to do is wait.

The youngest priestess, Božena, says that as long as I'm in a place of sanctuary, I should reflect on what brought me here. I think I like that word: *reflection*. At night, I go up the mountain to where the tree line breaks, and I sit on one of the little stones jutting out of the dust, and I stare up into the black. The factory at the mountain's base makes the stars faint, but don't worry. I can see you still. I can feel your eyes. Imagine if I reached up—or threw a stone—and watched the ripples go through the stars until you disappeared. I'm so careful, Gracia. I never throw anything at all.

In the morning, that stuttering radio operator takes this tablet away. For the temple's archives, she says. She goes so red when I laugh.

Why do I speak to Princess Gracia Caviro, in her pride and her heresy, even though she will not answer me yet? I suppose I am trying to speak to myself. I suppose that, in that Pearl you have made His prison, the god who loves me best speaks to Himself, too. And we are not alone, we are neither of us alone, and I know it because I know there was once a day when you chose me over Matheus Ceirran, even though he was a god. And you are faithless, but I am a prophet, and I tell you, one day, you will choose me over Ceirran again. You will send someone to this temple, and they will call my name, and on that day I will know you need something from me at last.

I do hope you enjoy reading over these reports she sends you. I hope the stuttering girl marks them as frightening, or writes *Danger Emergency Blasphemy Sedition* over their seals. Most of all I hope that reading these gives you as much joy as it gives me to write them, dear heart, and as much joy as it will bring me to one day see the Lord of All Things bite your putrid heart in two.

I remain—

queen of Szayet—
Oracle of Alekso Undying—
your loving sister—

ARCELIA CAVIRO DIOMATA
beloved of God.

Some of this is even true.

She's not lying in this letter. She's only missing some of the facts. Admiral Decretan never bothered to sign the paperwork arranging to put Ceian troops in the temple at Itsaryet. Admiral Julhan Ceirran had to send ships in their stead. Everyone stationed at the temple swore oaths to him, not to her.

Not that the princess cared. The agreement between the admirals did say that any intelligence gathered in the Swordbelt Arm would go to Decretan. And who Decretan sent it to, I can guess as well as Celia can.

The original of this letter didn't go into the temple's archives, of course. Once Decretan had been sent a copy, the person who collected the letter was ordered to destroy it. I expect no one thought she would care enough to read it first.

But she didn't destroy it. And she read it, after all.

In any case, in this letter, Celia doesn't know the difference between one admiral and another. To her it's all Ceiao: a hundred faces, one mind, one state. It's just that I do know the difference, and the truth matters to me.

—V.

"Shields," I said into the helmet's communicator. "Call in."

Electricity buzzed. Force fields flared. Before us, the leeward port to the satellite Khramya swelled like a steel eyeball, crisscrossed with strips of shiny red explosive.

"Shields in north and east wings, Ana," said a crackling voice in my ear. "We're a go."

"South is a go, too," said another voice. "We've got *Surpresan* at our backs, Admiral."

"West is a go," I said. "*Videiran*, that's a five on detonation."

"Thank you, sir," said the voice of *Videiran*'s comms officer. "Four." I nodded at my lieutenant Ludon to my left, who nodded back and bent his knees. "Three," said the ship. "Two—"

Back in Alectelo, my lady Szayet liked to ask me about the conquest of Madinabia, about my battles with barbarian chiefs. I liked to tell her a story worth the telling, whether or not it was true—substituting a duel for a long afternoon's treaty negotiation, a siege for three weeks counting supplies. She always knew, and she always laughed. *You have no talent for lies*, she'd say. *I'm sure that's what you would have done, if you'd been your own master. What's the truth?*

Well, now I was my own master, and so now there was no one to stop me and my men from applying explosives to every locked door. *Not everything needs to be brute-forced*, said a dry voice out of my memories, and, *You'll hurt yourself, Captain, one of these days.* It was such a pleasure to hear that voice.

"One," said the ship. "Go."

The door roared. Fire collapsed down in gusts, leapt away from my shield like it was spring-loaded. The sky tipped, wove, and settled, leaving my eyes watering, my throat choked in dry air.

"*Videiran*, are you still broadcasting our demands?" I said, when my voice was back.

"Yes, sir," said the radio, and indeed behind the officer's voice I could hear our ship's main comms system, fuzzy and echoing oddly in my ear: *Release the criminal-inal Patrícia Laubi-aubian into our cust-ust-ustody. You have one hour. If you refuse, prepare-pare-are—*

"Well, it's been sixty-one minutes," I said, and drew my gun. "West, fall in."

The satellite Khramya, when we'd reached it two hours ago, had been as dark as the grave. Abandoned, to the naked eye, but they hadn't counted on *Estrelan Polar*'s heat sensors. Through those, the place sparkled like Szayeti fireworks.

"Proceed toward the center. Call if you find anyone," I said into my helmet, and tugged it off before the chorus of acknowledgments had ended. Around me, the three members of *Videiran*'s crew I'd brought for the western flank were doing the same. We'd come through the second air lock into a long, gilded hallway, where the air was warm and only a little dusty. We could spare our suits' oxygen supplies from here.

No sooner had Lieutenant Cardean tucked his helmet under his arm than he frowned, sniffing the air. "Something funny here," he said. "Smell that?"

I did: a faint odor, green and velvety. "Flowers," I said.

Quietly we proceeded down the hallway, and quietly we

turned toward the strengthening odor of roses: Lieutenant Cardean with heavy tread and heavier breathing on my right, Lieutenant Ludon cat-footed on my left, and beyond him our translator, a Kutayeti-born crewman named Ruzhaya. At the corner we came to a glass door, so thick with leaves that no light came through it.

I fired at the lock. The door swung open, a tangle of deep green and rose blossoms sliding to the floor just over the threshold. I stepped over it and eyed the garden beyond.

Szayet had private gardens, small ones, along Alectelo's hilly coast: needlegrass and field sedge, cloud-headed golden yarrow, thin stiff things that grew sparsely to survive strong wind and salt. This garden had no such modesty. From every wall roses tumbled, yellows and parchment-whites, red-studded arches curving over the grass. Blossoms peered from either side of thin walking paths, over benches and sunlamps. Through a lattice on the glass ceiling, stars stared down. The whole place was dead silent.

"There should be guards," said Ludon behind me.

"There should be *gardeners*," said Cardean. "Why's all this so quiet? Where's the pruners? Where's the fertilizers? Where's a man with a hose for the aphids?"

He strode out along one of the stone paths. "Come out, come out!" he called across the massed scarlet, hands cupped around his mouth. "It's only a couple of soldiers, eh? What're you waiting for?"

There was no answer. Above us, against the night, the roses bloomed.

"Dead end," said Cardean shortly, turning back to us. "Admiral, we ought to try one of the other—" and a trellis curled down from the wall and smashed full-force into his back.

Ludon shouted and leapt for him. He was too late: Cardean went down like an oak tree and hit the floor face-first. The trellis swung back, ready to strike again.

"Back!" I shouted. "Back, back—" We scrambled, all but Cardean, and the trellis slashed into empty air. I shot wildly, and heard metal sizzle. The trellis creaked back against the wall, smoking.

"Ana?" said Cardean weakly from the floor.

I seized his hand, yanking him to his feet. "Eyes look all right," I told him. "Teeth all there." His chin was a mass of blood, but that could wait. "Brave man, you are. And a lucky son of—"

Light flashed in the corner of my eye, and I dropped flat, dragging Cardean with me. The sunlamp swung up, reversed, and hurtled back. I rolled upright, already firing. Glass smashed.

"We've got to get out—" I began, and every trellis in the room whipped down at once.

Immediately I was slammed backward into a rosebush. I screamed without breath, chest burning—the metal had caught me from shoulder to rib—and pure soldier's instinct alone made me hurl myself down, thorns tearing at my skin, before a trellis smashed again just where I had been standing.

"Forward!" I bellowed hoarsely. "Move, move, move!"

To my left, Ludon leapt over a flower box that swung toward his feet. Sunlamps whacked at nearby bushes, sending leaves tumbling. "Hold fire!" I shouted. "Don't stand! Don't fight! Get to the far door!"

Gunfire rattled on the other side of the room—someone too far to hear, or too frightened to obey. Hinges creaked. I charged, metal slamming into the floor behind me at every step, and skidded through the door just as a piece of archway sliced through my suit and sent my sleeve flapping loose at my elbow.

Ludon was pressed flat against the wall, breathing hard. Cardean crouched behind him, cradling his bloodied chin. "Ruzhaya?" I said. They looked at me blankly, and then Ludon swore and tried to shove past me.

"Stay, Lieutenant," I snapped, shoving him back. "That's an order—" and I whirled to sprint back into the garden.

All paths had vanished into a carpet of thorns, multiplied in the flickering lamplight. Every arch wracked and twisted toward me. "Crewman!" I shouted. "Ruzhaya!"

A shout to my left, where a bench reared up from the earth, pawing with two steel legs. When I kicked it back, the shock jolting through my ankle, I saw her—trapped in a wire arch. It had coiled itself wholly around her body, a steel snake.

"Leave!" she shouted. "Go back!"

The wire had stopped at her knees. I seized it, then let it go nearly as quick—it was sharp as a razor, and it writhed.

"—if they hear I got the admiral killed they'll," Ruzhaya was saying, then urgently, "Admiral—Admiral!"

I had stopped listening as soon as she'd told me to leave, but that last *Admiral* was urgent enough that I flung myself down. Another sunlamp slammed into the soil, clinked, and swung up again.

Now *that* sound was interesting. There was something under the dirt. "Talk," I murmured, and stabbed my combat knife down an inch from the wire. It sang into the palm of my hand: metal on glass.

"Behind!" shrieked Ruzhaya. I yanked my leg up. A sunlamp crashed where my foot had been.

That was interesting, too. It had been four feet away from both me and Ruzhaya. If it had aimed closer, it might have managed to kill us both.

I curled myself around Ruzhaya's body and dug rapidly in the dirt with my hands. Nothing dropped from the ceiling. Nothing slammed into my head. Around the Kutayeti translator, it seemed, there was a bubble of protection.

My hands were scraping glass, now. I smeared the dirt away. There was a tablet buried in the earth, covered in illegible script, a hole in its center.

"The corner," said Ruzhaya suddenly. "*Terrestrial Intelligence, Emergency Override, Reset Arch 194—*"

I slapped the tablet.

The wire wove around her legs, catlike. Then it looped gently away from Ruzhaya's body, coil over coil, until she was free. Its end wavered, then plunged into the hole in the center of the tablet.

Above and around us, the walls groaned.

I seized Ruzhaya's arm. "Time to go."

Thorns slashed as we leapt toward the door, trellises swung wildly, but not one of them touched Ruzhaya. I pulled her into the hallway behind me. Cardean slammed the door. We stared at one another in silence.

"Remote-controlled robotics," said Ludon weakly at last. "Security cameras. Someone's operating it from another room."

"About thirty someones, then," said Cardean. "And what robotics have you ever seen with that kind of coordination?"

"There were no formations," said Ruzhaya. "There was no pattern. But they never hit one another, they never—never got in one another's way. It was like the room had a hundred legs."

"It was like a spider," said Ludon. "Like a spiderweb."

I didn't like that at all, and by the looks on their faces, the squadron liked it no better. "Call the other wings," I said to Cardean. "I want to know what they've found."

He pulled his tablet out and murmured into it for a few moments. "South wing's lost," he said. "They keep trying to retrace their steps and finding dead ends they don't remember. East wing says the same."

"North?" I said.

He met my eyes. "No answer."

I dug my nails into my palms. Fear in the fleet was a plague. If I showed the least hesitation, it'd catch. "Onward," I said.

Like hunting dogs we moved, me leading and the rest streaking behind, down corridors, through doors, past a long glass wall dotted with rain. At its end I shot off another lock, and we slammed through into solid mist.

My boots told me the floor here was all mud—nasty, sticky stuff, hard to yank my feet out of. I slid on an errant leaf and skidded, spitting an Alectelan curse.

Red fire hummed an inch from my ear. Instantly we answered, shooting blindly, and someone howled. Good. "Fan out," I said, my voice oddly flat in the fog. "Find the shooter."

After only a few more feet, the crops began: green tomatoes, pale yellow squash blossoms, rows of deep green and purple bushes as tall as our knees. Warm mist curled at my hands, my neck. For long minutes we trudged onward, our only company the wet noise of leaves, our breathing, a faint hiss from the mist machines far above our heads.

Ludon's blurred silhouette stumbled. There was a yelp from the earth. "It's him," Ludon called. "He's alive."

"Good work, Duarte," I said, wading through the leaves toward him. "Turn the little bastard over."

We crouched in the mud by the Kutayeti. The flesh of his stomach was charred bright, and he was moaning like an animal. "Quiet," I said to him, and when the noise continued, "Ruzhaya—"

She snapped in Kutayeti. His whimpering didn't fade, but his eyes went as wide as dinner plates. "Who are you?" I said impatiently.

He spat a long furious stream of babble. "He says we'll be destroyed by the Holy Flame of Alekso of Sintia for disturbing the sanctity of the emperor's land," said Ruzhaya.

"Ana?" said Cardean.

"Szayet's palace guard say worse things to the street cats," I said. "Anything useful?"

"He's saying we won't leave the satellite alive," Ruzhaya said. "No—I'm sorry, it's—" She frowned. "Sir, he said when we get to the satellite, it'll kill us. But we're *on*—"

"Ana!" said Cardean. I whirled round, irritated, but his

grim expression brought me up short. His tablet was blinking an urgent red. "*Estrelan Polar* signaled," he said. "The satellite's launched its drone fleet."

"For this you interrupt me?" I said. "*Estrelan Polar* needs permission to shoot down drones?"

"There's over a hundred of them," said Cardean.

I sat back on my heels, struck silent. A satellite this size should have two dozen security drones, three dozen. It would take my men hours longer to destroy these, and that was hours in Kutayeti space I hadn't accounted for.

But that wasn't what put a knot in my stomach. It would take at least twenty men to operate that many drones. This satellite was tiny—twenty unproductive mouths to feed was inconceivable. Where in Alekso's name did they keep them all?

"Order Galvão to cover *Irene*'s engines," I said. "*Videiran* and *Estrelan Polar* can survive a scraped knee or two. I don't want to lose any men over this."

"Prepare for retreat, Admiral?" said Cardean, fingers dancing over the tablet.

"No," I said, turning back to the Kutayeti. "Not until we've gotten what we came for." The Kutayeti's breath had gone shallow. I smiled humorlessly and shoved his chin upright with my gun.

"Right," I said. "Where is Patrícia Laubian?"

The Kutayeti said something short and scornful. "With the satellite," said Ruzhaya.

"What—" said Cardean, but I held up a hand and said: "Ask him: Where's the satellite?"

"He says he can't tell us," said Ruzhaya once the Kutayeti had finished speaking. "He says we're—I don't know the word. Earthly. Dishonorable. Cursed?"

I looked hard at the man's face. There were little prayer beads at the end of his braids, kohl at his eyes. He was unmistakably a man of the Swordbelt Arm. Any decent Ceian would have been ashamed to wear his clothes. The expression, though, was the same as any man I'd ever killed.

There were very few people in this world who, when you had one way or another gotten them on their backs, still managed to surprise you. The Oracle of Szayet was one of them. This shivering thug wasn't.

"Ask him, would it make the cabbages holier to spatter your brains all over them," I said, then shook my head. "No. Ask him, who'd care more about your being shot in the head over dishonor: your king, or your siblings."

After only a few seconds of Ruzhaya speaking I knew the guess had paid off. His face went the color of bad meat. I jabbed the gun helpfully deeper into the soft place under his chin and was not surprised when he hissed out an answer, Ruzhaya murmuring the translation over him.

"Thank him for his help," I said. "Cardean—break his knees."

He was still whimpering distantly when my men joined me in the next hallway a few minutes later. I let them come at their own pace, examining and reloading my gun, and when they'd gathered, I straightened unhurriedly and looked over the hallway's ceiling. There was the black glint of glass: a camera.

"All right," I said, and I winked at it. "Ready or not, here we come."

The door to the garden slammed. All the lights went out at once.

I grinned invisibly into the dark. "Run."

We sprinted as a pack, eight boots slamming against the floor, shoulder to shoulder, breath to breath. Something high above us popped—thudded—the ceiling rained glass. My face sang with pain. Cardean cursed violently, and I heard the echoes rattle to my left: a hollow space. "Turn!" I shouted, and we turned and were running over clean metal again, groaning walls, squealing pipes, beneath them all a soft *tink-tink-tink* like a bird at a window: heating metal.

"Cover your faces!" I screamed. My tunic caught in my armor plates—I yanked—it tore, but it was over my nose and mouth. Around me three people panted through clothing, wet and strained. Heat crawled through my boot soles, licking at my feet.

The clinking had stopped. The walls shuddered. I blinked, blinked again, and found that my eyes were stinging.

Fortune's tits, I thought. Fortune's stinking feet. We were dead. That was pesticide.

There was nothing to say. There was nothing to do. I could only close my eyes, hold my breath, and run, praying to Fortune and to Hope and to the dead, deaf gods of the Swordbelt Arm that my men were running, too.

I threw myself to the right, arm out. My nails and knuckles burned—I had not noticed cuts there before, the glass must have made them, needles too small even to hurt, but now they stung and sparked fire up my wrist and I knew the poison was under my skin. Oh, I would die, I would die, I was going to die choking ten thousand light-years from home, but I had not died yet, and my hand had found the wall. Onward was all. Onward and onward, and under my palm a shape, something jutting out, cold metal. I yanked.

Someone ahead of me, shouting, incomprehensible. I shot—a yelp—a thud—a slamming door. My lungs howled for air. The pesticide would have seeped into this room. We needed another door. Onward. Onward.

Long ago on Sintia, I had seized stones in my fists and leapt into the dark deep pools cut into the cellars beneath my school. Down I had stayed, the weight of the water pressing on my shoulders and my skinny bird's chest, while I waited for the teachers to blow the whistle to say the cadets could come up again. I saw it as clearly as I had seen the blooming roses. And

I knew by this that my brain wanted to dream, and that when I dreamed, I would sleep, and breathe, and die.

One more step. One more step. One more. You could not choose whether to feel pain, but you could choose whether to endure it. I had endured pain before. One more step. Don't stop, Captain. That's an order.

Against my palm, a wall. I caught at something absently, and, half-unconscious, pulled. It had been darker than even this in the water on Sintia. I had jumped into that pool with Sonia Couron—how had I forgotten that? Couron, beautiful Couron, hair floating above her head in a thousand directions like snakes. The two of us, watching each other through black water. Sonia looked older now, I thought. There was a faint silver shimmer in her locks, in the shadows beneath her chin. That was strange. We were very deep now, she and I. Surely the teacher would blow the whistle soon.

"Admiral," said Ludon above my head.

My hands stung like hell. Around me crouched my crewmen, red-eyed and pale, breathing hard. We were in a server storage room, its walls lined with blinking lights. Behind Ruzhaya lay an unconscious Kutayeti, her shoulder charred red.

"We're alive?" I said.

"You were only down for a few seconds," Cardean said roughly. "I don't think we're—"

He was interrupted by Ludon, who said abruptly, "Fuck me—" and turned away. A second later I heard him retch.

"Yeah," said Cardean. "I was saying. I don't think we feel well."

I felt like I'd spent the last three days drinking myself into a stupor. My mouth tasted like acid, and my eyes were wet. We would live, but we needed doctors, and we needed them badly. "Call Galvão," I said. "Tell them to ready the medics. How are the rest?"

Cardean pulled out his tablet and swore weakly. The glass was flashing like Alectelan fireworks. My headache screamed, and I covered my eyes. When I could open them again, Cardean's already-drawn face looked like a skull.

He said, "The drones clipped off one of *Surpresan*'s wings."

"A wing lost?" I said. "To *drones*?"

"They're too fast," said Cardean, eyes scanning the tablet. "They maneuver like—like nothing Galvão's seen. They strike at the ships, and then they retreat too quickly for return fire. They move like—"

"Like a spider," I said. "Like a spider's legs."

"Ana," said Ludon, "there's no reason it couldn't pour poison into this room, too."

He was right. There was no reason at all. But it hadn't done it, I thought, not yet.

An automated security system would not have waited to release gas on intruders at all. A human operator, waiting in some camera room in the heart of the satellite, would not have waited, either, not if the poison were something to which he had ready access. Whoever it was that had deployed the pesticide, he must have rerouted it from the garden's misting system to the corridors where humans walked. But he had done it impossibly fast.

"It has a weak stomach," I said aloud.

The lieutenants looked blank. I inclined my head at the unconscious Kutayeti behind the translator. "Bind her legs," I said. "We have a hostage."

It took two of us to lift the injured woman, and all four to drag her out the other side of the server room and into the next corridor. We were worse than poisoned, I thought to myself, we were tired. And *Surpresan*'s wing was gone. A real repair team would need to fix that, not people whose usual job was assisting backwater gardeners. Galvão would tell me to leave her behind, along with her crew, so that I could get back over the border, but even the thought of that made me clench my jaw. No, I'd be grounded on Khramya for days—weeks, if we couldn't find Ceian shipwrights who would cross the border to fix her—and that was if the other ships survived the drones at all.

And yet this thing, which maneuvered clouds of drones as casually as I might wave my hand, had not been willing to kill Ruzhaya. Not until she had interrogated the prisoner—not until she had proven she was a traitor to the Kutayeti Empire—not until she had shown herself its enemy. And now it would not release pesticide onto our hostage.

I had known of only one inhuman intelligence with this kind of complexity in its decision-making before, and that thing had called itself a god.

The first two doors I flung open were stacked full of fertilizer and bleach. But the third was locked by a flat sheet of pearl. An iris scanner, or a genome tester. Whatever it was, it protected something important.

I signaled to Ludon. He grinned thinly, drew an explosive strip from his belt, and laid it across the glass. We retreated to the end of the hallway, the hostage's boots squeaking over the steel, and listened to the end of the corridor roar like a tiger.

From the smoking hole in the side of the corridor, someone cursed.

I knew that voice. I straightened slowly. "Bring the hostage," I said. "I'd like to take my time."

"Oh, hell," said the voice in Ceian.

I slid my gun back into its holster and went slowly, easily, stepping over the debris into the room. Yes, someone had locked it very well. She must have paid them most of what she had left.

"Nice place," I said. "Expensive, was it?"

The woman on the floor groaned again. The force of the blast had thrown a well-upholstered velvet chair into the back wall, and her with it. A deep purple bruise was coming up on her chin.

"Looks expensive," I said. "These paintings." They were murals, nice ones, as pretty as ones that any Ceian dancing girl might have had in her dressing room: ocher yellows, delicate pinks, pale tulips and gladioli. It was all very elegant and sophisticated, and a little wet. "I don't go in for this sort of thing," I told the woman. "Never had much taste, me. Still—put enough money into something and even a vulgarian can be impressed, eh?"

Councillor Patrícia Laubian stirred and began to push herself up on one hand. "Ah," I said, and swung my boot hard into her stomach. She folded around it like cheap foil.

"Expensive place to stay, too," I went on. "No paint-on-a-pig for a councillor of Ceiao! Fortune and wheel, you even managed to lead *me* a chase. Did you wait for Barran's ash to get cold before you ran to the emperor with your purse open, or did you hail *Dom* Harsaky as soon as you left Ceian atmosphere?" She made a gasping kind of noise. "Speak up," I said, pushing my boot deeper into her gut. "Can't hear you."

She worked her lips back and forth, then, with visible effort, ground out: "Please."

I clapped my hands together. "Listen to the great speechmaker! Laubian, Laubian, I never knew you were such a rhetorician. Whenever I saw you talk in the old days, you always just seemed like another piece of cheaply bought shit."

This was punctuated with another kick, this time in her ribs. She yelped. "Then again," I said thoughtfully, "you must have had some guts, eh? Enough to stab"—I kicked her again in her chest, hard—"a man"—her gut again—"in the throat"—her knees—"when he was bleeding—on—the—floor."

By the end of these last, she was whimpering, low and wordless, like a street dog. Half her face was smashed down into her carpet, and her rib cage moved up and down, shaky little bursts of breath. "If you'd asked me in the Libeiracópolan which one of you murdering sons of Fortune's stinking piss would've been the very last one alive," I said, "I wouldn't have guessed you. Not in a hundred years. Life has its funny little turns."

Her shoulders had begun to shake, too. I squatted down by her head, propped my chin on my hand, and squinted at her with interest. A year and a half had changed her—more, I thought, than it had changed me. Not only was her hair cut, but dyed besides, a cheap ugly red. Her nose had pimples. The narrow prettiness I remembered from council meetings had faded into hollow eyes, thin lips, skin stretched tightly over bone.

Over sixty people in that marble dome. All of them armed, and only two or three had dared to meet my eyes. She hadn't been one of them.

"Cipon made it to Sintia," I said conversationally. "I know—what a surprise! Always so slow in the stairwells, she was, but she bought a fast ship." I grinned. "Goes to show there's a difference between *fast* and *fast enough*, doesn't it? Bazeirron, well, Bazeirron barely made it out of Micavalli's orbit once the battle was done. We caught him not two hours after Barran burned. But you, Laubian! You were clever, weren't you? Didn't even bother with fighting for the liberty of the Ceian Empire. Saved your money, saved your skin. Never went near Micavalli at all."

She shook her head, slowly, tears trickling over the bridge of her nose. "I know," I said comfortingly, and patted her cheek quite hard. "It *was* clever. You thought: They'll win the war, and I'll scamper off to some back edge of the galaxy, eh?"

"I didn't think anything," she moaned, rocking her head back and forth along the carpet. "I swear, Decretan, I swear."

"And why should they chase a sorry little rat who hasn't even bothered to bite?" I went on. "No, I'll slip off, you thought. I'll lose myself in the cleanup, get all tucked away somewhere in the Swordbelt Arm, make myself rich settling a piece of colony land, and die a fat old woman in my bed."

Behind us, the Kutayeti hostage stirred and coughed. Ludon slapped her face hard. Laubian flinched, and I grinned at her one visible eye. "You should've gone up to the Shieldmirror," I said. "Maybe the boy would've forgotten about you. Then again, maybe not. With him, even I don't always know—hmm, what's that?"

Speaking, or trying to speak, was costing her some effort now. Flecks of spittle had gathered at the corner of her mouth. "Get her some water, we're not barbarians," I said. "Ruzhaya—" She proffered a canteen. I tilted it toward Laubian's lips. "That's it," I told her encouragingly. "Drink up. What's on your mind?"

She drank deeply. "A trial," she gasped when she had let the canteen go. "Right to a trial."

Behind me, Cardean sniggered, but he stopped abruptly when I held up a stern hand. "Don't make fun," I said. "This is the law we're talking about. No, Laubian, that's right. Clever, like I said! You're not an enemy combatant, are you? Just an ordinary Ceian citizen, with a right to a trial."

"Shoot me now," she whispered, "and it'll be murder."

"Murder?" I said softly. "A murderer—*me*?"

That struck her silent, but only for a few moments. Her jaw worked. "Ceiao," she said, hoarse. "Take me back to the Crossbar. I'm a councillor of the city. Take me to Ceiao or you'll—you'll be an outlaw. Enemy of the empire. Nowhere left to go."

"A trial in Ceiao," I said, slowly, rolling the words around in my mouth. "Well, I'm no magistrate. Ludon, you've got a rich mother, haven't you? Does a member of the Merchants' Council have the right to a trial in Ceiao?"

"Yes, sir," said Ludon by the door.

"What a shame," I said, and patted Laubian's cheek again. The tears had dried up, and now the only evidence of them was the shining tracks along her cheeks. Her eyes were red-rimmed. There was a weariness there, I thought, deeper than the exhaustion of sitting trapped in this room while the hallways sang with gunfire. She had been tired for over a year.

"All right, get up," I said. "Can't get back for your trial if you're lying on the floor, can you?" She was briefly speechless. I yanked her to her feet, letting her bony weight fall heavily against my chest.

"Now, let me think," I said. "A trial means a lawyer. Does a councillor of Ceiao have a right to a lawyer?"

"Admiral," Ludon said again, "she might want—"

"Yes," Laubian spat out, shoving herself back. Her face was brightening. "And if you know what's good for you, you'll let me call him on the ship."

"Expensive things, lawyers!" I said. "Let's hope you didn't spend *too* much money on those paintings. Your usual might be dead, naturally. Do you know any good lawyers, Lieutenant?"

"I saw a very good one at her trial six months ago, sir," said Ludon demurely. "She argued for the prosecution."

"At her trial six months ago," I repeated, and turned to look at Laubian. "You know, I seem to recall something of the sort."

She stared at me, mouth half-open.

"You should have heard her arguments," I said. "I tell you the judge nearly wept. Shame there was no counsel for the defense, of course. You like to see that kind of talent come up against a little challenge. But what's to be done? I summoned all the murderers to defend themselves! Put out the word throughout the Crossbar: Turn up at my doorstep, and I'll take you to the courthouse myself. And do you know, not a one of you came?"

"Lançan's dead," Laubian said, voice shaking. "They're all dead, please. Please—please, please, it's over. I'm—I'm—I'm a councillor of Ceiao—"

"*In absentia* is the term," I said. "So I'm told. As I say, I'm no magistrate. The boy, though—a little scholar, he is! A Ceian to make Túlio Cachoeiran proud. Well, almost." I leaned in close to her ear, and she flinched back. "Not much fun at parties," I said in confiding tones, "but he does get these ideas. Useful, some of them."

She tried to step back. I closed my hand over her wrist, and she pulled at my grip, frantic. "This is—is—it's cruelty," she said. "I don't understand, I'm Ceian, I'm a Ceian like you, please—"

"There are no Ceians like me," I said, "anymore."

She spat at my face. "It's true what they say you've become," she said, high. "It's true. A cultist. A—a death-worshipper, a witch-pawn, a—a—a savage's painted pet—"

I tucked my gun gently under her chin. She went silent. I could feel her swallow against the metal.

"You smiled," I said. "I was there."

She said nothing.

"And, you know," I said, "they make the boy happy, these things. Council meetings. Acts and trials. He likes records. Thinks it's important to have things written down." I shrugged. "Me, I don't see the point. I know who killed him. I was there."

She stumbled. I pushed her back, toward the wall, one step at a time. "I know who was guilty," I said. "I was there. I know Cipon, and I know Bazeirron, and I know Majericon and Sévero Selon and Veguion's daughter and Branquon and Lan-çan. I know, I know, I *know* Jonata Barran. I know their faces. I know who laughed. I know who applauded. I know who called out *Liberty!* and I know who called out *Justice!* and I know who dipped their hands in his hot black blood and I know how they sound when they beg for their worthless lives because—I—was—*there*—" and I shoved her in three great steps against one of the painted tulips on the wall.

Under my hand, her chest was heaving as though she had just run for an hour. Her hair had fallen into her eyes. Like as not, I thought, she had meant to cut it soon.

"I'll pay you," she whispered. "Everything I have."

"I have money," I said.

"Land," she said. "Land, I'll give you land. I have a farm on Belkayet. I have workers—"

"You think I want a *farm*?" I said, and laughed in her face.

The tears had begun again. Her whole face was wet and shining, her mouth red and open. "I don't know what you want," she said. "I'll do anything. Anything, please. Please tell me what you want."

I withdrew the gun. She sagged against the wall, gasping. "Thank you," she said. "Thank you, please, thank you."

I watched her chest heave. Then I said, "Kneel."

She had been wiping her face on her sleeve. Now her hand fell. She looked up.

"You heard me," I said, and jerked the gun at the floor. "On your knees."

Her eyes darted from side to side: the door, the desk, the madly flickering lamp, the painted flowers staring down at her from the wall. I wondered if she had ever seen a Ceian on their knees before in her whole life, besides me.

When she met my eyes again, she flinched. I didn't move. At last, trembling, she sank to the floor.

"See?" I said. "That wasn't so hard, was it?"

She said, "What n—" and I swung the barrel of the gun against her forehead and pulled the trigger.

The last of the assassins swayed, then toppled forward. Her arms fell limply against the carpet, trying to stop her fall.

"Going to need to repaint this wall," I said. "Make a note of that, Lieutenant."

"Yessir," said Cardean.

Two days' chase. A year and a half. The ash where the Libeiracópolan had stood, glass-glint in the tumbled marble, fragments of gold and green. Túlio Cachoeiran's head, eyes bulging, furred grey swollen tongue. A pyre, a jet-streaked sky— Jonata Barran, wrapped in my cloak, flaring like a sunstorm.

Please, Laubian had said, *please, it's over.*

"Sir," said Cardean.

"What?" I snapped.

"They're targeting *Irene*'s engines."

In my mind's eye, Barran's corpse shivered silver. I tore my mind deliberately away. The man in the vegetable garden had said Laubian was by the satellite, I thought, stepping over the wreckage of the door.

"Ruzhaya," I said. "We're looking for something called *Control Room—Satellite Room. Motherboard Room.* Go and find it."

She had only gone as far as the end of the corridor when she stopped. "*Terrestrial Intelligence Room*," she said uncertainly.

I walked steadily down the corridor and, when I was near the door she'd indicated, lifted one of the explosive strips in my belt and waved it at the ceiling. The walls shuddered. An oxygen vent nearby pinged. The door hinges, when I stroked the explosive over them, stung with heat.

You could not choose whether to feel pain, I thought again, but you could choose whether to endure it. Once to get myself to Laubian; now to get my men out again. "It's rude to be unfriendly," I murmured to a vent, and stuck the strip firmly onto the lock.

We backed up. The door blew. I stepped through the hole in the wall, and was immediately tackled from the side.

Pain lanced up my elbow. A herd of elephants was sitting on my rib cage—my attacker, who must be twice my size. I wriggled, twisted, jabbed my injured fist into their solar plexus—Szayet's Undying God, that hurt—and, while they were wheezing, smashed my forehead as hard as I could against their face. They howled, rearing back. I whipped my gun hand up and fired directly at their knuckles.

The body collapsed backward. I sat up.

We'd come into a wide, dark room lined with holoscreens.

I saw the garden where we'd come in, the cabbage field where the man we'd caught was still bleeding into the greenery, and on a far wall, blue cloaks: my men, sprinting frantically through another garden, solar lamps crashing toward them. One soldier lay still beneath a tangle of wires and glass.

The rest of the room was full of tables stacked with tablets. Skinny young Kutayeti lay beside them, making awful animal noises—computer operators, most likely. Between them, guards were beginning to sit up and fumble for guns. There—across the room, a small, plain door, inscribed in Kutayeti.

"Through there!" I bellowed in Ceian. "Leave the hostage!" and tore toward it. I knew I had made the right choice when the wounded computer operators began to yell. Their words were incomprehensible, but their faces were masks of terror. Some tried to drag themselves toward me, legs limp and useless.

This door had six locks. I shot them off, one by one—had barely reached the last when the gunfire began—pulled all four of us through—and slammed the door shut. "Secure that," I said, jerking a thumb back. Ludon braced his weight against the door, arms spread.

The room was hardly wide enough to turn around in. A sputtering bulb lit three splintering wooden walls and one steel wall at the far side. The only furniture was a narrow bed, its head shoved up against the steel. Something lay there under a white blanket. The air smelled distinctly chemical.

"It's a corpse," said Ruzhaya, sounding equal parts bewildered and relieved.

"It's not," said Cardean, peeling back the edge of the blanket. "She's asleep."

He was right. The chest of the girl on the bed rose and fell, gently, very gently. Except for that motion, she looked to be dead to the world.

At first glance I had thought she must be a child by the Ceian army's standards. Now I saw she was much older—seventeen or eighteen at the very least. But there was something still childish about her hair, which was in two fat braids, sticking out on each side of her head; about her hands, clasped together under her chin as though she were holding a doll; about her face, round and peaceful. Her head was not on a pillow, but on a metal column screwed into a plate in the floor. Inside it, her little face looked like the center of a halo.

"I don't like this," I said, staring down at her.

"The wall," said Cardean, jerking his palm back from the steel. "It's warm."

I'd been wrong—it was not steel at all. It was so flat, so thoroughly polished, that I had mistaken it for metal. Even the Szayeti never polished it this well, and they held it to be the substance of holiness.

"Pearl," I said. "It's quicksilver pearl."

Ruzhaya seized the girl's arm and shook it hard. The arm came up, then flopped down to her side like a piece of cloth. Her eyelids didn't twitch.

"Wake up!" Cardean shouted, and clapped an inch from her nose.

Beneath the blanket, the girl's chest rose and fell. I hesitated, then slapped her full across the face.

She sighed a little. The door shrieked on its hinges. Ludon shouted, shoving his body back against the wall.

Something was beeping—the tablet in Cardean's belt. When I looked at him, he'd gone pale. "Admiral," he said. "*Videiran*'s calling. *Irene*'s engine hull has cracked."

I put my fingers under the girl's jaw. Her pulse was steady and strong. Her skin, I thought, was unusually cold. This close, I could see the minute twitch of her muscles underneath her eyelids, darting from side to side, like a person deep in a dream. And yet I did not think she was dreaming.

"Sir," Cardean said. "Sir, *Videiran* wants to know if they—if they can begin their retreat."

Gently, very gently, I laid my finger on the girl's eyelid and pushed it up.

Her pupil was blown wide, so wide that her iris was invisible. It did not dilate when the light struck it. I had not expected it would, not from the moment I had seen it. It was a bright, shimmering silver.

"Admiral!" said Cardean. "If the ships don't retreat now—" The door slammed again, and the room shook. He stumbled and fell back into the wall.

I slid a hand beneath the girl's head and lifted it up. The quicksilver pearl cables slithered out from the hole in the back of her skull down into the column below.

From the hallway came the loudest explosion yet. Ludon screamed. Ruzhaya screamed, too, clapped her hands over her mouth, and backed against the wall.

"Get me a flask," I said.

There was no answer. I let the girl's head fall—the cables whispered as they retracted, a thin buzz like insects—and whirled. "A flask!" I said. "Wine, liquor, two-centono beer. The hardest steel in the world won't cut quicksilver pearl. One of you must have a drink!"

Their terrified faces gave me the answer. I swore. "Cardean—"

"Sir," he said. "Should I order the ships to leave us?" His face was drawn.

"Right," I said, snatched the tablet from his hand, and swung it with all my might against the quicksilver pearl wall.

It shattered instantly. Glass burst across the wall. I turned the tablet over and dug within, heedless of jagged edges, to pull out what I needed inside: a sharp-edged chip of quicksilver pearl.

"Lift her head," I said.

Cardean looked as though he were touching a slug, but he obeyed. The whole room shook, then shook again. Ludon's head knocked hard against the door. He staggered, fell to his knees, and did not get up.

"Ruzhaya, take the door," I said, barely looking away from the girl's face. The cables from her skull juddered and swung like vines. I seized one, pinched the chip, and began sawing at the cable with all my might.

The screech of pearl on pearl was terrible. The chip shuddered so badly I wondered whether it would crack. And then its edge caught on the cable's surface, and drew a deep scratch—

The room stilled.

"Admiral!" said Ruzhaya.

I turned to look, and nearly dropped the chip. The door was— not shaking, but writhing, a slow, sick, liquid twist that began at its base and rolled up toward the ceiling. Something was happening at its center—a warping, the whole steel pushing outward, as if someone had put their fist there and pushed with the strength of a sun.

Ruzhaya had let her arms drop and was beginning to back away. "Stand to your post or I'll have your ears," I barked, and dug the chip into the scratch again.

Beneath us, the satellite—

—hiccuped.

The floor jolted. We all swayed, scrambling to seize the walls, the bed, one another. The oxygen vents in the ceiling hissed, a garbled noise like the sea. As I sawed, the dangling light bulb changed, flickered, weak yellow to deep orange to scarlet. The vents screamed, and now the light was as green as new grass, blinking madly—and then the cable snapped, and it went out entirely and flared again, a flat, shadowless white.

Backup controls, I thought. Override to default settings. Its manual operator was gone.

I began to hack at the next cable, haphazard urgent strokes. The girl frowned. Her hands twitched, fingers curling into fists.

"Cardean," I said, "hold down her hands. I think—"

The girl wrenched herself out of Cardean's arms and sat bolt upright. Her mouth opened painfully wide, all her teeth showing to the back of her black throat, her grey tongue thrust out over her lip. Cardean yelped and backed away. I seized the cable, which had slipped out of my hand. There were still two left to go, and I did not know whether those drones were still killing my men. I dug the chip hard into the pearl's side.

From every corner, filtering through the crack under the door, vibrating through the silver wall, the room screamed.

I had heard the noise of rats in dark alleys, when they fell into the nastier kind of traps. I had heard the noise of street dogs when their legs were broken by passing litters. I had heard the noise of hawks, diving toward the field mice below. This scream was none of these. It was human, and it was afraid.

My heart was hammering. Fear, I thought, disgust, childish, unacceptable. Then I wondered why I could not quite seem to catch my breath—and then the third cable snapped, and the scream stopped, and the girl collapsed backward. I felt the air grow cooler as the satellite's backup oxygen rushed in.

Only one cable left. I could hear nothing now from the camera room—not screams, not bootsteps, not the hammering of the soldiers on the door. I dragged the chip deliberately over the pearl and watched as the girl's lips peeled back from her teeth, as her hands flattened on the table, as she gasped for breath—and then gasped—and gasped—in and in, without exhale. A vein pulsed in her forehead. Her heel kicked at the table, an endless, violent twitch.

"Oh, *shit*," said Ruzhaya.

I turned to look and nearly dropped the cable. Ruzhaya had been flat against the door, arms spread. Now she was almost half a foot away—and almost half a foot off the ground, arms windmilling, Ludon's unconscious body floating below her. A second later I found myself rising up, dragging the cable along with me—then slamming down, Ruzhaya and Ludon hitting the floor with twin thuds—and then we were all falling toward the door, first Ludon smacking limply against the lock and then Cardean, howling as his injured chin met metal. I clung to the cable with my uninjured hand, the strand of pearl cut so deeply now that it wobbled under the force of gravity, unsure whether to hold my weight—

It snapped. I slammed belly-first into the floor.

All noise had ceased. I lay there for a minute or so, panting, before I could force myself to roll onto my back. "Who's alive?" I said to the ceiling.

Cardean groaned, which was probably an answer. "Ludon's breathing," said Ruzhaya, from near the door, which meant that she was, too. That was four, at least.

I grabbed the bed and pulled myself upright. The girl lay there, very still. Her mouth hung open. I put my hand beneath her chin and closed it, as gently as I could, and for the look of the thing, I lay two fingers on the left side of her neck, where her pulse should have been.

"She's gone," I said. No one replied.

There was no noise from the camera room, either, not even grunts of pain. I limped to the door, opened it, and looked round.

The corpses took up most of the floor. It was difficult, through the blood, to make out their features.

I squatted by the nearest and gently turned them over. It was one of the security guards, a hook-nosed person with grey streaking their hair. I had seen dead like this before, soldiers who had set hand-bombs to blow and not thrown them away in time. I patted the floor around the guard's arm and lifted a wet fragment of a gun.

The next body, a computer operator, had been wearing an ear-piece in her right ear. I found the earpiece after a minute or so, about a foot to the left of her head. Shortly afterward, I found the ear. The next had been carrying his gun in his belt. The next had been wearing glasses, with a digital augment to the lens.

"Room's clear," I said, not bothering to raise my voice. Behind me came bootsteps and the sound of gagging.

Most of the holoscreens were sputtering or dead. A few showed my men: walking through rose gardens, bending over to rifle through the pockets of guards. More showed corpses, in Kutayeti uniforms and Ceian both. The rest showed the orbit around the satellite. There was *Videiran* at the west wing, her belly scarred, her wings burned black. *Surpresan* was missing half a wing altogether. She spun in slow circles, her viewscreen too dark to see through. I could see through *Estrelan Polar*'s, though: On a flickering holoscreen shaded a peculiar blue, her crewmen worked frantically to beat out a fire on the bridge. The drones had vanished. So had *Irene*, and all of her men.

One screen did not display either the satellite or its orbit. That holo was of a man's face, quite close to the camera. I did not like the look on his face. There was a terrible pity in it.

"Get on those computers," I said, "if any of them still work. Contact *Videiran*. Whoever's left, tell them to pull into dock, and get those medics. We'll leave the minute we're fueled."

"Anita," said Cardean weakly.

Slowly, very slowly, a ship was nosing into the corner of one of the holoscreens.

I shut my eyes, not praying, exactly—of course not praying—but hoping against hope for a blue stripe, a Ceian uniform, some sign that it was Julhan come to drag me back to Ceiao. There was no such luck. The Kutayeti ship slid in beside *Surpresan*, black as space. Beside her, *Surpresan* looked no bigger than a handspan across.

And there was the second Kutayeti ship, settling its bulk beside *Estrelan Polar*; the third, by *Videiran*; the fourth, the fifth, the sixth, in the empty space where *Irene* should have been—and more, yet more, too many for me to count.

The tablets on the computer operators' tables buzzed. "We address the rogue admiral Ana Decretan," said an accented voice. "We are responding to a distress signal issued at these coordinates. Ana Decretan, you are under protective custody until such time as the distress signal is resolved. Should you remain in custody, the imperial fleet is prepared to repair and resupply your ships. You will be immediately escorted—"

I had stopped listening. Every tablet displayed the same thing: text in Kutayeti script, handwritten, letters enormous and messy. A child's scrawl.

I did not want to ask it, but I asked: "What does it say?"

Ruzhaya had her arms wrapped around her torso. Without looking at me, she said:

"Doctor, will it hurt?"

The Kutayeti voice rattled on, on, filling the room with empty noise. I turned again to the screen with the pitying man's face. He was smiling at the camera now. Softly, tenderly, he lifted his hand toward the screen. I only just had time to see that it held a scalpel before the picture went black.

To: Admiral Ana Decretan, Demipotestate for Confirming the Freedom of the City with Conciliary Power, Lady of the Crossbar and the Swordbelt Arm / in Alectelo, Szayet

From: Otávio Julhan Ceirran, Demipotestate for Confirming the Freedom of the City with Conciliary Power, Lord of Arqueiran and the Shieldmirror, Commander Ceirran's heir / in Ceiao, Ceiao

Sir—

After our call this morning regarding your journey to Khramya, I felt it might benefit the both of us to discuss your governance of our territories in the Swordbelt Arm, without the strictures, witnesses, and dignities of the offices to which we have both so fortunately been called. Let me first acknowledge that both your judgment and your sovereignty over your territories are held in the highest esteem by the people of Ceiao and the veterans of the fleet. The advice that follows is intended in the spirit of absolute respect to their opinion.

Your personal attention to the Swordbelt Arm well befits your capabilities as a soldier and an agent of our empire. The opinions delivered with such passion in our holo call are clearly borne of sincere principle.

It is your capabilities as a statesman to which I now turn. I take this opportunity to respectfully remind you that it is now your charge, as well as mine, not to seek glory for the Ceian fleet, but to secure order, stability, and prosperity for the Ceian Empire.

I regret that your responsibility to our client kingdom Szayet—
no doubt paramount—so often prevents you from discussing the
documents, council records, and proclamations requiring your
immediate attention that have arisen in the last year. In addition
to ordinary matters (the collection of tribute; the arrangement
for disaster supplies; routine infrastructure repairs), I would like
to turn your attention to the issue of moral reforms.

Our predecessors held the policy that filth in the Outer City
was inconsequential so long as the Avenuan Libeirguitan was
clean. This policy has repeatedly failed. You must have realized, as I have, that in these last decades of disorder and war, the
people of Ceiao have fallen into disarray. Ceian citizens work in
unregistered brothels. Every inhabitant of the city, from the river
to the road, has amassed some level of debt. Even in the Inner
City, on a market-day evening, my captains report fights, bawdy
graffiti, and drunks asleep in the street. Gangs have run ram-
pant in the Outer City so long that even respectable people—I
do not like to name names, particularly when the name is that of
an admiral's sibling—are routinely known to do business with
them.

The result of this degradation is resentment among the people
toward the Merchants' Council and the people of quality. I have
done my best to address the symptoms—you may have heard
about my sumptuary laws restricting luxury foods and imported
cloth—but discontent still brews. Ceiao must have more wealth,
for the sake of the people's bellies, and Ceiao must have more
law, for the sake of their safety. Ceian society must have pride
and self-respect, for the sake of the empire. As an initial step,
I would be grateful to hear your thoughts on an incentive for
childbearing or crèche vi

Letter not sent.

To: Admiral Otávio Julhan Ceirran, Demipotestate for Confirming the Freedom of the City with Conciliary Power, Lord of Arqueiran and the Shieldmirror / in Ceiao, Ceiao

From: B— O— / in the ship *Videiran*, Kutayeti airspace, the Swordbelt Arm

Written from the flagship, under command of Admiral Ana Decretan, Lady of the Crossbar and the Swordbelt Arm. Please accept apologies for unavoidable irregularity in the timing of my report, per unexpected changes in fleet route.

Decretan entered Kutayeti airspace twelve hours ago with three fighter ships. All ships low on fuel, ammunition, and supplies. (Inventory below in secondary report.) *Irene* lost with all hands on board. *Surpresan* in dire need of repair and unable to fly without assistance.

Twenty-five Kutayeti imperial destroyers arrived to escort our remaining ships to Sancta Mirtalo, the planet housing the empress consort's currently abandoned winter palace. The offer, made by Kutayeti ambassador Sasha Vualo, included resupply, repair of *Surpresan* and *Videiran*, and negotiations for peace. After heated discussion with Captain Galvão Orcadan of *Estrelan Polar* on the likelihood that the remaining ships would survive any further battle, Decretan accepted.

According to discussion between lieutenants on *Videiran*'s bridge, Decretan intends to funnel a request to fund troops, weapons, and supplies through Flavia Decretan's allies at the next meeting of the Merchants' Council. Please expect my next report at its regular hour.

I remain your obedient servant—

Letter opened, but the name of his spy has been cut off. I'll write back to C. He may remember who it was.

To Captain Águeda Vipsânian—

See above from my spy. One expects no better from Decretan at this point. Whether this story she sent me about this creature on the satellite can be believed is another matter.

Who is Ambassador Vualo? Please perform background check.

Tell Captain Maicenan the rescue ship and ransom money will be necessary after all. Perhaps when Decretan's on her way home, I can force her to talk to me. The woman at least has a keen sense of indebtedness.

See me before council meeting tomorrow to consider next steps.

Admiral Otávio Julhan Ceirran

Julhan—

Expect head of Patrícia Laubian within ten days—you're welcome—

ANA

 The holo C. sent to me, the one that summoned me from the country house back to this ever-glorious all-victorious smoke-choked heap of bricks, said that he wanted to help me with the work. "You'll write better in Ceiao," he said. "You'll be able to hear the spirit of the city here."

 But the truth is that he summoned me because he's running out of time. The truth is that he broke the promise he made to me on that island when he and I were young. The truth is that he has failed to make me immortal, just as I failed to do the same for him.

 Every day his doctors can give me makes a difference, now. The truth is that C. is afraid that what I'm writing won't be finished before I'm dead.

 When C. summoned me, I thought of when I began writing for him. I thought of the thorn trees, and the tablet, and the island on the last night of the war. And I thought, as I always do, of the memories, which I have carried for so long, and about which I have never told a soul.

 The truth is that I'm afraid, too. I'm afraid that the worst has come to pass, and I've forgotten all the things I swore I'd remember. I'm afraid that the work I do for him, and for Ceiao, will be all that's left of me. I'm afraid that when I die, C. will call my name, and I'll answer him.

So I begin to write this second history. I keep it in my travel case, and I read it over while the spider-litter jolts me down the Rouan do Templon do Matheus Ceirran, toward the city.

He won't mind telling me the name of that spy. Like as not, whoever wrote that letter about the Kutayeti destroyers escorting Decretan to the winter palace has been dead for twenty years.

—V.

THREE

Our god, the Holy Flame of the Swordbelt, Alekso of Sintia," said the Kutayeti ambassador warmly into my ear, pointing toward the cliffside ahead, "dug the mansion of Roof-without-Rain into that rock in less than two weeks. He used neither ladders nor stairs nor ropes. In fact, no one has ever accessed one room of the palace from the ground without flying up in a waxwing—not once in the last three hundred years."

"Is that so," I said.

"It's so," said the ambassador. "And without a waxwing, no one has ever descended to the ground again. Isn't that remarkable?"

I'd understood the implication the first time, but at the moment, no one in the galaxy could be blamed for treating me like a fool. The waxwing was a tiny wood-and-canvas thing somewhere in shape between a canoe and a fruit basket, with two bronze griffins perched on each side of it, slowly beating enormous pearl wings. One of the bulky soldiers in the basket was operating them by means of a quicksilver pearl panel, labeled in graceful Kutayeti letters that I could not read.

"Imported from Szayet," the ambassador had told me on the ground, running a finger lovingly along one of the carved feathers. "Though I'm sure you know that—as you *are* the lady of the Swordbelt Arm." The mocking tone was faint but undeniable.

"So fortunate that their quicksilver oyster beds have been revived at last—so much less costly for *Dom* Harsaky to import from Szayet than from Ceiao. And the pearl looks so beautiful on the feathers, don't you think?"

The waxwings fit no more than six people. This one held me, the ambassador, and three Kutayeti soldiers, guns on their laps. Somewhere underneath me, within the numberless rising wings, sat my lieutenants, Captain Galvão, my remaining three hundred or so crewmen, and the corpse of the silver-eyed girl we had found on the satellite Khramya. So many vessels had been required that they were still stirring up the dust nearly two miles below, so that the earth of Sancta Mirtalo looked less like a planet than a drifting scarlet sea.

Out of that sea rose a hulking mountain. Its western side sloped steeply upward, its peak so high that even in this hot wind, the soil gleamed with ice. A few yards down the eastern slope from the peak, the rock fell abruptly in a smooth sheet of grey to the earth, as though some great hand had taken a cleaver to the stone. Rivers pulsed down the cliffside from carved open-mouthed marble faces; brass trumpets jutted outward, their music blown away by the wind; climbing vines wove through balcony railings; ropes stretched from one open window to the next, fluttering tunics and trousers pinned to them—all of these twelve thousand feet in the air. Kutayeti fighters darted from the battleships above to the black holes in the cliffside, as swift as flies. From the sky, the palace was entirely accessible. It was a pity that our own ships were sprawled with their guts torn out on the desert floor.

The ambassador had claimed that the waxwing, too, was Alekso's own design. It wobbled alarmingly. For our safety, I'd been tied tightly to its benches with straps of leather, which was putting something of a fine point on my situation.

"Please don't hesitate to let me know if you need anything from your ship, Admiral," said the ambassador cheerfully. Their family name was Vualo—a Malisintian word, which was strange—but they'd clapped me very heavily on the shoulder and told me to call them Sasha. "We'll send a messenger down immediately the moment you ask. Though, of course, the empress consort's staff has made sure to stock the palace with every luxury. I expect you'll be happy to leave our messengers alone. We've received a message from your fellow admiral on Ceiao, asking whether you're all right—so solicitous!" They chuckled. "Of course we were happy to reassure him you're well, and that there was no need whatsoever to send a ship, but he insisted. I believe he's bringing quite a ransom. Naturally we've told him it's not necessary for a guest, but if he *will* insist on paying us—well. Will you be hungry once we dock? Still on Alectelan time? I'll send a servant to your room to help you dress for supper."

"I usually manage to get my own clothes on," I said.

"Really? I'll need to dismiss my sources on Szayet," said Vualo. "They told me something quite different—ah, here we are. Duck your head, please."

For all its flimsiness, the waxwing was swifter and more maneuverable than any fighter I'd ever flown. It dipped abruptly and nosed us into a narrow tunnel in the cliffside, where we hurtled through a dozen twists and turns—I was suddenly glad of my bindings—before emerging into a half-lit cavern full of twenty or thirty empty waxwings. Our own wove into an empty space and thumped onto the stone.

"At last!" said Vualo, hoisting themself over the edge of the basket. On the ground, they had stood head and shoulders above their fellows and my own. Under the low cavern roof, they loomed even larger, thick-necked and broad-shouldered, legs like temple pillars. Their hair fell loose to their shoulders, a thick and unruly white mane, though by looks they could not have been older than forty.

They reached down across the wooden frame and took the hands of the sixth person in our waxwing: a skinny woman with masses of dark hair and very dark skin, dressed in baggy red trousers and a loose yellow mantle. Whether she was meant to be a soldier, a diplomat, or even a Kutayeti I couldn't tell. She'd introduced herself in Sintian as Carmela Lukhaya, given me a startlingly limp handshake, and spent the rest of the flight up the cliffside in silence, staring at me with the kind of expression that I usually associated with Alectelan palace cats awaiting scraps of dinner.

Now she allowed herself to be helped onto the cavern floor, Vualo's broad hands surprisingly gentle in hers. "Don't worry about standing on ceremony, Admiral," they said to me over her shoulder. "With the empress consort still back on the homeworld, we're very relaxed here. Two or three courses, perhaps a little dancing—all you'll need is a bath and some new robes."

"What have you done with my crew?" I said.

"In the lesser officers' docking bay," said Vualo, eyebrows going up. "And your enlisted men in the enlisted docking bay, while we sort out their quartering. Is it the Ceian custom to seat crewmen at the noblemen's tables for dinner? Charming."

"No need," I said. "Show me where their mess hall is, and I'll eat there."

"Charming," they repeated, and smiled. At once, and very much, I disliked that smile—too wide, too sharp, and far too thoughtful. "Well, Carmela will show you to your rooms. Carmela—when the bell rings, will you escort the so-called lady of the Swordbelt Arm to dinner for me? Roof-without-Rain is something of a labyrinth, I'm afraid," they added confidingly. "People have wandered for *days* before anyone found them."

Lukhaya had returned to her silent, eager stare. When Vualo said her name, she jumped. "Delighted," she said, offered me her arm, laughed when I did not take it, and gestured toward the far side of the cavern. "This way."

The tunnel opened into a wide corridor, its floor patterned with mosaic lions. Afternoon sunlight, bewilderingly, glowed on the tile. I looked up: The walls had to be something like five hundred feet high, and some thousand feet above that, a clear glass ceiling slanted gently toward the west.

"People always think Sasha's joking," said Lukhaya, "and you know, they hardly ever are. Take a waxwing at a high enough altitude over the mountain—well, don't do that, you'll melt the mechanism, but it *is* a maze. The empress consort doesn't believe me, but I think the King Eternal used to use it for His experimental trials."

The pleasure in her voice on those last words made me certain of what I'd initially suspected. "You're a scholar," I said.

"Oh, yes," she said. "Yes, I am. I'm an expert in quicksilver pearl. Sasha thought you might have found the events on Khramya a little upsetting."

I stopped dead in the corridor. Lukhaya came to a halt, stretched lazily, and turned to face me. "You really won't have much time to change for dinner, you know," she said. "Of course, it's your right to arrive in the hall all sweaty from running, if you want to. You *are* the lady of the Swordbelt Arm. Or so we hear."

"A little upsetting," I said. "A girl with pearl shoved into her brain."

"I meant your having murdered her," said Lukhaya, "but yes, all right, I'll represent my emperor's court, it's very important to respect that other people's cultures have sensibilities. Really, though. Forgive me if Sasha's misled me, but I heard you spend plenty of time around a girl with pearl shoved into her brain. What's the difference?"

I was briefly speechless. Lukhaya appeared not at all alarmed by this. She turned a sharp corner and laid her hand on an apparently blank stretch of wall, where a rectangle unsealed itself and swung inward.

"Sasha said to tell you they're very sorry that they didn't receive permission from the court to put you up in the empress consort's rooms," she said, "but between you and me, her cats piss on her rugs."

I stepped inside, half expecting the door to slam behind me. It didn't. The room was wide, carpeted from wall to wall in intricately woven red. A desk stood in one corner, a bed in another, and in a third, a wooden folding screen painted with golden horses. An enormous window looked over miles and miles of brown desert, the occasional ocotillo shrub jabbing out of the slope of a hill. The destroyers hulked like wasp's nests against the blue. *Videiran* and her fellows glittered on the ground, bright, friendly, and untouchable.

Still, the sight of her was enough for me to find my words again, and I said harshly, "Should I see no difference between the Oracle of Szayet and a girl caged in a cell on a satellite, dead to the world? Maybe you didn't see the holos from the Oracle's approach to Plyusna, my lady. She was capable of announcing herself. There was a barge."

"Don't let the real noblewomen hear you call me a lady!" she said. "It's an interesting problem, I admit that much. Doesn't your client queen claim to have Alekso Himself caged in His own cell, so to speak? I'm afraid even if that weren't a blasphemy I'd have to laugh at it—I mean, really, a god in a rock! As if it were the life of a sorcerer, in a children's story...And then there's the Terrestrial Intelligence—" I stared blankly. "Those who have undergone the procedure, I mean," she said. "The people who host the union of pearl and brain. That girl who runs the emperor's rose garden. Well—*ran*. A consciousness that possesses a thousand ships, or the whole of a satellite, pitted against a consciousness that possesses an earring...I don't know about you, but the size of my cage would matter to *me*. But of course the Oracle claims He doesn't mind staying in that rock. Perhaps she finds entertainment for Him."

She was looking at me expectantly. With a shock I remembered myself and said, "Ceirran's a god on Szayet now, too."

"Yes, I heard," she said. "Captured from the commander's memories at the moment of his death, and carried around for months like a book she was saving to read later. Fascinating. Are you going to change, then, or do you want to look at the view?"

"Ch—" I said, and she bowed slightly and gestured to the folding screen. When I stepped behind it, I saw a pile of cloth. "And you mean to—what, stand in the open doorway?" I said flatly.

"Sasha was very clear that you weren't to get lost," said Lukhaya cheerily.

I swiped up the clothes—very loose sendal trousers tied at my waist with a golden chain, deerskin boots, and a red robe of astonishing softness embroidered at the collar with black fishhooks— and stalked out from the cover of the folding screen to go sit on the bed. There I methodically stripped off my own dusty boots, my cloak, my tunic, and my thigh wrappings, in that order. Lukhaya's dark face grew steadily darker throughout this, and when I reached for the place where my breastband was tied at the back, she cleared her throat and at last turned to stare pointedly out into the hallway.

I took advantage of her averted eyes to explore the quarters I'd been given. There was a tablet on the desk; a quick wave told me that it could make holo calls, write letters, and keep a journal, but had nothing in the way of galactic maps or planetary maps or translation programs or news, which was not a surprise. A few books in the drawers—two famous Sintian poems, which I discarded immediately, a very old Sintian book titled *Sondri Outlondish and Barbarious Cerimonies Among the Savage of the Perle of the Sword-Belt Arm*, which I resolved to memorize so I could tell Szayet about it, and one book in Ceian titled *He Has All the Time in the World: How the Laws of Alekso of Sintia Can Still Free You from Wickedness!!* The small chamber opposite the window had a tiled bath—I was evidently considered either too important or too repulsive to use the noblemen's baths in the palace—and a large quantity of hair oil and perfume, all of which I applied indiscriminately to myself until I looked and smelled as if I had jumped into a pool of myrrh.

Lukhaya had been quiet all this while, but at last she cleared her throat. "You can go down to dinner naked if you like, of course," she said. "I can think of a few of the empress's bannermen who won't complain."

"Oh, good," I said, coming back into the main chamber. "Lead the way."

"King of Light help me," she said. "I never had any talent for arguing with toddlers. All right! Let's go! Do you know, I expect it'll make Sasha laugh."

That was a victory blow. "Fine," I said, and went to tug on the robe and boots. The trousers I tied with my own belt—the chain struck a little too close to home.

"But of course," said Lukhaya meditatively as we went back through the labyrinth—the sky through the glass above was a pale purple, now, with shocking streaks of red—"your Oracle might not have carried the computer you call Matheus Ceirran around like a book at all. She could have put that pearl in her ear at the very moment of his death. Is that it? Did she become an Oracle again on the night he was killed?"

The night Ceirran had been killed, she'd been naked in bed beside me, propped up on one elbow, watching me catch my breath. She'd had a face like a falcon, then, smooth and beautiful and not in the least human.

"No," I said.

"Then when was it that she put his wires in her brain, exactly?" said Lukhaya. "A month after your fellows stabbed him? Two? I suppose there might have been a kind of preservation mechanism to keep the programming in stasis. Was there?"

She was smiling, but that strange hunger from the waxwing had slid back into her face. It was not a hostile expression, but neither was it a kind one. In fact it was entirely impersonal, and I was conscious again of that sensation of being watched by a mind whose workings were quite removed from my own.

We'd reached a set of filigree-covered double doors. Behind them I could hear the murmur of voices, and the faint strumming of a tanbur. "You don't remember?" said Lukhaya, after I'd been silent too long. "Well, you can give it some thought. I'll ask again," and knocked once. The doors swung open.

I stepped forward into a vaulted hall. Enormous sandstone pillars lined its sides, red mosaic its floor. It could have fit hundreds, but there were only some three dozen or so people drifting round its edges, dressed like me in loose trousers and sleeved coats. At its far end, the floor dropped abruptly into absolute darkness. I saw stars winking beyond it, and the orange lanterns of the desert dock, and understood that I was looking at a wall of sheer glass.

"Ana Decretan!" cried a voice. The ambassador had changed into a rich velvet robe, their hair pulled back into a short queue. They lifted a glass to me. "The lady of the Crossbar and the Swordbelt Arm! What an honor for our humble court to entertain her as our guest."

Laughter rippled across the gathered noblemen.

"Sasha Vualo!" I said. A maid in black was passing nearby, her tray laden with dried plums and wineglasses. I snatched one glass up and lifted it. "The starship repairman. What a privilege to be serviced by such a generous host."

The laughter increased at that, but I did not think it was friendly. Vualo executed a shallow bow, surprisingly graceful for their bulk, and came forward like a shark through the noblemen.

"I hope you didn't have too much trouble on the way," they said.

I was very sure that this had been directed toward Lukhaya,

but I said, "Not at all. Thanks for the clothes. Obliging of you to find them on such short notice."

"Oh, they belong to one of my lord the emperor's natural children," said Vualo carelessly. "There's a quantity enough of those—we were bound to have something in your size." At once I regretted not coming down naked after all. Vualo smiled again. "Still," they went on, "I hope you'll feel we've been more than hospitable. Your men, I admit, have been a little troublesome themselves. Half of them have refused to eat until they've seen you're safe. I don't suppose there's anything you'd like to tell me to reassure them?"

"You're not getting any reassurances from me until I've seen *they're* safe," I said. "Let me go to them."

"Hmm," said Vualo. "Well, we'll see what your behavior warrants. Naturally we wouldn't want you to upset anyone. Carmela, what have you and the admiral found to talk about?"

"Pearl," said Lukhaya at my ear, before I could answer. I was conscious of her behind my left shoulder, Vualo pressed in close before my right—for all that they were an overgrown desk-riding bureaucrat who happened to have been nearby when I'd been limping away from Khramya, and for all that she was a stick insect who seemed to have no title or power to speak of at all, my hackles were up. "Admiral Decretan was concerned about Khramya."

"You don't seem *concerned* enough about the Oracle having made the second Pearl of the Dead," I said. "Shouldn't a pair of Swordbelt cultists be tearing at their hair and trying to have me burned at the stake?"

"Oh, that's priests' business," said Lukhaya. "You can't expect a simple scholar to understand crime against the King Eternal."

"Besides, everything to do with Pearls of the Dead should be nonsense to you, shouldn't it?" said Vualo. "A good respectable Ceian like yourself. Surely you hold the position we do—that quicksilver pearl, however complex, is incapable of hosting a consciousness that one can really call human. Haven't you found that to be so?"

"I don't speak to him," I said. A thought struck me, and I narrowed my eyes. "Your—Terrestrial Intelligence. It doesn't host a consciousness you'd call human?"

"Well, no," said Vualo calmly. "It's not as if our hosts can speak. Or feel, as far as we understand. We program them to be completely loyal to the aims of the Kutayeti Empire—"

"No voices? No wills of their own? That's inhuman," I said.

"Of course it's inhuman," said Vualo. "It's a computer. I understand that the so-called consciousness inside your Oracle's Pearl imitates a human voice. Well, naturally a programmer should prioritize whatever functions best suit the device he happens to be working with. I presume the Pearl would find its parroting of human language more difficult if its eyes were spread across a hundred cameras, and its ears spread across a hundred speakers."

"The girl on Khramya had a consciousness. She recognized that my translator might be Kutayeti," I said. "She recognized when we took hostages."

"Her programming would allow her to distinguish foe from friend, yes," said Vualo. "The Terrestrial Intelligence is all that is best about humanity—human intelligence, human creativity, and yes, human loyalty—brought to its highest extreme, with any impurity and confusion stripped away. Some feel quite privileged to become a host, in fact. Wouldn't you?"

"My lady!" said a cheerful voice to my left. With a disquieting sense of relief, I backed away from the pair and turned to greet a handsome heavyset nobleman, who bowed slightly. "Lord Yarikhy," he said, "baron of Ychlan Nebula, what a pleasure. I returned from the homeworld as soon as I heard you would be joining us. I hope you're enjoying Roof-without-Rain?"

"Plenty. Let me see my men and lend me a couple of guns, and I'll enjoy it more," I said.

All three Kutayeti laughed. "Perhaps we'll have time for a drink or two after dinner, Admiral," said the baron. "I flatter myself that you remember my name. You may recall the letter I sent Ceiao five months ago about Ceian pirates raiding my manors on three worlds."

"Admiral!" said another voice. I twisted again and saw a square-jawed woman. "Princess Tsiraya of the Asteroids Vorysna, what an honor," she said, bowing. "And in the off season, too! I'm glad I lingered after the empress consort left. But what a shame to see you alone. You'll remember, of course, the letter I sent you regarding my niece's three daughters? Unmarried! How lucky that they're coming to visit this court in the next week. I do hope you won't leave Sancta Mirtalo too soon."

"What a courteous hope!" said Vualo. "I'm sure we can all wish for its fulfillment." They raised a glass.

"Lady Decretan," said a third voice, and before I could finish my turn, there was a fourth, and a fifth, Kutayeti noblemen in droves reaching out to clasp my hand, to bow deeply and look up at me with laughing eyes. "Of course, you'll have seen my protest on your recent tariffs on silk," said one, and, "You'll have heard about this terrible trouble with these bread riots on my lesser satellites—I'm so grateful that you took my advice to leave well enough alone," said another, and, "I do appreciate the trade for antimatter that your predecessor the commander arranged with me, Admiral, but I *am* beginning to wonder just a little about your timeline for payment."

I had answers for none of their questions, and though the trays of food drifting around the room never seemed to come near me, servants kept appearing by my elbow with newly filled wineglasses. My face was growing steadily warmer, and my replies steadily less coherent. When the dancing began, I found without surprise that I knew none of the steps, and had to make do with tripping over my own feet in time to the tambourines and kicking high enough that the fabric of the sendal trousers fell up to my thigh. This only seemed to delight the noblemen more, and when each dance was over, every one of my partners bowed deeply again, kissed my hand or the air by my cheek, and drifted away, usually with a whispered word in Vualo's ear. At last Lukhaya tapped me on the shoulder and cleared her throat.

The duke who was currently letting me step heavily on his feet as he told me about his recently widowed and very accomplished son—he'd been doing this for ten minutes, despite my repeated explanations that a marriage to someone without Ceian citizenship would never stand in Ceian courts—raised his eyebrows and sneered. "The ambassador wants a chance to speak to the lady of the Swordbelt Arm," Lukhaya said to him.

There was a faint stress on the word *ambassador*. What this meant I could not guess, but it had a profound effect on the duke, as well as the two other noblemen who'd gathered to put themselves forward as dance partners: They startled as if they'd been smacked and drew back. "Do come back to see me in the baths later," said the duke after a moment. "Roof-without-Rain is famous for its hospitality. I'm sure you'd find them—enjoyable."

"Enjoyable," Lukhaya muttered under her breath as Vualo's wide hand descended to steer me firmly toward the window at the end of the hall. "Greasy smock-merchant."

"You realize, of course," Vualo said when we had reached it, "that the emperor's hospitality toward your ships and your person is given entirely in spite of your unprovoked act of war."

My face was still very hot, and the night and the empty air looked wonderfully cool. I pressed my forehead against the glass and shut my eyes.

"What was that girl's name?" I said.

Vualo was a great silent presence behind me for a minute, a breathing mountain, and then they said thoughtfully, "I really admire it, you know, the way you talk. I could almost forget the holos from Khramya." They laughed a little. I could feel their breath against my shoulder. "The people who'd been holding computers that the Terrestrial Intelligence inhabited, I mean. But of course, one can't leave out the other deaths—the slit throats, and bullet wounds, and so forth. Well, and my lord the emperor is terribly upset about his roses, but don't tell him I let that slip."

"Is Kutayet an empire of peacemongers now? What good news," I said, turning my head so that my cheek met the glass instead. "I didn't realize you held all your colonies and pacified your tribesmen with chocolates and flowers."

"Flowers!—very good," they said. "Admiral, let's be sensible. We know Ceiao doesn't desire war. Your fellow admiral has assured us of as much in his messages. And my lord the emperor is not an unreasonable man. All he desires is to live in a galaxy ruled by law. An attack on a civilian facility—"

"Civilian facility?" I spat. "With a murderer sleeping in its beds and breathing its air?"

"If you say there was a criminal there, I don't like to doubt your word," said Vualo, very kindly. "I'm afraid there's no record of such a person in our entry logs—but I can see, of course, how the idea upsets you, and who among us has not acted in anger? In fact, the only deaths we recorded in our report on Khramya were those people carrying computers in which the Intelligence resided, and of the host for the Intelligence. And then, of course, all the casualties the host of the Intelligence inflicted on *your* ships before you murdered her."

I shut my eyes. It did not shut out Vualo's voice: "The emperor, in his infinite charity," they said, "does not desire that any more Ceians should lose their lives unless they must. If Ceian sensibilities are revolted by the Terrestrial Intelligence, he will keep all its hosts in his own territories, in his own lands. He only requires a demonstration that he retains his dignity, and then, Admiral, even someone carrying your sins can be forgiven."

"What the hell is a *demonstration of his dignity*?" I said hoarsely.

"You don't look well," said Lukhaya abruptly. "Should you lie down?"

"Hold on. My men—" I began, but Vualo stepped back, observing me with a shrewd eye.

"She does look unwell," they said. "Overindulged, perhaps? Take her to her room, Carmela. She'll want to lie down. And perhaps she'll want to pass that last message onward to her Ceian colleague, who has so generously insisted on sending a ship to take her home."

"Demonstrate what dignity?" I snapped. "When will you let me see my soldiers?" But Vualo was turning away, catching at the sleeve of a baroness who'd introduced herself to me earlier. My instincts told me to spring after them and hit them, though it seemed probable that there were reasons I should not do this, and I was almost certain I could remember what they were. My body told me with increasing insistence that I had eaten nothing since I had arrived on Sancta Mirtalo, and lying down seemed as inevitable as it was anathema.

When we reached my quarters, I folded myself down on the bed, head swimming. The lanterns were unlit, the shapes of desk and wardrobe and bathroom door black ink under the hard moonlight from the window. "Now what, scholar? I lie here until you come to fetch me, or I wander out into the labyrinth and hope something eats me?" I said to the ceiling. "Pretty cages you people build. So much for the emperor's generosity."

The darkness hid Lukhaya's silhouette, but I heard soft slippers on the floor. Her fingers were in mine suddenly, and then something snapped hard against my skin.

"*Ow*," I said, flexing my pinkie. There was a cool pearl band encircling it. I pried at the edge immediately, and with a creak, it unwound and lay flat in my palm.

"That's a tracking device," said Lukhaya. "When it's bent into a ring, every minute, it sends out a radio pulse on an extremely low frequency. Strong as you like—I could hear it from space. Go on, wander deep in the labyrinth. Try to find a monster or two. You can even try to find your men, if it pleases you. I'll fetch you when it's time for dinner."

"I don't recall the treaty or the law that gives the Kutayeti court the right to band a Ceian like a bird," I said. "Must have been asleep that day in school."

"If you want to deactivate it, just unbend it to kill the signal. And lie here until I come to fetch you," she said. I heard her footsteps shuffling back, toward the corridor. "Sasha's trying to keep *you* happy, Admiral. Is it their fault if you don't want to be?"

"What do you want before you'll let me see my men again?" I said to the ceiling. "What price are you asking? Just tell me. I'll pay."

Lukhaya was a silhouette in the doorway. I could not see her expression.

"Your friend," she said. "Is he altered from life? When you speak to him in the Pearl, is he the man you knew? Or is there anything—wrong with him?"

"Talking to my friend is the Oracle's business these days," I said.

Lukhaya sighed slightly. "Well," she said, "let me know if you think of anything else," and I heard the door close.

The nausea had retreated in our walk to my chamber. I could not bear to light the lamps, but I could bear to sit up, and I knew where the tablet lay on the desk.

Sure enough, there was a letter from Otávio Julhan, asking at great length whether I was injured, and telling me in no uncertain terms that no matter how the Kutayeti claimed I was not a hostage, he would be sending a ship from Ceiao to ransom me immediately at his own expense. My men, he said, could be rescued later, when the city was sure that I was safe. At this

I snorted, and sent back a message reading only, *Don't bother.* Whether he'd listen was another question, but at least I could tell myself I'd refused to abandon the three remaining crews— and besides, it preserved my pride.

There were no messages from Szayet. It was possible that they had been sent and intercepted, and that Ambassador Vualo or some other Kutayeti nobleman was holding them until the moment of best advantage. Even for me, though, this was wishful thinking.

I might ask for her forgiveness. But I had done nothing wrong, said my heart, bitter and hot. I might send her a military report—the last of our enemies was dead, I had made thousands of enemies more, I was stationed among them, and they would not stop asking me insistent questions about her Pearl of the Dead. That was what I would have written to her, had she been an Oracle in truth, and had Ceirran been listening when I spoke to her. Or I might send her a dire warning: that we had encountered a half person, some kind of monster beyond my understanding.

In the end I contented myself with sending the Alectelan palace my coordinates, a note that Otávio Julhan was sending a ship for me, and after some hesitation, signing the missive *Disciple.* That was what she had asked for, wasn't it?—and it was only a word. What was a word? You said one, and then it was gone; even mayflies lived longer. Words walked out of your skull without leaving so much as a footprint behind. Szayet proved that every day.

The tablet's holo calls, I saw, could reach as far as the Crossbar. I hesitated. In Ceiao it might have been any hour of the day at all.

Well, if Flavia was too tired to speak, she could always say *no* to me. Was I her keeper? I flicked the holo call request toward the blinking dot that represented Ceiao, and less than a second later, my sister's head shimmered in the tablet, hair half-unbraided, a pink sleeping robe wrapped round her shoulders. "You're awake," I said, pleased.

"You owe me thirty thousand dekar," said Flavia.

"What? Take it out of the council treasury, I don't care," I said. "Blame it on the usual suspects. How are you?"

"Short thirty thousand dekar," said Flavia flatly. "I don't have the least idea what you do all day, but it certainly isn't *answer your letters*. I don't know if you've noticed, darling, but you started a war a few days ago. Of course, if you'd prefer never to touch a centono of the military budget again, that could be arranged! In fact, your esteemed colleague would be happy to arrange it for you—"

"My esteemed—what?" I said.

"Your esteemed colleague," she said, "the Demipotestate for Confirming the Freedom of the City with Conciliary Power. Which he did call you at dinner tonight, to my face, and with the way he said it, I'd rather he'd called you a pig. Do you even know that today he argued that the council should cut off your war funds?"

"How are you, Anita; how was your flight, Anita; how's Kutayet, Anita," I said. "Was the monster with cables where her brainstem should be upsetting, Anita; yes, it was, thank you for asking, Flavia. Did you survive the battle, Anita. Couldn't say, Flavia, I'll tell you later."

She paused in her unbraiding and pinched the bridge of her nose. "I was hoping it was another of Julhan's half-truths," she said. "He was being honest? You've gotten yourself taken prisoner?"

"I'm not a prisoner," I snapped. "I'm negotiating a peace with a Kutayeti ambassador. How's that for *what I do all day*?"

"Of course you are. Then when will you come back to Ceiao?" she said. "Unless you mean to let Julhan's warship ransom you, that is?"

I pressed my lips together, and she closed her eyes and sighed. "He had the votes to cut off your war money for good, Anita," she said. "He said he felt terribly sorry for you, and everyone makes mistakes, even admirals, and he'd pay out of his own pocket to get you out of the mess you'd gotten yourself into, and that would be an end to it. I had to bribe seven separate councillors to open up the council's pocketbook just to make sure your troops in the Swordbelt Arm are funded through the end of the month. And now I'm short thirty thousand dekar."

"He's obsessed with peace," I said. "He'll grow out of it."

"It's not peace he cares about," she said. "Or if it's peace, it's not the kind of peace that'll keep *you* safe—no, nor me neither. He held a dinner tonight for Matheus Ceirran's dearest friends— all of us lounging in Matheus Ceirran's sitting room, eating off Matheus Ceirran's plates, while Matheus Ceirran's servants served Matheus Ceirran's wine. Now he's sending a warship to collect Matheus Ceirran's right hand and bring her back into Matheus Ceirran's territory. Otávio Julhan Ceirran. He's growing into it, if you ask me."

"Don't call him that," I said softly.

She sighed through her nose and closed her eyes. When she opened them again, her temper had cooled. "I don't, you know," she said, reaching up to begin unbraiding the other side of her head. "Some of our friends don't. Others try not to, but I hear them slipping. But Matheus's servants do, Anita—and the bath-house graffiti does, too. It's his house in law, now. It's been his name in law since the moment Matheus died. It's been his money in law as long as he's been able to spend it, dear heart—and I'll tell you freely, he has more of it to spend than we do. That means something to the people."

"It means he's not sleeping on the street," I said. "Much joy may that bring him."

"It means the people *see* him," she said. "On the streets, in council meetings, at public games. Laying flowers at shrines. Kissing his fingers by Matheus's boarded-up bedroom door."

"When I was young, we'd have called that base superstition, and put a guard on his porch to keep an eye on him," I said. "Not much of a patriot, is he? And the council will never think much of him if he doesn't behave like one."

Flavia tugged a ribbon out of a braid and began to wind it around her thumb. "He wouldn't have been a patriot back when we were young," she said. "Anita—we're not young anymore. The people see him allotting lands on Madinabia to Matheus's veterans. They see him relaxing requirements around which Ceians are allowed to live in the Inner City, and pushing Medveyeti and Sintian servants out to make more room for citizens—that was one of Matheus's pet projects, and everyone knows it. They see him arguing to the council that the fleet should expand Matheus's conquests, and bring them more money and more servants from other worlds. They see him building memorials to Matheus on the grounds of the Libeiracópolan. They see him demanding that the people of quality speak Ceian instead of Sintian at their parties, of all things. That's patriotism to them, now, not *liberty*, or *disestablishment*, or any of the things that Barran and Lançan died for."

"Any of the things that you and I killed them for," I said.

"Yes," she said. "Do you know what Eva Papinian asked me at that dinner at Ceirran's house?"

"I flew twelve thousand light-years to get away from questions like *what Eva Papinian asked*," I said.

She ignored me. "She asked me why I hadn't lent as much coin to the Outer City as Otávio Julhan had," she said. "*Me*—the widow of the man who was patron of every Outer City gangster for ten years! And do you know why she asked me?"

"She's a twit," I said.

Flavia bent her head to tug out another ribbon. "She asked me," she said, muffled, "because she couldn't ask *you*."

"Nor should she," I said. "What right has that piece of paste-jewel-decked froth to know how I spend my money?—or

Ceirran's money, for that matter? Why in the world would it ever be any of her business?"

"She's in the market for a wife," said Flavia bluntly.

"Undying! Too awful to bear dwelling on," I said.

"She's not the only one," said Flavia, whose lip had curled a little at the oath. "You made money after Ceirran died, Anita. You're the lady of half the galaxy. But where's that money going? Where are *you*? Are you looking for a Ceian spouse? Are you going to have Ceian children? They're not wrong to ask who'll inherit what you leave behind."

"Of course they're wrong to ask. You'll get it all," I said.

"Anita," she said, sounding very tired, "you can leave your reputation to me if you like. I'm nothing but a kindly old widow, and I'm not on the council, besides. I can act freely. But I'm not a miracle worker. Yes, the people remember you were half the reason the worship laws were repealed. They remember all the money you put in their pockets during the proscriptions. They remember that you killed Ceirran's assassins—"

"I didn't do it so that they'd remember it," I said.

"But they also remember you're a woman who went about on the arms of actresses," said Flavia, over me. "A woman who played dice games on her tablet in council meetings—who once threw up inside her shirt at a public ceremony—"

I snorted. "Lady Fortune, woman, I'd like to see them forget it if you keep bringing it up."

"I don't like it when you make me into a scold," she said. "In fact, I like it even less than you do, and that's saying something. Don't treat me as if I'm trying to make you upright and proper—me, of all people! But what in the world are you doing out in the territories, all alone? What kind of life is that? You need a partner, dear heart, you need someone to help you get away with it all. And now the only person helping you do that is me—and I do mean the *only*, Anita, because you aren't helping yourself."

"Helping me do what?" I said. "Do I want to spend all my time playing politics on the Avenuan Libeirguitan? Cleaning up my reputation with the magistrates at the Major Gate? When did I ask for that?"

"You became demipotestate of Ceiao, and lady of the Swordbelt Arm," she said. "On purpose, Anita, as far as I'm aware. Was that only so you might find it easier and more lucrative to drink on Szayet? You wanted Ceirran's killers dead—well, they are. The war's over. You must want something from Ceiao now, darling, and if you'd only try to *get* it—"

"I don't want anything from Ceiao," I said. "I want nothing. I just want—"

At first, in those early days after Barran's and Lançan's deaths when I was newly become lady of half the world, I'd wanted whims: to build a bath here, a tavern there, to drink and dance from the Major Gate to the Minor for free, to befriend every tavern-keeper and actress in the Outer City. But it hadn't satisfied. I'd slept half the day, and I'd still been tired. I'd drunk taverns dry, and I'd still been thirsty. I'd danced until my feet were bleeding, and I'd still woken in the hot blue hours of the early morning and wanted to peel out of my skin.

All right, I'd thought. It must be that I wanted to rule. So I'd gathered all the soldiers I could get, and then I'd run across the near parts of the Crossbar and the Swordbelt, threatening chieftains, raiding little independent satellites and bringing them under Ceiao's sway, giving golden rings and silver cups as loot away to my men and taking in return their laughter, their attention, their easy warm love. And that hadn't satisfied. I couldn't sleep more than an hour at a time, not in my own bed or in any of theirs, and I'd paced the corridors of my own ship night after night like a caged tiger, misery crawling in my bones.

Then Szayet had come to me in her barge, blazing music through the clustered stars, and called me disciple, and told me a story. In Alectelo I had been far from the river and the road, from the ruins of the Libeiracópolan, from the council and my sister and everyone who had ever known me. I'd had the love of the Alectelan people, as well as my soldiers, and I'd had evenings when Szayet and I put on old clothes and climbed over the palace wall and pretended to be citizens, and I did not even have to remember my own name. And when I woke in the night on Szayet, the queen was with me, and the itch under my skin mixed and melded into a different kind of need, and I could very nearly forget which was which. That had nearly satisfied. Nearly, in the same way that the girl on Khramya had been nearly alive.

What did I want, now that all the assassins were dead? I wanted nothing. I wanted to have nothing, I wanted to do nothing, I wanted to know nothing. I wanted to remember nothing. I wanted to be nothing at all.

"Listen," I said. "You said you have—how much money in reserve from Ceirran's treasury? Ten million dekar?"

"Three million, seven hundred thousand," she said. "And I tell you we don't have it. *You* know where it is—gone to councillors' bribes, or to games, or to lining the pockets of a thousand petty thugs down by the end of the Rouan Valquíria Ba—" She made a face. "The Rouan Matheus Ceirran. You're missing the point. The boy looks like a patriot, and you look like a fool."

"That's never stopped me doing anything I like before," I said.

The holo was so faint and staticky that Flavia's face was more color than shape. Even so, I could see how it went flat. "You're worse than Ceirran was, you know," she said.

"I hope so," I said. "Kindly old widow, my foot. Flavia, how'd you like to take my job?"

She shut her eyes and said pleasantly, "Darling, sometimes I could kill you dead."

"What's stopping you?" I said.

"Answer your letters, Anita," she said. "If you're about to be carried home in Julhan's warship like a captive for his triumph, give me some way of at least seizing back a little control on your behalf. An old scandal, a piece of gossip. Isn't there anyone that boy's taken a bribe from? Isn't there anyone who's seen him drunk? Isn't there anyone who's seen him naked? I remember you telling me that Ceirran saw him sitting at the camp followers' fires on Far Madinabia."

"If only he'd been there for the usual reasons," I said. "I'd bet a dekar he was taking polls on the disease rate in the infantry." I rubbed my chin. Flavia bristled at the least Ceian gossip the way a horse bristled at flies, but she'd been right when she'd warned me that Julhan had wanted to humiliate me, and I had been wrong. I wanted very badly not to tell her so. It was one thing for my pride to be injured by an upstart boy with no reason to love me, and another thing entirely for it to be injured by my sister. It made my blood boil to be grateful to people.

Well, there was a way to give her what she'd asked for and at the same time remind her that once she'd had to be grateful to other people, too. "What's that term Ceirran used five or so years ago," I said, "when he was prosecuting that man who killed Eliana Ludon's uncle?"

Flavia's eyebrows went up. She remembered that trial very well. It had been after her husband, Teo Pulcron, had been caught trying to overthrow the Merchants' Council. The city had been in turmoil, the traditionalist councillors hungry for blood. There was talk of mass arrests. One of the conspirators' widowers, a man Ceirran loved, had swallowed coals.

Ceirran had publicly accused one of those bloodthirsty traditionalist councillors of a murder everyone else had long forgotten. It had been worse than mere killing, he'd said in the courtroom, worse than even treason. The old crimes from the theomachy era would need to be revived, the crimes punishable by death. The jury had found the man guilty almost at once.

Someone had shouted fire in the courtroom before the verdict could be read, but Ceirran had made his point. A fragile truce had been restored among the councillors. Flavia had only had to swear on our mother's name that she'd known nothing of Pulcron's business, Pulcron's philosophy, Pulcron's work. She'd done it, utterly expressionless. Afterward, in private, she'd thanked Ceirran. Three days later, she'd raised a mob in the streets to give her husband a funeral.

"Enemy of the state," she said now.

"All right," I said. "Put this motion through the Merchants' Council for me. Conduct or speech inimical to the war against Kutayet shall be classified as acts of an enemy of the state. It is forbidden from this day forward to attempt to interfere with the success of the fleet of Ceiao, or to attempt to cause disloyalty within the ranks. Those who do shall be stripped of citizenship— so on, so forth. You write the rest, you're the one who can stand lawyers."

"That's one way to teach him to respect his elders," she said, eyebrows high on her forehead.

"He puts a knife to my throat, I put a knife to his. It's not personal," I said. It wasn't. When I'd been in school, if I'd spoken up wrongly in lessons, the teachers had slapped my hands. The boy had to learn, and learning hurt; that was the way of the world.

"You mean *I* put a knife to his throat," Flavia said, "and he looks to see if my neck is there for cutting. I love you, Anita, and I know you love me, and I'm glad of your attention, if only for a little while. But I'm the one who's in the city with him."

"Then take all the glory when you humiliate him, I don't care," I said. "You're the one who's taking the little brat seriously, for Fortune's sake. So he's stolen Ceirran's friends in the Inner City. What's the Inner City to me? The people might think they love him now, but as soon as rent's due, his little reforms about speaking Ceian at parties will seem a million miles away." I ticked off one finger on my hand, then tapped the next: "The city guard don't love him. Back when we were arresting people during the proscription, it was me that handed them their bounty money, not him. You ought to remember that—you were the one who made sure of it." A third finger: "And the fleet doesn't give a damn about him, either. He was sick all during Micavalli, d'you know that? Shouting troop movements through the door of *Laureathan*'s head."

"No, you've only told me seven hundred times, you'd better do it again," she said.

I frowned at her. It seemed to me suddenly that my sister was very tired. "Are you all right?"

"He's too clever. He's too cold," she said, low. "You're right, Anita, he won't take this personally. He'll only decide whether it's a problem, and then he'll decide how to solve it. Nothing is ever personal for him. That's what's frightening."

"Don't try to pretend you're frightened of anyone," I said, aiming for tenderness. "I know you too well."

"But I am," she whispered. "I wish you were here with me. I don't like being afraid of people. I haven't been afraid of anyone in over a year. He wears the name like it's a crown."

That got rid of my fondness in a hurry. "There are no crowns in Ceiao, in names or in any other place," I said. "Jonata Barran made sure of that."

"Jonata Barran can't make sure of it anymore," she said.

"Be careful, before I start to think you regret that," I said sharply. "When I let the boy come to war with me, he was a gadfly. As far as I'm concerned, he still is. This is your war, not mine—win it, lose it, take what money you need to bribe your way out of it. I have troubles of my own here."

"Troubles of your own there," said Flavia. There was a real bitterness in her voice now. "If I didn't know better, Anita, I'd think you make trouble in the Swordbelt Arm just so you can't come home."

"So I won't come home," I said, and flicked at the edge of the tablet very hard.

Her voice garbled, and her face grew thinner, and then thinner, until all I could see was the edge of one glaring eye. "*Anita*," she said. The connection died.

I buried my face in my hands. Through my fingers, the colorless lights of the desert moved in the dark below: scattered lanterns, the harsh sharp shadows of hills, drones floating in lazy clouds around *Surpresan*'s twisted starboard, a coyote darting along the ground toward some helpless thing.

A snap broke me from my half dream. The missive I'd sent Szayet floated in the corner of the tablet, where I'd discarded it while Flavia and I talked. My Ceian admiral's seal glinted there, cracked in two. Someone on Szayet had read the letter.

I sat at the desk for I did not know how long, watching that broken seal slowly fade over the tablet's wax-white surface. There was no reply.

To the usurper Altagracia Caviro, death-fed and death-doomed, the spider who squats on the sea, god-robber, crown-looter, whose footsteps summon vultures, whose tongue summons flies, whose blood shall sanctify the hand that spills it, sore-ridden, rust-eaten, reeking and ruined and undeserving even of hope, self-styled Patramata:

Weather continues hot. Not even the priests want to work. This morning they asked me if I could weed without supervision, and I said of course, and I went to the garden and lay down in the dirt and stared at the sun. I thought: I'll dry up like a berry, head to feet. They'll find me under the bushes with the grasshoppers, and when they ask me what happened, my tongue will be so shrunken that I won't have to say a word. But after about an hour or so Božena came over to cry on my shoulder because her lavender had died, so I had to get up again.

The other prisoners in this temple are little people, suffering for little crimes. On our way to the cellars we passed the cell of a singer from some far-flung colony of Ceiao, who wrote ballads protesting the destruction of their city's walls at the hands of the fleet. They stay in their room, and sleep all day, and when our shadows crossed their door, they hammered on it and complained of the heat. Another prisoner is a counterfeiter. She is a very old woman, and I think she will die soon, and then we will have a funeral and some excitement at last.

The last room on the way down to the cellars was empty—that room is for a smuggler, who in captivity has become terribly boring and is always helping the priestesses make soup in the kitchens. But outside it Božena and I found that stuttering Ceian, translating letters from Itsaryeti to Ceian. Eneida, she called herself. Shy as a deer, she is, but one of the only soldiers who speaks Sintian with any skill. What barbarians your Ceians are!

She ummed and ahhed at us for a while, which made me laugh, and eventually managed to say, "You ought to be working," and I said, "Try and make us, why don't you," and bullied her all the way down the winding staircase to the cellar where the air is at least a little cool. The roots of the fir trees hang through the ceiling there, and best of all, it is where the priests keep all their worst wine.

Eneida, who was still blushing and didn't want to speak, went from wall to wall, pressing and kicking and smearing at the dirt with her hands, even while Božena and I were breaking open the first bottle. "Are you trying to knock the place down?" I said. "You should have it done by next century, I think!"

"One of the sergeants used to tell me ghost stories about this backwater," she said, in that funny little singsong accent. ("What backwater?" said Božena.) "All the way out from the Vronashi network she'd keep me up at night while we sat by the brig. She said how I'd be eaten by a snake with a hundred eyes, and how I'd be put to work mining radium over rivers of magma, and how you people had cellars full of the skulls of pretty girls. I'd like to prove she's wrong—about one thing, at least."

"What would someone do with a pretty girl's skull?" I said. "That's not the useful part, is it?"

But she just kept rummaging. I went to find another bottle, but we'd only managed to finish half of it when Eneida yelped. I thought she'd been bitten by one of the rats—every time a Ceian finds out about the rats is funnier than the last—but she thumped twice at the wall, and then came over to us and snatched the wine bottle and, before I could kick her shins, swung it round as hard as she could at a patch of moss.

Božena shouted. I shouted! I thought she was about to threaten us with a handful of broken glass, and I tell you I was ready to look round for a bottle of my own. But it wasn't the bottle that broke, but the wall, and behind it there was another room.

I helped her pull the rotting wood away. It was a cupboard, really. Do you remember, when the hurricane came through Alectelo the year we were ten, and you and I went searching in the empty wings for a place to curl up and hide? The room in the cellars was hardly big enough for me and Eneida to fit inside, pressed against each other—though I'm taller than I was when we were ten, and she's half again as tall as I am. We could hardly cram ourselves through the hole before our knees knocked into something big and made of stone.

I shouted at Božena until she helped us drag it out. It *was* a stone, more or less, square with Itsaryeti writing around the sides. I expect you would have known how to read it, but I didn't, and of course the Ceian didn't, and Božena wouldn't translate. All she said was: "This was an altar."

What for, what for, we said.

"Sacrifices," she said.

You can imagine how big Eneida's eyes got. "Oh," I said to her, "don't you know that they sacrifice people here? They get them on the altar—they have a few more upstairs—and they tie them down, and they call on Alekso Undying, and they take a stone knife—"

She was growing paler and paler throughout this, and I was hoping she would faint, but then Božena told me off for telling lies and taking the name of the Holy One in vain. Well, it was worth a try. They never have enough of a sense of humor, these priests. *You* would have laughed.

"Sacrifices, nothing," I said to her when she was done with the scolding. "We never sacrificed anything in Alectelo," and she sniffed and said, when the men and women of Szayet had surgeries to make their bodies right, like the priestesses here, wasn't that a kind of sacrifice? No, I said, of course not, that was giving up nothing, it was only rectification. And she was appalled, and said if I thought rectification wasn't holy, then no wonder the worship we did in Alectelo was so ugly, and Eneida had to hold me back for a while. But at last Božena explained to us that in Itsaryet they had sacrificed animals to Alekso Undying once. And now they didn't, or at least not anymore.

"Not for twenty years," she said, and stared at the Ceian for a while, in case she hadn't guessed whose fault it was. "But there was a time when we took our lambs and fine young birds, and we laid them on our altars. And when we opened their throats, the god would act in this world. He would light passages in hymns for His priestesses to sing, He would write His commands on the tablets of the high priestess. That was a time when the temple did works of faith! Now all we keep is wine, and gardens, and traitors and thieves." She kicked the stone, and then she clutched at her toe and apologized to the god at the top of her voice while I laughed.

"Well, I don't understand, anyway," I said. "What should Alekso Undying want with a pigeon? Even if He could eat or drink, surely He'd ask for something fattier."

"He's not a merchant!" said Božena. "He's not a shopkeeper on market day—one doesn't use sacrifice to *bargain* with Him. It's not that He expects to—to—to be paid for His services!"

"You mean you kill living things for him and he doesn't even give you what you want?" said Eneida. She'd climbed on top of the altar by this time, and was lying across it with her head dangling off the end.

"He keeps the turnings of the universe in their times and in their seasons," said Božena to me. "He causes the stars to run in their rightful riverbeds. He makes it so that what rises falls again, and so that what's dead feeds what lives. He wants

THE SEA ETERNAL   103

sacrifice because sacrifice is the law. He wants sacrifice because He is the Lord of Justice. If you don't know that, no wonder you're *here*, instead of ruling on your own planet."

They aren't meant to mention about my being the true chosen of the god, you know. Perhaps they think if they don't tell me about it, I'll forget. (Though I know you haven't.) "I'm here because I'm a very penitent prisoner of the queen," I said, which made Eneida laugh.

"I've never met anyone like you before," she said to me, "who speaks like she's entitled to the love of gods."

"Don't I have a right to be entitled," I said to her, getting angry, "for isn't my title princess and Oracle?" and she laughed and she only meant that it gave me a kind of dignity.

"You're like a pillar of fire," she told me. "Are all princesses like you?"

"There's only one other like me," I said. "Tell me again, though."

"You're like a pillar of fire," she said, smiling, and then she asked Božena why the stars hadn't fallen to pieces now that the priestesses weren't killing pigeons about it.

"I don't know how the god manifests the disorder of the universe," said Božena. "I'm only one of the juniors. Disorders of the universe are after the initiation tests." Then she scolded us for laughing. "Maybe a hole opens in reality and gobbles the impious up," she said when we wouldn't stop.

"That's something to drink to!" said Eneida, and went to grab another of the bottles.

"Surely you ought to be spitting this out like poison," I said to her after we had finished about half of it, "and telling us about how much better the vintages are on Ceiao."

"I've never been to Ceiao," she said.

So we spent the next hour drawing maps of the Crossbar and the Swordbelt Arm in the dirt, she and I, while the priest sulked by the open hole in the wall, and when Eneida drank enough she lost her stammer at last and told me the story of her life: a godawful refugee camp on a godawful backwater moon in the Crossbar, a terrible tragedy of some type or another, a glut of orphans. A draft from the Ceian governor. Every household to give up a daughter, a son, a child, to board a ship and carry a gun across the Ceian Empire, just to threaten poor defenseless girls like me.

"I can hardly shoot this gun of mine," she told me when I said that. "They give that kind of job to the citizens. I take a soldier's oath, but I'm a false soldier, really. I translate, and I decipher signals, and I keep logs for the officers, because I write more beautifully in Ceian than the Ceians do. That's what colonials are useful for!"

"Ah, a chronicler, an archivist, a walking history book," I said, to annoy her or to make her laugh, but she didn't do either.

"Eneida isn't my name, anyway," she said, "or not the one my father gave me. I thought I'd get along better in the fleet if I used a proper Ceian name instead of my own." I asked her what her name was, then, and she shrugged and said she didn't think she knew me well enough yet to tell me that.

So I asked then whether she was angry that she was in the fleet. "We're guests on their land," she said. "If they closed the camp, we'd have nowhere to go. So we give up a little piece of our people to them so we can keep the whole. Only a little piece. We all owe something to someone. And what would I have done if I'd stayed? Sit and watch my neighbors going to the sickbeds one by one? It wasn't as if staying would have meant I could become whatever I liked."

"What would you have liked to become?" I said.

"A poet," she said.

At this point Božena began a terrible yelling. We found her in the open cupboard—she'd grown bored with rolling her eyes and sighing pointedly, and she'd gone to climb in to show us how neglected she was and how sad she was about the false soldier's earlier blasphemy, and right away she'd cut herself, clumsy thing that she was. (In some ways she *does* remind me of you. Do you still puff and pant going up the stairs of the western tower? When you write to me to beg for my help again, tell me.) We thought it must be a nail, and I was half hoping her jaw would lock up—well, it would've been exciting, wouldn't it? If you care for your sister's conscience, you might send me friends, or circus acrobats—but when the false soldier shone a stylus light in, we saw that there was a knife on the floor. It must have tumbled down from the altar when we pulled it out. I don't know how the false soldier and I didn't hurt ourselves, rummaging around as we did. Well—as for me, I imagine I was blessed, but surely she should have been cut to pieces.

Let me tell you what was strange about this knife. The hilt was made of ordinary bone, carved in the same Itsaryeti as the altar had been. The blade, though, was quicksilver pearl. That's why it hadn't rusted, and that's why it was still as sharp as anything, even rotting down here in the dark.

Then Božena and I understood: lambs and birds, laid on altars, throats cut. Once the sacrifice had been made, the god would light passages in hymnals, write commands—a computer in the knife, speaking to whatever computers were near it.

Božena was very impressed, but the false soldier wasn't. She told us it was as big a waste of resources as she'd ever seen to use pearl to kill innocent animals for the sake of a few parlor tricks with computers. "Now, if the knife was meant to, oh, jump up and strike at their throats on its own," she said, "that'd be different," and then we all had the same thought at the same time and Božena yelled and threw the thing away, and the blade went straight into the wall and stuck there, so that not even the false soldier tugging for near on ten minutes could bring it out again.

So she sat down and told us another story instead, which her father had told to her in that repulsive refugee camp: about a king restored to his rightful throne.

Whatever the priestess believes, the stars are still running in their courses, and this planet still turns. Now that the night is come, all the heat's drained out of the temple, down to the other side of the world. I'm thinking of you, Gracia. I always am. I am wondering what I will say to you, on the day you come for me again. I wonder what you owe to me.

I remain—

queen of Szayet—
Oracle of Alekso Undying—
your loving sister—

ARCELIA CAVIRO DIOMATA
beloved of God.

Midnight, later.

Ordinarily, after she takes my tablets away in the evening, she hardly looks at me. But today she came back an hour later and dropped the tablet in my lap. "You can't keep calling me a false soldier," she said. I said I certainly could, since she wouldn't tell me her name. "You're the stubbornest prisoner in the world," she said. "I wish we'd had ten of you in my camp." I told her again that there were only two of me, and she said, "Well, my name begins with a *V.* Does that make you happy?"

It made me very happy, because I could see V. was trying not to smile.

Back in the old country, when wishing still worked, there lived in a city by the Saltless Sea a good and noble king. He was courageous in his battles, wise in his laws, and fair in his judgments, and he was as beloved by his people as any king in the world of the living may be.

Now, my dearest, a day came about when the king had to fly to war in a faraway part of the stars. He had neither son nor daughter nor child of his body, and so he left the kingdom in the care of his trusted vizier, and he gave into the vizier's hands an enchanted stone.

"If you should ever fear for me," he said, "take this stone to the crossroads, and call my name. If it turns red, I am in mortal danger. If it turns black, I am dead. But if it is silver, I am as well as you."

A year went by, my dearest, and the vizier had no word from the king. "I am afraid he is wounded," he said, "and I must ride to his rescue." So he left the palace and took the stone to the crossroads. But when he returned, my dearest, he said, "The stone is silver, and the king is well."

A second year went by, and the vizier had no word from the king. "I am afraid he is lost," he said, "and I must seek out his path home." So he left the palace and took the stone to the crossroads. But when he returned, he said, "The stone is silver, and the king is well."

A third year went by, and the vizier had no word from the king. "I am afraid he is dead," he said, "and I must do rites for his soul." So he left the palace and took the stone to the crossroads, and when he returned, it was as black as winter night, and he said to the people, "Your king is dead, and I am become ruler of this country."

So there was a great weeping in the land. And soon there was a greater weeping, for the new king proved himself to be a tyrant. And on the Saltless Sea there arose that band of brave and rebellious pirates of whom my father told me a hundred and a hundred stories.

It is said that one summer day, the band of pirates were sailing about the Saltless Sea when they came upon a little ship—so little that it had only one sailor within. The ships surrounded it and ordered it to halt and surrender all its coin. But when the sailor inside stood up, they saw that she was Death.

The captain of the pirates, who was a brave man, said to Death: "You are fairly caught by our fleet. Release our beloved king from your house, and return him to the throne of our kingdom, and we will let you go unharmed."

But Death said: "He is not in my house."

For the truth was that the good king had not died, but had only suffered a great wound. The vizier had smeared the stone in ink in order to claim the kingdom for himself. And the good king had been carried away to that fabled moon where the sages of this spiral arm guard the Waters of Life, and when the kingdom's need was greatest, he was destined to wake, and come home to his people again.

So the pirates released Death, and they went about many more adventures on the Saltless Sea in those days. And they spent all their life in the hope that tomorrow would be the day the great king would return to them, and next year they would feast with him in his city. And it was their children, my father said, who founded our village.

Yes, of course *our* village. It was my father's, and his father's before him, and so it's mine, too.

The king? Well, it must be that he is still sleeping. But one of these mornings—

*   *   *

For the last three days of the spider-litter journey, I slept. The dreams were fever dreams. I saw the day I landed on Ceiao. I saw C.'s face. I saw the Ceian dinners with the poets, once peace came—me, Vera, Horácio, Propercion, all of us thinking we were philosophers and speaking like children. The feasts, the dishes so rich and sweet I never even thought of sharing them. A lamb laid on the table, and C. passing me the knife to carve it up. And then, in the dream, the dinner table was a stone altar, and the lamb was not a lamb at all, but a girl, wrapped up in silver ribbons.

"Well?" said C. in the dream. "We're hungry." And so I looked into the girl's eyes and pushed the knife in.

And I woke. And our spider-litter was crossing through the Minor Gate, into the city.

During the war, just after C. began making me promises about land and the future, I told him about my people's sickness—the sickness that killed my father and my neighbors, everyone I ever knew. He said to me, "Don't think of the dead. Don't think of dying. Don't die. Only write. Haven't you and I heard the voices of a hundred Sintians who are rotting in the earth of faraway worlds? Words are the only creatures who ever triumph over death."

"Yes," I said, "words outlast death. What would be the point of them, otherwise?"

I rest in the imperial gardens, most days, and I sleep in the sun. I drift, I dream. I forget things. The doctors whisper over my head, and feed me bitter medicines, and never leave me alone, except in the afternoons. C. comes to visit me then. And I sit up and read to him from the story that I've written so far, the first history, the one he demanded of me, and I watch his face—that narrow face that the world has come to know so well—and I wait for him to tell me whether those words will last.

—V.

F orty minutes, sir," said Galvão.

"Tell me again how long it's been and I'll throw you to the dogs," I said.

The good news was that, after five days of drunken dinners among the Kutayeti noblemen, ending with a flat refusal on my part to say another word to either Lukhaya or Vualo until my demands were met, I had been allowed to see my captain and my *Videiran* lieutenants. They were alive and apparently well, and assured me that my men were in the same condition, aside from one who had taken a swing at a Kutayeti soldier who'd refused to lead them to my quarters.

The better news was that Julhan had not yet landed, and Szayet had replied to my messages. We had been freed from the luxurious labyrinth in the cliffside—albeit temporarily—and we now stood at the bottom of the half-dried shallow gorge that, in Sancta Mirtalo, passed for a harbor.

The bad news was that there would be no wandering off into the desert. Vualo had politely insisted that I snap the tracking device onto my pinkie finger before they would activate my wax-wing. "There are wild beasts down there, Admiral," they'd said blandly. "If the device deactivates at any point, we'll come down immediately to help you escape them."

"Sir—" said Ludon.

"I see them," I said. Black flecks were expanding in the sky, resolving themselves into prows and hulls. Fifteen were frigates—painted in Szayeti red, but I recognized the Ceian steel beneath—and these came to a stop high above us, some half mile or so from the dozen Kutayeti ships. The rest folded their wings and dove. The river shattered.

When the splatter had cleared, a handful of ships floated two hundred yards upstream, their leader painted in gold. Its door stayed sealed. The other ships weren't so coy. Portholes opened, figures crawled out, and soon a neat row of red-cloaked soldiers crunched along the shore toward us. Behind them came a crowd of servants, some carrying tablets, some carrying tall staffs with standards at their tops, one carrying a long bronze horn.

"Good morning," I called down the riverbank in Sintian. "Thank you for—"

The man with the horn raised it to his lips and blew a long note.

"Hail to the Oracle of Alekso Undying and Matheus Ceirran!" he cried. "Hail to the Protector of Caviro Orakolo, and the Guardian of His Grave! Hail to Altagracia Caviro Patramata, father-beloved and father-loving, the Bearer of the Pearls, the Crown of Alectelo, the Queen of Szayet! Hail! Hail! Hail!"

The Szayeti flung themselves to the wet earth, arms outstretched. The ship's door hissed, unsealed itself, and fell forward, collapsing into a pearl-wire bridge. Onto it stepped the Oracle, reaching out one delicate hand backward to balance on her bodyguard's shoulders.

The last time I'd seen the queen of Szayet enter enemy territory to conduct negotiations, she'd come via carpet. Then, her hair had been tangled, her kohl heat-smeared, her dress sticking with sweat to her belly and her thighs. Today she was draped from head to toe in cloth of gold, sleeves long and voluminous, the skirt hem sewn with coins that clattered and whispered at her feet. Red jasper blossoms studded her long dark braid. Her eyes were painted in thick, careful black, her mouth and cheeks red with ocher. A silver belt encircled her waist, embroidered with the figures of lions, and around her neck she had draped a collar of red jasper beads as wide as my hand, and around her forehead she had set a golden diadem. The Pearl of the Dead sat in her ear, marked with a black spot.

She strode to the shoreline, not letting go of her guard's arm. On dry land, a bowing servant held out platters of bread and salt. She took a pinch of each, laid them on her tongue, and swept into a deep curtsy.

"The Oracle of Matheus Ceirran greets the lady of the Sword-belt Arm, the Honored Disciple of God," she said, "and offers her all obeisance and fealties due her office."

"And what an honor it is," I said, "to greet the Oracle. Did you enjoy your flight, Szayet?"

"When the lady sovereign of the galaxy sees fit to summon her servant, her servant comes without complaint," said Szayet, rising. Her face showed no expression at all.

"What would she have to complain of?" I said.

"I will ask, if I may, my lady, why you summoned your servant with such haste," said Szayet, her eyes fixed an inch over my shoulder. "Do you now find Alectelo too small for your armies? Have you collected such trophies that our warships are become your freighters to bear them home? Has your glory grown to the height that the queen of Szayet is now given the privilege of following you like a jackal across the galaxy, waiting outside your camp for the leavings of your kills?"

"Do you expect your lady to apologize?" I said softly.

"Expect? Never," said Szayet, and snapped her fingers. A servant sprang up, brushing sand from her front. "My bags to the high ground," said Szayet, without looking away from me, "and

Zorione to what rooms our hosts have seen fit to prepare for us. No doubt they will wish us to dress." She curtsied again, very deeply. "We look forward to when Ceiao's demipotestate next sees fit to grant us an audience."

Then she was gone in a wave of Szayeti palace staff, soldiers and servants pouring past. I recognized half of them—friends from the barracks, cooks and cupbearers, a half dozen of my card game partners, and of course old Zorione, already arguing fiercely with a teenage boy over a bag.

My men and I followed at some distance. The gorge was distant enough from Roof-without-Rain that, by the time we reached the dry dock, I was sweating like a pig. Our ships still lay there with their hulls peeled back, engines open to the sky. The repairs, Vualo had assured me with a smile, were in-depth and difficult. Out of a sense of generosity, the Kutayeti intended to return our remaining ships to us better than new. For now, they sat here in pieces: *Surpresan*'s broken wing, the burns and scars across *Videiran*'s hull, the bright sphere in *Estrelan Polar* that held her invisible, seething atom of antimatter.

There had been two dozen waxwings at the base of the mountain when we'd come down from our rooms. Now there were only two left, and the shadows of the others shifted over the dead earth: the Szayeti party, moving swiftly up the cliffside. They were too far away already even for shouting.

Carmela Lukhaya was waiting for us in the docking bay, dressed today in bright red trousers and a silver-patterned coat. "Your client queen is a very charming woman," she said, giving me a slight bow. "Sasha is busy, but I wanted to be sure to catch her when she arrived."

"Naturally," I said. Every minute Lukhaya had managed to get me alone—and these were often, as the tracking device ensured she appeared at the same time every evening to fetch me to dinner, no matter how deep in the labyrinth I managed to lose myself—she had barraged me with questions about the practice of the Szayeti faith. What prayers did the Oracle say before going to sleep? What prayers upon waking? What prayers after passing through danger, or after experiencing great joy? Was there any limit on how often Szayet could speak to Alekso, or to Ceirran? Had marking Ceirran's Pearl with ink made any effect on his ability to speak to her? "None whatsoever," I'd said truthfully.

"Tell me something," I said as we entered the labyrinth now. "Why is a scholar the only person in Roof-without-Rain who calls the ambassador by their first name? And why is a scholar patrolling palace hallways? Wouldn't you rather be in a library? Or are there no decent libraries in the Kutayeti Empire?"

"There are none in Ceiao, either, as far as I understand," she said, smirking a little. "Sasha has been kind enough to fund my research these last years."

"What do they get in exchange?" I said.

"Has Ceiao not yet invented friendship? What a pity. What was Commander Ceirran to you, then?" said Lukhaya, and ducked under my swiftly upraised arm to unseal the door to my quarters. "I'll be back to take you to dinner," she said, and fled grinning down the hallway.

"She may be too late," said a voice from the bedroom.

Lukhaya and my fury flew from my mind like birds. "You liar," I said, stepping through the door, "you nearly had me fooled."

"I never have you fooled," said Szayet, and crossed the carpet, took my face in her hands, and seized my mouth with her own. She kissed meticulously, methodically, as if my mouth were a map and she wanted to mark her place, and she dug her nails into the back of my neck until I went helplessly soft and opened for her.

"You *are* a liar," I said against her cheek, when at last she had let me go. "How is it you can navigate the labyrinth? Did you wander for hours, calling my name?"

"You have an imagination," she said, a laugh in her voice. "I have a dozen ships floating half a mile above this mountain, Anita. *I* didn't make the mistake of trapping myself and all my men in enemy gravity."

"Still," I said, "you didn't need to hide behind the door to say hello. Too good to be seen with the lady of the Swordbelt Arm?"

"Oh, always," she said, and slid her arms around me and pulled me against her. She had changed from her golden dress into green silk that whispered against my legs, and she had unbound her hair, so when she bent to me it fell round us like a curtain, soft and dark. I had meant to tease her in return, but she was warm, and there was the faintest scent of myrrh at her neck, and I found myself sliding my thigh between hers, canting just a little into her heat.

We were on the bed, she in my lap and I with my fingers skating along the small of her back, dipping interestedly into the waistband of her leggings and out again, when she pulled herself away with an effort and said:

"It was no lie. Anita, you have done me wrong."

I had not really thought that she was lying about being angry—kissing had never been at odds with anger for her. Even in the first days after we had met, when her nights had been spent in Ceirran's arms, I had seen how often she looked at me. I had thought that, once Ceirran abandoned her, I'd coax her into a little fun, and then my commander and I would return to the work of war. That had been a very serious mistake. But I knew she had thought in those days that her pride, her queenship, and her better judgment would be a barrier between her and my mouth. That had been her mistake, and it still was.

"Yet you did come when I called for you," I said, "and you cut it very fine. Julhan can't be more than a day or two behind you." I reached for her hips again, but she rolled off my lap altogether and sat cross-legged on the bed beside me, looking for all the world like a child at a lesson except for the old and stony expression on her face.

"Did you expect me to pay ransom for you?" she said.

I laughed. "Bought and paid for by my own client queen? That would be the world turned upside down. Flavia would have my head. No, you've come to spirit the whole lot of us away in the night, haven't you?"

"Who's to say I came for you?" she said. "You must know that I have business of my own with that great beast I met in the corridors. Vualo, did they say?—I swear I've seen their face somewhere before." I must have looked blank, because her lips pressed together tightly and she said, "Has there been no word from the Merchants' Council? No reports from your officers? Did the news go unread, or does Ceiao not find Szayet's troubles interesting enough to report to her lady?"

"I haven't heard a word from Ceiao in five days except that Julhan means to cart me back there like a lost lamb," I said. "Flavia delegates a hundred things to my officers. That's nothing remarkable." *Or she doesn't tell me about them*, said a cool voice at the back of my mind, *if they're Szayeti troubles, and she's as good as demanded I leave the Swordbelt Arm and do my duty by the city*.

"Nothing remarkable," said Szayet, and laughed a little under her breath, not happily. "Tell me, then, before I bare my heart to you. How is it that the hero of Madinabia and Micavalli leaves my shores with four good ships and then finds herself trapped in a maze like a rat? From Cátia Lançan's fleets you found no trouble, but you were overcome by one rose garden?"

I was quiet a long while then. I wasn't like Szayet; I had no art for facts and lectures. And I still saw that girl when I closed my eyes at night—those silver eyes in that child's face.

"Swear you'll believe me," I said at last.

She looked no less angry, but she looked much more serious. "I swear," she said.

It took some time to tell her what I had seen. When I had finished, she stared for a while out the window at the dead earth.

"This girl," she said.

"Szayet," I said, "she frightened me."

"Because she was dangerous?" said Szayet. "Or because she reminded you of me?"

I was silent awhile. It was a strange, crooked thing that lay between us. It was a strange, crooked thing that Szayet was, a cold queen in the courtyard and a laughing burglar in my quarters. Sometimes, like this afternoon, she felt as distant and empty as the far side of the Black Maw. Other times, like now, I remembered that she had entrusted me with the most precious things in her life: the falsehood of her queenship, the falsehood of her prophecy. The meaninglessness of the black spot in her Pearl, a pupil in the center of a sightless silver eye.

"You're a liar after all, Szayet," I said, "if you will sit with me and try to tell me that you aren't dangerous."

She sighed, subdued, but her expression was still bitter. "Do you know the planet they call the Ogre?" she said.

"Isn't that the dwarf planet on the outskirts of your system where we had that picnic at midwinter?" I said. "Irregular orbit, a sister moon?"

"Fifteen Kutayeti reconnaissance ships landed there and made camp five days ago," she said.

It took me a moment to understand, and when I did, I sat up and spat on the floor. *Demonstrate the emperor's dignity*, indeed. "I'll wring that bull's neck of theirs," I said darkly. "They as good as told me—as soon as they managed to get me and my soldiers a few thousand light-years away from you—"

"You did your level best to get yourself thousands of light-years away without their help," said Szayet.

Guilt pricked at me, which I did not like, and doubt, which I liked still less. "Give me their position," I said. "Julhan's warship can make itself useful after all. Say the word, and he'll come with a thousand frigates, and those reconnaissance ships are dust."

"And dig myself into an early grave," said Szayet harshly. "Why do you think they've come, Anita?"

"To threaten Ceiao's client planet, of course," I said. "Why else?"

"Because of opportunity!" she said. "Undying God, we've been selling them half the quicksilver pearl we grow in the new oyster farms. Of course they want us under their thumb—they want that pearl as tribute! If all they wanted was to threaten Ceiao, they'd go to Medveyet, Cherekku, any of my other neighbors that Ceiao has colonized. They want to threaten a planet that seems vulnerable—and they believe I'm vulnerable because they believe my sovereignty is a fiction, they believe I depend on you! They think that on Szayet, when Anita Decretan flies to war, all of Szayet's self-defense flies with her, that my own fleet is worth about as much as my broken moons! You won't stay on Szayet? Fine. But as long as you wear Szayet lightly, as long as you treat Szayet like a toy to be played with and cosseted and then locked away from thieves while you go about your business, you do my people harm! All you'd do by destroying those ships is painting me to be weaker still!"

By the end of this speech she had rolled off the bed and was standing at the window, arms crossed. For my part, I could not seem to meet her eyes, which made me angry. "Fortune's feet, Szayet, you've been blinded by pride," I said. "You think it makes your fleet worthless to be outnumbered by the whole damn Kutayeti Empire? You'd need to be an empire yourself to stand against them without help!" My voice was rising. I took a deep breath, and tried a coaxing tone: "Can't Ceiao be of use to you? Won't you say yes to that even once?"

"It wouldn't be once!" said Szayet. "Is the whole galaxy to be told that I'm helpless once the empire turns its gaze from me?

Should I leave my people fearful of constant war, distrustful of the peace, unhappy with their work? Should the whole of my dominion treat the Empire of Ceiao as a capricious and distant master, a schoolteacher or an elderly father or a cuckolded husband, to be thwarted and lied to and depended upon—"

Heat flooded to my face, black and dizzying. "So that's how the Swordbelt Arm sees Ceian armies, when they put their support behind a client monarch who can't win a war for the throne on her own?" I said. "Useful information. I can think of a friend of mine who would have liked to know that."

She looked at me for a long moment, then exhaled and turned away, facing the door. I could only see the very edge of her face. She said, her tone controlled, "I believe I have as much a right to speak truthfully of him as you have."

"Is that what you believe, Madam Oracle?" I said. "No, don't answer that. Satisfy your poor stupid lover's curiosity on this, instead. When I first met you, with whom were you cuckolding your husband Ceiao?"

What I could see of her face went absolutely, frighteningly blank.

"Perhaps it would be best if your usual escort accompanied you to dinner after all," she said. "I'm afraid my dress is ill-suited for this high company. I should change."

"Szayet—" I said, regretful, ashamed, and stubbornly furious, but she went to the door.

"Szayet, Szayet, Szayet," she said lightly. "Do you know, I liked the world better when there was somebody in it who thought of me as Patramata," and then she was gone.

I stewed for a long while before I could bear to sit up and go to the wardrobe, not least because it was the second time in as many meetings that she had had the last word on me. One of these days, I would need to learn how to be the one who said goodbye.

There was a message waiting from Julhan, naturally. His ship had reached Medveyet when he had received my message saying the Oracle had arrived. He would now begin the five-day return flight to Ceiao—he did not quite keep his frustration out of this, which managed to wrench a smile out of me—and he would take the opportunity to collect some of the tribute owed by our colonies in the Swordbelt Arm that I had, doubtlessly due to my busy schedule, failed to collect and send to the council treasury in recent months.

Toward the end, his tone softened:

> I understand that, in recent days, your sister may have inadvertently been given—and may even have conveyed to you—the impression that I meant you ill. Please rest assured that I meant what I said as you left for Khramya: It would not benefit me to sabotage you. I intended to negotiate with the Kutayeti for your release as a gesture of my good intent. If that opportunity is no longer available, allow me to demonstrate goodwill in some other way.
>
> I hope that the Oracle's decision to involve herself in Ceian-Kutayeti negotiations is the eagerness of a client queen to act for the benefit of the lady of the Swordbelt Arm, rather than the mark of a more selfish, less loyal ambition. It is, of course, your right to trust your safety (and the safety of your men) to foreign warships owned by a sovereign state. Please know that, should you call at any time, several of my own cruisers are not far from Szayet and can be dispatched to its atmosphere at any time to protect your person.
>
> Alternately, I would be glad to make you a loan— at favorable interest rates—of some thousand tons of perfumes, clothing, fine woods, silfion, and other luxury items from my holdings in Madinabia for you to sell to

the Szayeti people. Glad as I am that the crown's debt to
us has been repaid in full, it would do no harm for a little
Szayeti coin to begin to come into Ceian pockets again—
that is, of course, to yours.

Or you could simply come to dinner. My gardens are
bearing figs this year, and my cook has discovered a unique
recipe for mushrooms. It pains me that in recent days your
sister would rather dine with Outer City gangsters of
Kutayeti birth rather than people of quality. I would be
pleased to invite her as well.

With all due respect, I remain your diligent
colleague—

Good. He'd learned his lesson about crossing me, and he'd
learned it thoroughly. It was a pretty piece of groveling, too. The
note about putting Ceian warships in the Szayeti atmosphere
pricked bitterly at my pride. At least there was someone who
understood that for the generosity it was.

There weren't enough fine dinners or luxury goods in the
galaxy to induce me back to Ceirran's house. But Julhan's offer
tugged at something deep. Yes, I wanted that life I'd had before
Ceirran had died. I wanted power, I wanted the chance to get
my knife bloody every so often, but above all, I wanted carelessness. I had learned in those days the very particular and wonderful carelessness that came when you cared for only one thing.

If Szayet would only let me care for her in that way! If she
would only let me turn Ceiao's eye upon her, let Ceiao's mouth
devour her enemies—did she not understand what good fortune it was, what an honor, that the lady of the Swordbelt Arm
chose to eat at her table every night? Did she not understand
that no other Ceian in the world would have whiled away all
these days at the court of a client queen? She asked too much of
me—my patience, my silence, my inaction, for me to hold on to

the nightmarish awareness that the world watched what I did. Why could she not be satisfied with my devotion? Why could she not let me spend half my time as the Ceian fleet, raining destruction on all my foes, and half my time as a mindless creature blinded by fireworks and sick with feasting, and none of my time as Anita Decretan?

There were tables laid out in the hall when Lukhaya and I arrived, laden with roast quail, fresh biscuits, squash scattered with fragrant bee balm, and, naturally, dozens of flasks of wine. The Kutayeti had not stood on ceremony tonight, either: The duchess was smearing butter onto the biscuits, and the baron of Ychlan Nebula was sinking his teeth into a quail leg, fat gleaming on his chin. Vualo sat at the far end of one table, left of its head. As soon as they saw me, they rose and gestured with great graciousness to the chair across from them.

I had not had time to wait for the servants to pull the chair out before the door flew open again. This time the whole court rose, noblemen looking with bright, hungry eyes at the door.

"Altagracia Caviro Patramata, Oracle Queen of Szayet!" Vualo called. "I have the honor to be Sasha Vualo, messenger of the Emperor of Kutayet, the King of Kings, the head of *Dom* Harsaky, the most reverent keeper of the Flame of Alekso of Sintia. In his graciousness he has granted me the honor of passing to you, his sister queen, his deepest respects. He begs that your lands should bear fruit, that your animals should bear children, that your earth should be blessed with gold and your people should be blessed with wisdom, that your beauty should remain eternal, and that your ships should never rust."

Szayet had, after all, gilded herself further after leaving my rooms. The dress was the same, but her hands and wrists were draped in white pearls, her neck with silver. I was very sure that I had smudged the red at her mouth, but now there was no evidence of that at all.

"The emperor does me a great honor," she said. "Please bear my brother king my compliments, and my hope for his health, and the health of his kingdom, and the health of the empress consort, and the health of the six children of his elder husband, and the health of the seven children of his younger husband, and the health of *Dom* Harsaky in its entirety, and the health and fruitfulness of his lands and his seas and his vassals, from the Oracle of Alekso Undying and Matheus Ceirran, Bearer of the Pearls of the Dead." I imagined that I saw a curl to her lip when she said *and Matheus Ceirran*, and looked away to hide my expression.

Vualo bowed to her, very slightly. She curtsied in return, very shallowly, and crossed the hall to the head of the table. The court sat as one and burst immediately into whispering.

"How kind of you to grace us," said Vualo to Szayet, low. "Will you allow me to attend on you?"

"Certainly," said Szayet, and watched them, expressionless, as they poured her wine from the jug. I could not catch her eye. When they had sat down again, she said, still without the least flicker of feeling, "Szayet has been informed of the monstrous perversion you have made of our lord's great work."

Vualo looked positively delighted. "My lord is pleased to honor those brave souls who have given their bodies into the empire's service through the Terrestrial Intelligence," they said. "And his officers and his sworn lords, whose service is no less than his satellites and warships."

Szayet shrugged. "The Terrestrial Intelligence?" she said. "An apt name. There is nothing heavenly in it. May I return the favor?" She took the wine jug from their hand and bent gracefully over their cup.

"You may," said Vualo, "if I may ask what Alekso of Sintia has to do with the work."

"It is Alekso's intelligence you warp," said Szayet. "Our lord's intelligence, which you use to mutilate children. "

"I see the confusion," said Vualo cheerfully. "Ah—a little more wine, Your Majesty. Thank you. How kind you are to me! Of course a Szayeti would assume, believing so charmingly as you do that Alekso is in your quicksilver pearl"—Szayet's hands jerked, and the wood of the table bled purple, which Vualo ignored—"that it is His wisdom that guides any innovation that has to do with pearl at all. I'm afraid you're wrong there."

"And what is it you expect the Oracle to believe?" Szayet said to Vualo. "How did this blending of quicksilver pearl and the human soul come to the emperor, if not by the wisdom of the Eternal King?"

"Your Majesty," said Vualo pityingly. "Surely you aren't suggesting that every one of my people's secrets be laid bare in mixed company?"

At last Szayet looked at me, and I felt myself blush again. It was a look I had not seen on her face since the day we had met almost twelve years ago on Ceiao, when I had laughed at her for telling me that her father was the Oracle of Alekso Undying. But then she had been a petulant child, and now she was a woman, silk-clad and certain of her own beauty, and her eyes were the eyes of a hawk.

"Kutayeti ships will remove themselves immediately from Szayeti space and return to their legal borders," she said, turning away. I exhaled at last. "Does the emperor object to that much being said in mixed company?"

"Are they in Szayeti space? I was under the impression they hadn't breached your border," said Vualo. "Surely you of all people understand why the emperor must assert himself against Ceian aggression." *You of all people* made me start, but they went on as if they hadn't noticed, "He's appreciated so deeply Szayet's generosity as a trading partner this last year. He has no doubt of her continued neutrality in this unfortunate conflict." They smiled slightly at me. "But the queen herself must understand the emperor's difficulty, having such a close ally of the Ceian people on his doorstep. Particularly if Ceiao threatens to do to Kutayet as it has done to Belkayet—to Itsaryet—to Medveyet—to Cherekku—to Madinabia..."

With each successive name of a Ceian colony Szayet's face grew tighter. "What are Kutayet's intentions on the Szayeti border," she said, "in the name of *asserting itself against Ceian aggression*?"

"Nothing but to ensure our security until Ceiao's ships depart from our territory," said Vualo, spreading their hands.

"Ceiao's ships are happy to depart from this territory tomorrow morning, if you like," I said. "Now, even."

"And miss this lovely quail?" said Vualo. "Ah—and the musicians!"

They were filing in alongside the great sandstone pillars: tanburs and flutes, drums and panpipes. Some of the noblemen were beginning to rise to dance. The duke who had been telling me at length about his handsome son threw me a wink. I looked desperately away, stood, and held out my hand to Szayet, making myself smile as if there were no doubt about whether she would take it.

I heard her sigh. She laid her fingers in my palm, and I pulled her into my arms.

In this, at least, there had never been a shortage of comfort between us. She danced lightly, whirling out of my grasp as if someone had wound her up and let her fly, and when I drew her back against me, I could feel her heartbeat in her ribs. I slid my hand down to the small of her back. She shivered, but her face was still hard.

"A hostage shouldn't be as happy as you are," she said.

"I'm not a hostage," I said. "I'm negotiating the peace."

"I'm passing the word to Zorione to have two of the warships descend to this palace's entrances with docking bays open," she said. "Your men are leaving Sancta Mirtalo. If you want to keep *negotiating the peace* with that sneering brute, I can't make you leave. Nor do I intend to try."

"You're angry about what they said about your god, aren't you?" I said. "Really and truly. You'll say whatever you like about"—I dropped my voice to a very faint murmur in her ear—"using a god when you need him and then tossing him aside. But it drives you mad to think that anyone else might feel the same way."

"Say what you will of me," she said tightly, "but they're lying that Alekso's work has nothing to do with their Terrestrial Intelligence. I'm sure of it. Making Ceirran's Pearl of the Dead was difficult enough for me with Alekso's help. What fumbling efforts would come from *these* people as they tried to unite pearl and human consciousness, I dread to think."

"You don't think Alekso might have—" I said, and raised my eyebrows, attempting to convey in silence that she had given her god very good reason to help her enemies, starting with the fact that he had preferred her sister as his Oracle, ending with her public false insistence that he was no longer the sole god of Szayet, and including in the middle a fair number of times that I had privately mocked to her his tastes in clothing, lovers, and poetry. How much of this came across was not clear. She shook her head.

"He can't have had the power to speak to them," she said. "He can see within the bounds of the palace at Alectelo, and he can send dreams, as he did to Celestino Xicaran the night before Ceirran died, and—" She raised her eyebrows, which I understood to mean the dream that had told her sister she was his chosen queen. "Though you know that takes great effort for him. But he has never spoken to anyone more than a half mile from him, and certainly he has never spoken to anyone outside the Szayeti atmosphere. What's more, no one except his Oracle can ever speak to him. He is mine, and mine alone."

"Caught and caged like a bird," I said against her jaw, hands drifting down her waist. "You're fond of doing that, aren't you?" At that a reluctant spark lit in her face at last. Reconciliation without any apologies at all, I thought happily, and pressing my advantage, I murmured, "Think how good it'd feel if you let me kill them. I could open up their throat right here on the floor. Let 'em bleed out before the musicians start the circle dances."

"They have done some very neat work to protect themself from your doing exactly that," said Szayet quietly. "It would be no better than your vaporizing their ships in my asteroid belt."

"Of course it'd be better," I said. "You'd be here. You'd see the body. Very well, you won't let Ceiao protect you today. Will you let Ceiao entertain you?"

I felt her laugh without hearing it, and the sudden softness in her shoulders, in her hands where they pressed against my ribs. "You always entertain me, Anita," she said. "But you know very well that you're not at my mercy—not once we leave this desert, anyway."

"I'm always at your mercy, Szayet," I said. "At the top of a mountain, when I want a ship and only you have it. In a labyrinth, when I want a way out and only you know it. In the middle of a dance, when I want a kiss and only you can give it. How could I be at your mercy any more than I am?"

"Want?" she said. Her eyes were glittering.

"Yearn for," I said softly against the shell of her ear. "Starve for. Need. If my lady holds that I should go unkissed, I'll obey her, but Fortune! I'll die for the lack."

"You've suffered wanting far worse than that without dying of it," she said, smiling.

We'd come up against the great window, that sheer drop into black space, the ground as grey as thunder below. My head said we were entirely safe. My eyes said that if I lifted Szayet in my arms, and took another step—

She was looking at me expectantly. I grinned. "Name one thing I've ever wanted more than—" I said, and then stopped. The pipes were dying into silence, and her eyes had gone wide in warning.

"Your Majesty," said Vualo's voice behind my shoulder. I turned, bracing myself. They held out one broad hand and bowed, and I saw to my shock that they were bowing to me. "Will the Oracle be so kind as to lend me her partner for a little while?" they said.

Szayet was thrown, but only for a moment, and then she bared her teeth at Vualo. "Given the circumstances," she said, "I'm sure you'll understand if I wonder whether you'll let me have her back."

Now Vualo surprised me for a second time: They caught my eye and winked. "It's your right to keep her all for yourself, of course," they said to Szayet. Perhaps it was that—*all for yourself*, catching at the base of my spine and shivering all the way up to my neck—that made me put my hand in theirs, and say:

"I'll dance."

"Anita," said Szayet warningly, but whatever she would have said next was drowned out. The horns rose up. Vualo's thick fingers closed over my hand, and they drew me out toward the center of the floor.

Their size was deceptive. They moved with a leonine grace, careless and utterly sure of themself. Those great hands, I thought, would not have to put in any real effort to bruise.

"Your ships really will be finished shortly," they said. "Not that I expect I can convince you of that. Do you mean to leave them rusting here under the sun?"

"Of course not," I said. "We'll all leave when they're repaired, as you say."

I'd never had a talent for lies. Vualo smiled thinly. "Are you always so cavalier about cutting ties with what keeps you tied planetside?" they said. "Your ships. Your lover. Maral os-Margad."

I stared, and they raised their eyebrows. "You asked the name of the host of the Intelligence that you murdered," they said. "Had you forgotten?"

The girl, silver-eyed, mouth open like a fish. That wasn't a Kutayeti name. She must have been from one of the emperor's colonies—or one of his client kingdoms. I'd dreamed of her last night, and the night before, too.

"No," I said. "No, I didn't kill her. Your doctor got there first."

"Are you the Eternal Judge, that you should judge us?" they said. "This from the people who make their children into murderers when they are no older than fifteen?"

I thought, uncharitably, that I would like to see Vualo's face if I told them a few of the things I'd been doing to the enemy when I was fifteen. Killing had been by far the least imaginative part of it. It might have been that they saw this in my expression, for theirs grew thoughtful.

"What I wish you'd understand is that the Intelligence unites us," they said. "A ship to its crew, a satellite to those living on it. Those people who become vessels for it are only giving themselves a hundred mouths with which to speak, a hundred ears with which to listen. Their bodies may be stilled, yes, but their souls fly free—freer than yours or mine, Admiral. Don't you use your tablet to connect yourself to your family when you're far from Ceiao?"

"That's not the same at all," I said. "I'm not a—a *half* of my tablet."

"Are you not?" said Vualo, broad thumb sliding along my spine. "A speaker is half of a conversation. A queen is half of her kingdom—far less than half, in fact, a fraction. As a world is a fraction of an empire, as the present is a fraction of history. As a lover is a fraction of love."

"You're liable to lose that hand," I said.

They let go of me at once and held their hands up, smiling

a wide white cat's smile. "I'm afraid that we've reached a stale-mate," they said. "Both of us are blinded. Me by love for my lord, and you, of course, for yours." They jerked their head to the side, and I looked and saw Szayet, dancing in the arms of one of her handmaidens.

The princess of the Asteroids Vorysna was about to barrel into us. With reluctance, I caught Vualo's hand again and pulled them into a turn. "She's my lord, then? Weren't you telling her to assert herself against my aggression twenty minutes ago?" I said.

"Hm?" they said. "Oh, I see. I meant Matheus Ceirran. What an interesting misunderstanding."

Hell, I thought. That was a slip worse than I'd made in five nights of drunkenness and loneliness—though it had not, really, been a slip at all. Ceirran had not been my lord. He had been my officer, my commander, my friend. The people who had thought he was more than that had been wrong. The people who had thought he'd *wanted* to be more than that had killed him.

They'd been entirely correct, of course. "On Ceiao, Matheus Ceirran's dead," I said.

"But you're not on Ceiao now," said Vualo. "And, if the reports we hear at court are reliable, you've been avoiding Ceiao for some time. Do your talents lie in dancing rather than fighting these days?"

The dance had brought us left hip to right hip, my arm across their collarbone. I pushed my forearm up with some force against their thick neck. "Step outside with me and I'll let you judge for yourself," I said.

"Or perhaps it's simply that your lord is a jealous god," they said, not even sounding breathless, "and he wants you to be always at his side, and as the queen of Szayet is his keeper, Sza-yet must keep you." They shrugged. "If you were the Oracle, and you had that Pearl in your ear, I suppose you'd simply bring him to the battlefield."

I slid my foot in between theirs. They stumbled. "I'm not," I said, "the Oracle."

The music was fading now. I cast my eyes about for Szayet, but she was on the other side of the room, and Vualo's hand still had my waist in a strong grip. "Not so long ago, Szayet had one god and one Oracle," they said. "Now it has two gods, and two people who call themselves a god's best beloved. How good it is for divinities to dwell together in such harmony."

"Call it a miracle, if you like," I said.

"Oh, certainly true friendship is always a miracle," said Vualo. "A miracle made in the hands of man, as we say on Kutayet. How well do Alekso of Sintia and Matheus Ceirran communicate with each other, do you think?"

"Spectacularly," I said flatly.

"How do they manage it?" they said. "What in the Pearl of the Dead allows that sort of harmony to bloom?"

"How should I know?" I said, irritated and bewildered. "That's a question for the Library of Alectelo."

And then I was bewildered, because their face was abruptly alight with wolfish triumph—but behind me, Szayet said sharply, "Anita." I turned, relieved, and caught her outreached hand. She nodded to Vualo. "I see I was right to be afraid about whether you would return her."

"How could I bear to part from such pleasant company," said Vualo, and bowed to both of us, deeply this time. "Thank you for the dance, Admiral Decretan. If I don't see you tomorrow, please know I've enjoyed being your host more than you can understand. I hope to see you in Sancta Mirtalo again very soon."

The pipes began again, high and sweet: an old Belkayeti circle dance. Szayet pulled me away, along the outer circle. "Do you really want to stay?" she whispered.

"No," I said feelingly. "How soon before my men are safe in your ships?"

"We have six of my fighters running relay now," she said. "Move toward the far corner. Is there anything you need in your quarters?" I shook my head. "I don't put it past them to put a guard there," she said. "We'll go out the door."

The crowd was thin but plentiful enough for us to slip casually between servants. Easily, as though fidgeting, I tucked my hands beneath my cloak and pried at my pinkie. The tracking device sprang free, deactivated. I tucked it into a pouch on my belt and cast one last look back, afraid, but for once my instincts were wrong. Vualo was not looking our way at all. They had caught Lukhaya by the elbow and were talking to her urgently by the window, and Lukhaya's eyes were bright.

"Come," said Szayet. I felt her warm hand in mine, an unspeakable relief, and turned to follow her.

We fled through the labyrinth, she guiding us as her pilot above instructed her, through a crystal-blue pool, gleaming mechanical fish moving swiftly in its depths; an enormous pit where tiny waxwings fluttered from side to side; walls plastered with moving holos of scantily clad Sintians, thankfully empty of anyone but us; and at last another cavern, much like the one I had entered, but this one filled with red and blue cloaks—my soldiers and Szayet's own. I reached out to them, clasped hands, embraced lieutenants, fussed briefly over the soldier who'd been hurt trying to come see me. "You'll have first pick of the looting at our next victory," I told him, and he laughed.

"This way," said Szayet urgently from the far end of the cavern. I ruffled the soldier's hair and scrambled after her. The tunnels we'd entered by waxwing were not quite comfortable for a person walking upright—even Szayet, who was short, had to duck her head—and my back ached by the time I smelled creosote and emerged onto the edge of the cliff.

Wind whipped at our faces. Five feet below, a Szayeti fighter bobbed against the cliffside, the door in its roof open. Beneath it was a sheer drop to the desert floor.

Szayet held out her hand. "Do you trust me?" she shouted over the wind.

"Never," I shouted back, and jumped.

The Szayeti warships were all old, rusted things, especially to my Ceian eye. The one set to take us back to Szayet was older than most, her hull creaking with every shift of the accretion-tide. I knew as soon as I heard the engines cough to life that it would be a slow journey back to Alectelo.

"And what are you in a hurry to reach?" said Szayet when I said this, her arms sliding round my waist. The captain's quarters on this ship were pure Szayeti luxury, jewels strewn along their doors, ceilings carved intricately with scenes of shattering moons. The window was as long and tall as my arm, and with Sancta Mirtalo a shrinking red-orange fist below us, I felt strongly that was a luxury, too.

"Szayet, of course," I said. "Always."

She hummed. "I notice you haven't died yet," she said.

It took me a moment to remember our conversation in the ballroom. "Oh, I have," I said, turning round. "Starved and perished. Dead and gone and in the grave."

"Do you think I can't tell the difference?" she said, and before I could think of some reply to make her laugh, she had me pressed against the window, her mouth on mine, her fingers working at the fastening of my cloak.

"Say it again," she said a while later, on the bed. She was straddling my thighs, the heel of her hand pressing between my legs. "What you said when we were dancing."

"Say what?" I said breathlessly.

"Say you need me," she said, and bent to kiss me, so that I was trapped entirely beneath her warm sweet weight.

All I could do was rock my hips up against her hand, and this I did, eager and unashamed. "I need you," I said.

"Say you missed me," she said fiercely, muffled against my mouth.

"I missed you," I said, "I missed you, I wanted you—I want you—in your power, at your mercy—" She hissed at that, and sat up and began to work her hand in earnest. "Always," I gasped out, "always, Szayet, no one else's. Just don't stop—please, please—I want, I want, all I want, all I want is—"

I rose the next morning and dressed myself with no particular haste. The sun was thin and watery through the curtains—it always was, this time of year, and I had hated it since I was a child—and I threw my warmest cloak over my shoulders, so thick that shoving the pin through its fabric took me nearly a minute.

The snow had melted, at long last. The buds were nudging through on the linden twigs. I could hear the screeching of the spider-litters on the cobblestones, as rusty as usual in spring, and the distant roar of ships grown louder in the dampness of the air. The river was cracking, I thought absently. Sooner or later, we would see the waters of the Nevede burst.

The door of the Libeiracópolan, too, was streaked grey with last night's damp. I ducked through, not quickly enough—ice slid from the doorframe directly down the back of my neck, such a swift shock that I laughed aloud.

"What's so funny?" said Ceirran.

He was at the far end of the dome, in his own seat, raised above the rest. Some councillor was by his side, clutching his arm. He waved her off impatiently. "Come here," he said, smiling at me.

"As my lord commands," I drawled, picking my way through the benches.

"If I didn't know better, Captain, I'd call your tone insubordinate," he said. He hadn't stopped smiling.

"Fortunate for me that you know better, isn't it," I said, stepped over the last bench, and fell to my knees.

Above me I heard his laugh again, almost inaudible, more breath than sound. On my head, faint pressure: his hand.

"Rise, Ana Decretan," he said.

I rose. I loved his face at these times: a lion's face, eyes half-lidded. The councillor, just behind his shoulder, looked very put out.

"If you'd only give me a signature on these, Lord," she said.

"At my own pace, child," said Ceirran, without turning, "if that's allowed to me."

He could not see her flinch, but I could. "Of course," she murmured, and turned away.

"Have you eaten yet?" he said to me, nodding to one of the dark arches around the edge of the dome. "Come walk with me."

In one of the hallways of the Libeiracópolan there was a feast laid, pottage and berries and little fried fish, which burned my fingers when I picked them up and my tongue when I chewed them. "You're in no hurry to do business today," I said.

"I have plenty of time," he said, and smiled at me. And then, incomprehensibly, I was watching two Ceirrans—or rather, there were two of me, watching the same man: one who recognized that smile, who knew it as fondly and familiarly as she knew her right hand, and one who had never seen Matheus Ceirran look so blankly, brainlessly, stupidly hungry in his life.

"Show it to me," he said softly.

Half of me did not know what he meant. The other half said, a laugh in her voice, "I thought you told me not to carry it around."

"I did," he said, and, "You shouldn't," and then: "Show it to me anyway."

The half of me that was so certain put my hand in the inside pocket of my cloak. Something rested there, cool and hard. I withdrew it, and turned my palm over, and Matheus Ceirran lifted the quicksilver pearl from my hand.

"Anita," he said, "can I tell you a secret?"

"Anything," said my voice teasingly.

"I'm glad you took it," he said. "I'm glad it's not Patramata. I'm glad it's you," and I woke screaming.

It must have been a little after midnight. The lamps in the captain's quarters were blazing—they had woken at my motion: I was sitting bolt upright.

"What is it?" said Szayet sleepily. "What's wrong?"

"Nothing," I said. "Nothing at all."

Sir:

Your captain gave me to understand that distracting the lady of the Crossbar with day-to-day concerns could be misconstrued as impeding the war effort. Your captain also advised me that the lady of the Crossbar is in any case unavailable. Accordingly, it was suggested that I redirect the following report to you.

I have always been devotedly loyal to the name of Ceirran, and I have nothing but the greatest respect for your title and family. Please let me know if any of the above is unacceptable, and if so, please understand that my error comes purely from ignorance and not malice.

All the best,
Ângelo Pinhan
Secretary to the Governor of the
Vigesimal and Trigesimal Minor Colonies

Status Report on the Colonial Subjects
of Ceiao 20M3

The purpose of this report is to survey the situation of the surviving colonial subjects of Ceiao 20M3, formerly known as "Tenessa," and to recommend a treatment plan for their successful integration into Ceian society.

<u>Recommendation</u>

An end to funding of the partial medical care authorized under Council Act 1423§2A, "Treatment of the Displaced Colonials of Tenessa [*sic*]." An end to funding of the housing assistance authorized under Council Act 1423§2B, "Settlement of the Displaced Colonials of Tenessa [*sic*]," and liquidation of the remaining temporary camps. Moving forward, this committee recommends that the special status of the colonial subjects be ended. Those subjects who are candidates for Ceian residency, or, in extreme cases, citizenship (see "Veterans" below) should be permanently resettled on unpopulated or underdeveloped worlds.[1]

<u>Ceiao 20M3</u>

The star Ceiao 20, located 15.2 light-years from Ceiao Sol, is orbited by eighteen planets, including the gas giant Ceiao 20M. The moon Ceiao 20M3 was the only terraformed body in the

---

1 E.g., the Madinabic moons.

system. As of recent events (see *Inciting Incident* below), further terraforming efforts are underway to enable resettlement by Ceian citizens.

Due to the similarities between the dialect spoken on this moon and the Ceian language, historians theorize that the original inhabitants of Ceiao 20M3 are descendants of early proto-Ceian galactic explorers. These proto-Ceians likely split off from Ceiao's own ancestors shortly before the settlement of Ceiao.

The inhabitants of Ceiao 20M3 can therefore be seen as a living snapshot of the moment of Ceiao's founding, with a corresponding value to historical and anthropological study.

Inciting Incident

Twenty-two years ago, following the construction and terraforming of the satellite Altabau as a rubber plantation by Councillor Mauro Monteiron on the Kutayeti border,[2] the Kutayeti Empire launched an unprovoked and outrageous attack on the farm, claiming afterward that the satellite had been acting as a base for Ceian soldiers. Over 1,300,000 dekar worth of rubber trees were destroyed in the bombing, and 361 local workers (40.1% of the satellite's population) were injured or killed.

Though Councillors Quinha Semfontan and Matheus Ceirran argued for immediate military retaliation, Councillor Thiago Veguion noted that council funds were limited due to the recent conquest of Belkayet.[3] In a compromise brokered by Councillor Túlio Cachoeiran, a smaller budget was directed instead into development of orbital weapons to provide for defense of the satellite. After initial research, engineering, and testing, a newly developed shield was found to destroy up to 15% of incoming atmosphere-to-planet missile fire. Funding was

---

2 See *Altabau Crisis* in separate report.
3 Enacted by Councillor Quinha Semfontan.

provided through a personal loan from Councillor Semfontan, in exchange for council approval of Councillor Ceirran's exploratory expedition into the Madinabic moons.

It was agreed by all parties that the initial tests for the orbital weapon should be conducted on Ceiao 20M3, as it was both largely undeveloped and highly pacified (see Council Act 1392§4D, "Providing for the Defense of Life and Property on the Kutayeti Border," subsection: "Tenessa [*sic*]").

Immediate Aftermath

When the environmental effects of the orbital weapon became apparent, the 745,672 inhabitants of Ceiao 20M3 were evacuated and resettled on a moon near Sintia in council-funded camps.

Modern Day

Of the 745,672 inhabitants of Ceiao 20M3 at the time of the incident (not counting Ceian citizens or aid workers), 102,098 survive to the present day. It is apparent that the funding initially accorded to their ongoing care is far greater than sufficient to meet the needs of such a reduced population. For this reason, we recommend ending the housing assistance funds specified above.

In addition, we note that the resettlement program across various Ceian worlds has resulted in a merge of their local dialect with the Ceian language among the moon's inhabitants, and the acclimatization of their descendants to Ceian schools and into the Ceian workforce. Approximately 8,450 survivors of the incident currently speak an unaltered version of their local dialect at home. We anticipate this number declining to between 1,000-2,000 in the next thirty years, accounting for further acclimatization to Ceian civilization, and for the deaths of older survivors.

Though the camps were intended to be temporary shelter until their inhabitants could find more permanent housing, many survivors (55,824) remain in camps today, having failed to obtain other accommodations. In addition, the rates of declining health[4] among those present on Ceiao 20M3 during the weapons test represent an increasing burden on the medical infrastructure. We expect camp hospitals to be overwhelmed by the number of patients within the next four to five years.

Veterans

Though the draft has been expanded to the Ceiao 20M3 camp, current rates of enlistment in the Ceian fleet are insufficient to significantly relieve the financial pressure on state welfare. We note that crewmen currently enlisted in the fleet are overwhelmingly made up of descendants of survivors, rather than survivors themselves (634 born in the camps; 97 born on the planet Ceiao 20M3; 1 born on the evacuation ship). As a result, members of the fleet are far more likely than nonmembers to be native speakers of Ceian and recipients of a Ceian education. Due to rates of illness and death among survivors, most have few ties to living camp residents.

Recent years have resulted in the expansion of the Ceian Empire to terraformed but undeveloped worlds such as the Madinabic moons and Far Madinabia. The remainder of the funding set aside for aid to the displaced population of Ceiao 20M3 would more than account for loyal veterans' transportation to these colonized worlds.

In regions such as New Ceirranoro City (see attached report from the Commission on Madinabic Development), a state of competition exists that requires innovation and industry from

---

4 See attached reports on breast, cervical, gastrointestinal, and lung cancers; chronic fatigue; intrauterine growth restriction; leukemia; miscarriage; swelling of the limbs and neck; stillbirths; thyroid neoplasia (benign, malignant).

all new settlers. Transportation to such an environment would incentivize descendants of survivors of Ceiao 20M3 to avoid becoming recipients of state charity and transform into self-supported entrepreneurs. Failing this, transportation would allow them to find employment with Ceian-owned businesses in the region.

As noted above, there is significant historical value to the culture of the former inhabitants of Ceiao 20M3. We recommend the creation of a panel which may, with the cooperation of fleet veterans, perform anthropological, linguistic, and historical study of this culture before its disappearance.

Recommendation conditionally approved. Águeda, you know I dislike making enemies without prior planning. If any veterans were sworn to Ceirran before his death, find them decent farmland. Not too near Ceiao.

The note on historical value of their culture is interesting. Find veteran for interview?

On the subject of making enemies, you will have heard by now that F. Decretan has chosen to increase tensions. Please discuss with our men temporary strategies to avoid arrest as enemies of the state (limiting written correspondence, etc.). The proposed conflict de-escalation strategy (traveling to Sancta Mirtalo to collect A. Decretan for ransom) has also failed. Problem areas in the city: gangsters, veterans, working poor. More extreme measures will need to be taken to correct power imbalance between self and Decretan sisters.

Come to Ceirran's house for dinner to discuss next moves.

Otávio Julhan Ceirran

I asked C. for letters from those months, letters that mentioned Ana Decretan or Flavia Decretan by name. I suppose I got what I deserved.

I was a novelty at parties, at first: the colonial who quoted Sintian poetry like a trained parrot. Then C. heard me describe the river Nevede, and the speech of a councillor I'd met a few days ago—one description flattering, the other less so—and he heard the name of the planet where I was from. Then, when the dinner had ended, he pulled me aside and asked me: Is it true? Is Ceiao 20M3 the moment of Ceiao's founding, frozen in time?

Of course it wasn't. The same thousands of years that had passed in this city had passed on Tenessa. Who can preserve anything—a planet, a city, a person—in a single moment? Yes, I said. Yes, it's true.

You have an ear for the way people speak, he told me. You have an eye for the way the world looks. You write Ceian the way the old poets write Sintian—you write as if it is just as good a language for poetry as the other. You write things down the way they really are. Come to my house tomorrow morning.

And who was it, which Ceian gossip or dissatisfied officer or clever councillor, whose conversations he first asked me to listen to? Whose whispers were the first that he asked me to write down? Whose letters did he first ask me to steal?

"1 born on the evacuation ship." Did he ever ask? Would he have cared that that was me?

As far as I know, this report is the end of Tenessa's history. How could there be any more? Where are Tenessa's schools? Where are her libraries? Where are her scholars? Where are her storytellers?

In the gardens of Ceiao, I suppose, falling asleep in the sun.

—V.

If Julhan wants to pay off the city's debts, good for him," I said. "Teo Pulcron did the same thing back when you were married to him. Why are you complaining?"

"Teo wanted to overthrow the council and institute himself as sole ruler of the city, which I really wish you'd keep in mind," said Flavia. She was made up for dancing, glitter on her eyelids and smeared in the rows of her braids. Star fields glittered through her face in the holo, the light almost indistinguishable from her skin. Her voice, when she said *Teo*, was very flat. "And once he'd done it, let me assure you, he would've been happy to let all those same maidservants and farmhands and migrants in the factories across the river fall right into debt again, but this time with his hand holding their loans."

"So your gangster friends are upset, are they?" I said.

"*Friends*," she said dismissively, which was fair. They'd been Pulcron's friends, and it was because of the devotion she'd shown him at his funeral that they'd kept faith with her. "Of course they are. With all the loans they'd made, at the interest rates they were charging, that's millions of dekar vanished into thin air. Which is the boy's aim, of course. He's told the council they breed prostitution, promiscuity, gambling, fighting, and overdrinking."

"Lady Fortune, I should hope they do," I said. "What's his point?"

She waved a hand. "Disease, injury, disability," she said. "A strong people, a strong Ceiao, the usual things we used to hear from Thiago Veguion. The example of our ancestors, who built a virtuous society, from which some of us have unfortunately fallen." She shook her head. "He didn't mention you by name. I don't suppose he had to."

"Maybe he didn't want to mention my name," I said. "He wants to keep the demipotestacy strong, too, doesn't he? Besides, at least he's being honest about what he wants."

"Do you think that just because he insulted you, that means he's being honest about what he wants?" she said. "He's trying to strike at *me*, darling, and you through me. If there's any kind of power in the city that he doesn't control, he'll kill it dead. The debtors were your best friends in the city, and the gangsters were mine. You said the poor would forget about Julhan as soon as rent was due? Well, they won't now, and I'm scrabbling to keep my friends alive and out of jail. What happens when they're gone, and all the power that's left to stand against him is me?"

"Good fortune, you're bleak today," I said. "Lend your gangster friends some money. Take it from the treasury. They'll bribe the guard and they'll pop back up like cockroaches. It'll do them good to stop leaning all their weight on the people of the Outer City awhile, won't it? Do it till the boy sees he's fighting against the tide, and we'll all be friends again. And in the meantime the poor will get a chance to breathe. Even you can't complain about that."

"If you think that boy feels friendship, you're dreaming," she said, but she looked mollified. "More to the point, since when have you had moral principles?"

"Moral, nothing," I said. "I sympathize with the poor debtors of Ceiao. They know that."

"I can believe you sympathize with them readily enough," she said, "given how *you* spend money. But—forgive me for this, dear—for the poor debtors of Ceiao, believing in your sympathies and believing that you mean to help aren't really the same thing."

That made me frown, and I was still frowning a half hour or so later, when we passed into one of those strips of space unreachable by tablet and she had to end the call. On the bridge, Szayet had the captain's chair. Two Szayeti officers knelt before her, one of them holding a tablet covered in dense writing. "Ceirran Undying says the contract—" I heard her say softly to one of them.

I turned promptly around and winked at one of the navigators. She sprang up. I sat at her post, flicking through her records to amuse myself until the Oracle was done speaking to the dead.

I was used to chatter from holos while I was on the bridge, and these dead zones with their periods of silence didn't suit me. Seeking out the navigator's records of star fields did. It was soothing to see the billions of clustered stars, as bright and noisy and living as any Alectelan feast. Here was Sancta Mirtalo, only a few dozen light-years inside Kutayeti space. Here was our ship, and the other Szayeti ships beside it, blinking steadily across the roll of accretion-tide, very near now to the yellow dwarf star that marked our destination. Here was the official border of the Ceian Empire, a vast cloud stretching from spiral arm to spiral arm, straight across the Black Maw. That was a funny thought: that a Ceian ship could fly to the very center of the galaxy and proclaim itself to be within its own borders, even as gravity stripped it into strings.

"You look melancholy," said Szayet behind me. I felt her knuckles run lightly over the nape of my neck, and arched into her touch, pleased.

"Melancholy? Me? Never," I said. "Flavia called. Apparently, as soon as he landed back on Ceiao, the boy paid off the debts of half the city."

Szayet frowned. "That's kind of him," she said. "I wonder what he gets out of it."

"What a nasty, suspicious mind you have," I said, grinning. "Says it reduces crime. And prostitution."

She let go of my neck—I shivered—and I heard her sigh. "I wish I'd met him before Ceirran died," she said. "I'd expected he would write to me."

"Why should he write to you?" I said, more sharply than I meant to. My dream of Ceirran was now five nights in the past, and unlike my near-nightly dreams of the silver-eyed girl— Maral os-Margad—it had not recurred. Still, the thought of it pounced upon me at the worst moments: laughing with my men down in the ship's hold, eating dinner in the mess hall with Szayet's foot brushing against my calf. "Szayet isn't *his* property."

"Szayet is no one's property," she said, eyebrows raised. I rose and followed her back down to the captain's chair, and tucked myself against her side when she sat, perched half on the armrest, my arm wrapped round her shoulder. She reached up and caught my hand, her face still thoughtful.

"It's only that he calls himself Ceirran," she said. "It was never a secret on Ceiao that Ceirran cared for me. If I were Ceirran's heir, I would want to keep Ceirran's friends."

"You're not Ceirran's heir," I said, somewhat shortly. Szayet flicked a glance at me that, to my mind, had a good deal too much pity in it. What I had meant was, *Nor am I*, and I was certain that she'd heard it. That irritated me.

"Well, what did you tell Flavia to do?" she said. There was a little crease between her eyebrows, which I knew from experience meant that half her mind was with me, and the other was deep in contemplation of some scheme or mystery of the universe. I reflected on what she might be trying to work out—how to get me from the Alectelan harbor to her bed in the palace with the greatest speed, perhaps—and smoothed the crease fondly with my thumb.

"Told her to bribe who she needs to," I said. "Ceirran used to solve half his problems that way. If it was good enough for him..."

Before us, in the bridge's window, Szayet's sun was growing wider and brighter by the minute. I could see the pinpricks of the planets around it. It was shocking what a relief that sight was. The gladness of familiarity, I thought, though that wasn't quite right. I was familiar with Ceiao, and flying into Ceiao did very little to make me glad.

She kissed my knuckles absently. "Perhaps Julhan didn't write because he didn't want to acknowledge the Pearl of Ceirran Undying," she said. "He has his new cult of Ceirran on Ceiao, after all. He might think contacting me would give legitimacy to his rival."

So that was what she'd been thinking about. "He doesn't think you're his *rival*," I said, laughing a little to cover my annoyance. "He doesn't care what your people do. He told me you could worship a seagull, for all he cared, as long as I didn't go along with it."

Now Szayet was in our sights, its seas hazy with the grey of moving storms. The ship groaned with a starboard turn. I saw in the corner of my eye one of the pieces of Ostrayet, the broken moon, cresting over the atmosphere.

"But you do go along with it," said Szayet. "Do you want to make him angry so badly?"

"He's not angry," I said, thought of what Flavia had told me, and revised my opinion. "He's not angry with me. He thinks I'm a fool, I don't doubt, but what else is new from the people of quality?" I ducked for another kiss, but she pulled away.

"Is he angry with me, then?" she said. "Very well, he may

believe I am not his rival for Ceirran's name. Am I his rival for your time?"

I sat up sourly. "Szayet, do you mean to spend our whole descent talking about what a Ceian schoolchild thinks of us? I'd rather chew iron. If he's angry with you, I'll lay down my life for you, or whatever the done thing is to say. If you don't want me to go back to the lower decks and run drills with my men till we dock, let's draw up a menu for the next feast day, let's make plans for the new chariot racetrack, do something worth my time—"

Over Szayet's horizon, the third moon rose. Behind it was the Kutayeti fleet.

It massed in silver at the edge of the atmosphere, a single pulsing muscle of hulls and wings, four hundred or more warships set engine to engine, nose to nose—dangerously close, impossibly close. Beneath it, on the Szayeti sea, was that same grey-white spill that on the far side of the world I had thought to be a thunderstorm.

It was not a thunderstorm. Not three seconds had passed before that greyness began to warp on itself, edges curling in, thickening and darkening, rising at its center into a point. It was a shadowy pyramid on the sea—and then it was pouring upward, it was a river made of a million fighters, it was flowing into the mass of warships. In a single, unified motion, the ships opened the jaws of their docking bays to receive them.

The mouths shut. The cloud of warships hung still—briefly, terribly swayed toward us—then it, too, collapsed in on itself, was a drop of water, was a current, was a long silver tail that swished, dove toward Szayet's asteroid belt, and was gone.

I stood numbly upright. Slowly, as if in a dream, I went to the window.

My men I had left here, the blue-striped Ceian ships, were in chaos. They floated piecemeal over empty sea, spun in wild circles by the poles, huddled together by Alectelo and its neighboring isles. Round the equator, fire flared in the atmosphere: wings, hulls, cannons, tumbling to the sea. There were no Kutayeti stragglers, no ships left behind from a break in formation. There had been no formation. There had only been the swarm.

"God, help me," said Szayet, her voice raspy. "I'm burning."

Usually, from the exosphere, the islands of Szayet were only flecks of brown and white, even where they had lately been built out for miles. Now we did not need to see land to mark where the buildings stood. Over miles and miles of ocean rose ten thousand columns of smoke.

Behind, at the navigators' computers, one of the tablets coughed, spat, and sizzled. "—agship," it said frantically. "Flagship, flagship, report. We need repair ships, repair ships immediately—" A second voice joined it, then a third. A fourth. A fifth. A seventh. A chorus. We had been out of range for all of ten minutes.

"I should have known," said Szayet on the palace steps, many hours later.

It was just past noon, and the sun shone dull red. Alectelo's roofs reflected a sky the color of old wax, dirty yellow on untouched pearl. In fact, said the reports from the ministers and my officers and the governors of distant islands, nearly all of Szayet's cities were untouched, too. Perhaps two hundred Szayeti had died, no more. The ships had fired on fallow farmland, on automated refineries and shipyards, on remote-operated treasure diving drones, on the shining island-spanning bridges across which crab-litters ran laden with cargo. They had fired on statue after statue of Ceirran Undying. Some of my men had destroyed themselves flying into the quick-moving Kutayeti ships, and some of them had destroyed themselves flying into each other, but the rest had been merely humiliated by their failures to down even a single fighter. A good half of Szayet's wealth—the hand of gold that she had laid across her planet, the places where she had raised her people out of hunger and dependence—had been lost. But her people had lived. The emperor's kindness, said Vualo's mocking voice in my head, the emperor's generosity. The emperor's generous and gracious and infinite control.

"How could you have known?" I said roughly through my helmet. The terraforming machines were already at work scrubbing Alectelo's air clean, but it would be nightfall before they were done. We'd had to walk through the burning islands in red-feathered helmets the servants had brought from the flagship. Now, along the Bolvardo del Tombo, dark lanterns and empty food stalls marked the path to the sea.

Szayet was in far worse shape than I. Her beautiful satin dress was covered in soot up to the waist, her jewelry lost digging in the ash. "What could you have done if you had known, then?" I said, when she didn't reply. "Keep your fleet here, and leave me and all my men in the desert to rot?"

"Yes," said Szayet. "I could have done that."

That struck me silent. Szayet sighed, reached up, lifted her helmet from her head, and shook out her long dark hair. Without looking at me, she said, "If my fleet had stayed, we would have been annihilated. Did you see on the map what the swarm didn't burn?"

She had gone over it with her ministers earlier, acre by painstaking acre of Szayeti islands. "The Aleksan temples," I said, taking off my own helmet. "The libraries. The treasuries. Antiques, things you couldn't replace."

"Antique things that were no part of *my* legacy," said Szayet. "But that isn't what I mean. The quicksilver oyster farms, Anita. Not a one of them was singed. Whatever her loyalties, Szayet remains a pearl of great price."

There was such bitterness in her voice that I grasped for her hand, instinctive, and only then thought that it might be unwanted. To my surprise and relief, though, she seized it and turned urgently into me and pressed her face into my neck. Her cheeks were not wet—to my knowledge, she had wept only once in her life—but against my own chest I could feel the hammering of her heart.

"It spared your people," I said into the tangles of her hair. "You're not the Oracle to antiques and pearl refineries—you're an Oracle to them. And towns can be rebuilt."

"I'm an Oracle to gods," she said, sounding unhappier than ever. "I'm an Oracle to the planet Szayet—oh, Anita, how many of these swarms does Kutayet have?"

That was the question I had been trying not to ask myself. On its heels came another: "If this is what one swarm can do in ten minutes," I said, "why did they bother to propose peace talks? Why didn't they launch a full invasion of Szayet? Why not invade Ceiao?" Why, I did not say, had they spared any lives at all? The thing that had been half Maral os-Margad had flinched at killing, before I had cut the cables out of her brain. Whatever body lay senseless inside one of those ships, was its human half young enough to fear murder, too?

"Holiest," said her war minister from the street.

I felt Szayet tense, but to her credit, she did not shove herself out of my arms, only withdrew herself and stood gracefully. "You may rise," she said.

The war minister pushed himself up from his knees and climbed the steps. Aside from the smoke in his voice and the redness to his eyes, which everyone on Szayet today shared, he looked nearly pristine in the brown sunlight: beard oiled, cloak the smooth red of a poppy petal, a stack of tablets tucked under his arm.

"Are you well, Delio?" said Szayet. "Is your household well? Are your lands intact?"

Delio bowed briefly. "My mother and father survived, Holiest," he said. "My daughter is—" He hesitated. "There is a chance that her lungs may recover. I pray it will be so. My paddies will be replanted next spring, should the Undying bless me with life through to that time."

"With all certainty they will bless their faithful servant," said Szayet.

Delio inclined his head. "I pray I will see how to serve Him faithfully," he said. "What does the Undying God say, Holiest? Why did He open our gates to disaster today?"

There was no change in Szayet's demeanor when she lied, not the least alteration in her voice. This had unsettled me before, but now there was an odd comfort to it when she sighed and said wearily, "The gods say that the emperor of Kutayet has committed the highest of transgressions against their favored children. He has used the wisdom that made our Pearls to work a heresy in fire. They say that even now, the people of Szayet are before the gods' faces. The emperor is their enemy from this day forward, and their love will not pass from this world, not from your daughter, nor from your lands, nor from any of our neighbors and friends. Not until all that is burnt has grown green again, and all that is broken has been repaired."

"And how will He repair it, Holiest?" said the war minister. That time I caught the singular pronoun. I narrowed my eyes at him, and he looked at me blankly and bowed again.

"They will give us the same wisdom that rescued us from the plots of Cátia Lançan," said Szayet thinly. She had caught it, too. "We will soothe those who would devour us, and then we will show them our wrath, and they will know that Alekso and Ceirran are the kings of the heavens. Why do you approach the Oracle, Minister? What news do you bring?"

Delio cleared his throat. "The matter of the Kutayeti who were living on Szayet, Holiest," he said. "I have done as you asked. They gave us little trouble—most live in Alectelo, besides an enclave or two near the porphyry quarries. Those are in the brigs of two fleet barges now. They will arrive in Alectelo within the week, and should we receive their ransom from the imperial court, we will ship them back to Kutayet at that time."

"Thank you," said Szayet. "And the Alectelans?"

"Yes, Holiest," said Delio, and hesitated. There was a peculiar expression on his face. "The arrest pens in the Summer Market are holding them, Holiest. There's been—some trouble."

Szayet stiffened. "Have they attacked our people?" she said.

"No," said Delio slowly. "Holiest, some of them have asked to speak with you. They claim to have information that will benefit the kingdom. We believe they wish to broker deals for their freedom."

Szayet and I shared a glance. I shrugged. "They may certainly make what offers they wish," said Szayet. "Take us to them, and we will decide whether we accept."

The Summer Market, too, had much changed from the first time I'd seen it, when it had been strewn with bitter graffiti and empty stalls, burnt and broken from the damage of Szayet's coup against her sister. This last year I had known it in a hundred different lights: mornings buying mussels and perfume bottles at the stalls, late nights half asleep on tavern steps, evenings with musicians playing the old Sintian songs, whirling Szayet in my arms as the sun sank into the sea.

Today, under the fine stinking grey of the ash, the terra-cotta tiles were colorless, the canvas roofs speckled with black. Some three hundred or so people clustered under one roof, helmet feathers brushing the canvas. Some were old and some young, some finely dressed and some plain. Some were even in the uniform of Szayet's palace guard—Szayet had always preferred not to limit the guard to Sintians, saying that Alekso of Sintia's policy had been to make a fighting force of many peoples and many tongues. It was best, the old god had said, to have eyes and guns among all the peoples he wished to rule.

If Szayet felt any hesitation now in keeping his methods, she did not show it. She inclined her head when the assembled guards went to their knees. "You are all welcome before the faces of the gods," she said, and turned to the prisoners. "And you, too," she said, "once your emperor repents of the evil he has done."

Someone spat on the ground. A baby's cry rose, deep in the crowd. A young man in a creased raincoat glared at me with red-rimmed eyes.

"I was told that some of you wished to speak to me," said Szayet. "Do you need gold, or care? Are any of you injured? Do you need boats replaced—businesses—homes? You, sir?"

The man she'd pointed to flinched back and made a gesture I knew to be the sign against evil. Delio cleared his throat. Szayet's eyebrows went up beneath her helmet, and the man flinched again, then drew himself up to his full height.

"Unholy," he said in a rough accent, jabbing a finger. "Unholy—cursed."

He was pointing at me. I stared.

"Holiest," said a voice near the front. "Holiest—"

There was some kind of scuffle going on. Two muscled women were trying to hold back a third, who was pushing her way forward. "Let go!" she snapped at them. The guards sprang to drag her fellows away, and the woman stumbled forward and fell to her knees.

"Holiest," she said, "I've seen how the divine has worked through you, I've seen how your prophecy brought up the gold from the sea, and I'm one of your people, I am. I came here and I married an Alectelan and for thirty years I'm an Alectelan myself, now. Don't put me up for ransom. Don't send me back to Kutayet." She glanced at me and, to my bewilderment, made the same sign against evil that the other man had. "You need to know," she said. "You ought to know—"

"Heretic!" shouted someone behind her, and someone else

cried, "Traitor!" Voices were beginning to rise. One of the women who'd tried to hold her back scrambled forward, but a guard shoved her away.

I fired my gun three times into the roof of the tent. "Very good, boys and girls," I said, when silence had fallen. "You were saying, madam?"

A pale girl with glasses, no older than fourteen, had wiggled her way out of the crowd to stand next to the woman. "It was my grandmother that told me," she said. "She said the Kutayeti shouldn't tell outsiders. Holiest—don't send me back to Kutayet with the rest of them. If I help you, Holiest, if you could find the mercy not to—"

"My mother told me, too," said one of the people in a palace guard's uniform, a plump boy with freckles. "But I don't remember Kutayet one bit. So she's told an outsider already." His voice wobbled a little. "At least I think that's so."

"Told you what?" I said, losing patience.

"The revenge of Alekso Undying on the disobedient, Disciple," said the girl. "The curse that He let loose on the heretics of Kutayet. The monsters with the silver eyes."

To the usurper Altagracia Caviro, desecrater of Fate, the monster who breeds monsters, soaked in blood and twisted of tongue, the hulk of flesh that rots by the sea, the pillar of heartless stone, the larvae that cling to the skin of the whale, the fly which crawls across the eyes of cows, she who blasphemes the name of the Undying, she who would always steal my honey dumplings at dinner, she who cannot possibly be doing anything more interesting than reading this, self-styled Patramata:

How to begin to tell you about today?

Let's try this: Famine came to my prison on Itsaryet.

"It isn't famine, fool," said the priestess who runs the kitchens, when I went to tell her that if she starved the prisoners I'd gut her like a trout. "It's only rationing, and if you panic now, there'll be less to ration later on." Then she made me scrub out all the henhouses. But that was her mistake, for I stuffed seven eggs into my pockets and gave them to V. for safekeeping.

Here's some excitement at last: The Kutayeti Empire are blockading a whole Ceian asteroid belt, and among those asteroids lies the farm that sends this temple its milk and its meat. For the last two weeks we've been cutting the heads off hens and eating goat's cheese from the farms down the mountain. But today was an Itsaryeti feast day, and the head priestess insisted that the temple slaughter our remaining bullocks, and that we put our faith in the future. "For He delivered us from Kutayet, when He seized their capital three centuries past," she said, "and will He not deliver us again?"

I don't know about that, because He's not very handy at delivering letters. But a feast day meant a little laxity for prisoners and soldiers both, and I went out to the great marble steps at the front of the temple and ate my skewers of beef and hot peppers and drank my wine and thought about how Alekso Undying might have broken a blockade, if He had wanted to.

I asked V. why they'd bothered to go to war, once she found me. She said she'd heard rumors, but she didn't believe half of them. She said that her officers had tried to tell her that your lover discovered a hundred-handed pearl giant, or a sort of plague of pearl locusts—she explained it clearly, but I wasn't paying attention, because I was more interested in the way she moves her hands. She's lost the stammer entirely with me, now, but she still affects it when she's near the Ceians. She won't even look at them.

She has the nature of a spy, I think—two-faced, I mean. "It's not two-faced," she says, "only practical. I'm patient, and I obey, and I speak Ceian very well and I act Ceian even better, and I work my way into Ceiao's good graces." I called her a few names when she said that, and she told me, "I mean to make a bargain with them. When I've been in the fleet a long time, and I have some money, and I've earned a little reputation, I'm going to find a piece of good land out in the colonies. They're letting veterans buy land there, you know. So there I'll build a place where my people can dig a new Saltless Sea, and build our city just the way it was, and speak their own tongue, and keep their own ways. And I'll take my father's bones from the camp and bury him there."

I said if I were her, I'd make war on Ceiao and take that land for myself. "Well, I suppose that's why you lost your civil war," she said. So we scuffled, and naturally I soon won easi

"Careful with what you put down on that tablet, princess," she says, "or I'll have to take it from you. For good this time, not just for archiving."

"You could try," I told her, but all right, very well. I didn't win. One of the eggs I'd given her broke, and she threatened to crack the rest in my hair, and I cried uncle. Though I don't see why it matters what I write down, since no one reads my letters but you and her, and of course truth has nothing to do with you.

"Doesn't it matter to you what you write down?" she said. "And you call *me* two-faced! Your name's on these letters."

"Why does my name matter?" I said.

She thought about that for a very long while, long enough that I would've been impatient if it had been the youngest priestess talking, or you. It's different with V., I suppose. I like to watch her think. She's not nervous or smug. She goes away somewhere to try to find the right words, and then she talks quietly to herself for a while, and I watch her tongue.

"When I was a child, and my father was looking for me, he would call my name," she said. "And I'd answer. We have names so that we can be called. A name lets the universe know where you are—what you are. My people believe that before there was a galaxy, all things were chaos, every atom in every star and planet mixed up with all the others, so that light was unable to be light, planets unable to be planets, the sea unable to be the sea. When I write lies, when I write to the world that it is not what it is, I begin to forget how to tell myself that I am what I am. I dissolve a little into the world. When I die, and my father's spirit calls my name, I need to be sure I can answer, *Here I am.*"

"Not two weeks ago you wrote me a story about a pirate ship speaking to Death," I said.

"That was a story, not a lie," she said. "Stories can be true differently."

I thought of you, and I wasn't at all sure that she was right, but I said to her, "You lie about your name to the Ceians every day."

"That's not a lie," she said. "It's protection. I tell you, we have names so we can be called. When the Ceians called for me, I made Eneida. Then I put myself safe inside her, like a seed in a fruit. Eneida went into the Ceian fleet in V.'s stead, and V. will come out again when she's safe in her father's country."

I would have replied very cleverly and won the argument, but I was deprived of doing it, because something nearly ripped my hair out from my scalp and I screamed and leapt up to hit whatever it was. It was out of reach already. Never, never on Szayet did either you or I ever see a bird of this size: wingspan as wide as my arms, tail like a winnowing fan, white as the sun. There was another with it, so alike to the first that it would have taken me years to tell them apart.

"I bet I could shoot one of those doves, if you would give me your gun," I said.

"I bet you could, too," she said, but didn't give me her gun, which was rude. "Let's follow them."

For such wide-winged things they moved very slowly. They lit on every tree and broken-down pillar and overturned marble block that showed where the temple used to stand in wealthier times, all the way around the back of the temple and down the mountain. If I'd gotten that gun, they wouldn't have lasted a minute, but V. told me no again, and when I went to grab it, she seized my hand.

Very soon the trees around us grew more gnarled. V. cried out, and we found that they were growing thorny, too. Such strange trees they were! I broke off one of the little branches and held it up to the lantern, and I saw the sap was red, and smelled of iron.

V. had torn her hand badly, and her skin was going red around the scratch. "I ought to suck the poison out," I said to her, "to make sure of your safety."

"Then you would be poisoned, too, and besides, your mouth would infect the wound," she said. So I told her how insulted I was, and how terrible it would be if her stubbornness was her doom, and how I had once been in the barracks at Alectelo and how willing I was to take on danger for a comrade, until she laughed. And for all that I am still well and writing this letter these many hours later, and her wound only tasted like blood, which was something of a disappointment.

"Are we comrades, then?" she said when I was done.

I told her we had to be something like, because hadn't we come through danger together, and defended each other against deadly enemies? She laughed at that, too, and asked if buried stones and trees were deadly enemies now. "Well, it's not as if they're our friends," I said.

"Is everything an enemy if it doesn't give itself over into your hands?" she said. I said that was a ridiculous thing to say, and what was more ridiculous was that she intended to spend a beautiful day taking the banner up to defend some trees, especially considering she was the one who had been hurt.

"In the camp where I grew up, my father used to tell me a story about a husband and a wife," said V. "There was a god who wanted to have the husband for his own, and they fled across the forest and came to a cottage and pleaded for sanctuary there. And as it happened, two rival gods lived in that cottage, and they were so impressed by the couple's devotion that they turned them into oak and linden trees, and forever afterward wove their leaves into crowns."

"Why didn't the gods in the cottage attack the god who was chasing the mortals?" I said. "Weren't they strong enough?"

"Maybe they would rather live in a garden in peace than start a war between gods," said V.

"Then they were poor gods," I said. "If a god turned me into part of a thorn forest, I would have something to say about it!"

"What would you say about it, princess?" she said.

"I would say," I told her, "that though you have captured my body, my mind is my own. And I will not rest until I have justice, though I should burn down the world to see it done. Tell that story, please."

"I don't think that's my story to tell," said V. "I don't think my father liked to tell stories that ended with the burning of the world. It would've frightened him."

"It wouldn't frighten me," I said.

"Nothing does frighten you," she said, "not when you're angry. It's wonderful. Why don't you tell it, instead? It could be a Szayeti story."

"My father didn't like to tell that kind of story, either," I said, and went off among the trees to look for a stick I might use as a spear to kill the birds. But when I'd hardly gone a foot or two into the undergrowth, I had to call out to her again.

"Are you all right?" she said. I showed her what I'd found. It was a bough from one of the trees, but there were no thorns on it at all. Instead, there was a fruit—a pear, I suppose, because it looked a little like the round sand pears that come from the islands north of Alectelo in the late autumn. Though I have never before seen a pear whose skin was made of gold.

"I can't reach it," I said. She has almost half a foot on me, so she stretched up, but she couldn't manage it, either. I had to help her up onto one of the branches, and as soon as she touched the stem of the fruit it broke like spiderweb and came into her hand.

"The twig was gold, too," she said, when she'd returned to the ground. I looked up and saw more gold above—a second fruit on the branch, I suppose, though I hadn't seen it at first. It seemed to be growing just in the place where the first one had.

She gave the pear to me and bowed and said, "Princess." But as soon as I put it to my mouth I found that its skin was not just the color of gold, but the texture of gold, too, and very hard.

"We'll need a knife for this," I said. She drew one from her pocket and went at the stem, but it barely scratched the surface. So we went once more to the cellar. I sat on the altar and watched her pull at the quicksilver pearl knife in the wall, then she sat at the altar and watched me pull at it. Then we lay on the altar together and panted for a while.

At last I got up for another try—but my palms were so sweaty that they slipped, and I cut myself right from heel to fingers on the part of the blade that stuck out of the wall. I cursed, and told the knife that it had better free itself, or it would be sorry. And as soon as I had, it came out into my hand—so perhaps Božena was telling the truth, after all, that it used to answer little prayers when it was given sacrifices.

We divided the pear between ourselves. I kept the knife. The fruit's flesh was soft as silk, and sweet as cinnamon, and though we looked through every slice, we could not find trace of a seed.

So I thought of what V. had said about her name—that it was a seed in a fruit—and maybe she was thinking the same, because she said, "Do you think that, if I'm called Eneida enough, I'll forget that I'm V.? Do you think I'll begin to tell myself that I am what Eneida is?"

"It's only a name," I said. "My name, my royal name, is Arcelia Caviro Diomata. It means *beloved of God*. My god loves me as much as He did the day I was crowned, and my sister reads that name in each of my letters, and knows it to be true. And one day, when she comes back for me, she will give me back my god, and I dream that He will call me Diomata again. But since my sister usurped me, no one has called me by that name outside of dreams."

"Arcelia Caviro Diomata," V. said.

Despite all I'd told her, I suppose I thought that when someone said that name again, something would happen. Alekso Undying would arrive with gold and trumpets and take me up into the heavens. The wind would change, and the stars would run in their right orbits. I would feel, for at least a few moments, that nothing and no one was missing from me.

"I can see it again," she told me, "that dignity you have. It always comes into your face when you're thinking of your god. It makes you look beautiful."

"Beautiful?" I said.

"Yes," she said, "beautiful. And terribly sad."

"Since my sister left me," I said to her, "no one has called me Celia."

"Celia," said V. "Celia, let me tell you my name."

One day, you'll come back for me. I believe that. I know it. I lie awake at night, waiting for it: tomorrow, I think, and tomorrow, and tomorrow. Yet still—

I told you once that you only loved material things, things you could hold and steal. Of all things I think you loved books the best. You loved them because when you read them, you saw a mind or a memory nailed to the page like a butterfly, a piece of someone that you could tear off and swallow down. In books, you could dig your claws into someone who belonged by rights to another planet, or to another century, or to the grave.

Perhaps stories that go untold are nothing, mean nothing. Yet still, my usurper, my enemy, my best-beloved sister, still, still, still: I don't think I will write down what that girl and I did down in the quiet dark.

I am tired, and warm, and the lamp is burning orange. There are planets in this universe still unconquered, and there are feelings in this body still unconfined. There are freedoms that one person can yet give another, which have nothing to do with knives or thrones. Outside I can hear the wind and the trees, whispering to each other in a language neither she nor I have ever learned. Their secrets are their own.

Perhaps I don't need to wait for you at all.

I remain—

> queen of Szayet—
> Oracle of Alekso Undying—
> your loving sister—

> ARCELIA CAVIRO DIOMATA
> beloved of, among others, God.

Four or five years ago, a crony of C.'s went up to the temple mountain. I asked him if he would go to the thorn wood and look for that golden fruit, though I gave him to understand that I'd found it without any help. Anything for C.'s friend, he said. But when he came back, he told me he hadn't seen a thing. Maybe you dreamed it, he said. When I said I hadn't, he shook his head. Burned, then, he told me. It must have gone up in flames along with the other trees.

—V.

Effects of salt water on quicksilver pearl, trial fourteen," said the priest's voice. "Discarded navigation computer from Her Majesty's Starship *Faro de Alectelo*. Let the record show that the navigator is eight inches in circumference, weight of four pounds. Salinity of water at thirty-six parts per thousand. Trial begins."

There was a splash.

"When I was young, I used to go up the Ponten Emília and throw melons into the river next to the fishing boats," I said wistfully. "See if I could get the sailors wet."

Szayet ignored me. "What are the readings?" she said, leaning forward on her stool.

I folded myself back on the laboratory bench. The saltwater boat, into which the priest had just dropped a lump of pearl, threw shadows on the ceiling. It was two weeks since the Kutayeti swarm had set Szayet on fire, and it had not returned.

Nor had the endless feast of Alectelo. At taverns, people could barely make eye contact with me. At the first theater performance since the attack, the actresses had flinched when I'd applauded. When I went to find a game of cards or dice in the palace barracks, no one would play with me but my own men. This week I had had to break up three fights between my crewmen and Szayeti guards, and though no one had been willing to tell me what the matter was, the glares at me from the Szayeti and the way my crewmen bristled told me enough. One by one, Szayet's best noblemen were disappearing from court—the lords of the polar islands deciding abruptly that Alectelo was far too hot this time of year, the minister of justice called out to address bribery in the new satellite ports, the minister of war gone to care for his daughter's lungs in his faraway paddies.

Long, long ago, said a voice from the computer they'd dropped in the saltwater bath, *the emperor of Kutayet had a palace that was a wonder to rival all wonders.*

That was why. The story that the Kutayeti had told us, which the computer was now playing aloud, had been an entirely different kind of wildfire from the one Szayet had suffered already, but it had been no less devastating.

It stood in the rings of a great gas planet of many colors, said the computer's voice, *on an island of pure diamond. Its staircases were made of jade, and its arches of turquoise...*

It was not only among the noblemen that hearts were troubled. The priests of a dozen islands in the remote northwest quarter of the world had formed a pact, pulled down their statues of Ceirran, and declared that they were returning to the old faith and ready to be martyred for it. Philosophers from Sintia and Itsaryet had begun to trickle slowly but steadily out of the Library, murmuring about censoriousness and accusations of heresy from their priests back home, and when I stopped by the Summer Market, I heard no more than three languages spoken over the course of a morning. Temples to Ceirran had emptied overnight, their altars bare, their priests singing hymns to empty pews. A large island full of wealthy merchants and their idle children, who had rebelled against Szayet's great-aunt many years ago over the tax rate, had begun a second rebellion. They demanded that the Oracle abandon her new god, and also, as a sign of her penitence, decrease the tax rate.

When we were out in the street, Szayet carried herself with all her usual self-possession and grace. But when we were alone, I saw how deeply her first real brush with unpopularity had struck her. At night, she paced back and forth into the small hours, sometimes murmuring to herself, sometimes climbing into my lap and pressing her face into my shoulder while I rubbed her back. In the day, she came down the Library ladders to these forges, drawing up test after test based on what we had heard in the Kutayeti story. She had tried to splice quicksilver pearl into the nervous systems of fruit flies and zebra fish. She had wired it into the xylems and phloems of the palace orchards' tangerine trees. She had burned it, boiled it, and washed it in acid and alkali solutions. In desperation, she had ground it up and injected it into rats. She had been left with dead trees, dead insects, dead fish, rats from whom the palace doctors were removing tiny kidney stones, and pearl computers absolutely unchanged from their state on the day they'd been made.

"There," she said above me now. Her fingernails clicked against glass. "The memory rate decreased by almost two milliseconds—that's something."

"It could be, Holiest," said the priest thinly, "but I feel compelled to remind you that the margin of error is up to twelve milliseconds on that point. The Kutayeti ambassador is almost—"

"The Kutayeti ambassador," said Szayet, "can wait above the harbor until the moons crash down, as far as I care. The tests will yield data if I must wring their necks like chickens to make them do it. Is there any alteration in the rate of data received?"

Now, it happened that Alekso of Sintia came to dwell there—said the voice.

"Szayet, they used to say back in the dark days of the priesthood on Ceiao that Alekso of Sintia flew to Paradise, plucked the sun from a tree, and ate him for dinner," I said. "The man liked to make war. He made an empire out of it. That part of the Kutayeti story's real. But as for the rest of it—a mythical plague of having cables shoved up your brainstem, as if it were the grippe—"

"Stories come from somewhere," said Szayet.

"Yes," I said, "from liars."

I heard her controlled exhale. "You're dismissed," she said to the priest. "Make the forge ready. I want to see if fire has any effect on the computers."

"Holiest," said the priest, and a door clicked. A moment later, Szayet's face appeared above mine, frowning.

"This is the fifth time, by my counting," she said.

I rolled upright and stretched showily. "Fifth time for what?" I said.

"That we've had this fight," said Szayet. "Say it, if you're going to say it."

"Very well," I said. "You could try to talk to him. No law against it."

"It won't answer me," said Szayet. "You know that, Anita. You have seen me trying."

"Try again," I said. "So he's acting like a child, sulking in a corner. He'll break in the end. He has no one to talk to but you, after all."

"It does talk," she said, "but it doesn't answer. It talks nonsense, it sings scraps of songs in Malisintian, it screeches and hums. It won't even show a real face to me—it appears as an upside-down cat, or a flickering red candle flame, and then it disappears again. Alekso has always been a child, and has decided to be a child until I give the Pearl to my sister, and that is an end to it. Besides, you know what it told me after Ceirran died. Half of Alekso's work was Caviro's, and without Caviro it's at best half a mind. No answers will come from that quarter."

"You never used to call your god *it*," I said.

"You never used to believe hysterical girls crying at you about wild stories their father told them," said Szayet sharply. "Caviro's archive will tell us what this silver-eyed curse is, and my tests will tell us more. I will not look like a credulous barbarian in front of the Kutayeti ambassador. We need real wisdom, and we need it to come to us from some friendlier source than—"

"Than a god who's laid a curse on you for preaching blasphemy and disobedience?" I said.

She stared at me, expression flat. I shrugged, pushed myself to my feet, and strolled to the computer that the priest had thrown in the saltwater bath. Above it floated the pale girl with glasses we'd spoken to in the Summer Market.

There is a river, far from us and near, and on its banks there is blue sedge, and by the sedge there are white flowers, and among the flowers there is a cat, she said. *And he crosses the river this way, and he crosses the river that way, and each time he crosses, he tells a story.*

Long, long ago, the emperor of Kutayet had a palace that was a wonder to rival all wonders. It stood in the rings of a great gas planet of many colors, on an island of pure diamond. Its staircases were of jade, and its arches of turquoise, and in its halls hung the faces of every emperor back to the beginning of the world, with eyes of obsidian and gold. And it was said that the first emperor of Kutayet, who was a woman of wisdom, had laid in its foundation a stone made of a single summer day. So the palace walls were always as new as the moment they had been built, and the palace's tapestries never faded, and the air within smelled always of lilac blossoms.

"May Fortune smile on blasphemy and disobedience," I said. "Are you afraid of him?"

"Of course I'm not afraid," she said sharply.

Now, it happened that Alekso of Sintia came to dwell there, the holo said, *and his people loved the palace, and called the rings of that planet the Fortunatas. But a Sintian courtesan grew jealous of its beauty. She whispered in Alekso's ear that its glories rivaled His own, and she persuaded Alekso to set the palace alight. So the King Eternal burned it to the ground, and left to conquer other worlds.*

But the Undying's beloved remained behind in the Fortunatas to watch over His brightest jewel. And when Alekso departed that world, He kissed His beloved's hands, and said to him, "With these, you will lay a curse upon any who rise against Me."

I could see her very slight wince at that. "You *are* afraid of him, Szayet," I said, shaking my head. "You, of all people? You caught the thing in the Pearl in a net of lies and stories a long time ago. You know which one of you has real power."

She looked away. "When my god, and the god of my ancestors, was alive," she said, in a strange, flat tone, "he burned books."

"Libraries?" I said, uncertain. "Like Alectelo's?" Her face was quite still. I went to the bench, crouched down, and took her hand, drawing my thumb along her knuckles, but she still stared at the floor.

In the next days a rebellion did rise against the rule of the Sintians, because the people had loved the palace, said the holo blithely. *But the beloved of Alekso of Sintia walked among the Kutayeti people in the Fortunatas, across the many fragments of those rings, through their towns and their villages, and he touched their faces with his hands. Then he departed to join his beloved in another spiral arm.*

"No city has a library like Alectelo's. But every city has books," she said. "Ostrayet had books. He burned the books on Sintia— the books about their old gods, the books of prophecy that he couldn't make fit his reign." Her lip curled. "He burned people, too, of course," she said. There was a thin irritation in her tone. She was having an argument, I thought, with someone who was not me. "But people do die. They shouldn't, but they do. That's the way of the world. But books—plays—poetry—stories— they're what the dead leave behind. They aren't meant to die, not ever. They're meant to last forever."

This, I thought, was philosophy, and I was annoyed that it was philosophy. It seemed to me sometimes a deliberate coldness that, even in the bed beside me, Szayet would wander somewhere that I could not follow. "But they don't last forever," I said, for lack of anything better.

*The children and spouses of rebels vanished from their families'
homes*, said the holo. *Many never reappeared. Those who did were
not as they had been. For they slept and did not wake, and some
starved in their beds, and others died of thirst. And when their families lifted their eyelids, their eyes were as silver as the stars.*

"They don't," she said quietly, "and they do. I have heard the
lost poetry of Sintia."

"In the Library?" I said.

She shook her head. "From him," she said.

The little pearl gleamed in the low red light of the forge. "He
told it to you?" I said.

And though they neither spoke nor walked, said the holo, *the
monsters with the silver eyes brought a curse on the people of Kutayet.
From house to house it spread, so that it was in the water and in
human touch and in the insects of the air, and milk soured in the jug
and grapes turned to dust on the vine, and the branches of the apple
trees that had been heavy with fruit blossomed and shrank and were
bare. And the people dreamed strange dreams.*

"He would mention it, before Ceirran's death, when he and I
were still speaking to each other," she said. "Quote lines, sometimes, the ones he had grown up with. I would ask him for the
rest, and he would disappear." She looked at her knees. "Perhaps
I was wrong," she said. "Perhaps stories don't keep people alive.
Perhaps it is things that are mortal, and people who keep them
alive, by remembering."

*"We have said in our hearts that a mortal thing was more holy than
the Holy One," said the people*, the holo murmured, *and so they went to
make atonement. They gathered the monsters and the sick and the mad
together, and laid them on a ship, and launched the ship from the bay by
the ruin of the emperor's palace, on the end of the diamond isle. And they
rained fire upon it from the sky, the pure and holy fire in which Alekso lives
to this day. And the ship and all its people burned and sank into the sea.*

The Kutayeti people departed the Fortunatas, and they vowed to destroy all writings which spoke of it, and all maps which showed where it lay. And they swore in the name of Alekso's fire that they would never reveal the location of the diamond island to another living soul.

From that day forward, the curse was lifted from the Kutayeti people. So winter came to the summer country.

"Szayet," I said, "if it were up to me, I'd throw him into a cup of wine, drink to your health and long life, and hold the planet by force of arms. But you know me—I never use a kind word where a kick will do."

That made her serious expression crack at last. She took my hands and lifted me up and kissed me. "I've spent my newfound gold on farms and books and our feasts, this last year," she said. "I don't have the men to hold the planet by force of arms. Not without relying on the Ceian fleet, in any case—" I stiffened in her arms, thinking of what she'd said on Sancta Mirtalo about Ceian protection, and she said, sounding tired, "Anita, you'll forgive me if I like Szayet's sovereignty a little too well to let my throne rest entirely on Ceiao's guns."

"Who said anything about Ceiao's guns?" I said. "They're my guns. I'm holding them."

The door creaked open. "The fire tests are prepared, Holiest," said the priest.

I let go of her hands. "My lady," I said. "I'll follow you as far as the forge."

"And if I did do—as you said," she said quietly to me as we followed the priest beneath groaning pipes, "and I gave you the wine to drink, what would you do?"

"Toast your health, of course," I said, raising an eyebrow. "What else?"

She smiled a little. It did not quite reach her eyes. "You always are too quick to trust," she said. "Within an hour of wine poisoned with pearl touching your lips, Anita, you'd go to sleep, and you wouldn't wake again."

I considered this. "I thought you were a better tactician," I said. "You should have kept that a secret. What if you wanted to poison me later on?"

"That would be a foolish method. You'd drain the cup, and there would be no poison left for me," she said, and stopped. We had reached the door of the forge. "We're under the southwestern wing. Don't tease the scholars, if you can manage it—"

"I never tease the scholars," I said.

"—and change before dinner," she said, sighed, and leaned in to kiss my forehead again. "There's no such things as curses," she said. "We have nothing to be afraid of."

It was a strange thing to be a Ceian on the receiving end of a warning against superstition. "Szayet," I said, "if someone laid a curse on you, I'd pity the curse," and turned to climb the ladder up from the dark forge tunnels to the Library.

I'd never been inside the Library of Alectelo in the old days, the beggar days, before Szayet had begun hauling the sunken treasure up from the seas. From outside, the place had been a threadbare coat: faceless stone heroes staring down from crumbling lintels, chipped mosaic, sandstone columns worn soft with time and ocean wind.

Now above me swelled domes painted thickly in gold. Scholars rushed across the gleaming black-and-white floor, some with books tucked under their arms, some gesticulating wildly to one another, some dragging trays piled with tablets. There was none of the harsh acid and sweat and iron from the tunnels I had just left, none of the wild Alectelan sea salt. When I breathed in, I smelled old paper, new copper. The morning was coming down in a hundred colors from a hundred stained glass windows: Ceirran enthroned on a field of stars, Ceirran holding an eagle on his wrist, Ceirran on a pirate ship with his hand raised in stern reproach. Ceirran lying resplendent on a purple bed. Ceirran ascendant, Ceirran holy, Ceirran divine.

"The boy's begun to write sermons now," Flavia had told me shortly this morning. "Anonymously, of course. The flyers turn up by the shrines, in the bathhouses."

"What a poet he is," I'd said. "What does he say?"

"Mainly that Ceirran loved Ceiao," she'd said. "That he conquered Madinabia for Ceiao's sake—*pacified*, the boy says—and made the galaxy safe for Ceian enterprise. That he wanted the city to be free of violence and corruption and the decadence and disorder of the old council. That he represented Ceiao's new age of glory, free of the long shadow of Sintian culture and Aleksan conquest. That he longed to come home to Ceiao—"

I snorted. The boy had been in service on Far Madinabia when Ceirran had been whiling away luxurious, useless months on Szayet. It had taken Szayet herself to persuade my friend to leave the planet, and then only by promising him immortality.

"How does he have the time?" I said. "Aren't you wearing him out with ruining his reputation?"

She had laughed a little, though she hadn't looked happy. "Dear heart, *I'm* worn out," she'd said. "I'm paying the soldiers' orphans and the old veterans to spread rumors and scribble graffiti about the boy, I'm paying *my* friends among the gangsters just to keep that faction of the city alive and out of Julhan's reach, and I'm close to broke. The troubles are adding up, Anita. You need to win back the people's love, and you need money, and the council is demanding to know whether they'll all be murdered in their beds by swarms of Kutayeti ships tomorrow, and Julhan claims he needs your war money to double the number of the city guard and enforce his moral reforms, and there's more enemies of the state in the cells every day besides—"

"You say that last like it's trouble," I said. "That's exactly what we asked for. The days of the proscriptions again—kill who threatens us, scare the rest into good behavior. Give it time, and that'll answer our other problems."

She pinched the bridge of her nose. "But it's not the days of the proscriptions," she said, "because in the days of the proscriptions, you were lining the city guards' pockets, Anita. When the dead gave up their gold, you always made sure to spread it around. Julhan called you too generous, back then, but now he's changed his tune. These days, when people are arrested, the council takes that money to pay for the dole and for your war against Kutayet, and the guards go hungry."

"When we were growing up, the guard were happy enough with the bribes they got from the gangsters," I said. "They didn't need admirals to line their pockets then."

"Half of the gangsters have been arrested on charges of being Kutayeti," she said. "Well, on charges of speaking in opposition to the war—but we all know what that means. As for the rest, Julhan knows well enough that I'm all that's keeping them afloat. If we lose the city guard, we've run out of any friends who aren't your sworn soldiers. The guards miss the days of chaos—peace isn't lucrative. They can't collect bounties, and Julhan is telling them that if it weren't for you, they'd have a higher salary. They're listening to him."

"Yes," I'd said, "those days are what they miss, aren't they. Tell them—oh, tell them I'll call them tomorrow, we'll sort out some funds."

"Will you?" she'd said.

"Don't give me that tone," I'd said. "Money for the guard, and a plan to win back the people's friendship, and an answer for the council on victory against Kutayet. The Oracle and I will have that last by sunrise." By nature I wasn't a liar, and I hadn't lied to her then. Sunrise was still a little over twelve hours away.

Through an archway on the northern side of the hall was a study hall full of long tables, their benches crammed so tightly with red-robed priests that the whole room looked like someone had had a bad accident. This was where we'd cooped up the scholars going through Alekso of Sintia's personal effects.

I sauntered across the tile and leaned in the doorway. The noise in the room was tremendous, and all of it seemed to be argument. I recognized Sintian, Ceian, the harsh consonants of Szayeti, high-pitched Cherekku from five wildly gesturing women with silver-painted mouths, some absolute nonsense that I suspected to be Belkayeti, and even what might have been Diajundot. As heads began to turn toward me, the voices faded, one by one, until the only sound left was a plump young woman at the head of the table, shouting:

"—would never act without purpose, but absolutely without merit to claim that all of His purposes are directed toward *us*, of all people. A god for all times..."

She trailed off into the silence. "Oh," she said. "Honored Disciple."

"Any luck?" I said.

The librarians exchanged glances. Szayet had put them in a difficult position. She had named me Beloved Disciple of Matheus Ceirran, walking symbol of their newest undying god, but most of them didn't much like me. "We're—unsure, Disciple," said the plump young priest at the head of the table reluctantly at last. "The Oracle's timetable has been—repressive."

"She can't make the ambassador fly any slower," I said, strolling toward the table. Stacks of paper sat on it: translucent diagrams of ships, a drawing of a crowned man in what looked very like a waxwing, an open leather-bound journal—real leather! The man's taste for extravagance would have made Sonia Couron jealous. Szayet had a priest's knowledge of Malisintian, the ancestor of the modern Sintian tongue, but my understanding of the neat handwriting covering its pages was fragmentary at best. On top was a hand-drawn map, marked with more Malisintian notes. I recognized *Swampland*, and *three days*, and *slept...knees*, that last by a drawing of a striped cat.

Some of these islands had vanished in the last three centuries, and some harbors had frosted over, but I knew that peninsula, the curve of this beach. In the center was a drawing of a tiny brick building, three smokestacks jutting from its roof. Beside it was a sheep. *Very ugly houses!* said the note.

"Ah, Ceiao," I said. "What's your name? Where'd you get these?"

"Sister Constanza, Disciple," said the priest, bowing her head briefly. "These artifacts are from Caviro Orakolo's possessions. They're little studied—"

"Little studied for some," said another priest sourly.

Constanza cleared her throat. "Most everything Alekso Undying says in these particular journals is repeated more clearly or more beautifully in His later writings, Disciple," she said. "We've pulled them for examination because of their dates. We believe that He sent them to Caviro in the period when He was conquering Ceiao—that is to say, the period when he left Caviro in Kutayeti space to maintain the peace."

"Kutayeti space," I said, "meaning the Fortunatas."

Constanza wrinkled her nose. "If such a story is true, Disciple," she said. "The Holy One made quicksilver pearl Szayet's great blessing. Whether He would favor a foreign people with His—" She saw the expression that had come over my face at *favor*, stammered, and was silent.

"I thought your god picked up quicksilver pearl on Ostrayet, before he broke it in three," I said. "Native to that moon, wasn't it?"

Her face twisted. "That's so, Disciple."

"He managed to curse the Ostrayeti well enough without resorting to enchanted sleep and soured milk," I said. "So what's the trouble with this journal?"

"It's absence of trouble that troubles us, Disciple," said Constanza uncertainly. "There's no mention in any of His journals of a diamond island, nor of a rebellion there. He might allude, here—" She tapped at a line in the journal, which to my eyes read something like *Ice child, odd but a countryman, I am bland*. "The Undying speaks of His difficulties adapting His new pearl navigational computers to His ships," she said. "He says, *It's all well and good for a ship to see the whole galaxy, or in any case, to see those parts of it that are still on the map. What I wish it'd see is other ships! They're worse than cats, these things; they won't network, they won't sync, it's every pilot for himself, and H—— help him if he isn't adept at formations. I'd like to write a program—*"

"What's H-blankety-blank?" I said.

One priest perked up. "The censored name of a barbarian god, Disciple," she said. "It's believed that nine hundred years prior to Alekso's birth, in the Years of the Generation Ships, the old Sintians developed a primitive yet philosophically intricate..." I stared at her until she trailed off, then nodded to Constanza again.

"*Those parts of it that are still on the map* is our point of interest, Disciple," said Constanza. "We believed for years that it referred to planets He had destroyed, but now, some think it refers to this apparent destruction of Kutayeti records. In the next entry, He describes the program He's written failing to sync the navigational systems, and He quotes a very famous Sintian poem in the journal—and again in the map, look here, Disciple: *For our days go by quickly, and great works come slowly*. Or the more literal translation—*for life is short, and art is long*."

It was so similar to what Szayet had said to me in the forge that I seized the journal from the priest's hands, ignoring the cries of dismay from around the table, and was surprised and irritated when all I could recognize was *long... life*.

All of that about the navigational computers was the same as what Vualo had said in the library: People could use pearl computers to send messages to other computers, but those messages were units of text or noise, they did not interface with the computers' own reasoning systems, and pearl could not speak to pearl in pearl's own tongue. Fleet formations were still made up of dozens or hundreds of pilots working together in practiced choreography—unless they were the swarms of the Terrestrial Intelligence, of course, who avoided the problem by being a single brain. "Get me that tablet with the translation," I said. "This is all you've found? Nothing on whether the god really did mean to curse the Kutayeti? Nothing on why being burned alive in the middle of the ocean ended the curse?"

The priests made apologetic faces. I sighed. "Work through the night," I said. "I don't want to see a one of you leaving the Library until you have something of use."

They didn't look nearly as put off by this as I had hoped. "I hope you'll join us for some research when you've greeted the ambassador, Disciple," said one of the priests, sounding very much as if he meant it.

"We all need to hope for something," I said. "I'll be seeing you, gentlemen."

Evening came, and with it mist, filling up the lawn outside the windows, drowning the half-moons and the stars. In the palace it beat at the skylights, slipped in through cracked windows, dripped from the high red rafters. Servants slung aluminum poles over their shoulders, clipped lanterns to each end, and went down to the royal harbor before me, the lights swaying wildly, throwing blue shadows over the roads. Fireflies zigzagged at our ankles and winked out in the pampas grass. Waves sighed. The summer nights were cold in Alectelo, but tonight the sea had forgotten to take back the sun. Sweat prickled at the crooks of my elbows, the back of my neck.

Szayet was already waiting at the harbor-gate when I arrived, running her hand up its pearl inlay. "The fire tests?" I murmured as the court began to file in behind us, whispering.

She shook her head slightly. "Something odd with the saltwater experiments, though," she murmured back. "I'll need to run more tests. When we send holos between computers that we've dropped in the same tank, there's odd variations in the metadata. Timestamps change. I don't understand..."

That phrase was enough of a rarity coming out of her mouth that I could've listened to any quantity of technical talk that followed it, but there was another splash out in the blurred dark, this one louder. "Look sharp," I said.

The warning was barely in time: The ship skidded through the harbor-gate half a second later, dust rising in her wake. She was a bright, sleek felucca, startlingly small, her prow capped by figureheads of a lion, a goat, and a snake. Two Kutayeti soldiers had emerged from the door in the roof before the dust had begun to die down, two more moving behind the glass of the viewscreen.

Szayet's herald cleared his throat and blew a long note on his horn. "Sasha Vualo, the ambassador of the Kutayeti Empire," he called.

"And friends," said Vualo genially, swinging themself down to the sand. They flicked invisible dust from their shoulder, then bowed deeply. "Altagracia Caviro Patramata, Oracle Queen," they said. "The Emperor of Kutayet, King of Kings, most reverent keeper of the Flame of Alekso of Sintia, has granted me the honor of passing on his wish that your fields never know fallowness, your people never know sickness, your scholars never know idleness, and your tongue never know bitterness."

Szayet gestured shortly. The herald half-heartedly proffered platters of bread and salt. "We welcome you home to the earth and the sea," he said.

"How kind of you," said Lukhaya, emerging from behind Vualo—I had not even seen her come down the ladder—and pinching both in her hands. "I feel so welcomed already."

"I am glad of your ease in my sovereign lands," said Szayet icily. "I have summoned you here to negotiate reparations for an outrage."

Vualo, to their credit, had lost that perpetual look of being on the verge of laughter. "My lord the emperor carries great sorrow for those of your people who were lost in the action," they said. "Much as he carries his sorrow for his own people, lost in the unprovoked attack on Khramya. He is most eager for the Oracle's goodwill, and for the goodwill of the Szayeti people."

"Your lord carries his sorrow," said Szayet thinly, "but he is not sorry."

Vualo bowed slightly. "Your Majesty, look to your sky," they said. "Where is the emperor's fleet? Where are his fighters? He has not sent his generals to Szayet, his sworn bannermen, his reconnaissance ships. He has certainly not sent an admiral who commands half his fleet, or proclaims herself lady of the whole spiral arm. He has sent a diplomat. He comes with open hands and an open heart to his sister queen, the ten-times-great-granddaughter of the beloved of Alekso of Sintia, in the name of our shared god, the love He bears us, and the love we bear Him. Will you take the outstretched hand? For His sake, if not for ours?"

The murmuring behind us had increased. The wind was rising. Vualo's hair, blue under the lanternlight, fluttered up to halo their face. I thought of their hands on my waist in Roof-without-Rain—*I really admire it, you know, the way you talk. I could almost forget the holos*—and dug my nails into my palm.

"In the name of our god, Alekso Undying, and for his sake," said Szayet, "until we can do so with clear eyes and a clear conscience, the throne of Szayet will neither clasp hands nor make alliances. Nor will Szayet ever bend the knee—to anyone—without first receiving the blessing of the divine." She put a slight emphasis on this last. The whispering softened a little.

"Bend the knee!" said Vualo. "Certainly not. Szayet's sovereignty is sacrosanct." They raised an eyebrow at me. "My lord the emperor would never ask such a price for his friendship."

"Would he not?" said Szayet. I suspected her dry tone was

more for the benefit of her courtiers than anyone else. "And yet I have bartered with your emperor for our pearl, and it seems to me very wise to hear his price before agreeing to barter with him for his friendship."

This was close to an insult. The volume of the whispering was rising again, along with the cold salt wind. Now Vualo did smile—the smile that had become dreadfully familiar to me, the wide white grin full of sharp teeth. "So it is wise," they said, "and so I will tell you. My lord the emperor demands that you release the murderer and pirate Ana Decretan, self-styled lady of the Swordbelt Arm"—they nodded to me—"into his custody for immediate trial."

The wind roared. Behind the ship, seagulls burst up from the rocks, squawking. "I'll consent to be shown to my rooms," said Vualo politely, "if the Oracle feels she needs time to think."

"I don't understand something," said Szayet later in her bedroom. "A little higher, please."

"Just one thing?" I said, dabbing the handkerchief nearer to her eye. She was sitting in her breastband, cross-legged on her bed, while I wiped the kohl from her eyes with a damp handkerchief. Most evenings, this was the maids' job, but I had asked her to send them away tonight and let me do it, if only to soothe the feelings Vualo had ruffled at the harbor. "I don't understand any part of it. They didn't even look surprised when you said no."

"Of course they didn't," said Szayet. "It's the question that's the attack. If I agree and hand you over, then Kutayet knows that threats and violence can break Szayet without trouble, and I put myself at war with Ceiao besides. If I decline and keep you here, then it seems to the people that I put Ceiao's interests above theirs. Like as not, the emperor is spreading coin among the rebels—" She shrugged at my startled expression. "It's what I'd do in his place, if I had an empire, and designs on my rich neighbor. That unpleasant scholar will be among the servants, I don't doubt, whispering that I'm governed by my fear of Ceiao. Worse, that I'm governed by my heart."

"Which you're not," I said, tilting her chin up with one finger.

"I'm governed by the gods, of course," said Szayet, smiling up at me. "You don't sound convinced."

"Me? I believe everything you say," I said, and then, a moment later, "No, you're right. Not that you don't make it sound convincing. I don't know, Szayet, I'm not clever—it's only that it *is* what you'd do in their place, if you had an empire. You'd charm, and you'd flatter, and you'd ask sharp questions until the other person didn't know up from down from rim from Maw, and their throne was crumbled to pieces. But Vualo isn't you."

"Vualo didn't seem like a charmer?" she said, eyebrow raised. "They were sweet enough when they were greeting me."

"No, they don't," I said, moving to the other eye. "That wasn't charm, it was—I don't know, playing with their food. What *is* the scholar doing here? She said she studies pearl—well, why isn't she in a laboratory in Kutayet somewhere, working at her research, or building more monsters for the emperor's army? What benefit does it bring her to follow Vualo around like a street dog?"

Szayet looked thoughtful. "When did she leave?" she said.

"What do you mean?" I said.

"When we were greeting the ambassador on the beach," she said. "She took bread and salt, I remember that. Then Ambassador Vualo went on about open hands and hearts, and we spoke of prices, and then of you—but I don't recall the scholar having a thing to say. I don't recall seeing her at all after that, as a matter of fact."

"She kept in the background plenty of the time in Roof-without-Rain," I said. "She's not an aristocrat, doesn't want to violate court etiquette. You know the sort of thing."

"None of the Kutayeti court are here, and none of my ministers or landholders give a damn for who the emperor's ennobled and who he's left common," said Szayet bluntly. "Why shouldn't she take advantage and push herself into the spotlight while she's here? Why *does* she have half a role in the Kutayeti court, anyway, if she's not noble?"

"She told me that she and Vualo are friends," I said.

Szayet snorted. "Friends," she said. "Well, for my—"

Outside the window, something thudded. The light in the bedroom flared gold.

I sprang off the bed, swearing profusely. Szayet followed a second later, dashing to the balcony with no heed to her half-nakedness. "This damned mist, I can't see a thing," she said. "There's moonslight—I think the sky's clear—oh, Holy Lord, preserve me." There were screams from the streets below. No, not screams, I thought, but shouting. Someone was calling in Szayeti, a single word, over and over again.

"Thief," said Szayet, her face grim and set. "Thief—thief. Anita—"

I was already fastening my gun belt around my hips. "My lady," I said, saluted, tore out of her room, and was halfway down the palace steps before I thought to question the salute.

There was a crowd on the Bolvardo del Tombo already, pushing and shoving. I saw a half dozen tavern-keepers I knew, and my own soldiers, and some of Szayet's palace guard. But strangely, too, there were priests—dozens of them, clutching at one another and shouting. One was scuffed with black marks straight up her arm and her face—I knew her: Constanza, the plump young woman I'd spoken to earlier today. As soon as she saw me, she staggered toward me, gasping:

"Disciple—royal harbor—they're—"

Harbor was as good as a gunshot. I sprinted, heedless of shouting and Szayeti diving out of my way, glad of the sleeveless tunic I'd thrown on for sleeping and for my good soldier's boots. Down the gravel path again—terribly dark now without the servants' lanterns, even the fireflies gone to bed, only the crashing of the waves to guide me, and the very faint moonslight through the fog. That brief golden light up in the city had faded. That meant no fire in the streets. A single explosion, the way I would have done it, probably demolishing just one door of the Library. *Thief, thief—*

"You smug little monkey-tongued piss-blooded double-dealing son of a pig," I said aloud. And then, my strides lengthening, shouting into the dark: "You *prick*."

In the mist, someone shrieked with laughter. I bellowed wordlessly and put on another burst of speed. Light was flaring ahead, blurred white, far brighter than the moons. Shoes clattered on metal. Engine fire rumbled, and there was a terrible scraping, metal over stone.

I was close, now, so close I could see the ends of the engines, the fire flaring up. I could make out the rungs on the side of the ship, the open door, the silhouette of a head. I had the lowest rung in my hand, I was clambering up, I was nearly there, I wrenched Carmela Lukhaya's arm toward me before she could close the door, and I shoved the barrel of my gun into her face.

"Land this ship, scholar, or I swear in the name of Matheus Ceirran I'll shoot you dead," I shouted over the engines.

Lukhaya tugged her arm away and wriggled down onto the inner ladder. The ship was bouncing over the ocean now, foam flashing. I seized the edge of the door as she reached up to slam it, and for a long moment we struggled, her weedy arms flexing fruitlessly. At last she let go and, as I was shoving the door open and swinging myself down, she smacked the gun from my hand.

I kicked her in the face as hard as I could. She cried out, a garbled, liquid noise, and clattered down the ladder, groaning when she hit the floor. I fumbled in the pouch on my belt—yes, there it was—and, in one swift motion, I pulled out the tracking device she'd given me in Roof-without-Rain, bent it into a circle, and dropped it into the ship before she had a chance to look back up.

That put paid to my hands' purchase on the ship. The wind caught me, and I fell backward and smacked into the water.

If it had been winter, the fall would have killed me. Even the summer current was cold enough to feel like knives. I flailed, kicked through the darkness, and surfaced, spitting salt water. The light of Vualo's ship was a little white star in the dark, was an eye-fleck, was gone.

The royal boat found me there, half a minute later, roaring over the waves in a cloud of steam. Two palace staff girls tossed a torpedo buoy down into the water and dragged me up onto the deck where Szayet stood, her arms crossed.

"Fetch a towel," she barked at the girls who'd rescued me, "a blanket, dry clothes, something. *Go*," and snapped her fingers. The girls disappeared through a door in the deck. Szayet turned to face me.

She had thrown on a patterned shift, tied at the waist with a ribbon—the plainest she ever dressed, these days—and her face was still bare of paint. In the dim moonlight I could see two white spots very high on her cheeks.

"A journal," she said. "The priests were studying through the night. They say she came in not ten minutes after Vualo's ship landed, wandered around until she saw them working, and asked them what the documents were. When they asked who she was, she said she was an old drinking companion of yours, come from Ceiao. She put on an accent. She called you Anita. She described how you drink, and how you dance. She made them laugh."

"Snake," I said bitterly through my chattering teeth. "What did she want in the journal?"

"The priests don't *know*," said Szayet. "It's Alekso's musings on pearl, that's all. And the people are saying—"

She cut herself off, glancing down toward the deck. Voices beneath it murmured in Sintian and Szayeti, interrupted by a few soft sobs.

The people were saying—it wasn't hard to guess. A queen whose enemies already said that she had roused her god's wrath. God's own word, kept safe in the Library for three hundred years, snatched away in the night. Fortune and misfortune, we'd have said on Ceiao, and even on Ceiao, we did not like to linger with the world's unfortunates.

She stared at me now with the steady, assessing eye of a bird. Despite her technical faithlessness, I had rarely, if ever, seen her in despair. Even now, unshaken confidence shone in her expression. "You chased them out onto the ocean for a reason, didn't you," she said. "You found a way to hunt them down."

"Will you let me?" I said, low.

She exhaled hard. The ocean hissed.

"Say please," she said.

"Let me leave you," I said. "Let me track down the ship. Let me steal back your god's word, and learn what it was stolen for. Rely on me, Szayet. Please."

"Disciple," she said.

"Yes?" I said.

"You answer to it when it suits you," she said quietly.

We were very near the shore of Alectelo now. Dim shapes were appearing at the harbor-gate through the fog, red and blue. "Szayet, that ship's getting farther away by the second," I said. "Another hour and we won't be able to tell that tracking device's radio pulses apart from neutron stars'. I need one of my liburnae, I need a crew—"

She nodded, eyes intent on my face. "I will," she said. "I'll let you go. But, Anita—"

"Oracle!" called a voice from the shore. I saw the captain of her palace guard, some priests, hobbling old Zorione, a crowd blurring behind them in the fog.

"Swear that whatever you find out there, you'll bring it back to me," Szayet said. "If it's treasure, swear you'll turn it over to the

Szayeti treasury. If it's wisdom, swear you'll let us use it to our advantage."

"I will," I said. "Of course I will."

"And swear—" she said. "Swear that you'll come home to me."

I lifted her hand to kiss it again, and then her forehead, and then her mouth. "I'll always come back to Szayet," I said. "Bleeding, bruised, drowned, ship burnt, throat slit. The road between us covered in thorns, or embers, or slavering dogs. The whole world flooded. No ships left in the galaxy. Barefoot, limping, carried on a stretcher. Nothing would stop me from coming back to Szayet—unless—"

She had half turned away toward the shore, hair fallen over her eyes. "Unless?"

"Unless they hurt my face, and I wasn't handsome anymore," I said. "But then you wouldn't want me anyway."

She laughed, or tried to—her voice caught halfway through. "Then take your crew," she said. "I'll go back to the forges for the saltwater tests. And when you return—Anita, when you return—"

The boat shuddered. We'd hit the dock. I waved at blue Ceian cloaks in the crowd, purpose filling me up again, light in a glass of water. "When I return, we'll do whatever you like," I said, striding toward the railing. "Lieutenant Ludon! Go to the docks. Take *Taraxandran*—"

The crowd poured down the dock toward us. The wind rose, and the fog with it, thin and grey. The Library was still smoking, priests cursing Vualo's name, people throwing dark glances our way, the tide clear for takeoff. Szayet pinned my cloak and leaned up dark-eyed for a kiss. My liburna's engines roared. It did not occur to me for some time that I had not precisely promised what Szayet had asked me to.

To: Admiral Ana Decretan, Demipotestate for Confirming something-or-other, Lady of do-you-really-expect-me-to-bother-with-your-titles-at-the-moment / in Alectelo, Szayet

From: your beloved sister, if you happen to remember her name / in Ceiao, and furthermore, a temper

Anita—

This is really the end. I can wish and wish you'd keep your appointments, but it doesn't mean much if you're not here.

You'll get the report of Julhan's arrest first, and you'll be angry about it. Well, it was your bluff he called, and it was up to me to either follow through or let the whole city know your threats are empty words.

Let me tell it as clearly as I can. Your esteemed colleague argued—yet again—to transfer your war money to the city guard. Did you answer my calls? Did you reply to my letters? Take a guess. I was the one who had to grit my teeth and put on my best clothes, I was the one who had to go from door to door on the Avenuan Libeirguitan begging money—you of all people, sister, know how that made me feel—and then I was the one who had to go to the captain of the guard and bribe him within an inch of his life. Only then would he bend enough to write out a warrant for Julhan's arrest as an enemy of the state. I write to you now from my front step, where I've been sitting for the last hour, waiting for him to deliver me the report that the arrest's finally been made.

Anita, this trick won't work twice. I wish I hadn't had to do it once. I'm afraid that a good lawyer will put him back on Ceiao within the month, and who knows what kind of revenge he'll tell his people to wreak on me in the interim? I'm tired, and I'm afraid, and I'm furious with you. If you ever loved me, come h

Letter not sent.

To: Admiral Ana Decretan, Demipotestate for Confirming the Freedom of the City with Conciliary Power, Lady of the Crossbar and the Swordbelt Arm / in Alectelo, Szayet

From: Otávio Julhan Ceirran, Demipotestate for Confirming the Freedom of the City with Conciliary Power, Lord of Arqueiran and the Shieldmirror, Commander Ceirran's heir / in Ceiao, Ceiao

Being a copy of the attached proclamation:

It being understood by this court that in light of the war against the EMPIRE of KUTAYET, the sworn enemy of the EMPIRE of CEIAO, and reflecting the great danger posed by their arts, there shall be an arrest of all those whose conduct is inimical to the progress of the war;
and
it being understood by this court that the corruption of the Outer City, and the corruption of noncitizen residents in Ceian territories, is a plague to the people of Ceiao, and financial and social dealings with the gangsters there is likewise a plague, and detrimental to the Ceian war cause;
and
it being understood by this court that the below-referenced defendant did, for many years, consort socially and financially with known criminals of the Outer City;

that she did request recordings of private Merchants'
Council meetings to which she, as a private citizen, had
neither privilege nor entitlement, and in order to obtain
such illegal information, committed acts of bribery;
that she did commit bribery with, and attempt bribery
of, members of the Merchants' Council, who have
testified to such effect before magistrates;
that she did urge convicted vandals to commit graffiti
intended to besmirch or mock the reputation of an
admiral of Ceiao, and pay them for such labor;
that she did attempt by further means of bribery
to effect the arrest of an admiral of Ceiao, whose
importance to the war is evident;
this court issues a
WARRANT for
the ARREST
of
ENEMY OF THE STATE:
FLAVIA DECRETAN
daughter of Mara Decretan
and sentences her to
BANISHMENT
from the city and planet of Ceiao.
She will have neither home nor succor. The road will
not bear her feet. The river will not bear her weight.
The doors of all houses are closed to her. She may
drink no water, and she may warm herself by no fire.
Her citizenship is revoked. All who assist her are
breaking the law.
She has until nightfall to find a ship.

This letter was never opened.

—*V.*

To Captain Águeda Vipsânian—

Glad as I am that you pressed me to have a contingency plan, I don't believe our bribe to the captain of the city guard outpaced Flavia Decretan's by more than a day. We cannot cut matters so close again.

Every threat must now be neutralized. Arrest the remaining gangsters. Ensure we are forewarned of Flavia's destination, and that we have sworn men stationed wherever she intends to land. Instruct our governors on the colonies that Flavia is not to be allowed into their palaces. Instruct our spies in Szayet to argue to the Oracle that Flavia represents a threat to her hold over Admiral Decretan, and the sisters should under no circumstances be allowed to meet.

The admiral must be dealt with separately. Until Flavia reunites with her, she is without a mind, but she still has her teeth.

We must prepare for civil war.

To: ALL FLEET—ALL FLEET OFFICERS—ALL FLEET CAPTAINS

From: Otávio Julhan Ceirran, Demipotestate for Confirming the Freedom of the City with Conciliary Power, Lord of Arqueiran and the Shieldmirror, Commander Ceirran's heir / in Ceiao, Ceiao

Effective immediately, all nonessential military personnel in the Shieldmirror and the Swordbelt Arm stationed on Ceian colonies, client kingdoms, and similar possessions are summoned home to the star system of Ceiao. See attached document from Captain Águeda Vipsânian regarding positioning and stations.

E very now and then,

time—

—a little too soon, I think—

In the evenings, when the light in the house grew red and the air filled up with the sweet choking silence that recalled deep water, I would lift our mother up from the couch, pull her arm over my shoulder, and lead her to bed, moving carefully so she wouldn't stumble over the tile. Sometimes she would fight me, but not often. Drunkenness would make me angry, when I was grown, but it only ever made her sad.

And after—after, when I closed her door and crept along the balcony and down the stairs on cat's feet—after, when we would drag the heavy mahogany table into the sitting room and shove up the windows so the clear cold air came rushing in with the noise of the street in its wake—after, when we would feast on sweets and leftover wine, tell rude jokes, wrestle until one of us begged for mercy, when we'd run through the streets to the houses of the other councillors' children, throw stones at their windows, kick over their statues and run—after it all, back home in the garden, Flavia and I would watch the stars. They watched back and said nothing. To them, we might as well have been sparrows, or oak twigs, or ash in the wind. I loved them for that.

But before—

"Ana!" Ludon bellowed.

"Keep our tail down!" I shouted. "Slowly—*slowly*—curse you to the Maw, don't take your hand off that lever—"

Taraxandran shuddered. I swore. She was only a little hot-engined liburna, lightly armed and prone to bursts of sudden speed, and all her comms had been deliberately killed: no messages accepted, no hails answered. That meant she was near-invisible, but it also meant she was alone. This close to the center of the galaxy, where the accretion-tide was wild and brutally strong, she tossed and turned like a leaf no matter how clear the space.

We were not in clear space now. *Taraxandran* had had a single chance: An hour after Vualo's ship had crossed the Kutayeti border, an asteroid storm had come thundering down toward the Black Maw like a band of horses, Kutayeti and Ceian patrol ships alike fleeing before it. We'd plunged into its wake, a fragment among thousands of fragments, and ridden into the Kutayeti Empire without so much as a warning shot across our tails.

"*Port!*" I bellowed. "It's barreling right for our engines, damn you, better that it clips the wing, if we lose the antimatter we're dead—"

Now we were paying the price for stealth. Ludon slammed his hand down on the ship's controls. The asteroid shot past, less than half a mile from our wing. In the misty map of the Kutayeti Empire over the control panel, the dot representing the tracking device on Sasha Vualo's ship flashed red.

"Any movement?" I said.

"Not so much as a twitch, sir," said my navigational officer eagerly.

"Three hours, that makes it," I said. On the map, the dot sat behind a triple star system and before a protoplanetary disk. Kutayet's empire hung between Szayet and the center of the galaxy, and Sasha Vualo's ship had crossed nearly the whole of it. That was wild land, the very edges of the territory, much nearer the Black Maw than any well-populated Kutayeti farmland or mines or city-worlds. Empty space, said the map, but the map was Kutayeti. And the people who'd made it, back in Alekso's day, when—

—when—

—whose when? Whose then? Whose now?

The river was as dark as stone. After only a few seconds, my feet were numb.

"It'd help if I slept with her," I said to the moving surface of the Nevede.

"That's unusual," said Flavia.

"Funny, I'd swear you'd met me before," I said.

"Oh, not the wanting to sleep with someone," she said, "but you don't often say it would *help*."

I sneered at her. "Do you think she'd ever had an affair before? She must've. Some slack-jawed cultist boy, desperate to please, writing her poetry. Your hollow rib cage holds prophecy like a bouquet of flowers, you dwell in sacredness like a grape dwells in jelly, how holy to kneel—"

"Why does it matter?" said Flavia coolly.

"Difficult road to plow, is love," I said. "For the young especially. It might be she's never kissed anyone before. Does she think he'll leave his husband for her?" I dragged my fingers through the smooth brown stones of the riverbank. "Does she think he'll get children on her?"

Flavia was silent. I spat into the river and watched it vanish without trace. "Be on my side," I said to her.

"She's a naive little fool who thinks the crown of Szayet is as good a lovers' gift as sweets and poetry," said Flavia, without the least bit of enthusiasm. "He'll tire of her and come home."

"No, she isn't," I said. "She's not a fool at all."

"Anita—" she said, and sighed.

There was a stone under my palm. I eyed the far shore and hurled it. It skipped twice, then sank.

"I always hated this river," I said.

"You never said," said Flavia.

"It was the only river I ever knew," I said. "Until I left the city, and I saw—oh, little streams in canyons, great slow wide brown tributaries running through fields, waterfalls, the sea... I thought I hated water. And what's the point in hating water? You might as well hate the world." I kicked my feet, watching the pale movement of them in the current, brown under moving black. "You might as well hate the city."

"Anita," Flavia said, "may I tell you the truth about something?"

"What have you been doing up till now?" I said, laughing.

She smiled thinly. "I think you'd be happier if you'd never sworn an oath to him," she said.

"If I hadn't sworn an oath to him, I'd be dead," I said at once.

"I know," said Flavia.

I sputtered, and she sighed. "I don't mean that the way it sounds," she said. "Of course I'd rather have you the way you are—awful as you are. Better than running off to be a mercenary in Arqueiran, or a thief, or cannon fodder in some backwater colony. Only whenever you leave, you come back like this."

"Like what?" I said sharply. "Last time I came home, we were wreathed in victory." The civil war won, the council's defenses smashed like so much glass, Semfontan's mansion empty, the city guard flocking hungrily to our banner, Ceirran standing triumphant on the steps of the Libeiracópolan.

"Yes," she said. "You were. The war's over, Anita. Sorry though I am to see Quinha dead—"

"You weren't sorry when the assassin came through your window eight months ago!" I said. "Fortune's toes, Flavia, you'll start to sound like *him*. All his weeping, and swearing undying friendship, and handing out pardons like there's a bargain on."

"Sorry as I am that I didn't see Quinha killed by a Ceian executioner before a crowd of thousands," she said, "she *is* dead. Matheus has won Madinabia—he's won Ceiao—now he's won Szayet, I suppose, or at least a bed in it. He has no battles left. When he's come back to the city, you should pay a visit to Cláudia."

"Cláudia Pulcron?" I said blankly. "Why?"

"Because she has a piece of seashore away from the crowds, and a dozen servants with nothing to do all day but rub your shoulders and feed you grapes," said Flavia. "Or you should go to Sintia and spend thirty nights in a row at the theater, and scandalize Sintielo with a whole fistful of actresses. Or better yet, go to some little satellite in the Shieldmirror, far away from Madinabia and its moons, where they've never heard the name Matheus Ceirran in their lives. And there you can drink until you've forgotten the difference between him, Quinha, and Altagracia Caviro of Szayet."

"Fortune forbid," I said. The wind was picking up. I could feel the hair on the back of my neck beginning to rise. "He'll come back, and he'll forget her within a day. Then we'll plan what's next. Far Madinabia. The borders of Kutayet."

"Do you really think he'll forget her in a day?" she said.

I shrugged one shoulder. My feet were quite numb by now. If I knew Ceirran, I thought, he wouldn't dwell on the Oracle of Szayet for longer than a month. He'd smile when his mind lighted on her. He'd tell the council that there was no use deposing her for a puppet or a governor, the way Semfontan and the rest of the council had deposed so many kings and princes throughout the Swordbelt. He'd swear up and down that he would think of her always with fondness, and when it came time for Ceiao's troops to seize the treasure in her oceans by force, he wouldn't stop them.

But I had thought I'd known Ceirran when we'd landed on those salt-washed little islands. The Ceirran I knew, when the princess had rolled out of the carpet in a flimsy dress, would have packed her away to Alectelo's dungeons. The Ceirran I knew would have sat smiling while she tossed her hair and widened her eyes and spoke to him sweetly, and he wouldn't have so much as sent me out of the room. He would have never sent me out of the room.

"Do you think you'll forget her?" said Flavia.

I looked at her out of the corner of my eye: her curls, her long limbs, her broad-boned beauty, so unalike to what I saw reflected in the mirror or in the moving water below. And yet when she turned to look back, I knew her eyes; I knew them like I knew my own.

"You're not on my side at all, are you," I said.

"I'm on Ceiao's side," she said, "like every loyal citizen. And Matheus's, of course. Aren't you?"

"No, you're not," I said. "You're on the side of that girl. You haven't even met her, and you like her better than me."

Unexpectedly, she smiled. "Don't mistake me for someone else, Anita," she said. "I'm never on anyone's side but yours."

"Swear it," I said, impulsively and childishly.

"On our mother's ashes," she said, "and on the ashes of my husband, and on the Nevede filled with waste and refuse and the Rouan filled with beggars and thieves, and on all the worlds you've ever conquered. I'm on your side, Anita, until the day I have to bury you. Only I wish sometimes that you were, too."

You asked for a story,
     but you wanted a confession—
          a litany of sins.
I have made promises, and then,

                                             later—

—broken—

At first I mistook the planet for empty space. It was black—not the greying shadow that fell on moons and asteroids on the leeward side of the sun, but a black so deep as to be nearly bright, richer than the night that fell to its east and its west.

But its rings spilled outward in circle after circle, white as salt, flecked here and there with black and brown and forest green. And as the planet grew in our sights, the crew put hands to their mouths, or softly cursed the names of Fortune and Justice, or made surreptitious Alectelan signs against evil.

In the time it might take a man to draw a breath, that impenetrable black shivered like oil and split. Scratches opened over the planet's surface, sea greens, glittering violets, iridescent oranges and reds. As if drawn by claws they streaked across the black, and in their wake I saw the swirls of black storms. Then they were gone, as quickly as they had come.

"Lightning, Admiral," said Ludon.

But the way his voice shook betrayed that he knew it was not lightning alone that cracked the planet into these jewel-veins. Even the most hardened veterans on this ship, who knew as much as a scholar about atmospheric iron and copper particles, gases of methane and refraction, bowed their heads and whispered sailors' superstitious charms. When I passed among them to clasp their arms and murmur comfort, they gripped my hand blindly and turned their faces away from that hard fractured light.

We lit the lanterns on *Taraxandran*'s cannon. She bore slowly down through the rings' steady ice rain, and her tunnels of light swept through miles of depthless freezing fog—no, not depth-less. Billowing mist gave way to dark, and then to the telltale fading blue of atmosphere. A moonlet had drawn a thick black line through the rings, ice and hail cascading into it like iron toward a magnet. And beneath that atmosphere—

There was no diamond isle. There were no seas. There was water, perhaps, the faint slick shine of it, along the trenches and valleys. There were shores—what had been shores, but now were glass, warped with deep creases and curves. Beyond them, the moonlet rose in crumbling towers, jagged waves, gleaming spikes hundreds of feet tall. The earth was the near-black of very old ash, pockmarked here and there where particles of ice had struck it. I had to look up to confirm to myself that there was indeed atmosphere in this place, and when I did, I saw the million glints where the rings' ice burned up and spattered down for hundreds of miles to the earth. Had we been mistaken? Misled? Had Vualo and Lukhaya found the tracking device, and dropped it on this moonlet, to guide us into a futile and dangerous chase?

No. In the stark shadow of one of the spikes, against the black and paler black of the moonlet, turquoise stone gleamed. Crumbled heaps stood beyond it, marble fallen over marble, deep blue and the glints of jade, and long shadows that were not shadows but obsidian columns toppled into the ash.

There were very few volunteers for the exploration party. Still, oxygen was abundant, gravity near Ceian standard. Once we had disembarked, Ludon was able to pull off his helmet before the four of us had trekked half a mile across the stone.

I followed suit, took a deep breath of the cold air, and looked up. The rings split the sky in two, a white arc from east to west, faint toward the horizon and bright at the highest point. In each half of the sky, tiny candle lights flickered: meteors. The planet was setting, and it washed the air in violets and blues.

"Ana," Ludon said suddenly.

I looked down. We were crossing onto one of those wide, warped fields of glass, cracks spiderwebbing through them at irregular angles. This one was narrower than the rest, only about fifty feet wide, and it sloped gently downward toward our left and into a deep valley.

At that center of the valley were hundreds of thousands of bones.

Some had slid together in a heap where the ground was steepest: mandibles fallen on tibias, ribs sticking out at odd angles. The rest lay neatly on the stone, side by side, barely overlapping, ilia over femurs, collarbones above breastbones, even the tiny carpals of a thousand hands barely moved away from the thin pieces of forearms. It was as if two thousand people had climbed into this valley, lain down side by side, and gone to sleep.

And pearl winked at me through eyeholes, pearl trailed out beside spines in thin strings. There were long cracks across foreheads, with pearl stitches sewing them up. There were jagged holes between the eyes, with pearl patches over them.

There were gaps, too, a spine lacking a skull, a rib cage lacking a spine. On the far side of the valley, a thin black trail wove through the ivory: toes knocked over leg bones, craniums rolling to the left of their mandibles.

"Someone's come through here," I said. "Someone took bones away."

We did not have much farther to go. Only a few minutes after we left the bone valley behind, we came to an enormous wall, cracked down the middle. There were scorch marks at its base. Once we were on its far side, I saw a felucca, capped with the figurehead of a lion, goat, and serpent, blurring faintly through the rain. Its windows were dark.

A snub-nosed young Kutayeti stood beside it—yes, I recognized him from Roof-without-Rain. He'd danced with me once. I crouched, aimed, and fired. The boy's hand went to his throat, eyes widening. He toppled without making a sound.

It wasn't the ship he'd been guarding but a round metal covering, much like the ones they used for sewers in Alectelo. I signaled to Ludon, and we dragged the boy's corpse carefully back toward the ship and eased the covering up.

Ludon staggered back. I clapped my hand over my nose and struggled not to gag. Sewers had been exactly right—the smell that billowed up was worse than a bivouac pit after two weeks' siege. Waste, sweat, the usual repulsive stuff of unhygienic human living, and more: blood, and something chemical and sour.

After me, I mouthed to the others, swung my legs over the edge of the pit, and—

—dropped—

—the bottle, which shattered at once.

"Vomiting son of a dung-eating ape," I said, kicked at the shards, and was rewarded by pain in my toe. "Spit-rain and piss-snow and boils and plague—" I kicked again. Dark smeared along the jasper tile. Sounds in the evening light were wickedly sharp: the drip of the atrium fountain, Flavia's breathing from the couch, the slow beeping of the heart monitor in the next room.

"Don't act like a child," Flavia said from her couch.

"Piss on you, too," I said, and went deliberately without limping to the fountain, leaving wet toe prints behind. The fountain was only a tinted trickle, staining the tiles rust dark. I pushed my foot under the water and hissed.

I heard Flavia's book thump down. "You'll poison yourself," she said.

Now when I put weight on my foot it properly hurt. Admiral Semfontan's lieutenants would curse me for coming back to them damaged, I thought. Well, they would curse me anyway. Six months inspecting shipments of computers and lanterns and rain boots and carpets at the harbor, six months watching

Semfontan's door while guests filed through her parties. What would discipline mean? Scrubbing out tanks of chemical waste by the Nevede, maybe? That would be a pleasant change in fortune.

I heard Flavia sigh when I began to limp toward the cellar door. When my hand touched the knob, she burst out:

"She'll be happier at the hospital."

"So now we give a centono whether she's happy," I said savagely. "When did that happen?"

"She'll be safer at the hospital, then," said Flavia. I turned. She was sitting up, knees tucked into her chest. In the last month she'd developed an affectation of leaving the house with her face painted, and this evening there were still faint traces of vermilion on her cheeks from her earlier dinner. "They'll make her—comfortable—"

"Comfortable," I said. "Of course. Why shouldn't she be comfortable? That's what she'll say, when she wakes up and doesn't know where she is—when she learns a dozen nurses saw her piss the bed, and told their wives and children and the actresses they meet in taverns and Fortune knows who else—"

"You don't know that'll happen," said Flavia.

"That's what she'll say," I said, "when she's in the spider-litter coming home and she's screaming that I left her with strangers and robbers and thieves, when Sonia's father slams the door in my face again, when Semfontan bothers to look at me at last and tells me she's terribly sorry and if she can do anything for me, oh, she'd be more than happy to have the Decretans owe her a favor. She'll say—at least I was comfortable."

Flavia unfolded herself. She had taken her braids down after she'd come home, and her hair was a wide soft cloud. Beneath the jade eyelid powder her eyes were very bright, and her knuckles were clenched white. "Anita," she said, "if we take her to the hospital, then when she finally—"

"*You* don't know that'll happen," I said, before she could finish.

"It might not be now," said Flavia. "But what about the third time her heart seizes? The fourth? You can't—" Her voice cracked. "We can't take care of her forever. You can't worry about what she'll say forever. She's not going to live—"

I yanked the cellar door open, hobbled into the dark, and slammed it after me.

In her bedroom after my baths, when I was very young, our mother would sit me down on one of her chairs, and I would pick at the wickerwork with my finger until she noticed and smacked my hand away. Then she would take her heat gun and run it over my hair, an inch or less from the scalp. It hurt, and it hurt badly.

She could never do it to my sister. Flavia had our grandfather's curls. A year from this day, she would have maids: women of her husband's household, Sintian and Cherekku girls who attended to her hair in the manner a lady should be accustomed to, pinned and woven with gold thread or bound with jewels. Now, though, she styled her own hair into wavering and uneven braids, carefully and alone. She never spoke about this to me.

The silence was deeper down here, the stone floor cool. When we'd been children, Flavia had used to say that the ancestors of the family Decretan, the wild refugees from the generation ships, had buried their servants beneath those stones. At night, she'd said, they rattled at the bottles, trying to claw their way out. Now I was grown, and the world was half the size it had been when I was young. The house, the assessor had told Flavia, was around two hundred years old. Our great-grandfather Luís had bought it fifty years after the theomachy.

"I might die tomorrow, too," I said to the wide and empty dark. "And who would come to point and laugh at me?"

There was a bottle I'd pulled from the racks here last night. I fumbled against the wall until I had it in my hands. Ceiao was an old city, for all that, an old land. For all I knew, there might be bodies here: victims of wicked priests, of Alekso of Sintia's conquest, of famine, of plague, of having lived. When I died, Flavia might bury me here.

Flavia might watch the grave dug, and lay my ashes in. Flavia might think of what to say at my funeral. Flavia might receive me wounded and dying, and sit by my bed, and measure the poppy into a spoon. Flavia might listen to my heart monitor, the way I had listened for the last week to our mother's.

"I shouldn't be down here," I said aloud.

I didn't know why I'd said it. I'd come down here to get the new bottle, hadn't I? Where else would I be?

"I didn't break the bottle last time," said my voice in the dark.

I put my free hand over my mouth, bewildered and unhappy. I was drunker than I'd thought. What was *last time*?

The wine, when I tipped the bottle to my mouth, had gone sickeningly sour. I swallowed it and tried not to gag. It happened, sometimes, down here in the dark. Somewhere in the cork, there must have been—

—a crack, a—

—scratch—

—and, over time—

—not yet. Almost—

"—with the new input," said the voice of Sasha Vualo.

I signaled for a halt. The river by now was up to our ankles, if you could call it a river. The Nevede, on a good day, was liable to catch fire from the sheer quantity of refuse in it, but even it was more water than waste. What we walked through now was black and viscous. The farther we had pressed, the more it had stunk.

But the walls were fine, well-glazed brick. As we'd passed, I had made out faded lions fighting faded bulls, lotuses against stained blue, strange long-necked creatures with bird's feet and forked tongues. Now, near the tunnel's end, the lamps blazed brighter, the floor sloped higher, the river ran deeper. Old bronze doors along the walls stood locked.

The door ahead, though, hung open. White light spilled through from the other side. So did voices:

"—naturally not heresy." Vualo again, a low drawl. "That's how I'll put it to the King of Kings in a week: She preferred failure to heresy. He'll be thrilled. You know how he adores rigid adherence to piety."

"You know how he adores a wild-goose chase," another voice said brightly: Lukhaya. "That's how *you'll* put it to the emperor in a week. What came of all that treating with Decretan, child? Ah, Imperial Majesty, you'll like this. No, the whole of the Terrestrial Intelligence is just as it was a week ago, but we sang the subjects some lovely lullabies—"

"I swear by Alekso of Sintia, Carmela, you'll address me properly or you'll regret it," said Vualo. "You learned bad habits when we were keeping a pet Ceian."

Lukhaya barked a laugh. "One of these days you'll have to follow through on some of your threats," she said. "And I wonder what you'll do then—my lord."

"Then," said Vualo, "I'll regret the necessity of what I have to do next. Don't forget that it was a wild-goose chase that brought you here, Carmela—don't forget that the empress consort called me a fool to my face every time I opened up my purse for you. Do you really mean to tell me you know best when it comes to the court? Me—after all these years?"

A long pause. I twisted back to stare at Ludon, who shrugged. Vualo had never once asked on Sancta Mirtalo or on Szayet to be called *my lord*. I had thought their title was *ambassador*.

"Never," said Lukhaya's voice eventually. "Spirits below, Sasha, you know how devout I'm not. It's the principle of the thing. I'm not looking through this old book for a Malisintian orison or a hymn. The cure shouldn't be a—a—a magic word. It should be neurological—it should be psychiatric. It should be in the subjects' focus."

"What are you suggesting?" said Vualo. "Oxytocin in the cerebrospinal drip?"

"Perhaps an amphetamine," said Lukhaya. "I mean it, I'm not serious about devotion—mine or theirs. It's the intensity of their feelings I'm interested in, not the direction." Footsteps clicked, and her voice began to grow louder. "Speaking of the direction of feelings," she said, "you did do an admirable job making nice with the heretic. How did it feel to prostrate yourself before a false god?"

There was the rumble of Vualo's low laugh. "The emperor should try it," they said. "Hauling up a few acres of sunken gold would certainly solve my budget problems... Carmelita, I'm tired, I'm hungry, and I haven't had a decent bath since we shipped out to the desert. Dose them with amphetamines, dose them with arsenic, it's your prerogative. I mean to go to my ship, send the emperor the news that the broken subjects haven't experienced a sudden miracle, and let you work while I finally sleep. Just indulge me—run a Szayeti orison on one of the pearl-linked skulls."

"The skulls are dead," said Lukhaya's voice dryly. "If they start talking to one another, that really will be a miracle. You learned bad habits when we were making nice with the Szayeti, *my lord*."

"You're only sick of testing false hypotheses," said Vualo.

"And what if I am?" said Lukhaya. The door hinges creaked. Silently, I drew my knife. "Listen," she went on, "I told you I didn't mean to question your judgment. All I'm interested in—"

The edge of a silhouetted face—a hand—a rubber boot. Light washing outward. In half a second we would all be blind. I squinted and threw.

Someone screamed. I broke into a run, gun raised, the other three following. A heavy splash, and footsteps—Vualo barreling toward me, another blade glinting in their fist. "Drop it," I snapped, not expecting to be obeyed, and wasn't disappointed. They bore toward me like a bull. At the last moment I dove and, before they could blink, had an arm around Lukhaya's throat.

"Drop it," I said again, and set my gun barrel against her temple.

Vualo froze, breathing hard. There were three more barrels aimed at their head, but if they saw them, they didn't care. They were staring at me—at Lukhaya's head—as if hypnotized. In their hand, the point of the knife wavered.

"I'd love to see you try," I said. "Might be your aim is better than your dancing." I shrugged. The gun barrel shifted against Lukhaya's scalp. "You want the artery in my neck, for preference. Either side's all right." I tilted up my chin. "Go on. Throw faster than I can shoot. That'll be a miracle worth seeing."

Their great hand wavered, then opened. The knife splashed.

"Clever of you," I said. "Ludon—" He snatched the blade from the river, nose wrinkling. "Where are your men?"

"Patrolling the hallways, with orders to check on us every five minutes," said Vualo instantly.

Resting, then, or far enough from here that it didn't matter. I examined Lukhaya. She had fallen unconscious. Shock, most likely. My knife had stuck shallowly into her thigh.

"She needs bandages," said Vualo, and looked at once as if they regretted it.

The dark patch on her baggy trousers was spreading slowly enough that I was sure I hadn't hit an artery. Vualo didn't need to know that, though. "She needs the wound cleaned," I said. "Who knows what nasties might be crawling around in this mess? Well—you would, of course. Ah, careful!"

Vualo had moved suddenly toward Ludon's gun, and I'd curled my finger warningly around the trigger of my own. They snarled and raised their hands again.

"Let's take a walk, Ambassador," I said. "Lieutenant, take lead."

Lukhaya had roused by the time we reached the end of the tunnel. I could feel her whimpering against my chest every time we took a step. "You stabbed me," she said, sounding bewildered.

"There's that keen scholar's intelligence," I said. The smell was nearly unbearable now. In the open door was a length of rubber pipe, sludge dripping blackly from its end into the river. Something electrical was humming. "Up you go. Keep those hands high, Ambassador."

"Admiral," said Ludon up ahead.

I shoved Lukhaya forward and followed her up a staircase, into a laboratory.

There were no metal beds here, no walls of sheer pearl, no columns supporting heads. The people lay facedown, shoulder to shoulder, hands dangling limp from their cots. The pearl cables in their skulls sprouted every direction—into the ceiling, into walls, into humming slabs of pearl standing between the beds. From here to the far side of the room, pearl cables hung like jungle vines, weaving and overlapping.

Some of the patients were as young as the girl in Khramya. Some were younger—one was a boy who could not have been older than thirteen. Some were much older: a woman with stringy white hair growing down to her hips, a woman with spots on her hands and veins heavy and blue in her legs, a man beginning to bald.

The beeping came from heart monitors. These sat at the head of each cot, blinking blue. Beside them stood tall poles dangling with full bags of clear or white liquid, and tubes ran from these into the backs of necks where spines began. More tubes ran from the bodies' mouths, from their arms, from beneath their loose grey shifts, feeding into the rubber pipe I had seen on the stairs.

The walls were covered in holoscreens. Text spilled rapidly

across them. It was in Sintian, but it might as well have been in the Muntiru tongue for all I understood it: On one screen I saw *oxygen*, and *phototachometer7845*, and *drone length not exceeding*, and nothing else.

But even I in my ignorance could see that this was strange computer code. One screen wrote rapidly: *Shiptype:ketch. Wegiht limit: 2500 sttone.* Another: *Color input YELLOW not recognized. Select a color: Salt / Acid / Honey / Fish*

And it was not only code. One screen said in Sintian, *Where am I?* And then, a split second later, *Doctor, are you there? Hello! Can you hear me?* And instantly again: *Hello, can anyone hear me? Is anyone listening? Is anyone there?*

"Quicksilver pearl thinks more quickly than the brain," said Ludon quietly. "Time moves slowly for computers." His face was grey.

Can anyone hear me? said the screen. *Hello, can anyone hear me? Can anyone hear me? Hello! Can anyone hear me? Hello! Hello! Hello, can anyone hear me? Can anyone hear me, hello! Can anyone hear me? Can anyone hear hello hello can any hello hear me hello can hello hello hello hello hello can anyone hear me hear me hear me hear me hear me hear me me me me me me—*

On the back walls of the bathhouses of Ceiao, there was graffiti to this effect: that Commander Ceirran's murder had been arranged by the Merchants' Council's clerks. Why? It had become so expensive to find meeting places, said the wits of the public baths, that the clerks wished the council were only half its size.

It was true, in any event, that the trickle of people down the front steps of the house was thin and slow, that though the evening was frosty some went without overcoats, that even those dressed in warm clothing wore neither silk nor velvet nor jewelry. It was true that a few bore old burn scars—this one on his hand, this one along the side of her face—and it was true that there were bags beneath their eyes, that they hung their heads and did not speak. It was true that when each reached the bottom of the steps, he peeled away from his fellows, and went with slow step and slumped shoulders into the windy dusk.

"Goodbye," said the woman at the top of the stairs, "goodbye. Goodbye, Adriene, give my love to your brother. Goodbye, Manoela, and do be careful on the road, there's gangsters out there! Goodbye, Heitor, and don't forget you've promised to have me for dinner. No, I thought you'd remember. Goodbye, goodbye—"

She stood in a pool of lamplight, blue stole thrown over her shoulders, velvet gloves drawn up to her elbows, wrists and neck gleaming with gold. In the windows of the house's upper story, the silhouettes of maids moved back and forth closing lamps, so that as the grey slid out of the sky, she was the only bright thing on the street. It was only a close and knowledgeable observer who would have seen through that brightness the new lines on her forehead, the mechanicality of her smile, how she pulled absently at the cloth on her hands.

When the last of her visitors had gone, she stood for a long minute and looked silently over the empty street. Now her smile had vanished. Now she wrapped her arms around herself, perhaps from cold or perhaps from another feeling, and she sighed.

"Are you Flavia Decretan?" piped a voice from the bottom of the steps.

Flavia Decretan looked down and frowned at who she saw there: a woman in black, scarf wrapped round her face, wearing the armband of a docks messenger.

"I am," she said. "What business do you have with me?"

"News from the front," called the messenger.

Flavia was not a young woman any longer, and her dignity had been earned at cost. She did not cry out, or clap her hands to her mouth, or faint. But her bracelets clattered from the shaking of her hands.

"Is she well?" she said.

"I was told to find you first," came the messenger's muffled reply through the scarf. "Flavia Decretan is to hear the news before anyone else. I've been ordered to make sure of that."

At the start of this speech Flavia had grown quite pale. By the end she was clinging to the railing of the stairs. "Come here and give it to me," she said. "For mercy's sake—"

The black-clad figure ascended the stairs slowly, reaching into her bag. "Here," said the piping voice. She drew out a bulky envelope, stamped in red with the seal of the Ceian fleet.

Flavia snatched it and ripped it open—then her brows knitted, and she tipped out two coins into her palm, but she had barely time to look up in confusion before I'd pulled the scarf down from my face and seized her in my arms.

"You pig!" she shrieked as I spun her. She had nearly half a foot on me, and was very difficult to carry. I staggered backward into her door, laughing, and we both slid in a heap to the ground. "You heartless thing—there's been nothing but evil gossip for days. I thought they'd come to tell me you'd died on the way home!"

"Cancel the pyres, and send away the flowers, and tell Ceiao's actresses to dry their tears," I said. "You'll have to put up with me for another year or two, I'm afraid. What's all this business at the house? You haven't become a councillor while I was away."

Flavia sat up and brushed at her arms with the affronted dignity of a cat. "Oh, one doesn't need to be on the council to offer them the use of one's house," she said archly. "One only has to be a patriot. If the council finds my house useful, I'm humbled."

"You're worse than a snake," I said, and grinned in perfect satisfaction at the sky.

"Anita," she said, serious now, "they told me the war had ended. Is that true? Are they—?"

I shoved myself upright against her railing. "Dead. Both of them," I said. "I burned Jonata Barran myself. There's still the rest to scour—Cipon, Laubian, Veguion's daughter...It isn't ended. But it'll have an ending. Here—" I scrabbled on the stoop for one of the ice-cold dekar she'd dropped. "Freshly minted. Check the reverse."

She took it in her velvet-gloved hand and examined first the obverse portrait, which was a man in profile, a faint scar on his chin. *CEIRRAN COMMANDER*, it read along the edge. Then she turned it over. Its reverse side showed a winged woman. Her left foot stepped forward into empty air, and her right foot rested on a globe.

"It's Lady Victory," she said.

"Look closer," I said.

She raised it to her eyes and squinted. "Anita—" she said faintly.

"Not a bad likeness, I think," I said. "They got the nose right. Of course in life you're uglier. Hey!" She'd shoved me. I fell against the door again, grinning.

"Ceians never put living people on their coins," she said quietly. "And never, ever civilians."

"These are new times," I said. "Our times. Ceirran's times. What do the people care who's alive and who's dead? It's the image they're spending, not the men." She said nothing, staring at the gold against the velvet, and I said, abruptly embarrassed, "You don't like it. I'll call it off. We'll melt the stamps—"

"Anita," she said thickly, and flung her arms around my neck. At first I was alarmed, and then I understood she was laughing— great, helpless gulps of air, very close to sobs. I put my arms around her, and held her while she laughed, until she was gasping against my chest.

"If you ever keep me in the dark again about whether you're alive, I'll kill you," she said at last.

"If I die, I won't send a messenger," I promised. "I'll come to you as—"

"—a ghost," I said.

"Sir?" said the doctor's apprentice.

I stared at him. The ceiling rattled. "You said *a ghost*, sir," he said.

"No, I didn't," I said. "Are you feeling all right, ensign?"

"Just undo one hand," said Lukhaya coaxingly, garbled through her swollen lip. "Just so I can apply the sedative. Just to the control group."

I shook myself. "Again," I said to the apprentice.

He put his tongue between his teeth, eyed Lukhaya—her bony shoulders, her hands tied behind the chair, the gag that we'd pulled down to her chin when her screaming had stopped—and struck her across the uninjured side of her face. She wailed.

"You won't get far," said Vualo wearily. We'd shoved their chair up against the holoscreens. Green Sintian lettering glimmered in their white mane. "That one's terrible with pain. Has been since she was a child. She'll say whatever you want to hear, and never give a damn for the truth."

The ceiling rattled again. Dust spilled into Lukhaya's hair. She and Vualo had refused at gunpoint to tell us how many guards patrolled the tunnels, and unwilling to waste men on protecting my person, I'd sent nearly the whole crew of *Taraxandran* to clear the compound. "By explosive, for preference," I'd ordered, which they had saluted gleefully.

In the meantime, I'd found *Taraxandran*'s doctor's apprentice. He'd cleaned, dressed, and bandaged Lukhaya's leg, and given her a shot of something that would make it feel like a block of wood for the next six hours. He'd also demonstrated a refreshingly practical attitude toward applying his recent learning in anatomy and in pain.

"How many of your Terrestrial Intelligence come off the laboratory table like this?" I said to Lukhaya. "Tubes in their arms, raving nonsense?"

"Errors aren't nonsense," she said primly. The apprentice raised his arm, and she said, "One in every fifty! At first—at first."

"At first?" I said, very coolly, so that Vualo wouldn't hear how the bottom of my stomach had dropped. There were forty people facedown on these beds. Just one had decimated Szayet. Did the Kutayeti have thousands?

"It took me ages to perfect the technique," said Lukhaya. She sighed. "Alekso's little bulldog wasn't any scholar. The only records of building the Intelligence that he bothered to keep in the Fortunatas were muster books, rations and casualty logs, holo copies of maps—and the skulls, of course, if you can call those evidence. Well, we couldn't have made the breakthroughs without the skulls—but I *did* still need to be a genius to make the breakthroughs, so—"

"To the point," I said pleasantly.

She flinched. "In the end we learned on our own how to combine pearl with the subjects' brains without killing them," she said. "After we'd done it, the subjects only had the ordinary number of software errors. Computer operators' mistakes, damage to the cables or argyropoeic wiring—we could fix those. That was what we thought had happened to the first of these, we thought the pearl was leprous, we thought we could replace the wires and try again..."

I looked at the Sintian text blinking across Vualo's forehead. *In the dark*, it said. *In the dark, in the dark, in the dark the dark the dark. Dark is like a mirror dark is like the sea dark is like the sunshine the red the blue the green—*

"The problem wasn't in their pearl," I said. "It was in their brains."

There was another thud from above, and the distant rattle of gunfire. "Some brains," said Lukhaya. "A few. Defective. Serfs, tribesmen. Uneducated people, you understand. We trained them before we transformed them, we fed them moly and coca leaves, sped up their neural activity, we thought it would help. But the subjects still broke once we tried to wake them into the Intelligence, they broke and they broke, they threw out errors we'd never heard of, they repeated themselves endlessly, and when we plugged them into ships—"

During this speech her eyes had fallen shut, and she shuddered again. "The ships tore apart," she said. "If the human hosts managed to survive the disaster, their brains were unusable afterward. But it was only a few of them. We disposed of them. We made more. We were making an army."

"And then," I said.

"And then more of them started malfunctioning," she said. "Hosts who had been working perfectly well, who had been functioning for weeks—for months. All of the older ones began failing, one by one. By the time we learned the warning signs, three dozen hosts had died. When we knew what to look for— the confusion, the retreat into memories, the little spelling errors or repetitions—then we could pull them out of their ships or their satellites before they had degenerated entirely, and then at least we could save the passengers. It might have been better if we hadn't learned. The emperor wouldn't let us remove the Terrestrial Intelligence from the satellites and ships where they were still embedded, not as long as we kept the casualty rate low. He said the Intelligence was too useful to abandon before we absolutely had to."

"But you had to," I said. "Because more of them were breaking."

"More," she said, "and more, and more. One in every thirty of those we'd made was broken. Then one in every ten. Not just the serfs but citizens too, tradesmen, scholars. A daughter of one of

Archduke Zuvany's lesser spouses. That was when the emperor agreed to halt production altogether, and it was lucky he did it then, because we didn't even know—"

Without warning, Vualo said, in a tone of deep boredom, "You should have stayed on Szayet." I turned to look at them, and they shrugged as best they could with their hands bound behind their back. "You'd have been happier there," they said. "Drinking your wine, arguing with your queen, letting a boy fight your battles. Do you think the emperor only sent me to Sancta Mirtalo to pry Szayet's secrets out of a loose-tongued fool? You still might negotiate with him, Admiral."

"Negotiate!" I said. "If I were the emperor at the moment, I'd be swearing to see the ravens fighting over Anita Decretan's corpse. Funny thing to offer, isn't it? Gag them." The apprentice tore a strip of cloth from the hem of the nearest host's shift and went about shoving it between the ambassador's teeth. Ignoring their grunts and struggles, I turned back to Lukhaya. "Go on," I said.

She looked wary, now. Vualo's interruption had done its work to warn her to guard her tongue. Well, I could make guesses. "You had to halt production," I said. "An archduke wants his daughter's mind in working order, hm? Even if he's sold her body into service. However you broke these people, you need to repair them. But you aren't clever enough to see how they're broken."

"Clever enough, nothing," she said. "Just undo one of my hands, won't you? Just let me take the tablet—" She struggled fruitlessly and subsided at my look. "The amount you don't know about my work," she said sourly, "could fill twelve libraries. What in the world do you think you walked in on? When we've found a cure for—"

Vualo grunted loudly. Lukhaya shut her mouth. I sighed. "Again," I said.

The apprentice swung his fist into her gut. Lukhaya shouted, breathless and noiseless, but said no more.

"Again, sir?" said the apprentice to me, but I shook my head. Vualo's face was a mask of black-eyed fury. I didn't need to make them angrier; hurting the scholar had given me time to think.

"You spoke about trying Szayeti orisons," I said. "You asked me how much time the Oracle needed to connect herself to Ceirran's Pearl. You asked me how Ceirran and Alekso could speak to each other, and I told you to look in the Library of Alectelo. You did look—and you stole a piece of Alekso's writing that was about forcing pearl computers to sync. You know why these monsters can't speak right or think clearly after all, don't you? You push a computer into these people's brains, and then you wake them up, and they wake up with cameras for eyes, with speakers for ears, without any way to touch another person at all."

I shrugged. "I've seen a soldier lose his eyes. Seen one lose her ears, too. It wasn't pretty, but it wasn't death. They got up, they went on, they took land in the colonies after the war and for all I know now they're fat and happy with three mistresses each. But when you wake your monsters, they have no one to speak to, no one to answer their questions, no one who says hello. No one but their own minds, their own memories—and half of their mind isn't even their own. That girl on Khramya, Maral os-Margad— what did you say about her? She could distinguish foe from friend, but she couldn't speak, she couldn't understand speech. Fortune, no wonder she was so desperate for us not to kill the satellite staff—they were the closest thing she had in the world to human company!"

From above, where my soldiers were, came the loudest thud yet. The floor shuddered. A holoscreen whined and died. "Do they sleep?" I said. "No, they've got to be life support, don't they? You can't afford to let oxygen and gravity dream. Ludon was right—computers are faster than the brain. Too fast. How quickly does time pass for one of these people? How long do

they spend alone in the dark? Weeks? Years? Oh, I'm sure some
can live with it, at first. Some of them can stand to be useful
to you for a few months—Undying Name, from their point of
view, it must be decades. But no one can live that lonely forever.
Alekso of Sintia might have spent the last three hundred years
in a pearl the size of my pinkie, but at least he had his Oracles.
These people don't have that. They need to speak to each other
in order to bear it. And speaking to each other is the one thing
they can't do."

I shook my head. "We wondered why you bothered to keep
them a secret. Why would you negotiate for peace, if you had
a weapon like that on your side? When that swarm of ships
bombarded Szayet, we thought the world had ended. But of
course you had to keep the Terrestrial Intelligence a secret—you
couldn't afford to brag about an army that was busy destroying
itself. And then I discovered the girl on Khramya, and you had
no choice but to bluff. You revealed that the Terrestrial Intelligence existed, but you had to pretend its hosts could stay alive.
How terrifying it must have been, that attack on Szayet! At
every moment you must have been afraid the ships would rip
themselves apart, and we would understand that every swarm in
your new army had an expiration date."

There was a strange choking sound from beside her: Around
the gag, Vualo was laughing. I nodded at the apprentice, who
yanked down their gag. "What's so funny?" I said.

They coughed and spat onto the floor. When they raised their
head again, they were grinning. "Alekso of Sintia had his Oracles," they said. "Not *has*? And he doesn't *have* your commander?
Another interesting misunderstanding."

I shoved the gag up between their teeth. They didn't resist this
time, but their eyes were bright.

"Unwire the hosts," I said to Lukhaya. "Disconnect them."

"I can't," she said sharply. "They're missing twelve square

inches of skull. Do you think that grows back? Even if I wanted to, I'd have to hack open their brains to pull out the wire. At best they'd be catatonic—" Her tone changed abruptly, sweetly desperate. "Admiral, let me apply the sedative. Just let me let them sleep. Just an hour's dosage, that's all."

"From their torturer, that's touching concern," I said. "Speaks well of you."

Her jaw set. "The subjects knew what I was doing here when they boarded the transport ships," she said. "They knew we weren't playing backgammon. It was my job to make them into the Intelligence. It was my job to work out how. Was it my job to be their keeper?"

Work out how, I thought. She'd found scanty notes, a few skulls. That was what she'd built her army from—that, and her own intelligence, just as formidable and dangerous as the Terrestrial kind. She'd said they'd found nothing else useful here. And so they'd come to Szayet, to charm the librarians, to discover what Szayet's people felt was important, and to steal whatever documents they could, in case they held a cure for their sick and useless monsters.

There had been no mention of silver-eyed people in that journal. I had thought that was strange. But now I thought that had been stupid, Szayeti thinking: the expectation that everything that mattered to Alekso of Sintia was something he had archived, the expectation that what he had wanted from the future was understanding rather than obedience.

"Untie her," I said to the apprentice.

Lukhaya's face collapsed into joy. "You won't regret this," she said. "My needles are in the storage closet. Just let me—"

"You're not going to your needles," I said.

The apprentice had loosed her ankles, though her hands were still bound. I hauled her upward. She landed on her injured leg and whined.

"Admiral," she said, "you should let me sedate the subjects. Please let me—"

"Ensign," I said. He snapped to attention. "When the crew is back," I said, "tell them I've gone exploring. And leave that one gagged."

Vualo grunted again urgently. "Don't miss me too much, Ambassador," I said, looking Lukhaya up and down. She seemed about as rough as a butterfly, but you never knew. "Ensign, if I haven't come back in two hours, send a search party," I said, and jerked a thumb at Vualo. "But shoot them first."

There was a pearl torchlight on one of the far tables, and a knife on another, both of which I tucked into my belt. When I opened the door at the far end of the room, cool air rushed in at once. It smelled like flowers, I thought in bewilderment. What flowers grew down here?

"Hurry," I said over my shoulder, and stepped through,

onto the street.

"I think I like it this quiet," I said. "Not so much a fuss with the crowds."

Ceirran said nothing, only looked long down the travessa Carenan, the overhanging trees. The spring flowers were coming in. My memory named them, despite my conscious intent to look elsewhere: blooming hawthorns, daffodils, purple crocuses.

"All the empty houses," he said quietly.

"Call the foxes and pigeons and rats," I said, "and open up the doors, and lay out crumbs, and then they'll all love you, too. Why such a dark face, Ceirran? You're the lord of the world."

"Yes," he said, "lord of the world," and shook himself and turned to me. "Of course. Call the city guard, and make sure the houses are kept secure—none of the gangsters should get ideas." I opened my mouth, and he raised an eyebrow at me. "Neither should you, Captain."

"Sir," I said, with malicious humor. There were two little marble dancers in Quinha Semfontan's house that I'd wanted for years. Well, and so. If he ever found out, he'd let me.

We set out walking again, down the alleyway and toward the broader expanse of the avenue beyond. Above us, in the eaves, birds were building their nests. No wartime for the sparrows, I thought. One councillor was exactly like another to them.

"I'll have to find a place to sleep," I said casually.

"Hm?" said Ceirran, looking down at me. "Your sister isn't in the city?"

"Ah," I said after a moment, "she is. Of course."

"I hope you won't mind me saying this," he said, "but it's still her husband's house, to me. I nearly expect him to come around the corner now, about to ask me to dinner."

We had reached the end of the alley. To my left stretched the blue tile of councillors' mansions, patchworked with yellow oak leaves. Here was Cleto Branquon's, lanterns extinguished, iron bars nailed to the door. Here was Filipa Geganian's, its front stoop empty of servants and of laughing women for the first time I could remember. Here, at the very end of the street, was a narrow house, a statue of Valquíria Barran toppled over at its base. Here were the gates Flavia and I had climbed over, and here was the tree Flavia had fallen from when she was nine. Here were the tall thin pillars on which Flavia's hand had lingered, nails painted and knuckles heavy with golden rings, the last time she had left: her wedding day.

"Come to dinner with us," I said to Ceirran. "We'll have the run of the markets. Let's eat thrushes in honey, and lift Narcisa Cipon's wine from her cellars."

"Did you ask people to stay with you and Flavia so casually when it *was* Pulcron's house?" said Ceirran, smiling.

Pulcron's house? I thought. *No, don't come to Pulcron's, come to my mother's.* And then I remembered I had sold that house years ago; and then I wondered, if I were thinking of it as the Decretan house again—if I were living again in that long, ragged autumn after she'd died, with the strawberries rotting underfoot and the roof shedding dusty tiles into the maple roots—why I had not thought, *mine*.

"Later, perhaps," he said. "My husband will want to see me soon. I'm afraid he's terribly upset. You know how fond he is of his moral qualms."

"Things could be worse for him," I said, and turned purposefully to the right, putting my mother's house at my back. "He could be fleeing toward Sintia with a handful of moaning councillors on his bridge, trying to work out how to fight his way through three-quarters of the fleet, cursing the day he ever promoted Matheus Ceirran to admiral. For instance."

"Captain," said Ceirran.

"*Sir*," I said.

"Quinha is my friend," he said quietly.

There was no reply to make to that. Ceirran loved his friends. And I—

—and I—

and I loved—

"About eight hours, I give you," said Lukhaya.

I turned in a slow circle. The torchlight flared out: bare rock, a long tunnel with a rough flight of stairs at its end, great stalactites hanging white and bruise yellow from the ceiling, and finally a circular door.

"Were we here a second ago?" I said.

"Here?" said Lukhaya, surprised. "Where else would we have been?"

"I was just with—" I said.

I had just been asking her whether this was the place she'd described. I'd asked if this was where she'd found the old maps.

We'd picked our way down the stairs, she stumbling forward, me carrying the pearl torch high. What else had I been thinking of?

"Never mind," I said, and passed the torchlight over the door. It was all rusting green: tessellations of suns, flower stalks, crowned and bearded men holding offering trays. In the center, an open-mouthed lion's head jutted out, a strip of pearl beneath its tongue.

"The empress consort likes to call me when she wants to dig her claws into Sasha a little," said Lukhaya dreamily. "She'll have twelve ships here as soon as they miss one of her hails." She was leaning on the wall of the tunnel, eyelids fluttering. She hadn't bled through the bandages, and whatever the doctor's apprentice had given her, she still showed no signs of pain. Still, it didn't take a doctor to know she should have been lying on a stretcher with one of those poles feeding blood into her wrist, not standing here with an enemy, drifting in and out of dreams.

"Good," I said, crouching. "The men will want entertainment by then." There it was: a rusted yellow ring by Lukhaya's feet. White calcium crept over the edges of every stone and discarded coin here, but not this. Someone had picked it up recently. It might even have been Lukhaya—she certainly looked unsurprised to see it.

It fit in the lion's mouth perfectly. I rapped it. The door groaned and swung inward. Thin light bloomed.

It was a wide, high-ceilinged room. The light came from a thin strip of glass arcing across the ceiling, and fell on steel tables, steel shelves, the rotted remnants of what must have once been wooden stools. Stalactites hung here, too. The smell of must was thick enough to choke.

Lukhaya yawned. "I think we found a list of his frigates' janitors here," she said. "And an inventory of all the perishable fruits and vegetables he was packing in his flagship. We took away all those tablets, of course. I believe the homeworld library has them now."

The shelves were labeled in Malisintian, a cramped chicken

scratch. *Correspondence, barons, princes, knights*, one said under my torchlight. *Symptoms of Kutayeti moons*, said another—no, *Tribute from Kutayeti moons*. *Maps, rim-something-something quadrant*. *Correspondence, Imperial Flagpole*—that was wrong— *Imperial Bannermen to Alekso*. I ran my fingers over that shelf, finding nothing but rust and unpleasantly sticky residue, which I wiped on Lukhaya's cloak. She yelped.

Correspondence, Olimpia to Alekso. Correspondence, river captains? Ah, *wing captains to Alekso*. Why hadn't Szayet's ancestor kept any letters he'd actually written? Something I couldn't read, something I couldn't read, something that might be *captives. Judges*—no, *justice. Condemnations. Correspondence, Alekso to Alekso. Correspondence, Emperor to Alekso. Tribute*—

"Hold," I said, stepping back to the shelf that had said *Alekso to Alekso*. "Why would he write letters to himself?"

"Oh, you found that?" said Lukhaya. "What a little narcissist." She made a face. "May His infinite mercy shine on all of us blasphemers. How should I know? I tell you that all these shelves were cleared out, except for a tablet or two. His dog must have taken those letters away to cry over in bed."

I frowned, trailing a finger along the shelf's edge. Something was nudging at the edge of my understanding. Szayet had told me, a long time ago, of a memory that the intelligence in the Pearl had shared with her. A war camp—the planet of Szayet, before the flood—and a boy on his knees, holding out a piece of fruit, saying, *You too are Alekso of Sintia*.

The wall behind the shelf was half mold, streaked with white where stalactites dripped down. But the torch's beam shone on a triangle carved on a brick in the upper corner, so tiny that had I not been looking for it I would have thought it was a trick of the light. A triangle—that was the Sintian alphabet.

"D," I said.

"D?" said Lukhaya. "Who's D?"

"Disciple," I murmured, and pushed the brick.

It slid back. The shelf swung out in a wide arc, hinges shrieking. Dust billowed from an enormous hole in the wall.

Without hesitating, Lukhaya bolted like a rabbit into the dark. Half a second later, glass crashed. She groaned.

"Enjoying yourself?" I said, peering through the doorway.

This was a smaller chamber, not nearly as well-preserved as the first. Badly rotted tapestries hung over a mold-choked bed and a rusty shelf stacked with a dozen tablets. There had been a red glass lamp on the shelf—had been, because Lukhaya had skidded into it, and the lamp had shattered on what had previously been her uninjured thigh.

"Ecstatic," she said thickly from the floor.

I swept the torchlight slowly over the shelf. I'd been sure that Caviro had hidden something in this laboratory, something the Kutayeti had not known how to find. *Disciple—Alekso to Alekso—* that uncomfortable prickling at my heart—I had been sure, very sure, that though Alekso had wanted above all to be worshipped, there was something of him that Caviro would have kept private, secret, shut away from all of his worshippers.

There was a label on this shelf, too, which read *Records, experiments, conclusions: the chimera campaign. Chimera* was a word I didn't know. I lifted the first tablet from the pile and knocked it awake.

"You read Malisintian, don't you?" I said to Lukhaya.

"At the moment? Not without anesthetic," she said.

I sat cross-legged beside her. She'd wrapped her arms around her torso, but the torchlight didn't show any blood there yet, and she was breathing well enough. There was still no sign that she'd bled through her leg bandages, either, and only a few dots of blood on the other leg where the glass had cut her. Nothing fatal, then.

"I can wait," I said. "How long does your friend Vualo have

left before the deadline I set?" It occurred to me, as I said it, that I didn't know. That was unsettling. I had as decent a sense of time as any officer who'd ever had to run a mission without looking at a clock.

Lukhaya was sitting up reluctantly, her arms still wrapped over her stomach. "Give it to me," she said, and squinted at the text. "Fire alive, my god has bad handwriting. All right.

"'A sweet green country I've found for us, Caviro, but the local barbarians are quarrelsome people. Even the ones in our camp can't get through the night without challenging one of their fellows to a fight. The god they worship here was a savage warrior, and they claim every one of them is descended from her, by way of two sisters who fought to the death over which of them she'd blessed. One sister killed the other with a rock and built a city. If you can call a hill full of shacks and engine smoke a city!

"'But in the tents of the camp followers they tell us that they are descended from a ship that fled a burning city, and that they were led by the son of the god of love.

"'I'm sending you back the diagrams of our latest bright idea, with my notes. Don't go soft on me, trezoro. It's your job to make sure I stay alive, not mine. Convince me that there's a way toward replicating me besides this fusion of pearl and neural tissue. Don't I always listen to you in the end? If you don't abuse my love by acting like an old woman, you'll know why I gave it to you in the first place.

"'What about the prisoners from that scuffle by the burned-up palace? Pick a few dozen who aren't useful enough in the galleys. I don't think the *quantity* of the pearl will be our problem, but its *shape*. I'm not afraid of perforating my bones. It's the softer tissues that will give us trouble. Find out how much trouble— I don't doubt we'll overcome the body's breaking points, once we're together again, but first you must learn for me where they are. Be creative. I trust you.

"'Soon you'll lay down harbors for me, and raise up towers, and go forth to do my miracles. And they'll look at your works and say my name—just as they always do. For my name is your name, as your hands are my hands—just as they always will be. Write to me.'"

Lukhaya's voice, through these last paragraphs, had been growing hoarser and hoarser, and at last she set the tablet down and leaned back. The mattress trickled dust into her hair, but she didn't seem to notice.

"He wanted to do it to himself," I said. "He thought that this was how he could become immortal." But his experimental subjects had broken, just as the subjects in the lab above had broken. Caviro had left all of them on this planet. Their families had thought they were suffering a divine punishment, rather than the unintentional effects of a divine experiment. They'd put them on a ship, burned them, and fled, leaving the pearl-infested bodies behind. That was when the Kutayeti had begun to tell one another the story Szayet and I had heard after the swarm attack. No one had seen those bodies again until Lukhaya had discovered this place, three hundred years later.

Alekso had decided to forget the secret that he had tortured all of those Kutayeti prisoners in order to learn. He and Caviro had let all evidence of them be buried here, the results never to be replicated. They hadn't thought anyone would be clever enough to do what Carmela Lukhaya had done—to reverse engineer the process from skulls alone, to learn the trick of making the Terrestrial Intelligence without their help.

Hell, they hadn't wanted anyone to be clever enough. Caviro had told Alekso what happened to the experimental subjects, I thought. He'd learned how their minds looped in on themselves, sightless and alone. He hadn't wanted to live like that.

He had lived exactly like that for the last year.

I'd told Vualo and Lukhaya that Alekso survived because he

had his Oracles. But he didn't have his Oracle anymore. He and Szayet had stopped speaking for a long, long time. And when she had tried to contact him at last, she'd said, he'd answered her in screeches, in babbling, in nonsense. He hadn't even shown her his face.

"I thought what happened in the old story was an act of justice," said Lukhaya hoarsely, startling me. "I thought the god was passing sentence on the rebels. I thought he was imposing order on the universe. Someone had to, I thought. If he wanted to hurt them, they must have deserved it. But it wasn't about order, was it? There is no order. The court didn't hurt people because they'd done something wrong, it didn't hurt them because they were wicked. People suffered because he decided to make them suffer. That's all."

Why this mattered to her I could not imagine. I looked at her hard. Her arms were wrapped round her chest again. Her face, under the dusty mass of curls, was tight with hurt. "What's wrong with your chest?" I said.

She stiffened. "Nothing."

"If you're damaged, I'll need to carry you up," I said. "Lean back. Was it the lamp?"

"No," she said, without moving. "Hand me the rest of the tablets. I'll help with them."

"Don't be a fool," I said, tugging at her arm. She was pulling back like anything, but she had muscles like twigs, and slowly I pried it away from her stomach.

Beneath the fabric of her tunic was a square, bulky shape. "Wretch," I said, yanking the tablet out from underneath.

Of course she'd wanted to be first into the room. She'd guessed there must be something—anything—worth taking. She'd nearly gotten away with it, too. Perhaps she would have dropped the tablet in the tunnel, to come back for later, or perhaps she would've tried to carry it all the way back up to Vualo.

Well, the good news was that I'd come in far too quickly for her to get a look at what it was. What had Szayet's ancestor used often enough to leave it at the top of his nightstand? I knocked on its surface.

Light exploded. I ducked my face to my chest, eyes watering. When I looked up, a transparent human skull was rotating slowly over the tablet's surface.

Inside it, a brain pulsed pink and grey. Thick silver cables spilled down from the stem.

I reached out as if in a dream and brushed a cable with my hand. Diagrams sprang up—circuits, tables, equations, electricity, paragraphs of text. *Part one*, said the highest paragraph, and then Malisintian. I could make out the words *Using a cranio*—something, and then, *proceed to*—sew? Stitch? No, *perforate*—

"Olimpia, mother of God," Lukhaya whispered. "It's an instruction manual."

The ceiling thudded.

I stiffened. A peculiar sound was rising at the edge of my hearing, one I could almost name. "Is that the empress's ships?"

"Ah," said Lukhaya. "I was hoping we'd have another hour."

I looked down. Now she was grinning, a faintly hysterical expression, white teeth beneath dust-white hair. "You should have let me give them the sedative," she said.

"Sedative? What are you talking about?" I said.

She jerked a thumb at the ceiling. "Aren't you lucky?" she said. "Your men will have their entertainment after all."

I looked up, and as I did, I realized the name of that strange sound: silence. As we had walked down these tunnels, as we had circled the storage room and this little bedroom, at every moment I had been listening to the patter of dripping from the stalactites, the trickle of water along the walls, the whispering of rivers in caverns somewhere far beneath. Caves were carved by water. Water always flowed.

Now I shone my torch over the ceiling, and saw a forest of sta-lactites, blue and yellow and white, water hovering at their tips, water frozen in serpentine lines along their edges, gleaming gold under the light. Not one drop moved.

The ceiling shook again. The water shook, too. It ran up the stalactites, into the ceiling, and vanished. And the stalactites began to shrink, folding up on themselves, growing thinner and thinner, shorter and shorter, until they were stone grass blades, until they were thin white fur, until there was nothing but a smooth stone ceiling speckled with white dots.

An exhausted groan, and a crash. I reared back, spitting dust. An enormous stalactite had tumbled onto the bed, as big as an elephant's trunk, sending clouds of white up with it. There had been no stalactite that large on the ceiling when we'd come in.

"Where did that thing come from?" I said, and as I said it, I saw: The dust was lifting from the bedsheets, the rot in the wood peeling away, the stitches sewing themselves up. The sheets were grey, were yellow, were clean white cotton. "Damn it, scholar, what have you done?"

"Did you think we stopped building the Intelligence because a duke complained about his daughter?" said Lukhaya. "The most useful weapon Kutayet's ever known? One of *Sasha's* projects?" She laughed without humor. "No.

Every now and then,

time—"

"—what's that on your hand?"

I'd been rubbing it. "Old cut," I said. "Showed up again the other day, you know how they do."

Flavia had been bending over her clothes trunk to fuss at one of her dresses, but now she took my hand. "It looks bad," she said skeptically.

It had been, at the time. On Micavalli I'd hardly been out of my ship before the traitors had been on me, and it had been one against a hundred, at least until air support had roared down to blot out the sky in fire and ash twenty minutes later, and even then I'd been hacking through them like garden weeds, blaster in left hand and knife in right, and hadn't so much as breathed from landing to Lançan's launch. It was then that I'd gotten the cut, as a matter of fact. One of her boys, so bloody-faced that I'd accounted him too weak to so much as stand, had wrenched the knife from me and slashed deep at my knuckles. It would've been a clever move, if he'd managed to hit bone.

"It's a scratch," I said, pulling my hand away. "If I die, you'll be the first person I tell."

She hummed. "You never slept in this room, did you?" she said.

"Not before the war," I said. "Semfontan's dinners were bad enough without staying the night. I slept here a few times, though, after I bought the house."

She frowned. "What was wrong with the main bedroom?"

I shrugged. There was something wrong with every bedroom. I'd gone from one guest room to the next, sleeping now upstairs, now downstairs, now on a mattress stuffed with wool, now one with feathers, now on the couch in my own office with the wine bottle resting on my stomach. Here Semfontan had served roast peacock's eggs and a rose patina to the councillors of old, here she had drawn a map of Cherekku with the point of a knife, here she had feasted me and Sonia Couron, here I had seen her laugh a deep belly laugh and pull Ceirran into her arms.

"Nothing at all," I said. "You're speaking to a hard-living soldier. Didn't I always sleep on your couch after I sold our old house?"

"You slept in other people's beds plenty, as far as I recall," she said tartly, but she stepped away, trailing her hand thoughtfully across the wall murals.

"Does it suit you?" she said.

"*Suit* me?" I said. "What—is it a dress in a new color?"

"Well, it's a house," she said. "You live in it."

"Oh, of course," I said. "I live in Semfontan's old house, I live on the travessa Carenan, I live in Ceiao. They all suit me. All I do suits me. Why are you fussing?"

Her hand stopped at a blank piece of wall. "How did you have the house painted?" she said.

"*How?*" I said. "With paint."

"You're obtuse, darling," she said, sounding almost pleased about it. "Did you scrub the walls?"

"You're frivolous, *darling*," I said. She smiled at that. I sighed and closed my eyes and thought. "No," I said at last. "Pointless expense. We painted over it all."

"Ah," she said, and she shut her eyes. "Then there's a mural just here, under this paint. In the new style, you know, so large, so cleverly done that you would have thought it was a holovideo." She smiled, a strange and small half smile. "It was a window, and through the window was the city of Ceiao—in fact it was the skyline of Ceiao, just as it is through the real window here, the houses and the orchard, even the shutters hanging out into air. If you stood in the right place, it was impossible to tell whether this window or that was the way out."

"She never bothered to get herself an imagination, that woman," I said.

"No," she said, opening her eyes at last. "No, she never did."

"There were things we did remove," I said. "One of the dancing rooms was lined with metal from the hulls of pirates' ships—can you believe that? This piece inscribed with curses in Sintian, and that one carved and painted with a great white eye, and that one still scorched—"

"I know, Anita," she said.

"Oh," I said, "of course you do." To cover my discomfort I

went to her clothes trunk and folded up the topmost thing in it, a long flame-colored mantle. "You should sleep here more often," I said over my shoulder. "Did you see the state of the roof? The garden? The whole thing fell to ruin after Semfontan's husband died. Maids drinking themselves sick in the cellar, spiders nesting in the office. She'll never know what a favor we did to her household by killing her."

"I have a household of my own to manage, Anita," she said dryly. "Generous though the offer is."

"You'd have two," I said, bending to retrieve a white skirt studded at the belt with carnelians. "The richest woman in Ceiao, you are. Aren't you lucky?"

"What would you do if you didn't have a sister?" she said. "Hire a housekeeper?"

"Die," I said cheerfully, bending over to the next piece of her clothing, and stilled.

At the bottom of the trunk was a charmeuse gown—deep, rich, the heavy thick red of sunset. Its bust was beaded in orange and black, the hem of its skirt sewn with garnets. It flared out at the hips—there had been at least five skirts under it, I remembered, each of them straightened and fussed with for long minutes before the next could be layered atop it by Teo Pulcron's hired maid.

"You kept your wedding dress," I said.

Flavia was silent a long while. At last she said brightly, "Of course I kept it. Don't you remember how much it cost? I'd have been a fool to throw it away!"

I ran the back of my hand down the beads. I'd barely touched it on the day. Pulcron's maid had snatched it away to smooth out the skirts, to do up the ties along her back, to pin her curls into place—already, though they were not yet married, Flavia's husband had been so generous to her that his staff slept in our house, ready to attend to her every whim. It was he who had paid for the dress, not us.

I held it out to her. "Go on," I said.

Her throat bobbed. Without meeting my eyes, she lifted the dress by the shoulders. Her hand passed over the beads, traced the seams at the waist, her expression intent.

Ceirran had once said to me—no. *People* said to me, sometimes, that it was difficult to believe that my sister was the same person who had raised a mob in the streets of Ceiao to demand Teo Pulcron have a proper burial.

That, I'd always thought, was a typically Ceian thing to say. Typically Ceian, to hold that there was a line down the center of the world, and on one side was Flavia's laughter and her gossip and her hand in Teo Pulcron's, and riots and fire were on the other. To hold that her parties and politenesses were any different than the politenesses of Semfontan, who had cut down pirates and rebels from Ceiao 11 and Cherekku by the thousands when she'd been young; the politenesses of Cachoeiran, who had demanded that the council not spare Pulcron the death sentence; the politenesses of every councillor on the Avenuan and in the Inner City who, when our mother had done with drinking through the money, had mocked us behind our backs.

No, it was the same Flavia who stood before me now, lifting the dress against her torso, turning her head now toward the window, now toward the opposite wall. Her movement was the same, careful and controlled. Her face was the same bare, hungry face. She was, it seemed to me, no older than she had been as a new widow, as a new bride.

"If you like it so much," I said, "why didn't you put it on?"

Put it on when? she should have said. But she folded the dress over her arm and said, "Oh, Anita, I don't know. It was summer. We were walking a long way, that mob and I. I didn't want it to get dusty."

I kept looking at her. Her face twisted. She said, "I wanted his gangs, you know. They were useful things. I wanted his ideas. I wanted the people who liked them. I wanted his anger—he was always so angry. I wanted his inheritance, I suppose. I wanted to be his widow."

"I know," I said.

"I didn't want to be his wife," said Flavia.

My forehead slammed against the wall.

"Fuck," I said, staggering back. *"Fuck!"* A hundred yards ahead, Lukhaya was bolting up the tunnel, the tablet tucked under her arm.

I sprinted after her, groping for my gun at my belt. Between the dimness and the starry pain in my head, I might as well not have bothered. My shot sparked off the tunnel ceiling, and a stalactite smashed to the earth, fifty feet short of her back.

I ought to have been on her like a mountain cat in a matter of seconds. But she was spry, especially for such a soft-handed weed of a woman, and my shoulder and my hip were throbbing, too, though I couldn't remember hitting them. And I must have been dizzy, because the tunnel was swaying underneath me—no, that was no injury, the floor itself was rippling, stalagmites thrusting up like cat's claws, crumbling and rebuilding themselves and bleeding down into the floor. Lichen furred down the walls and then vanished. The stone dimpled with pockmarks and slumped flat.

I hadn't been here. Or I had been here—I must have followed Lukhaya out of the records room, into this shifting nightmare—but some part of me, the better part of me, had been with Flavia, standing in Quinha Semfontan's old guest room. I'd been caught in a memory.

But that couldn't be right. Flavia and I hadn't spoken about one of my reopened old cuts, not that day and not ever. There had been no old cut. No one at Micavalli had slashed my hand. What had that been, then? Hallucination?

The earth was rolling, now, steady pulses that bore me up the steps, shoved me into walls and sent me stumbling. It was worsening the longer it went on—or was it the farther we fled up the tunnel, the closer we drew toward the unconscious things in Lukhaya's laboratory? The two palace guards back in Alectelo had said, hadn't they, that the monsters had soured the milk, rotted the grapes. Ordinary superstition, I'd thought at the time.

At the top of the stairs, the lamps flickered madly, rust fanning over them. The tunnel had begun to fill with my men and bound Kutayeti captives, staggering, groping for balance as the earth threw them this way and that. I was losing sight of Lukhaya.

"Grab her!" I bellowed.

The Ceian fleet is feared throughout the galaxy for its deadly efficiency, its relentless discipline, its near-inhuman correctness of form, and the absolute surety with which its men move as one toward a goal. If the galaxy had been able to see my men in that tunnel, the empire would have collapsed in a matter of hours. Soldiers stampeded, waving belt knives and blasters. Lamps spat sparks and died. Men shrieked in the sudden dark like infants. I waded forward, teeth gritted, elbows jabbing out. I was too short to see over my men. Was that Lukhaya's shaggy head of hair, bobbing round a corner?—or there, pushing her way through a door?

The laboratory was within sight, its doorway choked by the stampede. Green rust foamed on its door. Holes chewed themselves in the metal, carvings flaking away—and just as quickly, the door was shining bronze, bright as a hawk's wing, and I shoved it aside, stumbling into the room.

The hosts lay as still as the grave. But the holoscreens vibrated with text in a dozen tongues: *doctor DOCTOR is that you? who is this? is that Dimka Vova Lara? One fine summer day when the birds were singing Lara I thought you were I'm sorry I'm sorry I'm*

sorry and the lindens were in flower where am I? let me open the door.
and the sun had come to rest on the ripples how much for the ferry?
LET ME OPEN THE DOOR Lara I thought we laid your body in
the THE END THE END THE END THE END THE is that
really how it ends? Lara I thought we closed the door on your tomb but
you're here and you're in the river, a woman bashed her sister's you're
you're then who are you

Vualo was rocking back and forth in their chair, teeth bared. Heaps of raw, undyed wool fleece lay strewn at their feet—the remnants of their gag, I guessed. "Where's your friend?" I barked at them, or tried to. Sound was moving at the wrong speed. My voice was an octave higher than it should have been, an octave lower.

"How should I know?" they said disdainfully, as slow as honey.

"Does she know how to pilot a ship?" I demanded. Their grin was faint and wavering, a heat mirage. "Die with us then," I spat. "Ludon—" He'd appeared in the doorway, eyes wide. "Find sedative," I said. "Needles. Alcohol, if you can—"

"You have a rabbit's heart, Admiral," said Vualo. "We'll have to wait to die. Look."

I turned. *Doctor doctor doctor doctor,* said the nearest holoscreen, *doctoctoctoctor where am where where where searching. Searchiing 10 rods. 20 rods. 3,0 rods. 2 fields. Found: grass. Define: oxygen levels.*

And up and down the walls, the screens flickered, the text slowed, the frantic rattle looped into the repetitions and questions I had seen when I'd come in. Outside, the shouting had begun to fade.

"The flares will happen again," said Vualo—there was still a hiccup in their voice here, a drop in pitch there, but it was their own, rich and nasty. "I can't prevent them, any more than these half-wits the emperor gave her for staff could prevent them when she was with me on Sancta Mirtalo."

Ludon was sprinting back with a box of syringes. "You won't

even slow them down," said Vualo. "She's always kept the right balance of sedative to herself. *Clever* girl," they added, so warmly that I drew back in disgust.

"With me, Lieutenant," I said, and took off toward the door, in the direction of the filthy river. Lukhaya must have taken a quicker way out, one we hadn't seen. I'd make her pay for that trick, once I caught her.

The faded creatures on the brick walls were now bright and clear. The doors shone, the rust of three hundred years peeled away. Had it ever been the rust of three hundred years, or had it been from a thousand years' aging, or from ten? How little did age and youth mean in this place, if this was the chaos the hosts caused? Who had built this laboratory—Caviro himself, the Kutayeti rebels he had destroyed, the emperors that had reigned millennia ago?

The ladder to the surface was dangerously rusted. I cursed. "Don't start climbing until I'm up," I told Ludon, and scrabbled rung over rung, through the hatch, and onto a field of diamond.

The jagged black waves had smoothed. The ashy towers had melted away. Straight to the horizon, the world was a finger-printed glass, fragmented and shining, sparking here and there where rain struck it. Beneath my boots, crystal sang out like a bell with the planet's reflected hues, light splintering deep into the earth. A long stretch of white sand lay beyond the wall, and at its end, a tossing silver sea.

Light flashed in Vualo's felucca: a lantern. The door in her roof hung open. A limping silhouette moved within.

It hurt like hell to run, every step on that diamond jarring up my ankles, but I ran like a pack of hounds was after me, slipping and sliding on the rain-slick crystal. With fifty yards left between me and the ship, the silhouette jerked its head up and slammed a button. The door hatch began to creak down.

I shot up the ladder like a rat and shoved my leg under the

door just as it closed over my thigh. It was like being sliced by a butcher's knife—I screamed—but the mechanism shuddered and slowly creaked open again. I tumbled down the ladder, bounced off a sack, and landed in a heap on my injured leg.

"*Fuck* me," I said to the ceiling.

Around me the ship rumbled. Lukhaya had started her engine. I heard thumping on the roof, too, above the noise of the rain. That had to be Ludon, too late to slip through the door.

I struggled to my feet and limped to the end of the hallway. Lukhaya was bent over the ship's controls, flicking at the altimeter and fuel gauge lights, the instruction manual open on a stool behind her. She was whispering to herself in quiet Sintian: "Engage the gravshaft—damn—first advance the antimatter toward the pinion, then pump fuel through the duct—"

"Other way round, sweetheart," I said, and when she turned, I fired at the navigation computer: one shot, two—

There was a thud. The ship shook. My third shot went wide.

Lukhaya screamed. The control panel screamed, too, and coughed sparks. The blast had gone straight through her into the navigation display, smearing black right up to the glass of the viewscreen.

She sagged forward. I darted to catch her and ripped off my cloak, sending my admiral's pin tumbling.

"Don't faint," I said. The heat hadn't cauterized her wound. I shoved my cloak against the dark patch spreading over her abdomen. "Up—up, up, keep your eyes open. You're all right. You're not going to die, not unless I let you. No, don't—" She was sagging toward the control panel. I slapped her face, and she rocked upright.

A wet, cold wind was blowing up the hallway, smelling of salt and smoke. Ludon had done exactly what I would have done, exactly what he had seen me do a hundred times: laid explosives and blown the roof.

"You gave me a good chase," I said. "Nearly won the crown in long distance. But *nearly* never hit any rabbits, eh?"

She was moaning, a low, horrible, wordless whimper, mouth open like a child. Behind me, Ludon's footsteps clicked up the hallway. I didn't turn. The shot had entered just below her ribs, and the blood pulsed steadily against my hand. I'd hit a vein. "The warps in time," I said. "Is that what I wasn't meant to know about? What your friend the ambassador didn't want you to say?"

The hiccups rattled against my hand in sticky bursts. She was laughing, I realized. "My friend the ambassador," she spat, weak but clear. "You grass-witted spread-legged stink-drunk Ceian fool. You painted ape. You brainless, joyless, loveless heretic's collared dog—"

I slapped her again. She shuddered. "Look at it this way," I said, trying to keep my voice steady. "That instruction manual's lost to you. The journal's lost, too. There's no danger that the emperor will accuse you of giving them up without a fight—you're welcome for that. All that's left to decide is whether you bleed out alone in this ship, watching your enemies fly off toward the Crossbar, wondering if the whole moonlet will transform back into coal again before you pass out—or whether I send for the doctor, and you tell me what in the name of Fortune's guts and garters just happened and why."

She was shivering. "The emperor would order me to die," she said. "Hell, the empress consort would beg me to."

The planet, on the horizon behind her, flashed gold around her hunched birdlike shoulders and faded to black. Against its light she had looked very small. I hadn't meant to shoot her, I thought. A whining, childish impulse: I didn't *mean* to.

"Would Vualo?" I said.

She stared at me blankly, then her head sagged back and she laughed again. "You're wrong," she said. "There's no *if* the moonlet will transform. The flares come once every eleven hours by the Kutayeti clock."

I twisted to look at Ludon, who stood wide-eyed, face scuffed with rain and ash. "Grab that tablet and get the doctor from *Taraxandran*, now," I said.

He saluted, scooped up the tablet, and darted away. In the changing light from the planet on the horizon, my blood-black hand flared violet, flared green. Lukhaya was beginning to shiver. She'd go into shock soon.

"Does the diamond island cause these flares?" I said. "Is that what the story meant, when it said the palace was built out of one summer day—that this place warps time?"

Lukhaya shook her head. "Residual effects of the Fortunatas' location," she said. "We're nearer the center of the galaxy than any other inhabited world. The flares in time come from the Well of Ashes."

The Kutayeti name for the Black Maw. "It's a hole in the world," I said. "It doesn't *flare*."

"Fine, then," said Lukhaya blearily. "Have it your way. I'm too tired for Ceian cynicism."

Her eyes were fluttering shut. "Don't—" I said, and shook her by the shoulders. Her head flopped. "Keep talking, you fool. If you sleep, you won't wake. How does the Black Maw flare?"

She blinked slowly. "Do you know what would happen if you went into the Well?" she said.

"You'd die," I said.

Lukhaya shrugged. This moved the fabric of her tunic along her wound, and she groaned. "Eventually," she said weakly. "But before you died... There aren't words for it, not in Sintian. Distance wouldn't mean the same thing. Time would be measured the way we measure space. North and south replaced by *was* and *will be*." Her voice was fading. "An hour ago, three hundred years ago, all those moments would be like the rooms Mother swept. Do you understand?"

"No," I said. Her consciousness wasn't good—the rooms

Mother swept?—but her eyes were bright. Talking about this
was keeping her awake. "Explain it to me."

"Time is like a long, straight path," she said. "Every mile on
the path, there's a—a flower." She giggled wetly. "A rose. Say the
rose next to you is sick. If you look behind you, you can see the
same rose, healthy, and the rose behind it just starting to open
its petals, and the rose behind it just a bud. And ahead of you,
you can see a rose in front of it wilted, and a rose in front of that
one dead. Outside the Well, where time flows straight from the
past to the future, you'd call that a life. You'd say the rose grew,
bloomed, and died."

The wind was wet on my face—a bright briny wind, a sea
wind. I thought unhappily that I could see Szayet in Lukhaya's
face, Szayet looking over the city, Szayet in the Library, Szayet
leading her people in hymns. It was the same pleasure, the same
joy. "Outside the Well, you'd believe that dying is the only thing
that the rose *is*," she said. "That coal is the only thing the moonlet is—that rust is all the metal down in the laboratory is. But
if you were inside the Well, all the times that the rose was alive
and all the times it was dead, all the diamond in the island and
all the shining bronze, they would just seem like different places.
Time is a direction, as surely as space. It's just perspective, is all."
Her voice was growing faint again.

I shoved the cloak deeper into her wound. She groaned, low.
"What does that have to do with the Terrestrial Intelligence?" I
said.

She nodded slowly. "At the Well's center—" She lifted her
uninjured hand and pinched the fingers together. "That straight
path I was talking about, the path that's Time, it ends. Nowhere.
No-when. The rose, or anything else on the path, they all stop."

"They disappear," I said.

"No," she said. "No, because when matter disappears, time
keeps going. You can't ever vanish from this world, not really.

All you can do is make an empty space where you used to be. But at the center of the Well of Ashes, time stops."

The cloak was very wet now. "This speech should have less time, and more matter," I said, keeping my voice light, "or you'll be sorry for it."

She scoffed. She was sitting up properly now, and her voice was strong. "We think," she said, "we *think* that the people in the laboratory—the broken hosts, the lonely people—are reaching out with their pearl minds to detect signals. Electric signals, radioactive, thermal, anything they can get. We think they detect an energy that behaves according to laws quite, quite different to the laws we know. It's an energy that comes from inside the Well. An energy with laws that would ordinarily only apply on a scale smaller than the atomic. We think that in some way, mentally, neurologically, computationally, the hosts of the Intelligence *are* inside the Well. That, to them, time no longer means what it means to you and me. That the quicksilver pearl in their brains absorbs—and, every eleven hours, releases—an energetic force in which time and space variables reorient themselves so deeply as to apparently randomize temporal cause and effect. Do you understand me?"

"Your monsters get so lonely that they learn how to warp time?" I said.

"That's not right at all, but let's say yes," she said. "Every eleven hours, any pearl computer near a host whose mind has failed becomes—strange. Ordinary tablets forget things, or they know things they shouldn't, or they send messages to locations they shouldn't be able to reach. For even the smallest pearl chip, it's suddenly as if time means nothing at all. And the subjects, the subjects go haywire. I went through fifty tablets in twenty days. Fifty-seven. Sasha needs the budget. Sasha's going to be angry..."

The burst of lucidity had passed. Her head was drooping. The rain light flickered silver over her face. "So if you brought a broken host to Ceiao, the city would start to turn back in time?" I said.

"No," she said. "Ceiao's much, much farther away from the Well than here. The host wouldn't warp anything, not unless they'd already absorbed the Well's energy, somehow. The time warping wasn't even this bad on Kutayet—but it was bad, it was bad…Water boiled in a second. Paint stayed wet for three days. The empress consort's mirrors rusted over, she was so angry with me. Not that it takes much. We stationed all the functioning hosts we had left in places closer to the rim of the galaxy. Khramya. Szayet. And all the malfunctioning hosts, the empress made me move them here. Far away from anyone who mattered. So I went, too. Can't come home. Not until I find a cure." She laughed weakly. "Who minds exile? Everybody's always leaving every place. No such thing as staying put. Not in time…"

Her voice was fading. Damn her, damn her—I'd thought she had more time, but she wasn't any battle-tested Ceian crewman on the field; she was losing blood fast and she hadn't had much to lose. "Stand up," I said, and when she didn't respond, "Stand up or I'll—" A stupid threat, an empty one. Or I would what? Hit her, cut her? Shoot her again?

I lifted her gently by the elbows. She fell heavily against my chest. The mist had risen thick and fast, the world outside the viewscreen a moving whiteness. Had Ludon even reached the doctor yet?

"Don't close your eyes, Carmela," I said. "Keep talking. That's a Sintian name you have, isn't it? Who made a Sintian like you a spy for the Kutayeti Empire?"

She said something unintelligible, in which I caught *Sasha* and something that sounded like the Kutayeti word for *ambassador*. I shook her, and she said sleepily, "You're worse than the empress. Ana's a Sintian name, too, isn't it? Go join up with the Sintielan League. I was born on. On. Born and raised on—"

She tried to gesture with her injured hand and swayed. I caught her again but couldn't bear her weight, and we went together to the floor, her lanky legs sprawling.

"She got everything she wanted, the empress," she said to the ceiling. "Always does. It's good this way. The only person who gets hurt when I'm out here is me."

"That's not true," I said quietly, and gathered her carefully up toward me, her head on my thigh.

I thought, as I had on Szayet what seemed like a lifetime ago, that something was wrong with me, some twisted or broken or absent thing, some narrowness to my heart. Perhaps it was true what Lukhaya said about time. Perhaps there was some faraway place without borders or laws, where death was only one part of life, and not even the greater part. Perhaps there was a place where all those great ideals for which other people fought and died, all the righteousnesses and truths of other people's souls, were as real as the things that could be touched and spoken to and kissed.

But the part of me that was supposed to long for that place— to want it, to dream of it—never did, and never had. It raged, and it hated. But it could not remember that there was such a thing as evil, any more than it could remember that there was such a thing as good. And now that smallness in me saw a body dying in my arms, and remembered when a body had been in my arms a year and a half ago, and it stroked its knuckles over her forehead in comfort.

"It's not true at all," I said.

She huffed a laugh at the ceiling. "It took me," she said, "ten years to track down the Fortunatas. Ten years, and Sasha's purse emptying, and the temple mothers calling me insane, obsessed, a heretic barbarian and the daughter of a heretic barbarian, and all my bridal contracts falling through. So the subjects are lonely. Well, I know about lonely." Her eyelashes were fluttering shut.

"The island had to be real," she said. "It had to be real. There had to be a design, there had to be a plot, a plan, there had to be an order to the universe, or what was the reason for it all?"

"The reason for what?" I said.

She sighed and turned her face against my knee. "Are you sorry you shot me?" she said.

The rain clattered down onto the roof. "I'm never sorry for anything," I said.

"Good," she said. "I'm the same way. We ought to be friends."

The roof creaked. "That's the doctor," I said. "Stay awake." She hummed without opening her eyes. I tapped her face again, gently now. "Scholar," I said, "if it was all true, all of the legend— if this was once a country where a palace lived forever in a single summer day—"

"Oh, yes," she said, hardly a murmur. "Wouldn't it be pretty?"

The smell of brine was strong now. I could feel the sea wind on my hands, damp and cold. "You wouldn't need a pearl to make you immortal, not in the summer country," I said, though I knew she knew. "You would be able to raise—

Not yet.

—the dead."

"Why does the Oracle saying a prayer for the dead matter?" said Flavia. "Did it make the crowd angry? Did she want you to pay for killing the Szayeti boy?"

I pulled my feet out of the Nevede and lay on my back, river stones hard against my neck. "No," I said. "No one paid a thing."

The sky peered down, fingerprinted in deep greys. Soon it would storm.

"And that means you may do as you like," Flavia said, "and there will never be any price. You may hurt who you want, and destroy what you want, and cross every border in the galaxy until you reach the empty black, and no one will stop you, not once. Is that what's breaking your heart?"

No, I thought. No, and yes, because when I destroyed, when I killed, when I flew at the head of an army into Ceiao itself, it was not me who ensured no price was paid. It was not me who snuffed out angers and griefs and swept them out of sight—it was not me who made the world a place where you could throw an apple into the air and never see it come down again.

No, that wasn't breaking my heart. I loved him for it. I was sure I loved him for it. When love broke your heart, that wasn't how.

I laughed at the sky. "I know a secret about you."

"You know dozens of secrets about me, my dear," said Flavia.

"I know a secret about you," I went on as though she hadn't spoken. "You've never left Ceiao."

Flavia smiled. "I stand corrected. You don't know anything about me at all. How many times have I visited Cláudia at the seaside just this year? No, put that aside—I left school a little after you came, Anita, you saw me in Sintielo. Can't you trust your own memory?"

"My memory's as good as it's ever been. Don't mock me, I'll be an old woman soon," I said, enjoying her smile. "I'm not wrong. You walked over half of Sintielo, but you never left Ceiao. Who did you speak to, besides everyone you speak to now? Where do you go at the seaside, except among Cláudia and the other Ceians? You put the river and the road in your traveling bags and carried them on the ship. You've never left Ceiao in your life."

"*I* carry Ceiao in my traveling bags?" she said. "Then what are you doing, you and Ceirran, coming down across Madinabia like a pack of wolves in your warships and fighters?"

"Our duty to the state," I said. "Advancing the greater glory of Ceiao. Bringing home gold and captives so that the whole city can cheer Ceirran's name. Haven't you heard them?"

"I wish Sonia Couron were here to listen to you," said Flavia.

"She always hoped that one day she'd die of laughter. Your duty! You say it yourself, darling—it's Ceirran's name you're fighting for, not duty. And I'm sure that Túlio Cachoeiran would feel very smug to hear it."

I shook my head. "I'm sworn to Ceirran," I said. "No difference between his name and my duty, is there?"

"You swore your service," said Flavia. "Did you swear your soul?"

"My soul!" I said. "I wish Cachoeiran had heard you say *that*. I always hoped I'd see him die of apoplexy. Do I have a soul, then? It must be a stunted little thing. I don't recall getting much use out of it."

"Anita," said Flavia, her tone abruptly serious. I twisted to look at her.

"Ceiao is only the world because you make it the world, Anita," she said. "You don't have to."

"No," I said. "No, I'm not making Ceiao into the world."

"What are you doing, then," she said, "with your guns and your warships? With him?"

I shrugged one shoulder against the pebbled ground. "I'm making it into a tyrant," I said. "Whoever makes it into the world will have to be someone worse."

She looked down. "You call me provincial," she said. "Well, maybe I am. Certainly I was glad not to have to go to the front lines of combat—to cram myself into one of those starfighters and spend all of my youth and wits on thinking about where to aim and when to fire. You did—" I opened my mouth, and she held up a hand. "You did, and I'm glad you did," she said, "because you have your glory, and you have your oath, and—though you won't believe it—you have your honor, Anita."

I laughed aloud.

"Well, and you don't need to believe it," said Flavia. "You can lie to yourself, and I know you do. But you do have it, and though it's a strange and backward sort of honor, I think it's a better honor than Quinha Semfontan had in all her strength, or than the Barrans had in all their righteousness. And it hurts you when the Oracle prays for that boy. It hurts you that she's the one to rescue your honor, when no one else cares enough to do it. Not even the one who should care most."

"What's that supposed—" I began, but she said over me sharply:

"And you're easily hurt, Anita. Though you don't understand how easily. Not just yet."

The rain stung the back of my neck, ice cold. Great shadows moved behind the storm clouds. "She slept with my commander to get her throne," I said. "It's not meant to bother me?"

"I slept with Teo Pulcron to pay our mother's debts," said Flavia. "That doesn't bother you?"

I sat up. "Flavia. Why didn't I know—"

"Of course you knew," said Flavia. "What did you think happens in a marriage bed? No, Anita, I didn't fuck him before we wed, if that matters to you. It mattered to me, though at the moment I can't remember why. We married, and I was mistress of his household and his money, and you had a commission, and the magistrates had the bribes to get our troubles written away. He knew, of course. I never wanted to deceive him—and you'll recall that he had enough money to go around."

"He *bought* you?" I said.

"Certainly not," said Flavia. "You knew him, Anita! He liked us. He thought we were clever—or that I was—and that we were brave, or that you were. And I wanted to marry, and he wanted a wife. We can't all be noble enough to kill our way to prosperity." She shrugged. "And I loved him," she said, "of course."

"Don't say *of course* to me," I said. "That's love, is it?"

"Yes," she said. "It is. He had others, you know—the Itsaryeti priestess, Semfontan's cousin—and of course I had others, too. Eliana, Sonia—don't look at me like that. Do you think that after you broke Sonia Couron's heart, she just laid down to die? Well. The way poets talk, you'd think that love was a grand adventure. That love was the great army, conquering all, and we sought it out because it made us different, it made us people out of stories. People who don't ever have to wake up and be tired, or hungry, or unsure, or afraid, or ugly, or ordinary. And my affairs and his were the sort of thing that songs and stories are about, I'm sure."

The rain was falling properly now, smearing down the blush on Flavia's cheeks, the careful braids of her hair. She didn't appear to notice. "But what we did with each other," she said, "the bed we slept in, the city we might have built, and yes, the money we exchanged—that was love. It was love because it wasn't happy. It was love because it wasn't honorable. It was love because it wasn't free. To count up the world's cost, and to stare it in the face, and to say yes, I will, I will pay that price—that's what love is, Anita. It's love because it's what makes you real."

I rubbed my wet hand over my face. "Let me do something for you," I said.

"No," said Flavia.

"Let me kill Veguion for killing your husband," I said. "Let me make Ceirran buy you a new house, a better house, one that's all your own. Let me give you a place on the council, or let me turn every person on the council's life into a hell—"

"No," said Flavia. And then, more gently: "Anita, you don't have a king to serve. You have a sister. I don't want a right hand—I have one on my wrist, and I like it there. I have done what you needed done because I love you, I have done it so we might both survive, I have done it because it was right. Don't corrupt what you owe me into fealty."

I dug my hand into the riverbank and pulled up three wet shining stones: one red, one blue, and one silver-grey with a black hole in its center. I squinted at the red one and hurled it across the river. It bounced: one, two, three, four, five, six, seven, eight, nine—

"We never had this conversation, did we," I said.

"No," said Flavia. "I wasn't in the city that summer, my dear. Cláudia Pulcron kept me at the seaside. You didn't see me until weeks later, when the Oracle came to stay in Ceiao."

The stone on the Nevede was still skipping, down and up and down again, an endless arc of light. I held out my hand, and Flavia examined the stones, selected the blue one, and threw. It skipped beside the first, onward and on.

"Is this a dream?" I said. "Is part of me asleep, while the rest of me walks and talks in the felucca and the laboratory? Or is it that I really am somewhere else?"

"You're in history, dear heart," said Flavia. "You've reached the diamond island by now? Yes? Then I think this is the point when you've learned at least that much."

"I can't be in a past that never happened," I said.

"Perhaps not," said Flavia easily. "But history isn't the past, is it?"

I looked down at the silver stone, held it up to my eye, and examined my sister through the hole. "What is it, then?" I said.

"Memories," she said.

Through the hole in the stone, she was quite clear. It was the rest of the land that was beginning to waver: the river, the towers, the fast-falling rain. "Are you really Flavia?" I said. "Or are you something inside me?"

"Look at me," said Flavia.

I let the stone fall to my lap. Flavia smiled, and then smiled wider; and then her face opened up, folding outward like petals, lips and eyes and hair peeling back and away. Beneath it was a smooth liquid silver, flickering with blue and red.

"What's the difference?" she said.

The rain had turned to hard white sleet. The sand of the beach was all crystal, diamonds and ice. My lips tasted like iron and salt.

"Shove it out," I said.

The two Szayeti crewmen pushed the little boat as hard as they could. It bobbed and swayed across the water. A wave rose over the prow, and the corpse of Carmela Lukhaya vanished from sight.

The last of my crewmen were scrambling up the ladder from the laboratory, carrying medical kits and fuel. I must have ordered them to raid the place, though I did not remember it, any more than I remembered who had found this new steel ladder or where we had gotten a boat for Lukhaya's body.

I fell in beside the final crewman, who was carrying the journal Lukhaya had stolen from the Library of Alectelo. "Let me take that," I said. "Nasty bump on your head, there. How're you feeling? What do the men need?"

"Me, sir? I'm fine, sir," she said. "We've got a couple of bumps and bruises, sir. I think a girl down on bomb bay crew sprained her wrist."

"No—" I hesitated, uncertain how to ask and unwilling to press. "No injuries? No one—upset?"

"Oh, of course we're all upset, sir!" she said. "Sorry, sir. Didn't mean to sound like one of these barbarians, sir. Ready to jump onto the battlefield against 'em, sir, whenever you say."

I gave up. Lukhaya had said nothing about hallucinations or dreams, nothing about any members of the Kutayeti imperial court waking up with hours swallowed out of their memories. It was something about myself, then, that had caught me up in visions. A matter for doctors, not physicists. Telling my men about it would only make them worry about me.

The bridge was washed green in the planetlight. Ludon, waiting there, gave me a sloppy salute. Crewmen at the nav computers, the cannon, the comms, the engine gauges, sat poised to move. On the floor at the far starboard side, Sasha Vualo lay curled up, hands tied behind their back, their great lion's head bowed to their chest.

I stopped in front of them. Their gag had been removed, but they were silent. A deep purple bruise was coming up below their eye.

There was nothing left to say except the worst cruelties. I had heard them a thousand times, in the small hours of the morning, in the long nights hanging between stars, in the empty rooms where I could not sleep. I knew them like I knew myself. I said to them: "The two of you could have gone back to the imperial court when you fled Szayet with that journal. You could have crept into the Library under cover of night and tried to read it there, instead of stealing it. You could have told Lukhaya to cooperate, and perhaps she wouldn't have tried to run away from me."

They said nothing, they did not look up, their hair falling in coarse white strands over their face. "You could have run, you could have fought," I murmured. "You could have been faster or stronger or smarter. You might have reached the place she died in time. You might have stopped the bleeding. You might have heard the last words. You might have given comfort. You weren't there."

At last they looked up.

"I'll see you on your knees," they said hoarsely. "On your knees and begging, Ana Decretan, before I finally let you die."

"I know," I said, and rose. "Ready for takeoff. Take her up slow."

Taraxandran's hull scraped over the diamond, a nasty screech. "Keep us steady, boys," I said. "She's steel, not lace. Let's get into the black without springing a leak." Laughter rippled across my men, uncertain but present, and I breathed easy for the first time in what seemed like days.

Water splashed at last. The engines roared. The waves shrank into wrinkles, into light. Somewhere beneath them lay Lukhaya's body, and the three-hundred-year-old bodies of Alekso and Caviro's pearl-poisoned dead. Beside them, deep inside the earth, the people Lukhaya had tortured for what had seemed to them like centuries.

What would I want, I thought, if I were trapped for eternity in the worst moment of my life?

"Open the bomb bay doors," I said.

On the other side of the bridge, Vualo's head shot up in shock. I pulled my blood-stiff cloak around myself and paced to the edge of the viewscreen. Over the horizon, the great planet turned, crackling now purple, now gold.

I had once asked Szayet, when we'd been drunk on the shore together, what she would have wanted to do with her life if she hadn't been queen. *Oh, I'd be a scholar*, she'd said without hesitation, and kissed me, wine-sour. *You wouldn't like me at all.*

"Wake the communicators," I said, watching fire flare up from the surface of the moonlet. "Contact Galvão. Gather our ships on the border. We're going to war against the emperor."

"Sir," said Ludon. There was a note of relief in his voice. "All the ships?"

"Yes," I said. "All." I thought of the ancient manual, resting in the hold. Every part of me rebelled at the notion of touching it. Szayet wouldn't. Szayet would want it badly. Szayet would want the manual, and the letters, and the journal. I'd sworn to give them to her.

What would she tell the people I had found in the Fortunatas? Would she call those letters from her old god holy? Would she call them a miracle? Would she tell the people what they said, or would they be, like the god she had spoken to and like the god she claimed to have loved, at the mercy of what she wanted other people to remember?

"And contact the damned boy," I said. "Tell him what we found. He'll want to know."

Ludon saluted. I returned it, and turned away from the

spreading flames on the moonlet's surface, trying to hide my expression. It was, I thought, what Ceirran would have done. And I

I

I I I I I

IIIIIIIIIIIIIIIIIIIIIIII

i

Every now and then,

time

breaks.

Lukhaya was wrong. It's not a straight path at all. It's a circle.

I stand on the shore of a river. All around the blue sedge grows, and on the far bank little white flowers are blooming. A silver disc lies in front of me, buried in the slick, soft mud.

"Take that," says a voice, only a little louder than the river. "Don't let it go. Lose it, Captain, and you lose yourself."

I must go to my knees to dig up the disc, and so I do, and so I lift it. And now I see that it is carved, like a coin, or like a map of the galaxy, or like a shield.

"Who are you, Captain?" says the voice.

I know that voice. I would follow it anywhere.

And I look into the quicksilver pearl disc, and I see:

A high-towered city, so familiar that I almost say its name aloud. No, I'm mistaken; this city is not my home, but a place unknown to me. Two crescent moons hang in its sky, and its constellations are alien. It has no river, no road, but high, proud walls, and beyond its gates rolls the wide dark sea. And fire is pouring from its rooftops. And, in the way that bees flow upward together from a dead bull's carcass, a thousand ships swarm in desperation up from its windows toward the stars.

Now I turn the disc, and I see a river I know. On its shore, two women stand. Sisters, I think. One might be the other's mirror. But one woman is digging in the ground, and the other has raised a rock, and is swinging it at her sister's head. And I see the sister's corpse, and the woman staring down at the twin she has killed. And behind her, the walls of the new city, my city, are already beginning to rise.

Onward the wheel turns, and on, and on. Again the vision repeats itself, and again, and again. One man shot, one woman hanged, one man starving in dirty streets, ships pouring up from the ground. A fleet of warships, pulling the planet's north pole away from the sun. Houses burning, towers falling, hospital rooms and bedpans and tinctures of poppy, hurricanes roaring down from the west, earthquakes and wild beasts and plague. Towers rising, and the old city rebuilt. I know the shape of this city, too: an open eye. In its center, a white dome; and then the dome bursts, and smoke rises, and blood flows into the river, over the road.

And I turn the wheel, and I see captives filing down into the city prisons, I see a great bridge of ships from one asteroid to another, I see this city burning a second time. I see ships descending onto familiar worlds and unfamiliar ones, walls built across white-cliffed islands, temples falling until not one stone remains on another. I see the hacked-away stumps of trees stretching for thousands of miles, I see smoke billowing out of gashes in the land, I see seas boiling and mountains crumbling and storms rushing like armies over the earth, I see people walking together in chains, all of them going to feed the city, all of them burning in the guts of the city, all roads leading to the mouth of the city, the city returning to its beginning, the city held here in eternity, the city unending, the city that cannot find a way to end. And I see, cut deeply through these roads and towers, through the turning circle of the city's life, a silver scratch.

Someone yanks on the disc, hard. I trip, fall backward, and land on stone.

I am in a small, dusty room, filled with the smell of pine trees. The noise of water is now very far away. There is a woman standing between me and the door, crowned and dark-haired, but I cannot see her face.

With difficulty, I sit up. I am in no pain. I feel nothing at all, except perhaps a strange warmth, prickling in a line across my belly. But standing there, staring at me with wide eyes, face half-hidden in shadow, is

you.

You were born on a ship, and here you are, thief, alone on another, awake among sleeping soldiers, eyes red with weeping,

hanging between stars,

staring at a knife.

You say to me: Please. I'll do anything. I'll hollow myself out. Just so long as I can live.

And I tell you: Because I recognize your guilt,

yes.

I see the past—only four seconds ago,

and I pinch time, and take you there,

before it all went wrong—

"—*Anita*," said a voice.

My eyes flew open.

I was on the bridge, my cheek smashed against a leg of the captain's chair. Above me, *Taraxandran*'s alarm system shrieked. Voices babbled urgently behind me, on the bridge, in the in-ship comms channels.

Ludon's worried face hovered above mine, his hand outstretched. I took it and tugged myself upright.

The ship was back in the fog—no, not the moonlet's fog, I realized with relief. The windows showed a thick, steady white rain. We'd come up into the planet's rings.

The bridge was chaos: chairs overturned, cracked tablets strewn across the floor, officers and crewmen huddling in twos and threes, exclaiming when they saw me upright. "What happened?" I said.

"The engines cut out," said Ludon. "Our antimatter failed—we had to rekindle it from backup. We dropped like a stone. Lucky thing we weren't out of the rings, or we would've dropped out of lightspeed, too, and that would have been the end of us."

"Our computers, sir," said an ensign behind my shoulder. "The comms network—" She pushed a tablet into my hands. It showed a holo of a boy from the engine room, speaking urgently, hands waving, but I couldn't make out a word he was saying, and a moment later I understood why: The sound from the tablet was playing in reverse, turning his sentences into gibberish.

"Some of them are skipping every other minute, sir, or they're repeating every second," the ensign went on. "One of them started scrolling through old poetry from Cherekku, but that was a tablet we'd only programmed to be able to do bookkeeping, sir. A pearl hairpin from Szayet started singing very old Kutayeti dancing songs, sir. We think it must be picking up a signal that originated decades ago."

Lukhaya had warned me of this in the felucca, I thought. That strange Black Maw energy the Terrestrial Intelligence hosts carried—one great flare of it, exploding out from the planet, shooting straight through our ship. "Our vitals? Our navigation? The men? The instruction manual?" I said.

"Nothing fatal," said Ludon pragmatically. "The air supply went heavy on the oxygen for a minute or two. Our maps are all about fifteen years out of date, but the nav officers can handle the updated orbit calculations. The Terrestrial Intelligence instruction manual scrolls from right to left now, but that's the only change."

"If we run into any suns, I'll know who to blame," I said. Vualo, on the far side of the bridge, was beginning to stir. Not dead, then. "Did we contact Ceiao?"

"Not yet," said Ludon. "We're looking for a computer that has the capacity."

"Then find it," I said. My body was beginning to make a host of complaints known: my throbbing temples, the bruises on my shoulder and my hip, the ache in my back where I'd lain unconscious on the floor.

Whatever vision had come upon me had been a dream in truth, this time. It fled even as I tried to grasp it. My stomach had hurt. I might have smelled smoke. Someone had spoken to me, though I could not remember the words.

Julhan, I found myself thinking, wouldn't believe me when I told him. Well, perhaps we'd meet somewhere, he and I—not Ceiao, never Ceiao, but some colonized moon, one with laboratory facilities. It was he who'd want this manual, he who'd have a plan for how to use it. I'd promised Szayet—but Szayet would understand, wouldn't she, that this was the stuff of legends and nightmares, not a gift between lovers? Through the fog, the ice-sharp stars had begun to emerge. She'd be angry, of course, but she couldn't be angry forever. We'd go back to our feasting. I'd fight battles, if battles needed to be fought. And when we won the war against Kutayet, and I brought her the emperor's crown to hang in her bedroom, that would satisfy her. What better gift than that could a client queen want? And I'd sleep beside her, and miss nothing and no one, and dream no dreams at all.

"Admiral," said Ludon softly behind me.

I turned. He was holding a tablet. At its edge, two identical red seals bobbed up and down, a duplicated message.

"That's Ceiao?" I said. "You got through, then?"

He nodded. His face was grey.

"They sent us a message, Admiral," he said. "It's about your— Flavia Decretan."

"Oh, Ceirran's bones," I said wearily. "Ludon, unless she's descending from the sky of Szayet in a chariot of fire, I don't want to hear it any longer. I don't care if she says it's on my behalf. Her actions are her responsibility. Let her take responsibility for them."

He said, "Admiral," and his voice cracked.

I frowned. "What?"

"She was," he said. He swallowed. "She was sent into exile."

"*Exile?*" I said. "What, did the woman raise another mob?— no, don't tell me, I'll call her myself. Where's she run off to? The Trigesimals?"

"She was going to Itsaryet, Medveyet. Szayet," said Ludon. "The soldiers' camps, the veterans' farms. She had treasure with her— gold antiques—to raise an army. She meant to give a speech."

"A *speech*?" I said. "Now, of all times, she picks to be a politician?"

"She was crossing toward the Swordbelt Arm about forty minutes ago," said Ludon. "She took a route very near the Great Maw. Something happened to her ship."

"Speak sense," I said irritably. "What kind of something? Is she delayed?"

The fog had fallen away entirely. The rings curved up below us, white and grey, as blank and unseeing as all the stars. "No," said Ludon. "No, she's not delayed." His mouth worked. "Anita," he said quietly, "she's gone."

"To the Swordbelt Arm," I said. "I understand. But what happened?"

"The ship dropped out of lightspeed," said Ludon. "The—the bases near Sintia are going to send patrol ships. They're going to—to look for cargo."

"Good," I said. "She'll be angry enough that she lost any of it. Where did she dock?" He shook his head, and I said, voice rising, "Where is she? Where's she gone, Lieutenant?"

"They don't—they couldn't tell me," said Ludon. "Anita, they think her—her body—"

"Make them tell you, then," I said loudly over the end of his sentence. "She'll be looking for transport. She'll want to find me. Put out a broadcast to any moon or satellite in radius, override their communications—"

"They *couldn't* tell me," Ludon said desperately. "They think she was ejected instantly. They think—"

"No," I said, "you need to go back and ask again. You need to find out where she is, and then you need to bring her—"

"She died, Anita," said Ludon. "Flavia is dead."

"I understand why," I said, "I know why you think that. But that's a mistake. You need to start looking for tablet broadcasts. She'll be on one of the—the—the moons." Ludon was shaking his head, and I said, louder, "She's going to want a tablet. If you don't get her a tablet soon, she's going to be so angry. She's going to be so angry with me, if you don't find her right—"

To Altagracia Caviro, queen of hunger, queen of slavering jaws and starving dogs, queen of refuse and squander and waste, queen of rotting meat and curdled milk and stinking trash and bones, the worm that grows fat on the dead, the rib cage that seethes with the worms, who turns her face from the needy, who turns her back on the beggars, whose home is the hollowness in the center of the earth, styled Patramata:

The night you took me prisoner, I made an oath to our god. You had ripped Him from my ear by then, and He was a prisoner in your clenched fist. I did not know whether He could hear me. You had taken everything from me, Gracia, and I only had hope.

I said to Him:

Alekso Undying, my god, my king, father of my country, the man who loved my ancestor, hear this vow. If I should bend the knee before my lying sister—if I should call her Oracle—if I should pray to her, or if I should pray to You through her as Your messenger—

God, break me into a thousand pieces. God, cut my naked throat. God, make a trophy of me before my enemies. Strike me down as You struck down the moon, my god and god of my father, if I should ever break this promise to You.

Your lover's heir has called his troops home from the Swordbelt Arm. V. left me today.

For a while, Gracia, I could keep her from you. These pages had no claim on her, this pen could not touch her mouth. Your eyes, which ate my throne and my kingdom, which ate the love of our people and made it your own, could touch no more than the outline of her.

I knew how she blushed when she had been drinking, I knew the smell of her hair in the morning. I knew the tile on the roof of the temple where she once scratched a verse from one of the Sintian poets. I knew the taste of her hands, and I knew where touching her would make her laugh, and I knew where touching her would make her silent. I knew what she promised me when the sun had fallen and the priests were sleeping, and she crept from the soldiers' quarters into my bed.

I knew the stories she told me from her homeland. I knew how afraid she was the day the camp chose her to go to the Ceians, to be the offering to feed the hunger of the fleet. I knew how she stumbled over the words when she swore her oath. I knew how I held her, and what kindnesses I whispered to her in the dark.

History did not have her, the empire did not have her, this jail did not have her. I had these parts of her, I, I, I held her alone, I kept her, I kept her my own. I even kept her name.

They went like cowards, those Ceians, like rats from a cellar. I was weeding in the temple garden when the first ship went streaking across the sky. Maneuvers, I thought, though it grew smaller and smaller. And then it winked and vanished, and the second ship rose into the blue, and I knew.

And like a coward V. was waiting for me when I fled back to my cell, and like a coward her eyes were red with weeping. And like a coward and a fool, I told her to stay with me. Like a coward and a fool, I said, "Please."

"My life isn't my own, princess," she said. "If I could fly where I wanted, and pour out money like wine—well, then I'd build my father's house all over again, and lay down the foundations of his country in new earth tomorrow. But I am what I am, and when the empire calls me, I have to obey."

I called her a rat, a wretch, a weakling. How dare she say she is only what she is! Be other than what you are! Be more! Whatever she owed to the empire, she owed a hundred times more to me!

"I swore no oaths to you," she said.

"You tore yourself in two!" I said to her. "Desert the fleet. You will—you will. You will hide with me in the forest, in the grove of thorn trees, and in the morning, we'll steal down the mountain and flee to a village far away."

"And live like deer," she said, "waiting for the hunter?" Each of us living with a doom hanging over our heads, she told me. Living with forged papers, false names. A life that was a lie.

But I said to her, "A true life, because it would be a life together. You live for an empire that hates you! You fight for a wicked people! You die for them!"

"Will you keep my people, then?" she said. "Will you bring us food and medicines? Will you send us tents when we need to sleep, and ships when we need to fly? Will you carry our grandmothers on your back, and our children in your arms, and our memories in your mouth? Will you find land for us, here in the colonies, where we can rebuild our city?"

"You know how wealthy they are. They gorge on a feast and give you crumbs," I said. "You take their ragged tents, their scanty medicines? You should seize all they have and more."

"Yes," she said. "I should. But I can't live on *should*. Of course they're wicked. But the people who are righteous don't help. I have to live in this world, Arcelia. The gravestone where my father's name is written stands on Ceian land. Those are the bones I must build on. I have no others."

"Then forget your people," I said. "What do you owe *them*? Leave your father's name behind you! Forget Eneida and V. both! Why do you let your father's name chain you down?"

She spread her hands and looked so helpless that I wanted to put my hands round her throat. "Because it's my name," she said.

I spat in her face.

She wiped it off. "Arcelia," she said, "princess. Sometimes a vision comes upon me. A vision of the way the world will be—or the way it could be, unless something is done."

I asked her what vision a heretic had to share with the Oracle of Szayet, and spat again, this time at her feet. And she said:

"I saw the Ceian ship land on Itsaryet. I saw the priestesses protesting, and begging Ceiao not to come in, and I saw them swept aside. I saw Božena fall. I saw the garden left to rot. I saw the thorn forest burn up. And I saw Ceiao come to you, Arcelia. I saw a knife pressing into your throat."

Even if you were reading these letters, Gracia, I do not know how I would make you understand what her voice was like when she said those things. There was no stutter in it at all. I thought I was hearing her through water, so strangely she spoke, so soft and so hollow.

I said that I didn't believe her. But she said to me, "Liar." And she was right.

I took the knife from beneath my bed and threw it at her feet. "Take it," I said. "You gave me nothing when you gave it to me. Your father was no storyteller, your mother never bore you on a ship. You were born from crags and cliffs, and you nursed at a lion's breast, and your heart is limestone. I held you in my arms. When you had no home I was a home for you."

She went to her knees and took the knife from the floor. "I'm sworn to Ceiao," she said. "I am sworn."

"Then go!" I said to her. "Have I tied you to this bed? Ceiao has your oath. What does it matter that I have your heart? Love is nothing against words, nothing, nothing at all."

It might be that she wanted to say more, but I pushed past her, and fled down through the temple to the cellar. If she had been worth anything, she would have followed me. But I lay on the altar, and no one came.

I must have fainted or slept. When I came up again into the

free air, it was night. Smoke blotted the sky where the ships had been. At dinner there were no soldiers left at all. One of the other prisoners asked why half of the priests had gone away, and no one answered her.

Do you remember Pálide? Father brought him to the palace after our first tutor left, but before you left me to spend your days at the Library. He was only with us for a month or so, and I only took notice of him because he was so terribly ugly. His nose was all crooked—I told you it was an oak branch, and you hit me—and his eyes bulged out like eggs. He could not fight, or swim, or paint or play the kithara, or speak Ceian. But he knew astronomy. I remember your face when he would tell us about the stars.

He said to us, "The Holy One, in His wisdom, has caused our galaxy to move like a clock. The planets turn in their appointed order, at their appointed times. Stars, too, are born and die, according to the patterns that have moved them since the galaxy began. No matter how wide the spaces between the stars, they are joined by great laws, which know what matter is and what it will be."

He was wrong.

The stars aren't united, Gracia. They don't even know one another's names. The universe is moved by cruelty, indifferent cruelty, and by unguided, unlawful power. You are all that is left to me, and you are silent, and it is only by faith that I can still tell myself that through you and through the god I am not alone.

I have cursed her to the heavens, and I have cursed her to the earth. I have cursed her to the priests and the ships and the Ceian officers. And now I will do as I have never done before, and break the oath I made to myself when you threw me in the dungeons beneath Alectelo:

Bearer of the Pearl of the Dead, she who sits on the throne of Szayet, Oracle of Alekso Undying, false queen though you are, plead the lord of the heavens this plea.

Let Virgilia never find safe harbor. Let her drift between the stars and the comets. Let her starve, and thirst, and see no shore or sunrise. Or if she should breathe sky again, and walk in the light of foreign suns, let her watch the death of all she loves. Let her stand by the sea and see hope shatter and burn. Let her see a morning that brings peace without justice.

And when she comes at last to despair, let her call my name.

I remain—

your sister,

ARCELIA CAVIRO.

DIOMATA,
beloved.

—*V.*

PART II

—I FOUND MYSELF IN A DARK WOOD.

EIGHT

The air was like the inside of a mouth, thick and hot, towers hazed and faded toward their peaks. The smooth feathers of the Nevede had pockmarked with oil slick, tangled nets, chicken bones. It was coming on evening. Someone in the distance was shouting: hats for sale.

I lit the sílfion cigarette, took a deep breath, and held it. In dreams, that always woke me up.

The empty lot that had been the Libeiracópolan was sprouting over with clovers. There were footprints in the mud where it had drizzled this morning, greenless earth where rubble had been recently cleared away. At my feet lay a long twist of iron, woven through with shoots of new grass.

I sat on a rough, rain-streaked block of marble. It must have fallen from the roof. Wind and weather had once been its companions, and owls, and stars. Beside me stood a cairn of six or seven cobblestones, stacked as high as my knee. On the topmost stone, someone had written in charcoal the letter *C*.

Corpses are always the wrong size. To sit beside a corpse is to meet an actor that you knew only from holos. Even the least and meanest person, in death, is too small—not because something important has left them, but because too much of what is important remains. They are not meat, they are not dust, they are an animal, and you know how they once moved.

The least and meanest person, as I say. As for the great—

Szayet had once told me that she had seen his body. But I had thought to myself that this was that rarest of things: a lie Szayet did not know she was telling. She had never seen that body. She had seen a holo of that body. She had seen what the body would have looked like if the body had not been twelve thousand light-years away.

"Admiral," Ludon called from the edge of the lot. "It's getting late."

"Where is she going to go?" I said.

Steel blotted out the sky over the Avenuan Libeirguitan, and ships' shadows crawled between shadows of the leaves. At this distance, I could not tell my fleet from Otávio Julhan's. Above Flavia's house I thought the frigates hung lower, but I didn't trust my eyes.

The entrance hall of her house was cool and dim. Voices murmured at its end, falling silent when the door clicked shut. Conspicuously dustless patches stood along the walls where I remembered a statue here, a kithara there. Had her servants stolen them? Members of the council? Her friends?

But here was one artifact I remembered: a vase of delicately painted clay, showing Alekso of Sintia at a singing contest. Cinders were still smeared over the god's neck. I had pulled it myself from the Libeiracópolan's ruins. Of the hundreds of pieces of fine pottery lining the dome's walls, those painted stories that had survived three hundred years, survived a revolution and a civil war, only this one had survived me.

I wore a new black tunic with a tear in its sleeve, fine black trousers, and a black coat already plastered to my back by the heat. A nauseatingly sympathetic ensign from *Taraxandran* had brushed azurite on my eyelids, powder on my cheeks. I was missing the weight of my gun on my hip, and my admiral's pin at my throat, and a knife in my belt.

"Nothing up my sleeve," I murmured, and went into the sitting room.

It had been built to fit forty people. Now it held something like seventy, crammed into corners and couches. Someone had laid sheets over the fountain, the finely carved tables, the wall murals. A hastily painted sign on a vase read DO NOT SELL.

As soon as I set foot in the room, every person stood up at once. Seventy pairs of eyes silently took me in: finely clothed, face painted, hands empty, as unarmed as I had ever been.

"Ana," said the nearest, "I'm so *sorry*," and the wolves descended.

"—dreadful loss, Admiral Decretan, no one is sorrier than me, no one in the city—"

"—she was such a sweet person, the gentlest, the most innocent and soft-hearted, and she never forgot to help our family when we were in need—"

"—Anita, you know, I really wish you'd written to my household as soon as you heard, it's not like you to be so unfriendly—"

"—she was a dear friend of mine, you know, really my dearest friend, I thought of her as *my* sister—"

"—don't worry about anything, Anita, don't you dare lift a finger, I won't leave you alone for a second—"

"—and of course it's only natural to wish you could see this kind of thing coming, of course it's only natural to wonder if you could've done something to stop it, but—"

"—I always liked her, you know, no matter what people said—"

I shook hand upon hand upon hand, mechanical. Almost all these people I had danced with, drunk with, would have called a friend. None had come to visit me on Szayet, none had hunted the last assassins across the Swordbelt Arm. This was, I thought with a sort of distant interest, the most Ceian I'd heard spoken at one time in about a year.

They said prophecy had come in dreams to Ceirran's husband, Celestino Xicaran. They said it came in dreams to the sleeping heirs of Szayet, when the Pearl awaited a bearer, and all children of Caviro watched for a word that would name them Oracle.

The night after Ceirran had died, I had slept in Szayet's bed alone. And I had dreamed: that I stood on the marble steps of a building, and before me was a great crowd, surging and spitting and shouting, and all that separated me from their sneering faces was a stone table, covered by a shroud.

And I had dreamed: that I pulled the shroud away, and seen the corpse beneath. And the corpse sat up, and he said to me, "At last."

Night fell, colorless and heavy. Ludon went from lamp to lamp, flooding white over whiter sheets. A councillor arrived with Medveyeti servants, carrying cheeses and cured pork and sesame cakes, which someone arranged on one of Flavia's fine imported porcelain platters. Twelve more councillors arrived at once, caught allies or enemies by the hand, and tucked them away into corners to speak urgently in low tones about trading, property sales, and promotions for one another's sons. The civilian Joaquim Nequeiron took me aside to stammer out an elaborate speech that amounted to a request for either more sex or more money. I rid myself of him without finding out which and discovered that the first councillor had vanished, and Flavia's porcelain platter had vanished with him. Councillor Enxadan caught me by the shoulder, led me out to the garden, fed me two bottles of wine, and remarked that all the plants were dead.

"Neglect's a terrible thing," she said. "Someone should really take care of this place. The fruit trees don't know who's a citizen and who's in exile, after all. Why should they be punished for other people's misfortunes?"

For a woman who had been Jonata Barran's dearest school-friend and then given me all their troop positions for less than ten thousand dekar, this was very nearly philosophical. I stared at her.

"I have a very good gardener," she said. "I really take an interest in these matters, Anita. I do hope you'll let me know as soon as the house is up for sale."

Hours passed, and minutes. Rooms emptied. More dishes disappeared, as did glass bottles, ivory figurines, a little crystal statuette of a dolphin. "Goodbye," said jewel merchants, said weapons manufacturers and land speculators and holo-camera salesmen, "goodbye, goodbye—so terribly sorry—if there's anything, anything I can do—"

Somewhere around the sixty-fifth shutting of the door, consciousness returned. Sobriety didn't. I was sitting alone on one of the couches, a cup of spiced wine in my hand. Several people stood clustered around the fountain, talking softly about a romantic scandal between a bad poet and one of the city's best wrestlers. I didn't know any of them, I thought, almost idly. And then I thought: Have any of them gone to the shrines? Have they kissed the icons, or bowed to the cairns? Have they done it for the people's approval—for Julhan's—to meet the demands of the fashion?

I stood and crossed the room, stumbling a little with drink. In the hallway was the vase from the ruins of the Libeiracópolan. I lifted it from its shelf with careful hands, went back into the sitting room, and hurled it to the floor.

It smashed. Shards flew: the tiles, the shelves, the couches. Dust rose and fell.

The laughter stopped. A dozen pairs of eyes stared at me, silent, bewildered, enormously innocent.

"Get out," I said.

When the door had shut for the last time, the silence thickened. I watched it pool under the lamps and the tables and the fountain, around my hands and ankles.

A discarded dice game blinked on the couch, one of Flavia's tablets. I found the personal seal of *Dom* Caviro and tapped it with unfeeling fingers.

"Anita," said Szayet. I was, by now, used to seeing her in disarray, unkohled and loose-haired. But now her eyes were red, her face thin. She looked like her sister, I thought, and was startled at the thought.

"My lady," I said.

"Why haven't you answered my calls?" she said.

"I haven't answered anyone's calls," I said. I wasn't sure whether it was true or not. If I'd spoken to anyone besides Ludon on that long, numb slide from the Swordbelt Arm to the harbors at the Nevede, I couldn't remember it. I couldn't remember eating, either, or sleeping, though I could remember waking up.

Her mouth worked. "Did you not want me to come?" she said.

I stared blankly at her for a few seconds before I understood. The thought of Szayet at the funeral!—the thought of Szayet in Ceiao, kissing cheeks, speaking Ceian! Of course, she'd done those things before. It had not seemed absurd to me then. But then she had been Ceirran's woman, then she had been Ceirran's creature, and then I had been, too.

"No," I said shortly, unable to add flattery to it.

Again she pressed her lips together. Behind her, the holo was jewel green. Birds called—unfamiliar voices, not the cries of Alectelan gulls—and a voice barked in Szayeti. She was on another island, I thought, her army with her.

"I have news from the Swordbelt Arm," she said thinly. "Anita—I'm sorry to tell you like this. I wish it could wait. An hour ago, a Kutayeti swarm descended on the capital of Itsaryet."

I stiffened. "No."

"It was abandoned," she said. "Your soldiers have come home to Ceiao. How could the emperor have resisted?"

She paused for a reply—anger, I guessed, something spiteful.

I could not think of anything to say. The world was wrapped in quiet fog.

"My people have taken it badly," she said, when it became clear I was going to say nothing. "They say they're caught between the tiger and the wolf. I'm north of Alectelo, trying to keep this damned rebellion from spreading further. The Kutayeti took the farmland on Itsaryet, they took the cities. They took the—the temples—"

Her voice died. I said, "Your sister?"

She shrugged a shoulder. "They would not kill her," she said to her hands. "They haven't sent me any demand for ransom. They may never do it. Itsaryet is your colony. Its prisoners are your property."

That was something I could rouse myself to answer, a play with a familiar script. "If they ask me, I'll pay it," I said. "Whatever I have. Or I'll go to Itsaryet myself. I'll fight my way through and take her from the temple. I'm your servant. Say the word, and it's done."

She said, without looking at me, "Are you ever going to tell me?"

"Tell you what?" I said.

"Are you going to tell me you found that instruction manual in the Fortunatas," said Szayet.

My sympathy vanished like smoke. I bit back my first response, which was pure vulgarity. I had really thought, however briefly, she had called me to ask for help, and realizing it jolted me out of my waking sleep, into hot, easy fury.

"That's why you're angry?" I said. "Because you've been waiting through all this talk of my sister's funeral for me to—to confirm your spies' report? Gods alive! You haven't even told me you're sorry!"

This did not have the effect I hoped. Rather than stiffening with offended anger, she slowly shook her head. "You'd hate me for saying it," she said. "I remember—" Her throat bobbed. She said, "I remember when we buried my father. I didn't want all the old sympathetic words, the proper ceremonies, the weeping. I wanted him alive again. And if I couldn't have it, all I wanted was not to be alone. *I'm sorry* would be empty wind to you, Anita. I know you."

It was true, which made me unhappier. I wanted her to say *sorry*. I wanted her to say *if there's anything I can do*. I wanted her voice to blur into the indistinguishable, interminable voices of the Ceians, droning and hollow. I wanted her to look at me as they looked at me, with the blank dead faces of dolls. I wanted her to say exactly the wrong thing, to hurt me so badly that I would not be able to get up.

"Yes, you *know* me," I said, "you and your spies. Why should I bother to tell you anything, then? Why should I be berated for not answering your calls, if you already know all there is to know? If you're perched like a fat spider in the corner of my quarters, listening and waiting for me to come near enough to snatch, why should I come back to Szayet at all? What is there for me there?"

Her face flattened. "You might bring that manual home," she said. "You made a promise to bring whatever you found home. I suppose you never meant to keep it."

For a moment I hated her. It was only briefly that I had considered giving the manual to Julhan, only a breath, and I had been punished for it, punished beyond measure and reason. But of course she had seen it in me, her nose for my weaknesses like a bloodhound's. *When you can't find them*, I'd told her on Szayet, *you never hesitate to create them*.

I resented it, I resented her—not because she knew the worst of me, but because, seeing the worst, why did she still demand better? Why did she always ask me to be generous to her, though I was selfish and fearful and miserly? Why did she ask me to govern with her, though the whole Ceian Empire knew I was a thoughtless beast, a rootless dirty creature that couldn't even govern herself? If she knew I wasn't good enough to keep my promises, why did she ask me to make them?

"You pretend you're so frightened of Ceiao," I said, "so frightened that I'll hoard away a tablet for Ceiao, so frightened of Ceian ships, Ceian armies, Ceian power—*my* ships, *my* armies, my protection. You pretend you're so frightened that they'll hurt you, you pretend you're so frightened that I'll do you wrong." My voice dropped. "But that's a lie. Oh, yes, Szayet, I know you, too. What you're afraid of, *my lady*, is the truth. You're afraid that you're Ceiao's client queen."

"You forget yourself," she said, a low rasp.

"You've been forgetting yourself since you rolled out of that carpet," I said. "You *do* want a Szayeti Empire, don't you? Well, tell the truth to yourself, if you can't tell it to anyone else. You're no empress. You're the glorified governess of a client kingdom held together by a myth and a corpse. Fortune and misfortune, have you ever felt loyalty? Have you ever felt gratitude? Who put you on your throne, who gave you your crown? Who was it that made you an Oracle?"

"Not you," said the queen of Szayet.

That knocked the breath out of me. Under the sunlight of that far world, the Pearl in her ear was more light than shape. I could only just see that it had no black spot on it today, and I tasted gall.

"You ask for a report from the Fortunatas?" I said. "I'll give you one. Do you know what your humble servant found there, Holiest?"

"Energy from the Black Maw she was too foolish to understand," she said coldly, "and failed hosts she was too lazy to save."

"Oh, yes," I said. "Yes, my lady, you have it exact. But that's not all. I found that if you put a human consciousness into quicksilver pearl, he can't be alone. If he doesn't speak to anyone, he forgets what the world is. He loses himself. He forgets how to show his face to you. He talks static and nonsense. He screams. He breaks. He never comes back."

Her face went white.

"You're lying," she said.

"I'm not the liar here," I said.

She shut her eyes. When she opened them again, her face was blank, terribly blank. I had seen her wear that expression when speaking to Ceian councillors, when speaking to recalcitrant noblemen, when she had come back from the Island of the Dead the day she had been crowned Oracle. I had never seen her wear it when she was speaking with me.

"You're hurt," she said. "You only want to hurt someone."

I was; I did. "Whatever's left in that Pearl, it's Undying, but it isn't alive," I said ruthlessly. "You—Caviro's ten-times-great-granddaughter, Oracle of Szayet—you can't so much as breathe without biting the hand that's fed you, can you? You can't so much as breathe without wronging someone you owe because you can't stand owing them. Why should I give you that tablet? Why shouldn't I build swarms of ships? I'll kill that boy who's killed my sister, and then I'll take Itsaryet back—my colony, Szayet, *mine*—and I'll rescue that girl in the temple, but not for you. Not for you, because you left her there to rot, the way you left the thing in your ear to rot the second you didn't have any more use for it—"

"This has nothing to do with her," she said. Her voice shook. I was poisonously glad of it—glad that there was some part of me, through that distance and that dignity, that could leave a mark on that beautiful face. "You don't give a damn about her. You certainly don't give a damn about Alekso Undying."

"What do I give a damn about?" I said.

"Every day I have spent with you in the last year, half of your heart has been at Matheus Ceirran's funeral," she said. "I thought it was ego. I wish it were ego. That moment of your great rhetoric, your great riot, your great triumph—oh, it'd be just like you to want to live there forever, brat that you are—but it isn't, is it? What you want is the despair. Despair poured out endlessly and uselessly into a grave, just as you poured out your love endlessly and uselessly while he lived—"

"You don't know what love is," I said. "You used him to steal a throne—you're using his memory now to keep it—"

"I have done everything in my power to preserve Ceirran's memory, Anita," she said. "And hear this now—I've done it well. You want to know the truth? You want me to tell the truth? I have every right to use him. I have every right to use him—just as much as he *used* Szayet! Just as much as he *used* me! If that's ambition for a Szayeti Empire, then by the Undying Name, I'll keep that ambition, I'll do it gladly! He owes Szayet that much! I am sick and tired of your flinching when I make him into exactly the thing he told me to make him into! I am sick and tired of your flinching at the fact that that was what he wanted! That *I* was what he wanted!"

"Szayet," I said, "from the day I met you, you've made it clear that not a person or a thing in the galaxy will ever come before your pride. Whenever anyone is close enough to touch you, it eats away at you that there might be any cell of them, any atom, that you can't control. You get them under your thumb, or you throw them away. You threw away your own god. You left him to batter at the walls you'd put up around yourself, you left him to spend months screaming at you to listen. And why shouldn't you treat him that way? That's how you treated your sister—"

"That's how *you* treated your sister," she snapped.

It was such a relief to hear it. "Go to hell," I said, and swept her holo away.

Through the silence I waded to the back of the sitting room, against its weight I pushed open the door to the garden, and I walked through the foot lamps, and I went to my hands and knees before my sister's ash tree. For a moment I rested there, head bowed. Then I was sick in the roots.

Going back to Semfontan's old house was unthinkable. Going to the Outer City wasn't. There would be a Belkayeti or a Diajundot, fresh off the ship, who wouldn't know me by sight. There'd be someone who would let me catch their hips in my hands and press my face against their neck, who would let me push them down into their pillows, let me slide my hands between their thighs, let me forget for a little while that I had a mind or heart, anything beyond muscle and blood...

I hunched my shoulders. Even if I could lay hands on some fool who didn't know the name of the woman pawing at them, someone would see me. Someone would tell the person I'd touched, and they'd tell their cousins and their sweethearts, and soon enough some fresh-faced ensign pattering down to the kitchen for a morning snack would hear his servants chattering: *You'll never guess what the lech did, the night of her own sister's funeral—*

Behind me in the house, the front door rattled. I pulled myself to my feet, wine sloshing unpleasantly in my belly. It occurred to me that I couldn't remember the last time I'd eaten.

The second night after he had died, I'd slept in my own bed, and I'd dreamed again. And I had dreamed: that I stood on the same steps, and faced the same crowd, and the same table was before me, and I held the hem of the shroud in my hands.

And I had dreamed: that I pulled the shroud away. And I had dreamed: that beneath it lay a statue of green slate, unpainted and naked, its eyes unblinking marble. And I had dreamed that I screamed.

I opened the door. The heavy hot breath of the street rushed in. I looked at the people standing there, drew my head back, and spat deliberately into Otávio Julhan's face.

He blinked and held out a hand. The lanky, nervous-looking girl at his left rummaged in her bag, produced a handkerchief, and handed it to him. He dabbed his nose and cheeks.

"I came to offer my sympathies," he said.

"Your sympathies?" I said softly.

Julhan's expression was as flat as a painting. "Yes," he said.

"Let me make a suggestion," I said. "A piece of advice, friend to friend. Hold on to your sympathies. Hold them tight, you rat-tongued coward son of a whore. Hold them in your rotting fist and don't let them go, and I'll take them when I take your head."

"I granted you truce, Admiral," he said. "You swore on your name that, while you mourned, you would not raise arms against me."

"You *granted* me," I said, and spat again, this time onto his boots. "How's that for arms?"

"Admiral," he said quietly. "You and I made an agreement. When we avenged my cousin—"

"*Your* cousin!" I said. "As if you knew Ceirran! As if he thought of you! As if one man in Ceiao would devote one cen-tono's worth of care to you, except that he—" The end of the sentence would not come. Except that Ceirran had left him all he had. Except that Ceirran had devoted some care to him, before he died. Except that Ceirran's blood meant something. Except that it meant something that Julhan had it, and I had none.

He watched me with that narrow, dark face, so like my friend's, and after a long few seconds, he said:

"I didn't kill Flavia."

"Say her name again and you'll walk away with half your teeth missing," I said.

This did not appear to move him. "I am not a warmonger," he said. "I do not want your sister's grudges to weigh us down. I want peace, Admiral Decretan. All I have ever wanted is peace."

"Ceirran, Ceirran!" I said. "Come and look at your heir!

Ceirran, is this the boy who drags your name across Ceiao like a starfighter drags a corpse behind its engines? Is this the boy who wants your empire, this servant in his master's clothing, this soft-handed lawyer-hearted stone-tongued worm? Come and feast your eyes, Ceirran—Ceirran, come here, come and see—"

My stomach rebelled. I clutched at the railing of Flavia's stairs and counted the hard black pits beneath her cherry laurels until my body was under my control again. When I straightened, the bulky officer at Julhan's right hand was giving me a look of frank, unpleasant amusement.

"You have nine days left of mourning," said Julhan. "I am sorry that you lost your sister. Other Ceians have sisters, too, who lie among the dead of Khramya—who will lie among the dead of Itsaryet and Belkayet and even Sintia, if you abandon the war you started with Kutayet so that you can begin another with the people of our homeworld. Don't split your forces between Ceiao's enemies and her friends. Don't send more sisters onto the funeral pyre."

"It'll be your soldiers on the pyre, not mine," I said. "Do you have spies on my ships?" He said nothing, and I snorted. "You know what's in the tablet that I found in the Swordbelt Arm. That's why you come with your sympathies and your mewling peace, isn't it? It's because if you try to seize it from me outright, the way any decent soldier would, all the veterans of the fleet will eat you alive."

"So you would use that tablet in a civil war, then," he said. "On citizens."

I said nothing.

He inclined his head. "Whether my soldiers or yours," he said, "they'll be Ceians. It's understandable that you're inclined to imagine my death would help you. It's even understandable that you've given in to the urge to find someone to blame. But it's not too late to put aside your thirst for the death of innocents. Admiral Decretan, I have a proposal for you."

"If I'd killed one of your family, and you hadn't stopped me," I said, "you'd tell your handmaiden over there, who hasn't taken her hand off her gun, to draw it—and then you'd tell her to shove the barrel in your mouth."

The bulky captain whipped her hand out of her cloak. Julhan's face had been pale since I had mentioned Caviro's tablet, and now his nostrils flared, his lips drew back like an animal's. "I did not kill her," he snapped, and then shut his eyes. "Very well. Use the tablet, if you will. Win yet another civil war. What then? What kind of city will you build afterward? How will you make peace, if you do not make it with me? Do you think you live in a storybook, where the hero takes his vengeance and then is happy ever after? No matter how many you kill, when you're done, you will have to live in Ceiao."

"Oh, I *have to*?" I said.

Julhan sighed. "I intended to be courteous," he said. "I see you will not allow me. Admiral, you and I should marry."

It was some time before I stopped laughing. A minute or so in, I had to sit down.

"Don't mistake me," said Julhan, over me. "I have no intention of wooing you. Neither do I want to seduce you, or to otherwise do injury to either of our dignities."

"Oh, believe me, that's clear," I said, wiping my eyes. "Do you even know how to use it? Your *dignity*, I mean."

"Your sister instigated a regrettable violation of the Ceian peace," Julhan said. He did not resemble Ceirran, I thought, not really. They had the same long angular face, the same dark skin and modest build, but Ceirran's eyes had been bright, intent, sparrow-brown and startlingly alive. The color of Julhan's eyes was not quite black—a dead firepit grey. "She consorted with a criminal element, and encouraged corruption and bribery. I do not believe she was wicked in her heart of hearts. She was beloved among the people of quality in our city, and I do not deny that it was for good reason. I believe she only attempted to wrong me out of conviction that she was defending you."

"And was she?" I said.

"I *do not want* to hurt you, Admiral Decretan," said Julhan. "You do not want to hurt me. I won't insult you by offering romance—I want it no more than you. What I want is for this partnership of necessity, begun in vengeance and civil war, to become a lasting alliance with roots in Ceian tradition and Ceian law. I have a name, and a house, and coin. I have gained the loyalty of the guard and the people. You have the love of the fleet, and you have a very valuable manual. And more to the point—you have half the galaxy. You have a chance to make peace for the Empire of Ceiao."

"The Empire of Ceiao!" I said, and bent over laughing again.

"The Empire of Ceiao," said Julhan. "Yes. My country, Decretan. I have a duty to it. What would your sister say your duty was?"

"My sister," I said, "would say that my duty was to slit you from belly to throat and grind your guts into every bridge on the Nevede. She would tell me to bury you with Lançan—with Cachoeiran—with Semfontan—with every soldier of twice your years and three times your guts who I've put in the ground. And she wouldn't let me rest until she had seen it done."

In Julhan's mask there was no crack, no quiver of temper or of fear. "Very well," he said. "You and she are alike, I see. Águeda, Eneida, come." He turned to go, the captain and the lanky girl trotting down the steps ahead of him, then he sighed and looked back. "Admiral. However you mean it—I hope you want peace for the city, too."

"If he whose name you wear heard you now, he'd laugh you into an early grave," I said. "Peace! Tradition! He knew that talk for what it was. Men tell themselves a hundred lies to make greed and ambition sound pretty. The men who killed him certainly did. But Ceirran's blood should be more honest."

"You don't need to believe it's patriotism, Admiral, if you can't comprehend patriotism," he said. "Call it curiosity. You're right. I am young. I want peace in Ceiao because I want to see what it's like."

He was gone before I could tell him where to put his curiosity, vanished into the hazy darkness. The silence was thicker than ever, mud filling my lungs, mud slithering around my neck.

My men had docked *Taraxandran* on the far side of the Nevede. The water was sunk low enough that the river's mossy walls had begun to stink. In the ship's washroom I stuck my head under the cold sink tap, which did little to relieve the feeling that my whole skin was a rag that someone had used to wipe the floor. I pushed my hair back from my forehead, wiped my wet cheeks, and left in the direction of the brig.

I'd let *Taraxandran*'s crew scatter through Ceiao to see their families, and now her hallways were quiet but for the lapping of the Nevede outside her windows, wind singing hollowly at her aft engines. When I opened the brig's door, the figure hunched against the far wall made no sound, either.

"Nice night," I said.

Vualo didn't move. They weren't asleep. I could see the whites of their eyes in the door's shadow. Their mane hung lankly to their shoulders, and their clothes were still spotted with blood. We had told them that they'd be released to *Taraxandran*'s washroom whenever they asked, that we'd give them what spare uniforms we had that would fit. They had not replied—to that, or to anything. They had sat down against the wall of the brig, and they had not moved or spoken since.

"Ever been to Ceiao?" I said. "No? Sorry I can't give you the tour. Then again, you're not missing much, all told. A few bridges, an overgrown lot. Szayet wasn't much impressed."

Vualo sat silent.

I was still, despite it all, quite drunk. I leaned against the doorframe and spat acid aftertaste onto the brig's floor. "Get up," I said. "Come to the mess. Have a nightcap with me." No response. "No? I'll ask you for advice on my war plans. Tell you half the Merchants' Council's secrets, tedious as they are. Share a bowl of pottage. Bare my heart."

Not a twitch, not so much as a lifted eyebrow.

"The third night," I said contemplatively, "after the funeral—and the riots—I slept in Szayet's bed again. Never told her that, as a matter of fact. She'd fled by then. I had to break a window. Do you know, she was a terrible slob? Still is. Precious as a magpie about the things that catch her eye, but she'll treat anything like trash if it isn't beautiful. Centonos in the floorboards, kohl jars on the table, stockings under the wardrobe. I even found my own captain's pin in her hallway. Nothing there worth stealing. The place was just full of her, that was all."

They might have been a piece of stone, for all they seemed to hear me. "Dreamed, when I was in her bed, that I stood on the steps again," I said, "those marble steps I dreamed of before. And the crowd was before me, and the stone table between us, and the shroud. And I pulled it off—"

My hand twitched. I flattened it against my side. Vualo didn't so much as blink.

"There was nothing there," I said. "The table was cracked right down the center. There was no one there at all."

I already know he is dead, she'd told me when I'd come to her house that night. And when I asked how, *Prophecy*.

I was oracle to no god. I was not even a disciple. The first time I'd truly laid hands on something otherworldly had been in the Fortunatas, and as soon as I'd done it, I'd wrought death.

But I'd woken from my dream, the third night after Ceirran died, thinking: *He's not in any Pearl*. And the thought had brought with it a swift and wild and bewildering joy—

"The nightcap's still on offer," I said. "No?" Vualo sat there, head bowed, wordless. "Keep at this," I said, "and I'll start to think I've done something to offend you," and let the door slam shut.

Cardean had written to me. Our ships in the colony worlds, all but a necessary few, had gathered and departed the Swordbelt Arm. They'd join with my forces around the outer planets in this solar system, eyeing the boy's fleet, maneuvering carefully through the ranges of one another's guns.

Galvão had written, too. He'd reported the same as Szayet: Itsaryet was gone. The capital was occupied, the vast silver and platinum mines flooded, the ports locked down. The temple prison had been occupied by the emperor's men. There were no reports of any deaths—yet.

On Szayet, it was growing increasingly difficult to keep my men from panicking. Patrol ships swept the skies alongside warships, watching the outer black for swarms. Besides this, though, Galvão had had to dispatch fifty fighters to sweep the oceans to look for deserters, something I had never dealt with in all my years as an officer. My men had fought beside me for years. They trusted me to be at their side through death or victory. They had never before had to contemplate the thought of ordinary failure.

I had Caviro's tablet. I could make hosts of the Terrestrial Intelligence. I would doom each of them to a painful death, but I could make them. I'd shot and killed Kutayet's greatest mind on the subject, and it was now likely that I was one of the few left in the galaxy who did have the means to make them. Otávio Julhan knew that.

So you would use it, he had said. No fear in his voice, only interest, and a mild surprise.

The smug little wretch. I should have killed him the night we'd met.

Of course I wouldn't use the tablet. Of course I had to use the tablet. Of course thousands of men would die if I did not condemn a few to torture, to inhumanity, to solitary confinement and the loss of their reason. Of course the making of these things was a kind of murder. But when had I grown so soft? When had I ever flinched at killing?

I had in Alectelo, said my memory. When the soldiers who had fought for Szayet's sister—the soldiers I myself had taken captive in her war—had been under threat of execution, I'd asked Szayet to let them live.

Then, in Alectelo, when a boy not quite Otávio Julhan's age had come at me drunk and angry and armed because I'd cheated him at cards, I'd shot him dead in front of the palace. No matter how they remembered now that I'd pleaded for the prisoners, no matter how they pressed gifts on me and prayers and danced with me in taverns—that night, I thought, the people of Alectelo would have torn me limb from limb. Szayet had stood between me and the crowd. She had prayed for the dead boy's soul.

Outside the porthole, the light of Ceiao's lanterns flickered in the river. Ships roared. Faraway voices were echoing on the dock, speaking my mother tongue. In my heart, my own voice from an hour ago climbed to a child's whine: *You have to live in Ceiao. Oh, I have to?*

I had been so afraid to come here. I'd been so afraid of seeing those shrines. And what had happened, when I'd seen the one at the ruins of the Libeiracópolan? Exactly what I'd been afraid of. Exactly what was happening now, exactly what I felt at this moment: nothing, nothing, nothing at all.

I swept the tablet clear and stared at the ceiling. Above me the lamp burned and, when I blinked, threw green-grey shadows across my vision. My eyes felt so sore, so terribly tired and dry. Before me, the work, and behind me, the waiting bed. I could climb into it, I thought. I could lie down, I could close my eyes, I could rest. Then, the next morning, I would wake up.

Outside, the river whispered.

"Anita," said a voice.

I sat bolt upright. My quarters were dark. The lantern had gone out. My cheek was numb where the tablet glass had flattened it.

"Who's there?" I said.

Silence answered me. I stood and turned slowly, scanning the room's shadows, its corners. My combat knife sat on the table next to my sleeping cot. The voice had come from—where had it come from? The porthole? The bed? No one was there. I had imagined it. I was a fool, I thought with relief, I was a fool and I had acted the fool.

"Anita," said the voice, directly into my ear.

I spun and swung my fist. It met nothing at all. The room was as empty as sky.

"Who's there?" I called again.

There was no noise, not even footsteps in the hallway. I eased toward the bedside table, slowly, and closed my hand around the hilt of my knife.

"Show yourself," I said.

The world slowed.

The curtains by the porthole had been fluttering up in the night wind. Now they stopped, caught midway between ceiling and floor—and then reappeared, two inches higher than they had been. A particle of dust drifting past my face blinked out of existence entirely. I saw it a moment later, a foot away. The exhale in my lungs caught and held. There was no pain in my body, I thought. There was no pain at all.

"Anita," said the ghost, and stood up from the bed.

It had not appeared. It had not been there fifteen seconds ago, and it had been there all along. It was the same color as the shadows below the lantern, and against those shadows it was very clear.

"What are you?" I said, though I had heard its voice, and I knew.

"Your evil spirit," said the ghost, and it laughed.

"Why have you come?" I said.

Its face tilted. Then it shifted: colorlessness darkening, nose and jaw and cheeks emerging like ice from the winter river, scar spreading like a cobweb along its jaw.

"You called my name," it said, and with Ceirran's mouth, it smiled.

Back in that old, old country that we call history, when wishing still worked, when I was young and when I had a mother and sister and future and when I was only just beginning to name myself a pilot, the fleet instructors told me this:

Midway along the journey from one spiral arm to another, there is a border to a country that will not let you go home. If you lose the straight path near that place, no work and no labor will find it for you, and you will never again walk in the air of ordinary worlds. It is the center of the galaxy, and the empire without an ending, and we call it the Black Maw.

But I've traveled a long road since those days, and I've learned that there are more types of gravity than the physical. Here is another center of the galaxy: a city. Here is the center of the city: a garden of forking paths.

On one of these paths, you are going to die in pain.

Why in pain? you ask.

Your drugs will run out. It won't be anybody's fault. At the moment you die, the sun will be warm, and your attendant's feet will hurt, and his shift will be ending in less than half an hour. The agency for whom he works will have informed him that this particular client is an imperial pet. She only lives on generosity. In the days of peace—the great peace, the Ceian peace, the days of your agony—generosity, like flies, has found itself in such abundant supply.

There's a tablet on your lap. Above it float the words of a poem. You are holding a stylus, and trying to think of this half-line's ending. Beside you, on the bench, there sits a notebook, a hundred scraps of paper tucked between its pages. In these days you spend in the garden of forking paths, you have been writing, with great care, two different histories.

One is the story of the son of a god. He is the leader of a people from a dead, burnt country, a people consumed by endless war, a people who are capable of being defeated. He has come to a new world, and on it, he will build a new city: never betrayed, never mistaken, never dying, never-ending. This is a history for the city to hear. You are naming her, steel and statue, cypress and stone. You are telling her what she is going to be.

The other history is the story of a woman who kills her sister. This is for you.

When I was young, my teachers told me that it was not truth but lessons that were important. The lesson for me was that home is wherever you can take it.

But, of course, once you have a home at last, the home has you.

There will be a small, dense ache at the center of your chest. You'll think to yourself: Maybe I'll shut my eyes for a little while, and I'll finish writing in an hour or so.

The sun beats down. Later, when the attendant's shift is over, he will try to wake you up.

Who are you? you ask me.

Your evil spirit, Virgilia.

That's how your story ends. Abandon hope, all of us that enter it.

It had never been a library, really, or at least Szayet would never have called it one. The room was a little smaller than the Alectelan palace dining hall, its ceilings a little lower, its floor a forest of torn-up carpet, nails, dry fir splinters, holes. The book-shelves that had lined its walls, the blue-green map of Sintia floating beside the door, the velvet curtains tied back from the windows with golden rope, the cart piled with porcelain dishes and silver cups, the lamp crowned by a green glass shade painted with lions' heads, the dozens on hundreds on thousands of books—all these we had shoved to the sides of the room or flung into the fireplace. What we hadn't stolen, we'd smashed.

It had been Túlio Cachoeiran's seaside house. He'd fled here after he'd blabbed to the Merchants' Council about Ceirran's Pearl of the Dead, holing himself up like a rat while he waited to see what they'd do. Then, when they'd conspired, when they'd taken knives, when they'd come to the Libeiracópolan—he hadn't left. Not until Otávio Julhan had arrived from Sintia, flattering and begging advice, mentioning that he'd inherited Ceirran's treasury and hinting he was inclined to be generous—not until he had drawn Cachoeiran out to the house a mile away, where Flavia and I were waiting.

And in Cachoeiran's seaside house, afterward, the boy and I

had sat and made our list of names. This woman to die, though she was Julhan's distant cousin; this man to be arrested, though Julhan called for his execution; that woman to be spared, though Julhan badly wanted her cash. How late we'd bargained, he and I, while the stars wheeled over the sea. With any other man, that might have been the beginning of a friendship.

One of the few possessions of Cachoeiran's that Flavia and I had left intact: a gorgeous mahogany table. I had always half meant to send it as a gift to Szayet, if I'd ever visited Ceiao again. Now I sat at its head, Ludon on my right, holos of Galvão and Cardean on my left.

In the table's center sat the ghost of Matheus Ceirran, cross-legged. It watched me with its cheek propped on its hand like a bored child. As soon as I glanced at it, it unfolded itself, stretched, and slowly, sadly shook its head.

"Then we're agreed," said Cardean, scratchy with static. "There should be a laboratory at a second-rate university where the scholars will work for fewer dekar than the ones in Sintielo. One of Sintia's outer planets? Istruelo? Sancta Buey?"

"I don't give a damn," I said. Flavia would have told me which scholars she wanted to favor and which she wanted to snub, but Flavia could not want things anymore. Julhan would have known exactly where to get the best work for cheap, but Julhan meant to marry me, and I meant to kill him. "Whichever asks fewer questions."

"Are you sure we can't copy the manual, sir?" said Galvão, with strained politeness. "For your own piece of mind—"

"Stop asking," I said. "You used to give a damn about information security, as far as I recall."

The fact was, said a thin little voice in my head, the manual wasn't mine to copy. I'd promised it to someone else. I squashed that voice with effort. The tablet was in my own sleeping quarters on the third floor, slipped into my pillowcase. When one of the crewmen had tried to touch it, I'd cursed him for a useless pig. He'd slunk through camp like a kicked puppy all day, his friends shooting me glares when they thought I wasn't looking. I didn't know when I'd last made the men laugh. I could feel my black mood spreading like mud through the house and the grounds surrounding, the men walking on tiptoes around me and speaking to me as carefully as if I were a madman. I hated it, and yet I could summon up neither the energy nor the inclination to break it.

"Ana," said Ludon, "Julhan Ceirran sent me another message this morning. He says, in light of the Kutayeti conquest of Itsaryet, he wants to reiterate that he grieves with you, and that he's offering—"

"Burn it," I said.

"And another message from the Kutayeti court, too," said Ludon. "The court is very insistent on ransoming that ambassador as soon as possible."

"Why should we negotiate with them?" I said. "What do they have to threaten us with? Half of the hosts they have now will break in a matter of months." So would ours, once we built them. But Ceiao was farther from the Black Maw than Kutayet was, far enough that the breaking of the hosts would not cause the same warping in time we had seen on the Fortunatas—if Lukhaya had been telling the truth. "Vualo can spend some more time enjoying our hospitality," I said. "It'll do them good."

"A message from some of our colonial governors in the Swordbelt Arm, too, sir," said Cardean. "They ask whether we're planning to send back reinforcements from Ceiao to defend their borders. Given recent events."

Recent events: our attempt to get a handful of fighters through the Kutayeti patrol around Itsaryet, which had ended with two senior lieutenants lost and the rest of the officers fleeing through the Swordbelt Arm like rats down an alley, humiliated. "Doesn't matter, does it?" I said. "Not if we can get the Sintian scholars to help us make—" I tapped at the back of my own neck, unwilling to name the Terrestrial Intelligence. On the table, the ghost mirrored my movement, grotesquely exaggerated: digging its knuckles into the highest knob of its spine, arching its back like a cat. "We'll win any colony back soon enough."

"On that topic, Admiral," said Galvão's holo thinly. "The men were wondering who you might select to be the procedure's first—subject."

In the center of the table, the ghost grinned.

The men were afraid I would choose one of them, of course. They didn't need to be. Carmela Lukhaya had used—*serfs, tribesmen,* she'd said, *uneducated people.* The Ceian Empire held billions of colonials, immigrants, conquered peoples. Alekso of Sintia had used prisoners for his experiments, and Ceiao had no shortage of those, either. I could use Madinabic people desperate to earn privileges for their clans. I could use Sintians desperate for money. I could use Szayeti.

The ghost stretched its legs out on the table, yawned, and blinked at me slowly.

"I don't know who," I said shortly. And, when Galvão went to speak: "I don't *know*. Are there any more messages?" All three officers opened their mouths. "Any that can't wait?" I said, and reluctantly, each of them shook his head. "Fine," I said. "Fine. Dismissed." They traded glances. "Do you understand Ceian?" I snapped. "Dismissed."

"Captain," said the ghost, once the door had shut behind Ludon.

"Commander," I said.

It climbed off the table—or I thought it climbed. At its edges, its form was not quite clear. There was a peculiar rippling quality to it, like a shaken sheet of foil. Still, I could hear its footsteps, and the creak of the wood when it shifted its weight. When it was close to my chair, so close it might have touched me, it stopped and tilted its head.

"So they will follow you," it said, "even as far as civil war."

"The surprise is flattering," I said. I was lying, a little. It was Ceirran's voice—unmistakably Ceirran's voice—but there was no surprise in its tone. There was nothing at all, not even laughter.

"Or some of them will," it said, as if I hadn't spoken. "If you walked through the camps tonight, what would the soldiers be saying of Ana Decretan and her instruction manual from the barbarian land? Of her plans to conquer Ceiao by breaking some poor Ceian's mind?"

"What a brave and glorious general she is," I said. "And how handsome, to boot. Perhaps they don't want to die for me, but what does that mean? They want to fight for me—that's what matters."

It was smiling slightly. I said, wanting to knock that smile off its face—or at least to make it retreat a few steps: "You should know, I don't believe you're real."

Ceirran did not look offended. "Do you make a regular habit of talking to things you don't believe in?" it said.

"Ah, the Merchants' Council," I said, and grinned, more out of habit than anything else.

The ghost didn't laugh. "Do you think you've run mad, then?" it said conversationally.

I didn't feel mad, but of course a madman would have said so. "You're not much of a madness, are you?" I said instead. "Me, I think you're a computer program. You've come out of one of the tablets that were caught in the explosion at the laboratory. You're some piece of pearl that gives decent people hallucinations— that's all."

"Your vision of Flavia came before the explosion," said the ghost.

I had never told it about my hallucinated conversation with Flavia. "What do you say you are, then?" I said. "Is the boy right, and Ceirran is now become a god?"

The second before it replied was the longest second of my life. "You don't believe in gods," it said.

"I already told you that I don't believe in you," I said. It did not reply, and I said through the lump in my throat, "When I dreamed about Flavia, she called up a bridge and a riverbank and a wind and a sky. What world have you called up? Just Ceiao. What kind of god builds just—Ceiao? No. A hallucination, a ghost, a computer program. A god would have power. You're powerless."

"I might say the same of you," it said.

"I have an army," I said, smiling a smile I did not feel.

The ghost took a step back. I let out a breath. "All those men love you," it said thoughtfully. "But how many of them would rely on you? Are you their friend, who feasts with them and drinks with them and dances with them down the streets of a foreign town, or are you their leader, who walks before them into the jaws of death and brings them home again?"

"I don't need to choose," I said. "*You* taught me that much."

"Is that what I taught you?" said Ceirran. "I'm sorry for that."

On the table, the tablet blinked red. "Hell," I murmured, and went to wave it away, but before I could, the ghost dragged its fingers through the tablet's surface. The seal bloomed into Otávio Julhan's face.

"Listen to me," he said urgently, before I could slam my hand down. "Admiral, peace is still possible. If you'd only consider—"

"*Consider* this, you murdering half-wit," I said. "You don't want to marry me. What the hell's wrong with you?"

"We don't agree on the meaning of *want*," he said. "I proposed a solution. Naturally I want to see it carried out. You think for something to be *want*, it must be selfish—"

"A solution!" I said. "Ceirran Undying, you think you're clever. You think you can trade the rest of your life for peace, Otávio Julhan, as if it were on offer in a market stall. You—"

"Ceirran," he said. "Otávio Ceirran."

The ghost folded itself down until its nose was an inch from Julhan's, staring unblinkingly into his eyes. Through its flesh, the holo shivered like heat. "Die," I said.

"The rest of my life," he said, "was decided by councillors with knives in the Libeiracópolan over a year ago. You took half the Ceian Empire upon your shoulders, Admiral. So did I. Did you think Ceiao was a suit of fine clothes, to be worn on feast days and put away when you didn't care for it anymore? If you thought so then, listen to me now. We made a sacrifice—"

I smacked the tablet with the flat of my hand. It whined and died. The ghost twisted its head around—impossibly far around, a grotesque stretch—and raised an eyebrow at me.

"What did you do that for?" I said to it.

It blinked at me. "You were alone," it said.

"Alone?" I said, bewildered and repelled. "You were right here."

It shivered and vanished. I cursed under my breath, rubbed my hands over my aching eyes, and went slowly to go sit on Cachoeiran's stoop.

The afternoon was heaving itself seaward into hangdog night. Above me the stars blurred, below they flickered: ship lights, campfires. Here in the far east of the continent, the earth rucked up like an ill-fitted shirt, so the lights of my soldiers' tents crisscrossed and hid behind hills. My head knew the quantity, but my eyes said I had less than a hundred followers.

At the base of the steps a pair of guards sat, wineskins in hand, watching the horizon. Cicadas chattered. Behind the house, the sea, hobbled by Ceiao's moonlessness, hiccuped a halfhearted wave.

In Alectelo, we'd dress in old canvas tunics and sandals, braid Szayet's hair over her ear, and climb over the wall of the palace gardens. Szayet was no longer a sheltered princess seen only at ceremonies, I was no longer a stranger to her town, and who this was meant to fool I didn't know. Certainly, more often than not, our drinks came free. But on this world, if I found a threadbare crewman's cloak, pulled my hood up, walked out into the hills, sat by a fire, pitched my voice low, and asked...

And asked what? *Is Anita Decretan doing you wrong? Does it shame you to follow her? If she tried to run, where in the galaxy could she go?*

"No sign of trouble?" I said.

"None, sir," said one of the guards. "A flash in the sky earlier, but no noise since."

No land invasion, no siege, no downpour of Julhan's troops upon our position. Szayet would have been able to explain all the twisted reasoning: why the boy was so coolly certain that if he waited for us to strike first with a swarm, he would still emerge at an advantage, and how it could be that even now he was sitting in the city, writing proclamations that doubtlessly said, *Vicious—Aggression—Unprovoked—*

I made myself think, carefully and slowly, through every person in the galaxy who did not currently hate me. Then I revised the list to every person in the galaxy who was not currently justified in hating me. When I had finished, the list consisted of the emperor of Kutayet; Flavia, who was dead; and, bewilderingly, Otávio Julhan, who would be dead soon.

"Tell the men I'm retiring for the night," I said. "They'll find me upstairs." There was a bottle of wine in my room. I'd open up the windows and pour a glass or two. The ghost might come and sit at the foot of my bed, make itself comfortable.

Something of an attic, the third floor. These had been servants' quarters, not the master's. I'd left the main bedroom empty, and the decision unexamined. I walked silently across its floor, heel-toe, avoiding the noise of my own movements. When the wind blew, the whole place creaked beneath my feet, and when the air was still and the humidity crept into the wood, it creaked worse. Maybe the house had gone to seed since I'd murdered its owner, but I suspected it had never had anything but neglect from Cachoeiran. Purpose was a wonderful thing. It narrowed one's field of vision; it narrowed the world. And Cachoeiran, fastidious, scrupulous, determined to right an overturned Ceiao, must have felt so alone in this silent countryside, wondering as the wind rattled down the windows if he had fulfilled his purpose, if perhaps there was no purpose at all—

There was a light under the bedroom door.

I stopped. *You left a lantern on*, said my memory, but instinct said, *Not that lantern*. A moment later I knew why: The light bobbed and shifted, shadows creeping up the far wall.

I closed my eyes. Beneath my feet groaned the house's bones—and, yes, a few feet ahead, a creak that shouldn't have been there. Someone was walking around my room.

I crept to the door, silent, just as a hundred nights in the woods on the Madinabic moons had trained me—and threw open the door.

"Shit," said the girl, and dropped the instruction manual.

My first thought was that I had seen her face before. Good gods, it had been recently—it had been on the day of Flavia's funeral, and she had been standing at Julhan's left hand. There was a large pack slung over her shoulder. She was bent over my desk, and she'd yanked open one of my drawers.

"Not the first time a crewman's tried to surprise me in my bedroom after hours, funnily enough," I said, letting the door swing shut behind me. "But I don't recall you from *Taraxandran*'s manifest."

Her jaw worked, but she didn't speak. "Shy, is that it?" I said.

"You aren't dressed for that kind of surprise, anyway." Between the two of us lay thirteen feet of imported rug I'd taken up from the war room; four or five tablets I'd thrown onto the floor that morning; one discarded wine bottle; and, of course, the solid oak desk, which came up to her waist.

"Now let me see," I went on. "There's no men patrolling the eastern wall, but it's sheer sandstone, and if you're a spider or a lizard, you're wearing a very good disguise. Besides, there's no windows there—ah, but there's the skylight in the roof. And enough room beside it for a soft landing. I see. I used that trick myself once in Ceiao, did you know? Oh—don't, thanks."

She'd reached for the tablet. "I've had enough chases lately," I said pleasantly, stepping forward. "These knees aren't so young anymore, you know."

I hadn't been watching her hands, and without warning, one of them flashed to her hip. When it came up, she was brandishing a knife. "S-stay where you are," she said.

I cocked my head, considering. Then I shrugged and came forward across the carpet.

"I'm serious," said the thief, high-pitched, and slashed wildly at the air. "Don't move!"

"Of course," I said soothingly, and slid left, ducked her slash, seized her wrist, smashed her hand into the wood of the desk, and wrenched the knife from her unresisting fingers. "Who in the name of Alekso of Sintia trained you?" I went on, with some interest. "Is this what they're teaching in schools these days?"

The thief moaned, cradling her hand to her chest. "No, hold on," I said, hooked my elbow through hers, and tugged her in close. She was tall, but there was no grace to her. She stumbled and banged her hip against the desk. I tucked her into my side, so that I could feel her rapid breath against my body, and with my free hand I flipped the knife so that the blade rested flat on my palm. "This is a mercy knife," I said. "For the mercy kill—see?"

and I pressed my thumb to the ricasso and swung the knife in a neat arc until it hovered half an inch from the hollow of her throat.

She stopped breathing. Her eyes were as round as moons. "What you don't want," I said into her ear, "is to cut me. You see the edge?" I tilted the knife so its edge crossed her pulse, and brushed it very gently against her skin. "Much duller," I murmured. "Don't go slicing, not with this. A neck isn't a loaf of bread, eh?"

"Please," she said faintly.

"Did I tell you to be polite?" I said. "No, a mercy knife isn't a thief's weapon. It's for the field. The sharpness is at the point, see?" and I pulled the blade away from her neck and, before she could exhale, flicked that point up to her eye. "For men with gut wounds," I added pleasantly, watching her pupils dart back and forth. "Mercy. Do you understand?" I tossed the blade in the air, caught it by the hilt, and twisted my hand so that it disappeared. "Now who is it that hates you?"

She gaped like a drowning man. I shoved her away and watched her go stumbling into the wall with great amusement. "Who told you to carry a knife you can't use worth a damn? Hell, how *did* you come to your age without being able to use a mercy knife worth a damn? You're not some backwater Kutayeti. A good Ceian girl, aren't you?"

"I'm not Ceian," she said, so quickly that I knew it was reflexive.

"Colonial?" I said. "Your accent's Ceian. Where are your people from, the Vigesimal Colonies?" Her face went flat with fear, but I waved a hand and said, "Doesn't matter. It's where you're going that interests me. Sit down, won't you? You're giving me a neck-ache."

My bedsheets were cheap tartan, but they wadded up easily enough. I looped the makeshift rope round the girl's arms a few times—no point tying her tight; if she could unpick knots with any skill, I was a Madinabic goatherd—and leaned on the desk, examining the knife more closely. I had thought it was some cheap market trinket. Under the lamplight, though, the metal iridesced in a way that ordinary steel never did.

"Who'd make a knife out of quicksilver pearl?" I said, astonished.

The thief shook her head. I tapped it against my palm. "Who'd you steal it from?"

That got her attention. She shot upright in the chair, jaw jutting forward like a propaganda holo. "I didn't steal it!" she said.

Her outrage was so vivid that I was near sure it was truth, but I laughed anyway. "Break into some mansion on the Avenuan, did you?" I said. "Or one of the smugglers selling sunken treasure out of Szayet's atmosphere—did you buy it off one of them? Or did you take it from some prisoner of a Ceian war?" That last earned a flinch, and I leaned forward, interested. "Which part? The war, or the prisoner?"

"It was a gift," she said tightly.

"A costly gift," I said. "Fine, then. Tell me something else. Why'd Julhan pick a nice desk-job sort of girl who's never seen action rougher than a dogfight to do a cutpurse's job?"

Her jaw stiffened. "I'm not a—a desk-job girl," she said.

"My mistake," I said, and jerked the knife as if I were about to swing it at her cheek. She squeaked. "A real veteran, Lieutenant Thief," I said, grinning. "Has Julhan sent every gangster in the city into prison? Couldn't he find even one who'd work for Flavia Decretan's murderer?"

"I—I was only supposed to—to make a copy for the demipotestate," she said, voice shaking. "I read Malisintian." That made me raise my eyebrows—fluent Ceian from a girl born in one of Ceiao's neighboring star systems was one thing, but an education in Sintian history was quite another—but she continued, "He said, he—he wanted someone who'd been near the Fortunatas. Who'd been caught in your explosion."

I was startled, but I tried not to show it. I hadn't realized any Ceian ships had been caught in that explosion besides mine. "Why should that matter?" I said.

"The admiral s-said, it would work out all right if you caught me," said the thief. "Because—because, if you caught me, I could tell you what happened to your sister."

I sat down on the desk and laid the knife on my knee, its point toward her. "Start at the beginning," I said.

They'd left Itsaryet, by my reckoning, about a week before the Kutayeti invasion. I'd been right that she'd never really seen combat. She'd been a prison guard, she said—and then stammered a great deal, which I privately took to mean she hadn't been a good one—and her squadron had been one of the last to abandon the planet. By that time, they were chasing the rest of the fleet back to the Crossbar, and all cover for their retreat had vanished. They'd needed to find an odd route back to Ceiao, and so they'd found one: banking round the Kutayeti border, ducking and weaving toward the galaxy's center—

"The antimatter in my ship's engine failed half a million leagues from the Black Maw," she said.

"Liar," I said, reflex borne of a thousand piloting classes. *Protect the antimatter*, our teachers had said, over and over. *Let them hit your cannon, let them hit your wing. If the antimatter fails, there won't even be scrap metal for your parents to bury.*

She shook her head urgently. "I'd tell you a better lie, if I wanted to lie to you," she said.

"You are a piece of work, aren't you?" I said. That was an Otávio Julhan sort of answer. No wonder she'd caught his eye. "Who should I believe: you, or my eyes? You don't look dead."

"What does dead look like?" said the ghost into my ear. I flinched. It sat beside me on the desk, kicking its legs like a bored child. In life, Ceirran had never fidgeted.

"I was the only one awake when it happened," she said. "I was lying in my cot, looking at that." She jerked her chin toward the knife on my knee.

"When what happened?" I said.

She shut her eyes.

"The way that a wave rolls toward the shoreline in the river Nevede, only a ridge at first, then gathering speed," she said, "that was how the shock came over the ship. It rolled down from the bow, across the beds. It lifted me and my fellows from our cots. Then it passed, and we all tumbled onto our beds again, and yet no one woke." She frowned. "I got out of bed and went to the starboard window," she said. "I saw one of the other ships. All of its navigators were on the bridge, and why that was, I couldn't understand. It was sleeping hours. They should have had a skeleton crew. But they moved like—"

She opened her eyes. Her stutter had vanished altogether, and she was staring a little to my right, as though she were watching something on the far wall. But when I turned to look, it was only the ghost, and the ghost smiled and smiled and said nothing at all.

"My father used to say that, in the old country, when wishing still worked," she said, "there was once a man with a clockwork heart. When his wife wound him up, he would move twice as fast as other men; then he would go slower, slower, until he stopped. That was how the crew of the other ship moved—too slow, too slow... So I knew they were moving faster than lightspeed, and we were moving slower. I knew our antimatter had vanished. And I knew that we were going to die."

"Then how is it that you didn't die?" I said sharply to her. "What do you mean me to believe—that you got on your knees and prayed for the engines to work?"

That seemed to break the spell. The thief looked down, swallowed, and twisted her hands in her lap, once again the shy creature she'd been.

"I didn't get on my knees," she said.

"But you did pray," I said, astonished. "You really aren't a Ceian, are you?"

"The ship began to shake," said the girl to her knees. "My hands shook—I cut myself with the knife, on accident, right across my knuckles. And I thought of when I found the knife, and the priestess said—well, I thought of someone who I—I remember thinking: I'll do anything. I'll give anything. I'll give up everything I have, I'll give up everything I am, I'll hollow myself out, just so long as I can live.

"And then—" She looked up. "And then I was in my bed again. And the ship was still."

"You'd dreamed it all," I said.

The thief shook her head. "Untie my hands and look," she said.

I did not move to untie her hands. I knew it was there, as it had been there in my vision of Flavia unpacking dresses in my bedroom: that fading old scratch, the hurt I had never borne, the dream that had not been a dream.

What happened to your sister, she'd said. Julhan had guessed at something when he'd heard this story, something vital. The antimatter in the thief's ship had been destroyed—just as Flavia's had. But in that very instant, the pearl knife had changed. It had gained some power. It had answered the thief's prayer, and pulled her backward in time, into an instant when the antimatter had been in the engine again. So it had saved her ship from disaster and death.

Effect before cause, and future before past. Time, folded in on itself. Those of us at the eye of the storm had seen our ship thrown into disarray, the pearl in our tablets warped. There must have been some kind of computer in the knife—not a complex intelligence, not like the Terrestrial Intelligence or like the Pearl of the Dead, but an intelligence nonetheless. A priestess, she'd said? Had Alekso of Sintia himself made this knife?

Szayet said Alekso had been able to see most of what happened in the palace at Alectelo, and able to send dreams. If this knife had answered the thief's prayer then, perhaps it had answered little prayers before. If it had been anything very powerful, I would have already heard of it, and I would have heard that it had been stolen. But in the storm, it had gained new power.

When the laboratory had exploded, when all those isolated minds had screamed out at once, when that wave of Black Maw energy had gone rushing out from the diamond planet through our ship and through hers—it had taken the energy in, just as the pearl in the hosts of the Terrestrial Intelligence had taken the energy in. It had used it to save her life.

It had not saved Flavia's. If my sister had prayed to live when the antimatter in her ship had failed—when I had caused its failure—no one and nothing had been listening.

The manual still lay where the thief had dropped it. I went round to pick it up, and crouched there awhile, digging my fingers into the carpet, trying to breathe.

"Otávio pig-blooded half-souled Julhan," I said at last. "Boy calls himself grown and not an hour goes by that he doesn't send a messenger to whine and weep, *It wasn't my fault.*"

"So whose fault was it?" said the ghost.

"He sent her into exile," I snapped at it. "He put her on that ship." My eyesight blurred. I pressed the heels of my hands against my eyes, hard and aching. "She'd have been safe and sound on Ceiao during that storm if he hadn't—"

I looked up, and it was gone. I was speaking to empty air. The thief was staring.

I tossed the tablet into the desk drawer, rolled to my feet, and came over to pat her cheek, slightly harder than necessary. "I'm almost tempted to say sorry to you, since he won't," I said. "Lamb to the slaughter's not a pretty job. It would work out all right if I caught you, he said? Well, perhaps he thought it'd work out well for him. But if I started saying sorrys, the whole world would line up wanting one, and then when would I find the time to drink?" She shook her head, bewildered, and I said, "Do you know what that manual says?"

"I know that it's why we're going to have a civil war," said the thief.

The only people in the galaxy who did not have a good reason to hate me, I'd thought on the stoop: the emperor; Flavia, who was dead; and Julhan, who would be dead soon. Now the emperor and Julhan stood alone. I sat down again, grinning humorlessly. "Take my advice, little messenger-thief," I said. "Don't put too much trust in Julhan when he makes promises about peace. Did he tell you that if he had the same weapon as I have, the war would be over? He's Ceian, you know, the same as you and I. The only moment war doesn't govern us is when triumph does. And when the triumph's over..."

I slid off the desk and put my hand gently under her chin. "Don't tell Julhan thanks for the message. You'll be message enough, I'm afraid."

The girl swallowed. I could feel it against the pad of my forefinger. "Wait," she said. "Listen."

"Something else Julhan wanted to tell me?" I said pleasantly.

The thief shut her eyes. "Sometimes a vision comes upon me," she said. "A vision of the way the world will be—or the way it could be, unless something is done."

I laughed. "I've heard this kind of thing before. Spend a little more time on Szayet, thief, before you claim to speak in prophecies."

"It was in the Szayeti skies that I saw the ships," she said. "Ceiao's ships. So thick and silver that they blotted out the sun, and they rained fire. And the pearl city burned, and the islands burned. All that the Oracle loves became ash."

I reared back. Her voice had changed: distant, deep in her throat, shockingly hollow. Her eyes were shut.

"You think that what you risk in war is yourself," she said.

"It won't be. It's Alectelo that lies on the sacrificial altar, and it's Alectelo whose throat is under the knife. Even if you win against Admiral Ceirran, even if you make yourself sole power of Ceiao—what happens when you die? What will the next commander do to Szayet, when he knows the right rival could use that great war chest of pearl and gold to launch a rebellion? There will be no more Szayeti Oracles. There will be no more Pearls of the Dead. There will be no more feasts, no more dancing, no more music when the moons are high. There will be no more places where you are welcome. A Ceian governor will sleep in your lover's bed—if he bothers to live in the palace, rather than in some mansion bought with Szayeti tribute—and all the pearl of Alectelo he'll sell to pay for his children's dowries. And in a thousand years, the heirs to Ceiao will come to Szayet, and peer at the ruins of its towers, and shudder and laugh at its dead. And they'll wonder what it sounded like—that strange language the people spoke here, before the coming of civilization."

The knife had fallen limply to my side. This was why Julhan had sent her, I thought. This was why—not to thieve, not to copy, not even to tell me I had killed my sister, but to say these things to me, to paint this vision, colorless and terrible.

"You're a liar," I said.

"No," she said, but already I wasn't listening. From behind her, as if her shadow had decided to detach itself from her feet, a greyness was coming toward the desk. It stopped before me and reached out, not quite touching my hand.

"Anita," the ghost said, softly, kindly, "perhaps she's wrong. Perhaps it won't happen. All that matters is that you understand whose life you're putting at risk."

"I'll die first," I said. "Whatever happens to me, I swear I'll die before anyone touches a hair on Szayet's head."

"Perhaps," said the thief. Her voice was her own again, but raspy.

"Perhaps," said the ghost. "You swore to be my right hand, Anita. Perhaps Patramata will be more fortunate than I was. Perhaps, when she becomes everything to you—not just a lover you are generous to, a lover who makes you happy, but a lover to whom you have a duty, as you had a duty to your sister—perhaps a miracle will transform you. Perhaps you will become the Anita who is not selfish. Perhaps you will become the Anita who can be relied on. Perhaps you will not be the Anita who wasn't there when I died."

I raised the knife. But before the blade could pierce the awful blankness of the thing, it was gone.

The thief had flinched back on the bed. Her eyes flicked from the knife to the place where the ghost had been.

My heart was hammering. It was only words, I thought—why should it matter? It was only words and a strange voice, an actress's trick. But the vision would not leave me, the vision sat hot in my throat until I thought I must spit it out or cease to breathe: the ruins of Alectelo, crumbling and faded, and Ceians, stepping over blocks of marble, peering with uncomprehending interest at the temples, pulling out pocket knives and carving their names.

"Ceirran—" I said aloud, and blinked hard.

No rotting town of Alectelo. No shifting silver hole in the world. This was my room. These were my nails, digging into my hands. This was the noise of the men murmuring below me, and this the noise of the sea. This was my heart, my heart, my laboring and faulty heart.

What Ceirran had seen in me, the quality in me that had made him turn me into his right hand, was that I shared his own worst impulses. He had loved me because something was terrible about him, too. And when he bid me to do this thing and that and I did them, when he told me to kill and I killed, when he wanted me on my knees at his triumph before the city and I knelt and I kissed his hand, he controlled that terrible thing, he controlled himself, he made me safe for the world.

Two people in all the galaxy who did not have a justifiable reason to hate me. And one person who, against all odds—against my unreliability, my stupidity, my selfishness, the animal violence that had once been bound and bridled to a greater purpose, and now could only hurt—who, against everything that I was, did not hate me yet. I had failed Flavia, and she could not forgive me. I would fail Szayet, and she would never forgive me. I had failed Ceiao a thousand times, and Otávio Julhan—

Julhan thought he had something of Ceirran in him.

Oh, it would hurt. Ceirran's bones, it would hurt. When you were dreaming, hurt always woke you up.

The thief was staring up at me. I set the pearl knife down carefully on the desk.

"Call your master," I said. "Tell him—"

"What?" said the ghost's voice, directly into my ear, and I imagined that I could feel my friend's breath.

I said, "Yes."

Otávio Julhan Ceirran, child of Felipe Julhan (deceased), ranked Admiral, the Lord of Arqueiran and the Shieldmirror, Demipotestate for Confirming the Freedom of the City with Conciliary Power, citizen, aged 20, childless, consents to the following:

> that in a time not exceeding three market cycles, he will enter into marriage with Ana Decretan, child of Captain Mara Decretan (deceased), citizen, childless, aged 26;
>
> that his family will be considered at one with the family of Ana Decretan, and any parents, siblings, children, or other relations of the spouses will be considered siblings to one another, in the eyes of the law;
>
> that his name and property will be held in common with Ana Decretan, his wedded spouse;
>
> that, subject to the above, he solemnly swears that he is not subject to any heritable illness, bodily imperfections, or other conditions incapacitating him from service to the Ceian state;
>
> that he swears he is not party to any separate legal marriage contract at the time of signing; nor has he cohabited with another adult Ceian citizen for longer than a period of one year;
>
> that he will be considered liable for all violations of the marriage union on his part, including adultery, illegal violence, and illegal dissolution;

that the condition of any children resulting from marriage, by crèche or other means, will follow the legal condition of Ana Decretan, being Ceian citizens, and members of the Merchants' Council, and that in addition they will be considered natural heirs to all business, property, or money owned by Ana Decretan at the time of her death.

Ana Decretan, child of Mara Decretan (deceased), ranked Admiral, the Lady of the Crossbar and the Swordbelt Arm, Demipotestate for Confirming the Freedom of the City with Conciliary Power, citizen, aged 26, childless, consents to the following:

that in a time not exceeding three market cycles, she will enter into marriage with Otávio Julhan Ceirran, child of Filipe Julhan (deceased), ensign, citizen, childless, aged 20;

that her family will be considered at one with the family of Otávio Julhan Ceirran, and any parents, siblings, children, or other relations of the spouses will be considered siblings to one another, in the eyes of the law;

that her name and property will be held in common with Otávio Julhan Ceirran, her wedded spouse;

that, subject to the above, she solemnly swears that she is not subject to any heritable illness, bodily imperfections, or other conditions incapacitating her from service to the Ceian state;

that she swears she is not party to any separate legal marriage contract at the time of signing; nor has she cohabited with another adult Ceian citizen for longer than a period of one year;

that she will be considered liable for all violations of the
marriage union on her part, including adultery, illegal
violence, and illegal dissolution;

that the condition of any children resulting from marriage, by crèche or other means, will follow the legal
condition of Ana Decretan, being Ceian citizens, and
members of the Merchants' Council, and that in addition they will be considered natural heirs to all business, property, or money owned by Ana Decretan at
the time of her death;

Both parties consent that:

all military hostilities between said parties including, but
not limited to, themselves and members of the fleet
sworn to them, shall cease;

that reparations to Ceian citizens injured or killed in
advance of the signing of this contract shall be mutu-
ally forgiven, and paid from the treasury of the Merchants' Council;

that each party's titles shall not be considered among the
property held in common by the parties;

that residency shall be recorded at the house with address
at ———, the Avenuan Libeirguitan, belonging at
present time to Otávio Julhan Ceirran as inheritance
from Commander Matheus Ceirran;

that the dowry will be paid from the treasury of Commander Matheus Ceirran, in a sum not exceeding…

For some time, I could keep this second set of notebooks a secret
from C.—putting them inside my pillowcase, sliding them under
my tablets. Now, though, they're growing bulky. I saw him look-
ing at them on the bench beside me today. I thought he would

ask me what they were, but he only asked me why I wanted this contract. "How are you going to use it?" he said.

I'm not going to use it, I said. I just want to have it. It's just a part of the truth, is all.

"Only a part," he said. I asked him what he meant, and he said, "If you could open every record in the Archives—if you could read every Ceian's life, start to finish, birth and death, children—there wouldn't be one marriage contract among them that would look any different from this. If they loved, the contract just held a part of how they loved."

Then the attendant came with the drugs for the afternoon, and the two of them helped me inside, and C. carried in the tablet with my poem, and the notebooks with this second history. He hadn't spoken all this while, and when I'd been laid in bed and he'd tucked the blanket up under my chin, he said, "But it's the only part that matters, because it's the only part that lasts."

I was falling asleep, then, and I forgot that I was afraid of him. So I asked him whether he was going to take my second set of notebooks and read them while I was sleeping.

"While you're sleeping? No," he said. "I can wait."

—V.

CHAPTER

TEN

Flavia's face:

Rounder than mine. Her cheeks fuller, her nose thinner, a clean curve where mine was scuffed and scarred. Her chin, coming to a hard point, which gave her a certain decided air that she would not have otherwise possessed.

Her eyes, the cool deep color of scorched wood. Our mother's eyes had never stayed still—skittering from me to her, from her bed to her drink, from the laces of her dress to her shaking hands. Whatever strange alchemy had been present in the crèche, it had taken those eyes from us. Flavia, like me, had a snake's gaze, steady, patient, unbroken. She was, for nineteen years of my life, the only person I knew who could outstare me.

Her full mouth, ordinarily painted in burgundy, now bare and pinkish brown. The laughing twist to it, which would take so many years to grow cruel. She pinched her lips together and tilted her cheek. I swept the red paintbrush down.

Flavia's clothing, on the day of her wedding:

A wreath of hyssop and tiger lilies. A net of yellow threads, into which I carefully bound her hair. I fixed its knot at the nape of her neck with a golden hairpin shaped like a spear. Roses tied at her wrists, and roses tied at her ankles, above her soft yellow shoes. A red dress, orange-beaded and garnet-hemmed, bound around the waist with a girdle of glittering golden coins, which would be torn from her later that night.

There should have been a veil. This she had refused.

"It is the tradition, madam," said the woman Teo Pulcron had sent to bring our wedding clothes. "The oldest in the city. It dates from the years of the founding, when our ancestors took their brides and grooms from the nearby planets. They hid the strangers' faces so their families would not know them, and they built upon those marriages a thriving Ceian stock."

"I am not a stranger to Ceiao," said Flavia. She was looking at me. "I won't hide my face for this."

Flavia's feet on a soft white sheepskin. Flavia's right hand, bound in white thread with Teo Pulcron's. Flavia's eyes, glittering under the lights of the hawthorn lanterns. Her painted face, chin jutting upward, waiting for the kiss.

The rain had come down at last from its hesitation at the peak of Montan Bau, and it had come down hard. The air inside the little shed by the Nevede was close and hot. The windows were more motion than glass, and the lights of passing spider-litters snaked down the faces of the official and of Captain Águeda Vipsânian.

"Who will stand as witness for the first party?" said the official. She was an elderly clerk, an inspector stationed along the waterfront. Semfontan had appointed her a hundred thousand years ago, when Flavia had been living at Pulcron's house, and I had been sleeping alone in my mother's old bedroom with the grey mold spreading over the ceiling.

"I will stand as witness for Otávio Julhan Ceirran," said Julhan's captain, Cecílio Maicenan, "before Justice and the city." His voice was clipped and cool. He lifted his hand.

Julhan had been by the door. Now he came forward, put his hand in Maicenan's and faced the official. Someone had dressed him in red, someone had laid a crown of myrtle on his head, someone had painted the backs of his hands in rose madder. I did not think he had done it himself, because the leaves were spotted with black, the paint smudged along his left knuckle. Julhan, I thought, could be cursed for many things, but never for a failure to catch the details.

"And who will stand as witness to the second party?" said the official.

"I will stand as witness for Ana Decretan before Justice and the city," said his other captain, Águeda Vipsânian, and held out her hand. I laid my palm over hers. I had not been able to bear the thought of asking one of my men to witness. I did not want them to see.

"I'll watch," said the ghost softly from the wall. I didn't look in its direction.

The official looked from me to Julhan. "Since the most ancient days of Ceiao," she said, "when the barbarian tribes were driven out to the moons, and our ancestors' long flight from their burning city came to an end, the rite of marriage has been the great boon of our people. It is a union of not only property, but name; not only name, but fortune; not only fortune, but legacy. Do you enter this marriage in that full knowledge?"

"Do you want to do this?" the ghost whispered.

"I do," I said.

"I do," said Julhan.

"In your unity is a declaration of peace," said the official. "The past is gone. Your parents were never yours alone. Your siblings were never yours alone. Your children always belonged to one another. There are no sins of the fathers in Ceiao. Here in this room is the family, here alone is the family. Your union holds all your families' history, and all your families' promises. Do you enter this marriage in that full spirit?"

"I do," said Julhan.

"Do you know what you want?" whispered the ghost, dust-dry.

"I do," I said.

"May the marriage be witnessed," said the official. Águeda took the hawthorn lantern leaning against the wall and reached up to light it. On the other side of the shed, Maicenan was unrolling a sheepskin.

"May the couple be granted a home," the official said. Julhan glanced at me. I stepped forward, onto the sheepskin, and he followed.

"May the couple be united," said the official. In the light of the hawthorn lantern, Julhan's body was an outline of itself, sketched lightly on the air: here a cheekbone, here the whites of the slate-grey eyes, here his nails and the bones of his thin wrist. The official lifted a length of white thread.

"In the name of the city of Ceiao, and the—in the name of Matheus Ceirran," she said, stumbling a little over the second phrase, "I bring forth the thread of peace, which our ancestors spun in the houses that war had won them. Let all who are wandering come home to one another. Until now, you were two. From this moment, you are one."

She wound the thread round: my wrist, Julhan's knuckles, my knuckles, Julhan's wrist. The loop. The knot.

She drew it tight.

Turtledoves burst out of Pulcron's cages, a flurry of frantic grey and brown. The leaves of his apple trees rustled, hardly audible beneath the applause.

In Pulcron's ballroom, where Flavia would host a thousand parties in years to come, there had been imported custard apples and sweetsop nectar and broiled stingrays from faraway colonies; there had been gold leaf scattered on the tile, clinging to our sandals and ankles when we scuffed our heels; there had been musicians perched like vultures on the stairs. Who had I danced with? Sonia Couron, twice; Sérgio Catílion; Quinha Semfontan, avuncular, sneering; Jonata Barran, barely old enough for the fleet, who blushed fiercely when I touched their hand. Four corpses, waiting for their pyres. They would have them within the decade. I had laughed, stolen a kiss from Sonia behind a pillar, and gone out to sit drunk upon the balcony.

After a while, the rain had come. I had tipped my chair back and put my feet up on the edge of the balcony, and let it collect in the hollow of my throat, above the swell of my belly, between my legs. It had made no difference to the wine, or perhaps I'd been so drunk that I couldn't tell anymore what was salt water and what sweetness. I hadn't, I'd thought, been unhappy. It had been a very clear thought—certainly far clearer than the decision not to go inside, which had happened on some seafloor of my mind, far below the current and sunlight. I had not been unhappy at all.

After twenty minutes or so the rain had ceased, much more abruptly than rain usually did. I flopped my head backward and saw Teo Pulcron holding an umbrella over my face.

"Ah," I said. "I suppose this is where you tell me you really do love her, and you'll be sure to protect her, and all you want is my respect and approval?"

"Certainly not," said Pulcron. "There's nowhere else in my house to smoke sílfion privately. I expect you'll want me to share?"

I considered this—whether Pulcron might feel that it was a metaphor for something—and decided that no one who knew me would speak in metaphors if they wanted me to understand them, and that I badly needed a smoke. "Give it to me," I said, and held the cigarette carefully in my teeth while Pulcron lit the match.

We sat in silence, trading the cigarette back and forth. He had to smoke quite carefully, I noticed, because he was holding the umbrella over me, rather than himself. His right arm was entirely drenched. I thought I might be being manipulated, and tried to find it in myself to dislike it.

"Suppose I were to tell you," he said, exhaling smoke, "that I would make a bargain with you. That I would love her, and protect her, and sometimes you would do some little service for me or for friends of mine. Not often. Every now and then."

"Oh, I'd kill you," I said.

Pulcron laughed, sounding delighted. "You really would, wouldn't you? And not stop to think about whether it would help you at all. We're both very lucky I'm not that sort of person."

I had not realized that this was a sort of person it was possible to not be. I looked at Pulcron out of the corner of my eye, and found that he was looking back, studying me with a careful and not unkind eye.

"I could tell you that I'd love her and protect her, and in exchange, you'd try to have a little decorum," he said.

I snorted hard, and he cracked a grin. He was not, I thought, aging into grace. His thick hair was running to grey, his arms to fat. The family Pulcron was an old one, but there was a kind of vulgarity in his face of which I found myself abruptly, helplessly envious.

The grin twitched and became something unpleasantly sympathetic. "I have better things to do than to tell you to behave," he said. "It's my wedding night, you know. But take care when you want to brag that you can't be bought. If it makes a soft touch like me uncomfortable—and it does, believe me—I shudder to think how uncomfortable it would make someone with any proper civic feeling."

"You haven't even offered me any money. Who says I can't be bought?" I said petulantly.

That face was softer than I had thought. In the rain behind us, its edges were blurry, gleaming silver. "Then name your price, Captain," he said, in quite a different voice.

I stepped back against the edge of the balcony. The umbrella didn't move with me. The rain was in my collar, leaking down my spine, dripping into my hair. It shouldn't have been so warm, I thought. Spring was far too early for this kind of slithering dead heat. I blinked and scrubbed at my eyes. "Just up here," Julhan said, and I heard the door creak open, and scrambled up after him into the dry cool spider-litter.

It jolted and began to move. The lord of Arqueiran and the Shieldmirror reached across me and drew the curtain, leaving us in rain-speckled shadows.

"Groom," I said, extending a hand.

He stared at me, that blank grey stare, and took it. His hand was like snakeskin, dry and warm.

"Bride," he said. We shook. And when we let go, I reached inside my cloak and took out the instruction manual.

He turned his palm up. I laid the tablet there, and he grasped it firmly in both hands and looked at it, expression unreadable. For a long second I was afraid—then he laid it on the floor of the litter and stamped hard. The tablet cracked in two.

"You've allowed the inspectors into your ships and quarters to destroy the copies?" he said.

"Yes," I said. There were no copies. I'd told him so. He'd insisted on the inspectors anyway, and I had had neither the energy to blame him nor to fight.

"Then it's finished," he said.

"Yes," I said, and leaned my forehead against the cool window. Between me and the glass was the curtain, and the cloth itched at my forehead, and grew warm and damp where my wet hair soaked it. I had an ache along my shoulder blades that told me I had done nothing for several days but sit down, and I had an itch where my breastband met my ribs that promised two or three new spots would push up there soon. Besides Julhan's breathing and my own, there was no noise in the cabin.

I said, "Are you sorry that you asked me yet?"

"No," said Julhan.

Outside clattered the legs of other spider-litters, the shoes of Ceians weaving along the wet concrete beside us. "How about now?" I said.

He was quiet for a second or two, then said, "I have a piece of advice, Admiral, if you'll let me give it to you."

"Admiral?" I said.

"Would you rather I called you *darling?*" he said, mouth curling, and before I could recover myself enough from the fact that he'd made a joke to decide whether I'd laugh, he said, "You're not a prisoner. Neither you nor I came into this marriage with any illusions—not about each other, and certainly not about ourselves. I have carried the weight of Ceirran's name for a long time. It is no light burden. You are carrying your griefs, and those are heavier still. Why carry the intention to be unhappy?"

I looked up. The ghost was sitting on the cushion beside him. Its hand overlaid his hand, the one around which the official had tied the white thread.

"Well done," it said softly.

"All right," I said. "All right."

The litter stopped with the rain. On the Avenuan Libeirgui-tan, bronze puddles shone in the oak roots. Julhan slid out onto the street and went up the house's steps without looking back to see if I was following.

It was familiar, and it was a stranger to me. Hedges now sat to either side of the steps. The lamp above the door had been gold, and now it was paper-white. The front windows were invisible in the dark. Ceirran had kept a light on in the highest window, day and night. "Naturally. Why should our enemies know when you're at home and when you aren't?" I'd said, pleased, and he'd said—

"Why should my friends think there's an hour of the day when they aren't welcome?" said the ghost.

Julhan had stripped Ceirran's carpet from the entrance hall. When I emerged into the sitting room, his servants were lighting the lamps, drawing the curtains over the back garden windows, unlocking the shutters on the upper balconies and opening them to the damp cool wind. We sat on the couches, me sprawled like a dog, Otávio folding his long skinny limbs down with great precision.

It occurred to me, absurdly, that I did not know if we had spent four hours in a room together since we'd made the proscription lists. Now he looked at me, and I recognized the wariness on his face as identical to my own. My own words from before the wedding came back to me—*You don't want to marry me. The rest of your life*—and I felt a horrible kind of pity crawl up in my gut.

Why carry the intention to be unhappy? he had said.

Very well. I allowed myself to think it—and it was such a sick relief, such a lessening of weight: It would not all be misery. Some days would feel ordinary. Some days, I would smile. I would pity him, and he would pity me. We would work together. There would be fondness, after a few years. After a few decades there might even be love—the kind of love that came, whether or not you wanted it, when another person knew you. The kind of love Szayet would have given me, if I'd let her.

"To business, then," I said.

"To business," said Otávio, with visible relief, sitting upright. "I'm giving the order to restore our troops to the Swordbelt colonies. There are a few problem areas, which you'll know—" He snapped his fingers. A servant dressed in black appeared from behind the couch, laid a tablet in his hands, and vanished toward the kitchens.

"The bulk of the fleet's not behind these blockades," I said, tapping the lines floating around Itsaryet. "There's open movement for them, if I can use it. We still have the numbers—even these things can't wipe out all of us at once, not with our level of firepower. I'll take two hundred ships, rally around Belkayet—"

Otávio looked troubled. "Admiral, with respect—" he said.

"Fortune's sake, if we don't have anything else, can you be a human being?" I said roughly.

"Ana," he said, and looked down. "With respect, I'm requesting that you not return to the Swordbelt Arm for now. At least not without me."

"I'll have a hard time fighting battles from this house," I said after a moment.

"You have captains to fight your battles," said Otávio. "I know I am young, but it seems to me that an admiral's duty should not be to fight battles, but to win wars."

He had a point, which I did not like. "My men will miss me," I said.

"I know," he said. "I know that you're close to your men. The whole empire has heard that you eat meals with them, and gamble with them, and in the past have even—" He looked distinctly uncomfortable, and did not say *slept with them*, though I was dead certain he was thinking it. "You understand that we're married now."

"A married woman can eat meals with who she likes, as far as I know," I said, and regretted it at once when, rather than rising to the bait, he rubbed his hand over his mouth, looking far more tired than a boy his age should have known how to do. *The rest of your life*, my own voice sang in my ear, a mosquito.

"A married woman can," he said. "As for a demipotestate of Ceiao—" He sighed. "Do you know how I heard the news my cousin was dead?"

I shook my head mutely. When we'd met, he had been newly arrived from Sintia and already helping me plot Túlio Cachoeiran's murder. I had been wrapped up in Flavia and in bloodlust. Personal questions had not been of interest.

"When I met my cousin, in that battle against the pirates on Far Madinabia, I became very sick," he said. "The doctors sent me to recover on Sintia with my friends. Then Councillor Barboulethan sent my friend Maicenan the news that Matheus Ceirran had made me his heir. In the space of a second I had gone from an ordinary man to the owner of his money, his land, his place on the council—and his enemies, too. I thought I would die within the month, and most likely die penniless, landless, and powerless. I was terrified."

I stared. I had never thought, in those days, that hard-faced young man doubted his own victory—that he was capable of doubting anything. He ducked his head and went on: "But Maicenan told me, *No one can take the name.* That was true. The name was mine. I was Ceirran, and that was my place in the world. But if I were to escape Ceirran's fate, I would need to see that everything in the world had its place. My cousin did not know how heavy the name would be to carry. But what can I do but carry it? It is the only way I can restore order to the world. I must restore order. I will not be afraid again."

He sat back, looking now slightly embarrassed. "Eat meals with your men, if you must," he said. "It's only meals. But I'm afraid for you, Ana. There have to be boundaries between you and the fleet. There must be order. If it begins anywhere, it must begin with us."

The rest of your life, my voice whined again in my mind, *the rest of your life, the intention to be unhappy*—

"I want to talk about the cult of Ceirran," I said, as calmly as I could.

That threw him—or I thought it threw him; the vulnerability in his face closed over like a light, and I was left with that deadfire, curious stare. "Very well," he said. "We are married now. There are no secrets between us. All of my plans are an open book to you. What do you want to know?"

I thought of the windows in the Library of Alectelo, Ceirran enthroned, Ceirran's smiling face, Ceirran in glory, Ceirran who had slept in Szayet's bed. I thought of the long shadows of the statues, and the people calling me disciple.

Flavia had said to me, in a dream or something like a dream, *It was love because it wasn't happy—it was love because it wasn't free*. On Szayet I had been free, free to act however I wanted to act, free to be anyone I wanted to be. Here on Ceiao I was Ana Decretan, disgraced by my mother and by my own merits. On Ceiao I was all the things that Ceirran had loved, and I was incapable of being anything better.

"I want to play a part in it," I said.

"I was hoping you would say so," said Otávio.

He flicked the holo of the Swordbelt Arm away and tapped the bright red dot in the Crossbar that marked Ceiao. The map flickered to the Avenuan Libeirguitan: this house, Flavia's, the empty lot of the Libeiracópolan.

"You may have heard that I've written sermons for the Ceirran cultists in these last weeks," he said. "I suppose my plan begins with those. Our city was founded by a people who had come out of years of terrible war—as we have. They wanted to live in peace—as I do. So they lived purely. They married as the state advised, and they bore as many children as they could. They transformed the land—they made it bloom, they made it useful, they drew out every drop of wealth that it held and every hour of labor from the tribes there that they were capable of. They pushed their borders out, so that they would fear none of their neighbors. That was a world set to rights."

I looked at him, then down at the ruins of the Libeiracópolan. "Julhan," I said slowly, "that speech is priests' talk." He looked at me silently. "You aren't telling me you mean to restore the priesthood?" I said, shocked. "Kneeling, and tributes to the god, and all the rest of it?"

"No," he said. "The people can bear a god, if that god is Ceirran, but I think priests would still be a step too far for them. But

I might call myself the first among worshippers." He pointed to the Libeiracópolan. "This will be our first temple," he said. "The Temple of the Divine Ceirran."

I could only stare at him. A temple on the Avenuan Libeirguitan! On the site of the Libeiracópolan, where the priests themselves had kept their dungeons before they had been overthrown by the people a hundred and fifty years ago! It was impossible. The populace would revolt, surely—the city guard would arrest us, surely—the council would stop it, someone on the council would stop it, someone, anyone—Veguion wouldn't let it happen, Jonata Barran wouldn't let it happen, Túlio Cachoeiran would die before he let it happen—

"But I don't want the people to fear their gods, the way they did under the old priests," said Otávio. "I want them to love the cult of Ceirran." His hand drifted through the ruins of the Libeiracópolan: the clover, the cairns, the crumbled stone where its steps had once stood. "The people were best taught to love Ceirran by you."

It was suddenly difficult to find my voice. "It was Ceirran who taught them to love him," I said roughly.

"Maybe," said Otávio. "But when we build the new temples, you will be the face of the new Ceiao. You, the officer who remembered her oath to Ceirran and returned to her homeland." He leaned forward. "You can enforce the new laws. Punishments for debauchery, vice, adultery, disloyalty to the state. Rewards for bearing children. When we expand the empire, you can plant Ceiao's standard on new worlds, as you did with Ceirran on Madinabia. You can go before the people on the Avenuan Libeirguitan, as you did at his funeral, and swear loyalty and devotion at the temple. You can receive the divine Ceirran's blessing, and the divine Ceirran's forgiveness."

I could not speak.

He shrugged. "These are only ideas," he said. "Would you like me to give you a title? Champion? Most Faithful?"

I said to my knees, "Captain was always enough."

"Think it over," he said. "Find what the people would best respond to. There will be time." He hesitated. "I hope it will not hurt too much," he said.

I looked hard at him, tired-faced, thin-boned, grey from head to toe in the dim light. I had mocked him for being young a hundred times over. It struck me that he *was* young—two years older than I'd been when Ceirran had recruited me, but Fortune, that was young. He looked a hundred years old. And it seemed to me now that I could see the world through his eyes, as I sometimes had through Ceirran's, an unfolding star map of probabilities and possibilities, effects and causes, needs and desires and dreams; but where the world through Ceirran's eyes had been bright, drawn thickly with violence and fealty and hunger, the world through his was wavering, and sketched in fear and in the certainty of cost and sacrifice.

He was watching me back. "All of this can wait until the morning, if you want," he said carefully.

"Yes," I said. "All right."

He nodded and stood jerkily. "I'll wait up," he said, and went striding off toward the stairs.

Now I was alone. The night stretched out along the windowsills, crept over the floor. It was that time of evening when the light was sharper than it should have been, and it picked out every fleck of peeling paint, every exposed wire at the bottom of the wall, every slanted shadow where a chair or a table had not quite been placed parallel to its neighbor. The carpet here, too, had changed from a year and a half ago—this was rough golden stuff, Ceian-made, thick and hot and dry. Outside, by the back door, a waterspout dripped: *tick-tock*.

So this was the future, and this was being alive. This house, this boy, this world.

This wouldn't even be the first time I'd slept in Ceirran's

house. There had been a night here where I'd made myself too drunk to go home, a night there where I'd managed to stay two hours later than I'd meant to and pleaded I was afraid to walk the streets. In those days, there had been a longer couch in this sitting room—yes, here it was, shoved against the wall. Behind it, the atrium with its bubbling fountain, the skylight massed with clouds. The staircase there led up to the bedrooms. I hesitated.

He had said he did not want romance any more than I. He meant it. There would be the crèche, when the time came for our heirs. No one was going to touch me, and I was going to touch no one. I did not need to. I never would again.

Here was the corridor leading back to the entrance hall. Here was the room Ceirran had used as a library. I peeked inside, and saw bare walls, dusty windows. Here was the room where Celestino had kept his arched harp and his books of music—yes, those were gone, too, sold away. Perhaps even sold to Celestino himself, shipped to his little farm near Sintia.

Here was the boarded-up door: Ceirran's bedroom. I'd only caught glimpses inside. It had not been mine to see. Neither had it been Szayet's. That thought had once given me a fierce and terrible joy.

There was no joy now. But my heart leapt up in my chest like a turtledove, and sang, *Forgiveness, forgiveness, forgiveness.*

I said, very quietly, "Ceirran."

"Anita," said the voice of the ghost.

The relief was terrible and overwhelming. "I can't see you," I said.

"It's dark," said the ghost, with a hint of amusement.

I snorted. "Fine." And then: "Ceirran, I asked you once before." It said nothing. I said, "I'll ask you again. Are you a god?"

"I'm your evil spirit, Anita," said the ghost gently.

"Is it true what he says?" I said. "Can a divine Ceirran give me—would *you* give me—"

"What do you think?" said the ghost.

I thought that I hurt, hurt badly, aching deep down in my belly and in my throat, the way I had not hurt since the day of the funeral. I thought that the silence was falling over me again, enormous and billowing and grey, like a bride's veil. I thought that I missed Szayet, that I missed her so badly that my bones cried out. And I thought that I wanted him to give me forgiveness, and I was relieved that there was a cost to it, a terrible cost, a cost that it hurt to pay.

"Are you going to leave me?" I said.

"Not yet," said the ghost.

"All right," I said. "All right."

There will be time, Otávio had said. So there was time. We remained on Ceiao, the two of us, for ten more weeks. I did not go to the Outer City to dance or to find pretty strangers to dance with me. I did my drinking in private, and did not attend theater or races or festivals. I flew drills with my men, I inspected them, but I did not eat with them or take exercises with them. I came with Otávio to the altars, and said the sermons he wrote me. This was the least difficult of all things, because all of them began *Matheus Ceirran*, and all of them ended *mine, my own, my god*. The ghost crouched by the cairns and looked up at me with the whites showing round its eyes.

We did lay the foundations of the temple at the Libeiracópolan. Otávio drew for me the statue that he meant to put there: Ceirran bleeding, Ceirran in pain. "Others can remind the people that Ceirran is a commander, that he is a conqueror, that he is powerful," he said. "I want to remind the people that he is human. That, as he is human, they rioted in the streets for him. That, as he is human, they loved him."

I sent Szayet several letters. The first was cool, clinical, a demipotestate to her client queen: an announcement of a wedding. The second hemmed and hawed, inquired vaguely about the status of the rebellion, asked after some of my Szayeti friends in the palace, and angled without much subtlety for an invitation to Alectelo to discuss matters. To the first letter I received a reply from the palace staff: The queen of Szayet, Oracle of Alekso and Ceirran and my loyal client, congratulated the demipotestates on their union. To the second letter I received no answer at all.

The blockade of Itsaryet drew on. Our troops withdrew from the Ceian homeworld, launched themselves at Kutayeti fortifications, and failed to break them. Reports said the temple prison was operating in peace, the Kutayeti soldiers unwilling to break its sacrosanctity for a place now totally emptied of Ceian soldiers. There was no news of Szayet's sister. Delicate inquiries put to Otávio gave me no hope for extracting her—she was not a power in her own right, and she meant nothing to Ceiao. I myself had no good reason to want to please Szayet anymore. It was only the prickling memory of holding Arcelia tight so Szayet could rip the Pearl out of her ear, that night we had captured her, that kept me awake in the late hours.

We saw only one swarm, two weeks after our wedding day, which decimated all the ships we had waiting in Itsaryet's star system and then vanished. It was true what I had learned in the Fortunatas: The Terrestrial Intelligence was not reliable. To become a host for it was a death sentence, and it was difficult for the emperor to sentence so many to die, even colonials and tribesmen, when their deaths might warp time on his own homeworld, too.

Then a day arrived at the end of those ten weeks, when the wind had dried and the leaves were beginning to yellow on the linden trees, and Otávio came to me while I sat with a wine bottle in the garden, trying to remember whether this poppy bed was one that Ceirran's husband had planted. "The Kutayeti prisoner," he said to me. "They're still in your care, aren't they?"

"Vualo?" I said. "So they are." As a matter of fact, the Kutayeti court had not said a word about ransoming them since Otávio and I had married. It was as if they had forgotten about the ambassador entirely. I certainly had—I was not even sure whether I was keeping them in the city's prisons or in one of the frigates' brigs.

He nodded. "When the requests to ransom them stopped, I took the liberty of contacting my spies in the emperor's court," he said. "I thought you might like it if I asked them to investigate Ambassador Vualo's family—their history, their influence."

"Did you, now," I said, and thought of mocking him for being diligent in his schoolwork but could not summon up either the will to be unkind to him or the energy to talk further.

He took a tablet from under his arm and drew up a sheaf of letters, which he flicked through until he reached a thick black seal. "I'd like you to read this letter," he said, turning the tablet toward me.

Frowning, I peered down. It was the handwriting of a man I knew—someone who I'd counted one of my own spies in Kutayet, as a matter of fact. I hadn't realized he'd been writing to Julhan, too. I bent forward to read.

> As for the matter you inquired about: Our search of the imperial registries of noblemen in Kutayet is complete, as is our survey of sources in the Kutayeti court. No such person as Ambassador Sasha Vualo exists. There is no record of a Dom Vualo on the Kutayeti homeworld, nor among its colonies, and nor is there a record of such a family on Belkayet, Medveyet, Itsaryet, Cherekku, or any minor planet. Without a full facial scan or a blood sample, it is impossible to further determine this person's identity.
>
> There is also no record of a Carmela Lukhaya, or a Dom Lukhaya, in the imperial registries of noblemen on Kutayet, nor in Kutayet's academic records. However, our sources at the university on the Kutayeti homeworld note

that one Carmela Lucia Hashka registered for the study of quicksilver pearl some seven years ago. We were able to locate records of Lucia Naquena, a Sintian indenture, retained as a chambermaid at the Kutayeti imperial palace eighteen and one-half years prior to Carmela Lucia Hashka's university registration. Please note Hashky *or* Hashka *are the traditional surnames for natural children of the Kutayeti emperor.*

Please pass to Admiral Decretan our sincerest condolences for the loss of her sister.

Humbly, I remain—

I jerked back. "Natural children of the—" Oh, hell. I'd heard that before. Vualo had said that my clothes in Roof-without-Rain had been borrowed from one of the emperor's natural children. His bastards.

"The Kutayeti court was very eager to ransom the ambassador," I said flatly.

"Too eager," said Otávio. "I heard so from your camp."

Too eager. They hadn't wanted to give us time to think. Then, when that hadn't worked, they had gone silent—making it look as though Vualo was so unimportant that they had slipped from their memories. They had certainly slipped from mine.

A Sintian maid in the emperor's palace. A daughter. *The emperor would order me to die. Hell, the empress consort would beg me to,* Lukhaya had said. And she'd said, *Sasha's purse emptying, and the temple mothers calling me insane, obsessed, a heretic barbarian and the daughter of a heretic barbarian... So the subjects are lonely. Well, I know about lonely.*

"Vualo used familiar terms with Carmela Lukhaya—with Carmela Hashka," I said. "They were inseparable from her." When she'd died—when I'd killed her—it was as if I'd killed a part of them, too.

I understood that feeling, I thought. I understood it perfectly.

"Admi—Ana," said Otávio, "I believe we have leverage with *Dom* Harsaky to negotiate on the end of hostilities."

There was a woman inside me who sat up and spat at that. *Negotiation*, she said, *negotiation with the people who hid Ceirran's assassin from your guns? Begging to that family, groveling, getting on your knees—*

I ground my anger down. I was better than myself, now. I would be better, and I was learning to follow Otávio's lead. "We'll have peace?" I said.

"We'll have peace, and our colony returned," said Otávio. "We will have peace and Itsaryet."

To: PRISONERS' MAILROOM / in the Most Sacred and Reverent Temple of the Eternal, the Unconquered, the Seal of the Lion, Alekso the Great

From: unsigned / in the house of Admiral Otávio Julhan Ceirran, Demipotestate for Confirming the Freedom of the City with Conciliary Power, Lord of Arqueiran and the Shieldmirror, Ceiao, Ceiao

You won't get this letter, not until the Ceian army is there to deliver it, and by that time there'll be no point in sending it. But I write it down anyway, because when I see you, I'll be tongue-tied all over again.

No—that's a lie. Speaking to you isn't like speaking with these great admirals, or the other poets with their Sintian educations and Ceian jokes. It doesn't make me afraid. But I want to write this down, because I'm afraid that I'll wake up and all of it will have been a dream, and I want to have something of these promises that I can touch.

The admiral asks me to write things down, too. Conversations between councillors; the voices of farmers on the hillsides far north of the city; the way the Nevede moves when the smoke from the ships pours into it; what the people in the Archives say about Ceiao's founding, about the people who made it, about what they believed. The admiral wants to know all the prayers tucked into all the altars in the city. And I write these down, and read them aloud to him, and he asks me whether they are true, and if so, whether they are the kind of truths that a peacekeeper ought to keep.

Celia, here is the promise the admiral has made me. He says that, if I give him the years of work that a Ceian would, a soldier's term of service, he will give me land. The soldiers have nearly cleared out the wild tribes in the Madinabia E canyons, he says. Or they've carved out arable land over the pilgrim roads in Far Madinabia. Or he may remove the farmers at the bottom of the mountain and give me land on Itsaryet.

Your world, he says, which you say was so like the Ceiao of the old days. Of course you should rebuild it. We'll bury your father's bones wherever is right.

In Ceiao's smoke, I'm beginning to cough again, the way I did when I was younger. I think of writing to my people back in the camp—I could, now—but I haven't. I don't know how I would tell them what he promised to me—to me, and not to them. I try not to think of it.

Here is what I think of: your hair, and how you let me braid it around your head in my people's style, away from your strong beautiful neck. The knuckles of your hands. The night that we climbed up to the roof of the temple, and you told me first that the brightest star in the sky was Szayet's sun, and then you laughed and said no, Szayet's sun was the star farthest to the north, and then you laughed again and said Szayet's sun is that very blue star just overhead, and then you kept laughing and said, "Poet, you believe everything."

I told you that wasn't true. I hardly believed in anything, I said.

You said I was a liar. You could rattle off the whole of the last book you read to me now, you said. The way a fish, darting in the shallows of the harbor at Alectelo, swallows the fisherman's bait—that's how you swallow what you read.

I don't believe what I read, I said. I love what I read, I said.

I said, I read your letters.

And so I did want to write to you. I wanted to have these thoughts in a tablet's memory, etched into pearl, more permanent than promises. The admiral says words can outlast death. Maybe one day you'll read this letter, if you need to hold on to something that's outlasted me.

—V.

CHAPTER

ELEVEN

It was not night above Szayet, but neither was it day. The sky was the color of sickness, a deep ocher yellow, which struck out the horizon and blurred down into the dark. Round our chariot, the wheels churned fine dust. I could see through the window the plumes at my lieutenants' chariots, high thin whale-spouts of grey and brown. The chariots themselves were smeared like oils, the yellow hanging thick between their windows and ours. I thought that if I looked down at my hand on the seat, my body would have blurred, too, and I told myself not to look.

Angles and odd geometries nosed up from the horizon, a tall thin spike here, a twisting curve there. As the chariot drew onward, they grew higher, sprouted arms and spindly black legs, pressed briefly in toward the windows, leaned up toward the muddy sky. The chariot itself was traveling on a very narrow path, and had been for some time now. On the dashboard, a tablet projected a tangled green grid against the window glass.

When the black structures grew too thick and dense for the chariot to move forward, we rumbled to a stop. Captain Vipsânian unstrapped her wrists from the controls, detached the reins from the pearl dashboard, and twisted round to hand me three helmets.

I gave one to Otávio and set the other in the lap of the person who had called themself Ambassador Sasha Vualo. "Duck your head so I can untie that gag and put the helmet on you, princeling," I said. "Unless you want to breathe three-hundred-year-old ash."

Gravity was lighter here, though not as light as it should have been given the size of this moon. Otávio and I leapt softly through the crumbling grey earth, drifted under bent and broken doorways. Sasha followed a few steps behind, their stride made awkward and ungainly by their magnetic handcuffs. There was not the least breath of wind in this place, but every so often my boots or theirs or Otávio's would send a great cloud billowing up, and in the moments before it settled I could see the shapes of cobblestones, green mosaics, sidewalk curbs.

"Here," said Captain Vipsânian. We stopped dead, Sasha stumbling to a standstill beside us. I fumbled with a control in my sleeve and cut the speaking function on their helmet.

We had come into a little courtyard—I knew it had been a courtyard because two entire walls of it still stood, a gap in one of them that might once have been a gate. On the other wall, our shadows overlapped with other, smaller shadows, their arms flung wide, their legs lifted to run, cast by no one at all.

At the courtyard's far side, the world ended.

The horizon had been drawing steadily closer as we walked. Now we were at its edge. The earth plunged down, a sheer cliff of black basalt. Shifting sepias obscured its depths. Even had the air been clear, we would have seen no sea at its base, no river, only starry sky under our feet, and a half-lit blue jewel within: the planet Szayet, shining up at its shattered moon.

Sound carried well in this smoky air. We heard the first party a good minute before we saw them emerge from the left side of the courtyard: sixteen men in white helmets, white cloaks tied around the necks of their protective suits. At their head strode a very tall, heavily muscled woman, her suit painted with silver bulls, her helmet crested with plumes of gold. Her helmet visor revealed a dark, fine-boned face with thoughtful black eyes. She must have been nearing fifty, but still, the resemblance was uncanny. Carmela, I thought, must have never been able to hide.

She raised an eyebrow at me. "I see now why you claimed this territory was neutral," she said in lightly accented Sintian, "though I'll still insist on leaving before you do. I hope you don't mind the distrust. Stepping on billions of dead does sharpen my sense of caution. Hello, Sashenka! What mess have you gotten yourself into now?"

Sasha said something loudly, incomprehensible through the helmet. "I have no objection to your leaving first, as long as we both depart with what was agreed to in the holo call," said Otávio.

"Charming to meet you, by the way," I said. "I'm the lady of the Swordbelt Arm."

"Oh, yes," she said, waving irritably at the air as if swatting away a fly. "I have the honor to be Polina Harsakaya, Hand-maiden of the Holy Flame, heir apparent to *Dom* Harsaky, Crown Prince of the Empire of Kutayet, and so on and so forth. And you're Otávio Ceirran and Ana Decretan, and you have titles that we'll pretend I've said. I heard you've gotten married. I suppose congratulations are the done thing?"

Otávio coughed. "We'll pretend you've given them," I said.

"Excellent," said Prince Polina. "There's no chance of us moving directly to business before the witness arrives, is there? I've never had much patience for tardiness, and Father wants Sasha—ah, there we are."

This time the servants streamed in before their master: a dozen in red suits and red helmets, fanning out to each side, and then, picking her way slowly through them, wearing a suit brushed with dust of rubies, her shoulders draped with a deep red velvet mantle, her sleeves embroidered with gold, her eyes swallowed in black kohl, her head held high, walked the queen of Szayet.

"My lady," I said.

"Hail to the Crown Prince of Kutayet and the lady of the Swordbelt Arm," she said without looking at me. Her voice was hoarse. "You have seen fit to summon me to this hallowed ground of Ostrayet in order to witness your mutual peace."

"And to answer the grievances of our client queen, the Oracle of Szayet," said Otávio, after a pause.

Szayet's face was the face of a statue. "You are authorized to negotiate on behalf of the emperor, Highness?" she said to Polina.

"Good Lord, I should hope so," said Polina. "Yes, all right. Father will agree to the complete dismantling of the blockade around Itsaryet and to the evacuation of our troops there. I thought it was too generous, but he's not in the mood for argument. Who can blame him, I suppose? Poor Sasha." Sasha said something unintelligible again, and Prince Polina sighed. "Yes, and poor Carmelita," she said. "What an unfortunate duck she always was."

"And reparations for Szayet," I said. "You agreed to reparations for the attack on Szayet."

"We did," said Polina thoughtfully. "You neglected to inform us you'd been in the Fortunatas just before the explosion at that laboratory." I tensed, and she sighed. "Ceians do *talk*, you know, Admiral," she said. "In fact, the amount you people talk, I wonder you have time to conquer anyone. Father says he'll think about reparations once you can scrape two hundred years of rust off of half the mines caught in the backwash. Well, we'll say the way I phrased that sounded politic. I'm very sorry to disappoint you, Oracle—though it's really you who should be asking for this, isn't it? Maybe you'll do better when you do your own bargaining."

"I have no hostage to offer the emperor in exchange for any generosity he might choose to extend me," said Szayet roughly. "You may convey to him that the Oracle of Szayet was unsurprised."

"Excellent! I will," said Prince Polina. "And speaking of hostages—"

"Yes," I said, tearing my eyes away from Szayet. "All right. Let's get this over with."

Sasha stepped forward. I flicked the switches in my sleeve that disabled their speech and powered the magnet cuffs, and their wrists sprang free. They turned and fixed me with a long, hot stare, and I wondered with almost giddy anticipation whether they meant to hit me—but they only turned back and strode across the courtyard toward their sister. She pulled them into a short embrace, thumping their back with her fist.

"Polya," they said, and then a brief flood of Kutayeti. From the few scraps I had, I caught the words *Carmelita*, *pearl*, *God*, and what I thought was probably *sister*. Prince Polina's eyebrows shot up behind the helmet visor, but she hushed Sasha and patted at their elbow.

"Yes, rabbit," she said soothingly in Sintian. "Don't worry. I'll take care of everything." She smiled a little. "At least that's put paid to intelligence work in Ceiao for a little while, hasn't it? I'm afraid Mother's told-you-sos will be exhausting. Well, I'm sure you'll find an alias that'll hold one of these days."

"There's the mutual disarmament," said Otávio.

"Oh, mutual disarmament," said Prince Polina, clapping her hands. "Yes, of course. If you'll submit to a brief inspection by a neutral party to ensure you haven't set up laboratories to create hosts of the Terrestrial Intelligence, we're prepared to terminate our existing hosts by Ceian midwinter. And we're prepared to commit to a pact to create no new ones. Not that we have many doctors left who remember how! And not that it would be particularly easy to find a cure for their little problem without Carmelita, anyway. But knowing Father—and knowing you, Admiral

Decretan, no offense meant—I'm sure that if it had come to war, we'd both just spend ten years fielding an army with a one hundred percent casualty rate, if it let us kill each other quicker. So I suppose it's all for the best for you to return the manual and for all of us to give the idea a rest."

"The manual won't be returned," I said. "We're willing to produce evidence of its destruction, once the emperor provides evidence that the Kutayeti hosts have been—terminated."

"You've stolen property from what was rightfully our territory, you know," said Prince Polina, "even if we hadn't found it yet, and I don't know that you're much of a better person if your offer to make up for it is smashing that property to bits—better in God's eyes, anyway. I've heard you people care about gods these days? But Father said to accept that if you offered it, so there we are. Send us the pieces of the thing at midwinter, and we'll send you holos of the bodies."

"And a complete evacuation of Itsaryet," I said.

Prince Polina smiled again, slow and thoughtful. This time it was not a pleasant smile.

"Do you know," she said, "Mother always tried to discourage this sort of friendship—she was quite right to, of course—but I did like Carmela. One couldn't really help it. Strange girl. That Sintian maid who birthed her told her all those stories about the lost palace of eternal summer. Not very grown-up or reasonable things. I believe she thought knowing them would help the child fit in at court, but Carmela always took everything so *literally*. She told all of us princes she'd find the Fortunatas when she was six years old, but Sasha was the only one who ever believed her."

I stared. Prince Polina shrugged. "Give us a week," she said. "That should be enough time to pack up our things, say our goodbyes, patch up any windows we shouldn't have broken. And then the Itsaryeti can enjoy being conquered again by your people, instead. Does that sound all right?"

Szayet might have been one of those shadows on the wall, for all she was moving. "Acceptable," said Otávio. "Thank you for your cooperation."

There were no sunsets in that centuries-old smog, but by the time we'd made our goodbyes and returned to the chariots, the sky had deepened to the color of charred meat. Cardean had lit the chariot's lantern. Around it, a wide halo of dust bobbed and swirled. "Give me another lantern and the map," I said to Cardean.

"Admiral," said Otávio warningly.

"We agreed," I said. "Do you want her as an enemy? The largest treasury in the Swordbelt Arm, on the edge of Kutayeti space?"

His face said bluntly that I was fooling no one. He put his gloved hand on my arm. "There's no benefit to Ceiao in your being hurt," he said.

His exasperated expression had been painfully familiar, and his touch had made my back stiffen as though I'd been shocked. But when he spoke the illusion fell away. He meant exactly what he said, that boy, no more and no less. If Ceirran had said that to me, he would have really been trying to tell me that he felt—

I shoved the thought away. "Don't wait up," I said.

I'd taken the map because the world-edge against which we had negotiated was not Ostrayet's only sudden drop. The land was rent with fissures, most filled so deeply and invisibly with ash that an inattentive traveler could take one step off the road and vanish like a coin into water.

In a clearing within the thicket of scorched city, though, the earth sloped up and the cobblestones gave way to a field of obsidian. The Szayeti had erected a squat canvas tent in its center, with sealant smeared where fabric met ground. Holes in the sheeting, covered in translucent paper, beamed purple and green through brown air. The stone shivered with drumbeats.

"Halt," said one of the guards at the tent flap, before I could so much as put my hand to its seal. "Do you come as foe or friend?"

I gave them a look. They stared back, implacable. I had danced with them at least three times in the palace at Alectelo, and helped them seduce two different tavern maids. "Tell her I said friend," I said at last.

The guard's helmet murmured inaudibly. "She——" they said, and then, with great reluctance, "The court orders me to ask whether you're sure of that."

"Let me at her," I said evenly, "and I'll tell her how sure I am." Their helmet began to chatter again, but I pulled open the seals on the tent flap and slipped inside rather than waiting for a reply.

The court hadn't been a euphemism. There must have been a hundred people in this tent: merchants and noblemen who I recognized by their fine jewelry, priests who I recognized by their shaven heads, palace guards who I knew from long nights playing cards and laughing beneath the palace. Here was the long-haired boy who had lost the shooting contest with me during the Feast of the Ship Bokapalo. Here was Szlanya the minister of trade, Delio the minister of war—I thought of asking him whether his daughter's lungs had recovered after the attack, then thought better of it—here were poets and musicians and mathematicians and philosophers and physicians, pressed shoulder to shoulder at feast tables or tossing dice or slapping down cards toward the back of the tent or throwing their hands up in the center where a space had been cleared for dancing. The roof had been strung with winking stained glass lanterns. Colors blurred on the sheer black ground, whirled, and separated, red and blue into violet into the dark. On a dais at the tent's center, in a well-polished brass chair, her helmet tossed carelessly at her feet and a bottle of wine tilting precariously in her lap, sprawled the queen of Szayet.

The tent flap thudded shut. Like pooling fabric, silence spread, through the people at the tables, through the gamblers, through the dancers, toward the shining throne.

In this dense quiet my boots on the obsidian sounded louder than they should have. Szayet's hair was loose, her face bare, the thin golden circlet at her forehead her only concession to majesty. In her ear, the black-smeared Pearl of the Dead gleamed: Matheus Ceirran's false name, Alekso of Sintia's broken soul. She did not rise to greet me, did not wave a hand, did not say my name. Still I came, and when I reached her throne, I bowed.

"My lady," I said.

"Get out," said Szayet.

I straightened slowly. "Is this how you speak to the lady of the Swordbelt Arm?" I said, stretching my mouth out into an approximation of a smile. She did not return it.

"Then punish your client queen," she said. "Or let her alone. Do what you like."

"And if I like neither?" I said coaxingly. "What choices does Szayet leave me then?"

"Then you are free to do anything in the world," said Szayet. "You always have been, no matter what you pretend. You can disobey me. You can flee me. You can insult me. But you cannot make me love you for it anymore."

The silence in the tent was absolute. Above us, lanterns winked and faded away.

"I did what I had to do," I said quietly.

"You keep telling me so," she said.

"Then what else could I have done?" I said.

Now, at last, Szayet looked away. "You could have come home," she said.

"You would have been sorry I had," I said. "When you spoke to me, you were sorry you did. We would have fought like wildcats, Szayet, you and I. I would have called you names that you would have never forgiven me for—I would have shot out your stained glass windows, thrown your wine cellars into the sea—"

"And so, to spare my feelings, you married him," she said.

"I married him to *protect* you," I snapped. "To keep your world from becoming a casualty of a Ceian civil war—to protect these people, this court—to protect you from *me*, from how unhappy I made you—I married him to take myself and my ghosts out of Szayet, and to let your people prosper in peace!"

"You married him because you were selfish," she said, and I heard the roughness now in her voice. "You married him to make yourself the center of your own life again. You married him because you believed you would fail me. But *I* decide when you fail me, Ana Decretan. You were wrong to take that choice from me—you were wrong to take that power from my hands, which are a queen's hands, and the hands that held you in the night. Don't you know that of all things in this world, the safest is to make sure that you are only able to wrong yourself? You were a coward. You are a coward—and will be a coward, until I no longer have breath to call you one." She smiled, thin-lipped. "That power, at least, is left to me."

"Me, selfish?" I said. "Who's the woman that held the lady of half the Ceian Empire in her hand for nearly a year? Who's the woman who decided it wasn't enough for her? Selfish! From a woman who only demands more and more and more! I gave you love and more love and more love—I chose you over Ceiao, I told you I needed you because Ceiao wasn't good enough—I gave you my time, my attention, my service—but you'll call me selfish until you crawl inside my skin and squeeze my heart until it bursts."

"You'd give me nothing at all, if I let you," she said.

"Nothing?" I said. "I miss you! I love you! Ceirran Almighty, can't that be enough for you?"

"I'm not the one you miss," she said. "You expect me to believe you love Szayet because you fled Ceiao. What must I believe you love when you flee Szayet? Of course your own world's not good enough for you. It never has been—not any world, anywhere in the galaxy. You don't want it to be." I began to speak, and she said above me, voice rising, "You don't—because that would mean it's good enough without *him*."

I was silent. She said harshly, "But this world is good enough, my lady. Every world in the galaxy is good enough. It's you that's fallen short." She stood and stepped off the dais. "I tell you again: get out," she said.

I came forward, over the hard obsidian floor, hand outstretched. When I was near her, she flinched; when I stroked my hand over her arm, she shut her eyes. Her breath was coming shallowly in her chest. "What can I do?" I said, low, coaxing. "What will make you forgive me? Tell me, and I'll walk to the ends of the earth for a flower, I'll pull down the clouds and build them into towers, Szayet, I'll weave lightning into your braids and hang the sun from the end—"

"I don't want your devotion!" she cried, and now she tore herself away and backed toward the dais, as though I had a gun on her. "Anita, name me as you will name me, but I am not a world. I am not moon or sea or stars. I am not salt, I am not bread. I am not pearl. I am a woman and you have kissed me, and when you insult me, you will insult me because I am Altagracia. I don't want your service. I want your life."

Abruptly she turned away, and she put her hand over her face. "And I don't think you ever have loved like you want to live," she said. "I don't think you ever have loved unless you could destroy a part of yourself by doing it, and I don't think you know how." She swallowed. "And I tell you for the last time," she said, "get out."

The colored lamps were blurring faster now, and the light from outside the tent was gone entirely. Her face was a shifting mosaic of reds: here a cheekbone, here a shining eye, here a flat mouth. Only a collection of pieces, thrown together by accident, and nothing to keep them from drifting apart again.

I let myself look at her a long time. *When you have nothing else of her*, I thought, *you must remember this.*

"As my lady commands me, I obey," I said.

Night outside the tent pressed in too close. It weighed on my suit, it smeared over my visor. When I closed the door of the chariot and pulled off my helmet, the smell of it hung in the air, the bitter grease of rust grown old.

Otávio was awake. I could hear it in his breathing. But he said nothing as I stripped from the suit down into my ordinary clothes, nothing as I curled up on the seat beside him, and I was glad of that nothing, I was glad. I was sure he had not deceived himself that I was going to that tent to negotiate a friendship between Szayet's crown and Ceiao's admirals. I was sure that he had lain here, waiting, wondering if I would come back.

And maybe it was as Flavia had said, I thought; maybe this was what real love was built on. Maybe love was when you weren't free. Maybe real love was made of these moments, the moments when nothing in you was alight or singing, the moments without honor, the moments when you looked yourself in the face and knew that no one better was coming to live behind those eyes. And wherever you went, you would have to learn to live among those people who lied at funerals, who spoke in Sintian poetry and never left Ceiao, who mocked the sick for their sickness and the weak for their weakness and the simple for their simplicity, who praised your friends and let them die. And someday, when you too were on the funeral pyre, everything left of you would be what those people remembered. That was the world. If you agreed to live in the world, you had to live in Ceiao. You had to live with Ceiao.

I said, against the window, "I have something to tell you."

"Yes?" he said.

"The Oracle hasn't been in contact with the Pearl of Alekso Undying for over a year," I said. "He's gone the way of the creatures in the Fortunatas. She hasn't been his Oracle for a long time. She asked me to lie to her people about it. I did. She—"

And I meant to go on—to say the other truth, the worse one: *She told her people to worship a god that never existed*—but the words choked in my throat.

Otávio was quiet awhile.

"Did she hurt you?" he said. "Is that why you decided to tell me this secret?"

I said nothing.

"Is she still Ceiao's friend?" he said.

"No," I said. "No, I don't think *friend* was ever the right word for what she was."

The dark fogged onto the chariot windows. I sat curled up there, my forehead against the glass, and I thought of tradition and virtue, home and loyalty, and what they might mean; and what was wrong with me, that I didn't know what they meant by now. Say nothing, I thought fiercely at Otávio—say nothing, say nothing, please, nothing, nothing, please let me have nothing, please, let me be nothing at all.

For a little while, then, I had my wish.

Behind my dreaming eyes, the city assembles itself. Up climb the white pillars, the quicksilver spires. Up climb the pyramids, the cerulean pools, the museums and schools and libraries, the arching silver bridges covered in ivy and sweet red flowers. The great marble kings, crowned and enthroned, turning stern stone faces on the canals and gold-leafed trees. The streets, clean and white; the courtyards where philosophers shake fists at one another and drink wine and laugh; the children, running down temple steps, throwing themselves into the water; the poets, writing in the sunlight.

And this man refilling the philosophers' wine cups with his tongue cut out; this person scraping ink from parchment, thinking of their wife held captive on the planet below; this woman, and a hundred like her, whose hands made the pyramids and swept the white streets and spun silk thread and wrenched open quicksilver oysters, who walked sure-footed across the balance beams to the crenellations of the towers, whose captive hands raised those museums and schools and libraries high. But today she is gardening. Behind my eyes, she sets down her tools, and stretches, and ambles around the corner of the courtyard to catch her spouse's hand.

And the wave rises up from the earth beneath them, the color of noonday sun. And the sky grows bright and bright.

And here is what I dream then: The light fades. The city stands silent, but for the rattle of wind, of ash inside the wind. On the street, the burnt husks of litters. In the windows, nothing at all. The sky is honeycomb.

But in the courtyard, moving slowly, two sets of burnt-white bones. A hand in a hand, a grinning cheek against grinning cheek. Who can say now who was who? And how we dance—

I was woken by an insistent, burning itch at the corners of my eyes. *Pesticide*, said my memory. I hurled myself upright, gasping.

"Good, you're awake," said Otávio. He was bent over a tablet, sketching with his finger at a blueprint for some kind of bridge. "The accretion-tide shifts in our direction in forty minutes. Are you ready to go up to the frigate?"

My heart was pounding. My eyes still itched like anything— the smoke, I realized belatedly. I'd dreamed something I couldn't quite remember now, something very terrible. Broken glass, a black sky, pain in a burning line across my belly. "Yes," I said. "Yes, I am."

Sextilis was Otávio's frigate, not mine, though when I called it his, he insistently reminded me that our properties were held in common now. Most of the soldiers on it were new recruits, colonials and teenagers, too young to have fought under Ceirran or to be friends of mine. There were a handful of satellite ports between us and Itsaryet, each of which we needed to stop at for tribute, and so the journey would last us nearly a week.

Put in close quarters with those few veterans on board, I fell guiltily back into old habits: taking exercise on the lower decks with them, lingering in their mess hall for meals. My newfound discipline meant they now held me at a kind of remove, for which I could not blame them, but after three or four days a pair of crewmen unbent enough over bowls of pottage to tell me they'd heard rumors that I was no longer welcome on Szayet.

"Not welcome!" I said. "Bleeding misfortune, I'm the lady of the Swordbelt Arm, what's *not welcome*? I'll be back in Alectelo to collect tribute within the year."

"Right, sir. But we won't be coming down with you to stay for a month, sir, going through all the Szayeti tavern maids, is what I've heard, sir," said the shorter one, and yelped when his friend stomped his foot under the table.

"Might be a while before we go dancing again," I admitted. "I'm sorry."

It came out rougher than I'd meant it to. The two crewmen traded an alarmed look, and the taller one cleared her throat. "Can I speak freely, sir?" she said awkwardly.

"Of course," I said. A second later I realized that Otávio would have wanted me to say no, and kicked myself, but it was too late.

"I don't much mind your staying on Ceiao, sir," she said, ducking her head. "None of us who served with you much mind. It was fun, sir, but I've a wife and child at home, and I was sick of stumbling through the Sintian tongue with the cultists. I was nearly glad when the order came down that it was war with Kutayet, and I—well, we felt you weren't yourself, sir, and that's the truth. It wasn't that we thought you really believed in any of

that disciple talk, sir. But it would've gone to anybody's head."
She leaned in conspiratorially. "There was starting to be a touch
of Szayeti about you, if you'll forgive me saying it. Admiral Julhan Ceirran's men have been telling us what a good job it was
that he brought you back in time, sir, and I think we all agree,
sir. We're grateful."

The memory drifted back to me unwillingly of my face in
Szayet's mirror, kohl-eyed, dressed in the Oracle's red silk. But
rather than that roil of thrilled disgust I had felt that night, I
felt a deep stab of grief—and not only for the absence of Szayet's
touch. It shocked me, and I shoved the image away.

"You're right to be," I said.

With one last port left between us and Itsaryet's capital city,
on a long, quiet afternoon, I found myself in the quarters I
shared with Otávio, reading through a report from the Outer
City. It was a list of recent arrests, all of the names faintly
familiar: Galena Latynya, Pavel and Františka Doenten, Beatriz
Defolcão, the gang leaders that first Teo Pulcron and then my
sister had cultivated in the Outer City. For years these people
had run their pieces of the city using bad loans, protectionism,
bribes to magistrates, and a willingness to give their people the
clean water, building repairs, medical care, and attention that
the city of Ceiao denied them.

"These people were your friends," I said to the ghost, who
squatted unmoving at the end of my bed.

"Your friends, too," said the ghost. "They had their usefulness.
Their usefulness ended." I said nothing, and it said, "You don't
want to return to the old days, Captain? Sitting at tables filled
with councillors plotting and bargaining to put an extra dekar in
their pocket, slitting one another's throats and lying about liberty, leaving you and your sister to rot?"

"Not in the least," I said, with feeling. But it cocked its head
skeptically, and at last I burst out, "*I* was your friend."

"Captain," said the ghost, "before I died and afterward, you never, ever forgot what your usefulness was."

There was a rap on the door. I sat up. "Come in."

Otávio always knocked before he came into our shared quarters, a horrible kind of politeness that made me want to climb out of my skin. I nodded at him. He came to the end of my bed and sat down where the ghost had been.

"The crown prince landed on Itsaryet this morning in a private cargo ship," he said. "Prince Sasha came with her."

I stiffened. "They agreed they'd evacuate their troops within the week."

"They did," said Otávio. "They evacuated themselves, as a matter of fact, two hours later. Nearly all of the Kutayeti army departed with them."

"Nearly?" I said.

Otávio lifted one of my tablets from my bedside drawer, calling up a map of western Itsaryet with a flick of his fingers. "They left from here," he said, "here, and here," pointing to a town, a fort, a harbor. "But satellite cameras indicate that two or three soldiers remained—here."

Ice slid down my spine. "There?" I said.

"Yes," said Otávio. "They came in a cargo ship, as I said, but they unloaded no weapons. In fact, my spy says all they did was have a conversation with one of the inhabitants and give their soldiers some supplies. Do you know what business Prince Polina and Prince Sasha could possibly have with that prison temple?"

"What supplies?" I said. "What was in the cargo ship?"

"Pearl wires, my spy said," said Otávio. "Pearl wires, and medical equipment."

To my sister, Altagracia Caviro Patramata:

The next time I have something to tell you, by the will of God, you will be listening.

Here's the funny thing: I never liked Alectelo very much.

Not that there was anything really wrong with it, I suppose. It's a town. The market squares are made of tile. The beaches are made of sand. The people are made of people: young and old and thin and fat and talkative and tired and happy and eating and kissing and hiding from the rain and feeding birds and trying on clothes and dying sometimes. Or dying always.

There is a world where you said yes to me all those years ago, when I had you safe in our dungeon, and the city was mine, and I told you we could conquer the galaxy. You said then that the god would never abandon Alectelo. You said He loved it. You said that His beloved's corpse was there, that His corpse itself was there.

I tried to tell you then what He told me.

What is a city? It's only land and stone. Some ships, some bodies, some sky. In the world where you said yes to me, we built another city, you and I—two more, a hundred more. In that world, there was an Alectelo for each of us.

I don't know the way to that world from here. I tried to find it for a long, long time.

The prince from Kutayet said that they lay for ages in the brig of your lover's ship, thinking. They had all the time in the world to think, they said. They'd believed at first that your lover spoke the way she did—as if Ceirran Undying did not exist—because she was only the ordinary kind of heretic, the kind that thought the Pearl of the Dead was a magician's trick, a false idol. But then she spoke about Alekso as if He was as real as you or I. As if, though they were both Pearls, Alekso could truly live and speak, and Ceirran could not. They guessed then what Ceirran Undying was, said the prince. They guessed what he was not, and never had been. They knew.

You never chose me over Matheus Ceirran. There was no Matheus Ceirran to choose. You did not want me. You have never wanted me. You have never read these letters.

If I had known then what I know now, on the day you came to me in the dungeon, I would have hurled myself through the force field and ripped your ear from your skull. I would have put my fingers in your eyes. I would have burned myself to nothing and died, rather than let you walk away.

But the past is past, and I cannot rewrite history. I will not hear Him call me Caviro's daughter again. I will not hear you call me sister. I am alone.

Let me tell you about the doctor that the princes brought from Kutayet.

He's very young, you know, or maybe he only looks so. I don't think I've ever seen someone with such a soft face. There are no lines in it, not even when he smiles. I wonder, if he ever did anything as wild as laughing, whether his skin would peel open like the film under eggshell, but I'll never know. The other few soldiers sit snorting and joking in their ugly language, but he never laughs along, because he doesn't want to talk to them. He only wants to talk to me.

He's very honest, too. "I won't lie to you, Madam Oracle," he's saying to me. "I don't want to lie to you. It is dangerous. It will hurt. I will be blunt with you, Madam Oracle: I do not know how long your mind will survive."

I liked having a body, I think.

Well—it did what I needed it to do. It ran, it jumped, it danced, it shot. It spoke, it kissed. It saw and heard and tasted. It breathed. It touched and was touched in return. It would be greedy to ask for a body to do more.

Greedy always looked so pretty on you. Well, doesn't that mean it'll look pretty on me, too?

I suppose if anything makes Alectelo different, it's the arrogance. To the people I think it's common sense. Who wouldn't hold their heads up, if they knew they were keepers of the corpse of a living god? Who wouldn't walk tall, if they lived in the most beautiful city in the world, the Star of the Swordbelt Arm, the last living bastion of Sintia-that-was? Who wouldn't sneer at visitors, if they had the Library of Alectelo tunneling under their feet, holding all the words in the world? And Ceiao gathers to itself the money, the governors of the galaxy, the fleet that has borne down the world—but Ceiao can't take the name. Ceiao doesn't have a *history*. Ceiao doesn't have a past. It doesn't matter to them whether Szayet has a future.

I like to think of the moment when I wake up. To open my eyes, and then, to open my eyes, and open my eyes, and open my eyes again. I like to think of every new muscle I will stretch and flex: my thousand hulls, my thousand engines, my millions on millions of guns. How funny, after a lifetime of arguing over whose, really, was Alectelo—whose, really, was Szayet—whose, really, was our face, our hands, our voices—how funny to have parts of a body that will be really, truly mine.

Oh, Gracia, I hope you think they're beautiful.

There are so many people angry with you, Gracia. There are so many people who hate that Ceian who took the throne from the rightful Oracle—that Ceian who took divinity from our god—that Ceian who took your love from me. And they will hate me worse, when I tell them how for a year you have lied to them, how you have demanded that they bow to empty stone, how you have left our god to die in pain. And there are so many people who will weep for joy that I am come to lead them.

I sit on my bed. I pray. I listen to the lonely owl call on the roof. I hang my walls with garlands and wreath them with foliage from the garden. I walk where I like, this morning, and the priests are afraid to stop me. And the doctor unfolds his machines in the cellar, and I listen, and I wait.

You liked Alectelo, of course. You loved it. It was just inhuman enough for you to love. A city is a creature with a million eyes, a million tongues. Your eyes, now, your tongues. Your hearts.

I will come to you like the wind comes to you, Gracia Patramata. I will come to you like the rain. I will come with the voices of the living and dead, I will come in chorus, I will come in harmonies. I will come with a thousand eyes. I will come with trumpets and glory. I will come with sun and victory. I will come with my blood dragged across the sky. I will come to you in your palace, and I will come to you, and I will come to you, and I will come to you, and I will come to you, and I will come to you, and I will come to you, and I will come to you, I will come each part of me that is, I will come each part of me that will be.

I am coming to tell you what the fire tells the pine forest. I will sing you the love song that the locusts sing to the corn.

I remain—

yours—

ARCELIA.

Last night I dreamed I was on Itsaryet again.

I climbed down the temple stairs—alone—to the room where we found the altar, she and I. But instead of a cellar, there was a river, and on the near side of it grew blue sedge and on the far side little white flowers. Asphodel. And there was a boat, and in the boat sat an old man, and he told me that I should go to my knees and drink from the river.

Not yet, not yet, not yet, I said. Why not? he asked me. And I said, First I have to write it down.

Celia, when we were in the temple, you were made to give me your letters. For the archives, I would say, and then I would go red when you laughed. But I have kept these letters for twenty years, because I do not have your hands, your hair, your tongue, the brown of your eyes, how loud your laugh was, how sharp your smile, how your face lit up when you ran down the hill or aimed cherry pits at the back of the kitchen priestess's neck or wrestled with me on the rooftops, how you sang my company's soldiering songs under your breath when you were working in the garden, your pride, your anger, your fire. I have saved these letters, because they were the only piece of you that you would let me save.

C. visits twice a day. He says little. He only listens to me read the poem to him with what's left of my breath. Now the hero lifts his father onto his shoulders. Now he walks, with fearful heart and bloody hands, through the fire, toward the dark.

Now I copy your letters into this notebook, and I ask myself who you'll belong to when I'm gone.

—V.

*S*extilis's docking bay was empty but for the skiff we had taken to Ostrayet, a badly burned cartel, and two antique fighters. I recognized the smaller of the two, *Áspide*—she had helped chase Quinha Semfontan across the Swordbelt Arm. Her hull wasn't clean, but her fuel gauge was full. I swung myself up onto the tip of her wing, walked up to the curve of her viewscreen, and stopped.

"You run too fast," said Otávio breathlessly from the doorway.

"This fighter's quicker than your frigate," I said. "You'll need to provide covering fire for my retreat. I know you have no experience in that, but I'll talk you through it. All I'll really need is for you to give me a little maneuverability. When you've summoned the rest of the fleet—"

"We're staying here," he said.

The slope of *Áspide*'s nose was quite steep. I walked down like a cat on a fence, one foot in front of the other, and stopped just before the drop to the concrete bay floor.

"I was angry with her," I said.

"You were right to be," said Otávio.

"I don't care," I said.

Otávio looked at me calmly for a few moments, then held out his hand. I slid down the ship's nose to the floor and took it. His skin was cool and very dry.

"You know that you have not always shown clear judgment, Ana," he said, "but you showed it to me that night on Ostrayet. You said it yourself. The Oracle of Szayet is not Ceiao's friend. She wishes to destroy Ceian profit. She wishes to destroy Ceian influence. Her loyalties are malleable, her wealth is phenomenal, her remaining debt to us is negligible, she has no qualms about humiliating Ceians and subverting the plans of Ceian leadership, and even if she were poor, inexperienced, and humbled, she could not stay on the Szayeti throne. She is too cunning not to be dangerous."

"Ceirran put her on that throne," I said.

"Ceirran put her under obligation to him," said Otávio. "You have never managed that. But neither do you have any obligation to her."

I shook my head, unthinking, numb. "What are you saying?"

His hand closed over my wrist. "Prince Sasha Harskaye hates you," he said, "and wants vengeance on you, and they believe that usurping the Oracle will hurt you." I winced, and he tightened his grip and said, "Ana, listen to me. You are not obliged to be hurt."

I did not see the ghost appear. One moment there was only his dark face, his intent grey eyes, and the next there was colorless motion against the colorless concrete floor. It stopped just before his back and settled its chin on his left shoulder.

"What—do you mean me to feel nothing for her?" I said.

The ghost stared up at me, unblinking. "No."

"No," said Otávio, a beat behind it. "But you can love Ceiao more. Ana, you know I know what suffering is. You know how afraid I was when I became Ceirran's heir. But fear and grief can be small things, if you let them. Devote yourself to what the empire needs, and I swear, I swear on my life, you will forget your own suffering."

"What does the empire need?" I said—to it, not to him. I could not hear my own voice over my thundering heart.

"A governing body that can restore stability to the planet and the flow of trade," said Otávio. "And to the pearl farms that Kutayet relies on. And to sixty million miles of treasure, most of it still underwater. The work the Oracle does with a hundred excavators can be done with a thousand. There's jobs in that— building, operations. Not all of what's beneath the sea is gold and silver, much as I'm sure *Dom* Caviro would like to pretend otherwise. Bring up what's needed, clear out the rest, and for Fortune's sake, begin extracting resources to Ceiao. There are flooded mines—there are porphyry quarries that could stretch for miles more—there are hundreds of acres of space that were fertile land only a few centuries ago, now occupied only by rusted junk and calcified bones. Szayet might be Ceiao's breadbasket, if anyone bothered to make it bloom."

"You've been thinking about this," I said blankly, pulling away my hand. Otávio let it drop.

"It's my job to think about this," he said. "It's been yours. Ana, do you know the other reason why Kutayet wants to usurp the Oracle?"

The ghost's hands had crept over his shoulders. When it met my eyes, it winked. "What do you mean?" I said to it.

"The Oracle is not Ceiao's friend. But Kutayet still doesn't want an Oracle who was once a Ceian's lover," said Otávio. "They would much rather have an Oracle who will be dead inside three months. They know that she, a host of the Terrestrial Intelligence, will be incapable of communicating with the Alekso intelligence in the Pearl of the Dead. He, mad, will be equally incapable of choosing an heir. By winter, Szayet will be leaderless."

I took a step back. "I thought you wanted peace."

"There will be peace," he said. "When we have Szayet's treasury, when we have Szayet's pearl, when we have a Ceian governor in the palace at Alectelo, there will be peace. Szayet is our client. We have a duty to protect it—it, not its Oracle. We will go to war with Kutayet to fulfill that duty. And, with you as our general, we will win." He squeezed my arm, a little awkwardly. "I've given orders to my men to speak to yours about how glad we are that you've returned to us," he said. "I am glad. My cousin would have been glad, too."

"I would," murmured the ghost. "I am."

I stepped back again and let the fighter's nose settle between my shoulder blades. The steel was like ice in the cool of the docking bay, a swift, nasty shock to my nerves. Only by concentrating on that shock could I tear my gaze away from the ghost and say:

"Who told the princes of Kutayet that the Oracle hasn't been speaking to Alekso? Who told them that his mind is gone?"

On a ship it was never quite silent. Beneath us, the dull throb of *Sextilis*'s engines; above us, the hum of her oxygen vents. The distant laughter and footsteps of my soldiers and his, going about their everyday duties, as much a part of the ship as the antimatter or the steel.

"Well done," I said. "Full marks for the schoolboy, after all. You had me entirely fooled."

"I have never lied to you," he said.

"No," I said. "No, you didn't need to. You told me what I wanted to hear."

"Admiral," he said, "it's not too late for you. I should have told you, as *Sextilis* left Szayeti space, that I was about to contact Prince Polina. I was afraid that if you knew I was sharing it, your heart would overcome your good sense. I was right. Nevertheless, in the name of preserving your dignity, I will apologize. But can you defend the Oracle to me?"

"To *you*?" I said. "Who made you her judge and jury?"

"Matheus Ceirran," he said, "when he gave us this empire. Is she not volatile? Is she not proud? Did she not seek at every turn to keep you under her thumb? Did she not make you soft, did she not make you un-Ceian, did she not make you wicked, did she not shame you? Can you tell me she will treat you better if you return to her now? Can you tell me that, and then claim that she hasn't stolen your reason?"

I looked at the curved concrete ceiling of the docking bay and laughed a little.

"No," I said. "No, I don't believe I can argue with you at all, and do you know, I believe you know that. I don't think you want a reasoned argument, Ceirran's heir. I think you want a drunken libertine soldier who only got half the world in her hands by being loved by a better man than she ever was—and who knows it. You want someone who you can make sorry for the rest of her life every time she says *no* to you. You want a gun hand."

His lip curled. "Don't pretend that you have the least objection to demands of unconditional loyalty," he said. "What did Ceirran ask from you? The loan of your sterling reputation? Your well-considered advice? Don't make me laugh."

Ceirran grinned at me now. Its hand was at the edge of Otávio's shoulder, flat along his neck. Otávio showed no sign of noticing this, though he held his head with an odd stiffness. "What you had from me, you never had to ask for," I said to it.

"What I had from you was everything," said the ghost.

Otávio twisted to see who I was talking to, and turned back, bewildered and scowling. "Admiral, everything I have had from you, I have had to drag out through trickery, begging, or brute force," he said. "I continue Ceirran's policies—I achieve them, where he failed—I begin a cult in his memory—I let *you* come to the head of it, you who no one of sense has ever trusted with more than a centono! What belief have I abandoned that he promised to uphold? What policy have I rejected that he embraced? What did you ever want from him that I have not given you?"

"Ceirran," I said, low, "what do you want from Szayet?"

"I want what I just told you I wanted," said Otávio. "The

planet's instability has been a drain on Ceiao's resources for years. The client kingdom relationship—"

The hand on Otávio's neck moved, and it wrapped around his throat. "The same thing I have always wanted, Captain," the ghost said. "I want what she failed to give me when I was her lover. I want what you failed to give me when you let me die. I want what Caviro gave Alekso of Sintia."

"You want a reign that outlasts your death," I said. "You want to rule forever."

Otávio looked taken aback. "Are you feeling all right, Admiral?"

The ghost grinned—white teeth, a dog's grin. "Once you asked me whether I believed a man could live forever," he said. "And what did I tell you?"

"That you believed in the immortality of a man's name," I said. I remembered as though it were yesterday. The snow had swept over the Avenuan like eiderdown. At Ceirran's house, I had been given dinner, and I had sat at his feet by the fire, and he had stroked his hand through my hair. The morning after, he had died.

"Answer me," I said quietly, "and answer me truly. Are you a god?"

"What on earth?" said Otávio.

"I am Ceirran," said the ghost.

Now I could not see it at all. There was light at the edge of Otávio's face, by his knuckles and shoulders, and it glimmered silver when he moved. I reached out to it, as if in a dream, and when I dragged my fingers through the air by his ear, I felt a numbness there. He jerked back.

"Until the end of time," said the ghost's voice through his lips, "my name will mean *king*."

"Admiral," said Otávio cautiously, "I do not want to stop you by force of arms. Think of your men. Would you abandon them? Come back into the ship."

"Ceirran?" I said.

"Anita," said Otávio.

For a moment I thought I would be sick. The boy's lips had moved; his throat had worked. The voice had not been his own. He frowned at me, to all appearances entirely unconscious that he had called me by a name that was at all unusual for him.

I said quietly to the soft silver in the air beside his face, in which I could just see the edge of an eye, "He doesn't deserve this."

"You are a hysteric," said Otávio. He looked truly shaken, a sight that was a great deal less gratifying to me than I had hoped it would be. His mouth shimmered faintly with silver. "You are—and I'm sorry that she's dead, truly, but your sister was, too. It killed her. I wish you will not let it kill you."

"Why did you come here?" I said.

"Because you called me," said the ghost's voice. "You called my name on the stoop of Flavia Decretan's house, and I came from across the universe to answer you. He wanted me, too, Anita. He has said my name over and over and over again. What can I do but answer him? What can I do but come to those who want me?"

"I don't want you," I said. "I don't."

"You love me," said the ghost, through Otávio's closed lips.

I shut my eyes.

"I don't love you," I said. "I love the memory of you. I love who I was when I knew you. But if I can't live with you, then I want to live without you, Ceirran. I do. I want to wake up in the morning without you. I want to live."

"You are quite mad," said Otávio flatly. "I take it you mean to force me to destroy you."

I opened my eyes. He had retreated along the docking bay toward the next fighter, and was gripping its nose very hard. He looked, I thought, every one of his barely twenty years.

"Otávio," I said, "go home. Find a girl or a boy or anyone else—find a friend, someone you like well enough that you don't flinch at the thought of eating breakfast with them. Drink. Smoke sílfion. Sit by the river and read a book, if it pleases you. But lay Ceirran's name down. You're too young to be haunted."

He came back toward me, along the concrete. The light fell from the thin strips at the top of the docking bay, lighting his narrow face from above so that whiteness and silver moved at his eyes and the curve of his skull. "You have," he said, "the faith of a child. Do you know that, Admiral?"

"You *are* a child," I said.

"Perhaps I am," he said calmly. "But then I suppose I would rather be a child than grow into what you are. You loved Matheus Ceirran. You wanted his money. You wanted his name. You wanted his attention. Perhaps you wanted to fuck him—"

His reflexes were faster than mine, and he caught my wrist before my palm met his face. "Perhaps not," he said, and shrugged. "Regardless. Now you would rather be the disciple of a god who calls you to bloody revenge and foreign decadence than a god who calls you to duty and discipline. You would rather be governed by lusts and grief than by law—"

"By love," I said through gritted teeth.

"Love is human," he said. "Ceirran did not leave us the luxury of acting like human beings. You know that, Anita! But you would rather be selfish, you would rather have a single self, you would rather suffer, and you would bring all of Ceiao into suffering with you. Is this growing up?"

My hand was straining against his, but if I was exhausting him, it didn't show on his face. "Because I'm afraid I will have to stand in your way," he said. "If to stand against this makes me a child, then let me be a child. If to stand against this kills me, then let me be a corpse. But I will stand against you, and I will stand against your god, who is a god of war."

I stomped down on his instep, hard.

"*Fuck*," he said.

I was up on the far edge of the wing, lifting the door in her roof, before he could stand upright again. Yes, this was a ship I knew well: a very old model, Lançan-made steel, the pattern of the docking bay flickering in orange above the dashboard when I tapped it. As soon as I gripped her controls, I could feel her thrilling against my palm, humming in the bones of my hand. In the last years they'd built these ships for armor, not for speed. She'd fly like a songbird.

"Admiral," said Otávio, his voice muffled through the ship's hull. "Admiral, you won't leave your men."

That at last made me hesitate, and Otávio saw it. "They won't forgive you," said his voice. Disconnected from his face, it bounced and rolled through the ship, mechanical, omnipresent. "If you think they won't fight against you, you're mistaken. They loved you, but they never loved your mistress. My men have spent weeks telling yours how I saved you from her, reminding them that it's an admiral of Ceiao they love, not the Oracle's concubine."

I said nothing. He said harshly, "Admiral, if you start that engine, I'll have the Merchants' Council of Ceiao declare you an enemy of the state."

I shut my eyes then, and I thought of the city, I thought of Alectelo: the pearl on the Library domes, the gold on the beaches, the new buildings pushing up like grass from the shore, the water ships and drones dipping and diving into the harbor for treasure. The scars of bombs, new and old. The taverns, the alleys, the Sintian sentences with Szayeti words tripping through them and the Szayeti priests with Sintian names, the curving harbor, the seagulls and the poplars, the blazing constellations, the sky so blue that I thought sometimes if I flung my arms open I might fall up and never land. The palace. The Oracle's bed.

How it had felt to see my face made up in her kohl, not myself and yet myself, a woman I could have been in another world. The people, and how they had let me win the games we played, how they had danced with me, how they had called me disciple.

I had taken it as my due from a client kingdom, but they had never owed it to me. The empire had compelled their allegiance. The Oracle had compelled their devotion. But their love they had given freely. They had chosen to give it, and waited to see what I would choose, who I would choose to be, if I ever saw that choice was free.

"Enemy of the state," I murmured, and I woke the engine.

The hum rolled up my arm, through my spine, down the ship, until the floor of the docking bay began to shiver. Otávio whirled and bolted toward the doorway, and had barely slammed the steel shutter behind himself before I'd hit the call for the docking bay doors to open.

The void flooded in. *Áspide* howled. It was four and a half hours to Itsaryet, said my star map. I had no food, no water, no comms, and four clips of ammunition in my belt. The tide was with me, and it would turn against me soon. I gunned the ship.

"All right, then," I said to the grey triangle of Otávio's frigate, shrinking rapidly behind me. "I am."

The mountain range curved up the southern coast of Itsaryet's smallest continent, green peaks divided by long parallel white canyons, as though someone had dragged their claws through the earth. Hell, from all I knew of Alekso's conquests, some-one had. In its center, one mountain sat shorter than the rest, its blunt head emerging from a thick mane of forest. Not far below the tree line lay a quartz-white lake. I checked *Áspide*'s guns and dove.

The harbor was sparsely guarded. Sasha and Polina must have thought there would be no threat to the operation from Ceiao— after all, Ceiao's admiral had enabled the operation not a week ago. I was met with only two ships: a squat, silent liburna, wings folded up, and a fighter even smaller than mine. "This is the fighter *Krokodil*, hailing the approaching ship," said my comms in accented Sintian. "Ship, identify—"

I aimed carefully and fired *Áspide*'s cannon. The ships exploded. So, a second later, did half the woods behind them, crooked old thorn trees flaring up like paper. White birds erupted from the undergrowth, wings beating frantically at the air. I settled on the lake's surface and skidded toward the shore.

There was a path on the far side of what had been the forest. It wound round the mountain, crisscrossing through tall fields of corn lilies, weaving between pines and snowflowers, and ended at a set of marble steps. They tumbled down from the temple's pillars like carpet, under the sunlight so white and clean that even their edges vanished. Only on the very nearest could I see all the pits and grooves, the grey of three hundred years of footsteps.

The doors at their top were four times my height, carved of cypress wood. Ebony dripped in beads and cylinders at their edges, curled out in petals from the curve at their top. On the far edge of one door, neat Ceian letters read: QUINHA SEMFONTAN MADE ME.

"She didn't make them, really," I said politely to the priestess standing in front of the door. "She set fire to the first doors, and she handed over the gold for repairs when we'd won the planet. But that's what's written now. So how is anyone to know it isn't true?"

The priestess was trembling. She looked young: long-armed, doe-eyed, wrists and hands encrusted with bracelets and rings, her ankles bare where she was already outgrowing her yellow robes. Her hand held a little black gun. The barrel wavered, swung, and pointed at my forehead.

I grinned up at her. "Are you really going to make me?" I said.

"You don't have to, you know. You're not a Kutayeti. What have they ever done for you?"

"You're the heretic's lover," she said. "The Szayeti witch's dog."

"Guilty," I said. "And you?"

"My name is Sister Božena," she said, "and you will not pass the door of this sanctuary."

I eyed the trembling barrel of the gun. "I have a feeling I will," I said.

"This is holy ground," she said. "It does not belong to Ceiao. If you force your way through these doors under arms, you will be damned. I will curse you with the curse with which Alekso cursed the Kutayeti army at the Rimward Tide. I will curse you with the curse with which He cursed the great moon Ostrayet. I will curse you with the curse with which He cursed the lords of my land who prostrated themselves before idols. The heavens will not spare you. Alekso shall strike out your name from—"

Her finger twitched on the gun. I shot her through the head.

She fell as if I'd cut her strings. Dark spattered the cypress wood. Someone would need to scrub that.

The doors led to an entrance hall, and the hall to a long corridor, painted with figures of dancing women. Behind the first door I opened, I found the other priestesses. They'd been shoved into a cell big enough for one, five or six of them together, gagged with hands bound behind their backs. I ripped the gag out of the mouth of the nearest and sliced her bindings with my combat knife, and she babbled, "Thank the Holy One, thank Him, praise Him for His mighty acts. They put us here when we protested. We told the doctor that he couldn't—"

"Where is he?" I said.

At the sound of my accent she stiffened, and her eyes went to my knife. "You're not here to free us," she said. "The sanctuary—" and she snatched the knife out of my hand.

I scrambled back through the door, slammed it behind me,

and shot off the knob. Inside the priestess shrieked, rattling at the wood, but I was already running.

Two Kutayeti soldiers stood before a wrought iron gate, one bending to light the other's cigarette. When I rounded the corner, she swore and dropped the match. She was damn quick—before I could so much as get my gun up, a bullet ricocheted past my face—but speed wasn't skill. I cracked off two shots. They collapsed.

The gate was unlocked. With some complaint, it opened into a courtyard surrounded by a low peristyle. Terebinths grew in the corners, lavender in the center, and the rest were lettuce, red chilis, the parchment-yellow blossoms of pumpkins to come. I circled, moving silently in the manner I'd learned sneaking out of my mother's windows, bent knees, heel-toe, and saw a heavily padlocked iron door. I pressed an explosive strip over the lock and hurried back until flowers tore under my boots.

As soon as I stepped through the burnt hole in the wall, I was met by thick smoke. I coughed. My ear warmed immediately—a bullet humming by, an insect whine. I narrowed my stinging eyes and emptied my clip into the smoke. A grunt, then nothing.

The dissolving smoke revealed a uniformed corpse and eight locked doors along a very narrow hallway, bare and near lightless. An arch at its end held nothing but darkness. Voices rose through the doors: "Who—" "What was—" "It's my people, I knew—" "Come to slaughter us at last—"

"Where's the doctor?" I called.

There was a long silence. At last, through the door nearest me, someone said, "Burn in hell, Ceiao."

"All right," I said softly, and advanced, hand on my gun. The arch wasn't empty, after all: A flight of stairs sloped down into blackness. I halted at the top step.

"Come out!" I shouted down. It rattled down the steps, noise overlapping, fading nonsense. There was no reply.

So far, my enemies had been unprepared. That had been dumb luck. I had half a clip left, and I had lost my knife. Descending into the dark would be easy enough—I wouldn't even need to break down the door. Coming up would give me trouble.

In the staircase there was no light at all. I felt my way carefully, one hand on the cool clay wall, the other on my gun. It smelled like my mother's wine cellar here, damp and musty, sour with spilled wine—and faintly antiseptic, too. I thought unwillingly of Carmela Lukhaya.

Dim blue light illuminated the last step, where the staircase turned a corner. Footsteps shuffled faintly nearby. Metal clinked on metal.

"We can hear you, Ceian," said a breathy voice. "You'd better come out."

The cellar was wide, a blue lantern flickering at each of its corners. Empty bottles lay discarded on the floor. The far wall was swallowed up by a jagged hole, through which I could see nothing. A Kutayeti soldier paced warily along the left side, and at the right stood a long steel table, covered in scalpels, scissors, needles, a tablet, and a long black tube with a light at its end. A small man with tightly parted dark hair bent over it, pawing through tools.

In a tall steel chair at the center of the room, eyes shut, the body lay still.

It was not like seeing Szayet mirrored. It was like seeing Szayet as I did when I woke in the night, when the moonslight fell over her: strange angles of the tripled shadows, a looseness I never saw in the day; her mouth drained of red, her skin of brown, her clothes of hue and richness. Here was the hair, thick and raven-black, here was the lovely heart-shaped face. And then—beginning at the back of its neck, wrapping in thick ribbons around its jaw, spilling down over its bare shoulders, winding around its elbows and its wrists, crisscrossing its rib cage, flattening over its hips and outstretched legs—the wires of quicksilver pearl.

"The corporal signaled there was a disturbance," said the doctor, carefully removing his long red gloves. "Is he alive? No, no matter. You have come to bargain for the patient's life." He smiled, close-mouthed. "Consider the notion of leverage. The emperor—"

I shot him in the face.

The soldier flung up her gun. I shot her, too. That was the end of my ammunition.

Quietly, I went to what was left of Princess Arcelia, and looked her body up and down. The chair only served to keep her upright; both she and it rested on a large, flat stone, carved with writing I could not read. A bag of blood sat between her legs, a cannula running from its end under the pearl wires into her wrist. Another pearl wire ran into the tablet by the scalpel and scissors.

I rested two fingers beneath her jaw. Her heartbeat surged against them: *here, here, here*. Her skin was warm.

"Your sister runs hot, too," I said quietly.

A strand of hair had fallen over her face. I tucked it behind her ear. Her face looked entirely peaceful. I put my thumb to her eyelid and lifted it up.

A black pupil stared back at me.

Arcelia's hand swung up and seized my wrist. "Captain Decretan," she said. "You came all this way for me?"

I yelled and tore my hand away, backing up toward the surgery table. The chair's hinges screamed. Its back swung upright. The wires around Arcelia's jaw twisted and pulled tight, and around her chest contracted and expanded—it was through those wires that she was breathing, I understood with shock, those wires that were pumping her chest like a bellows. Her mouth wrenched open.

"See what God has wrought," she said.

It was unmistakably her voice, but it did not come from her mouth—that opened and closed at arrhythmic intervals, the pearl wires squeezing and relaxing, her teeth knocking together. It came in a static rush from the tablet by the scalpels.

"What are you?" I said.

"The Oracle of Szayet," said Arcelia, and laughed.

It was the laugh, absurdly, that calmed me. I knew that laugh, too loud, too brittle. When I had met Arcelia, she had been the queen of Szayet, she had borne the Pearl of the Dead, and its wires had extended into her brain. I had not been afraid of her then.

I came slowly toward the chair again, hands out and empty, watching carefully for sudden movements. The wires around Arcelia's jaw twisted. Her head swiveled on her neck to face me. "You can see me," I said.

"I can hear you," said the tablet, while Arcelia's jaw worked up and down. "I could see you, if you opened my eyes. He said he would leave me my senses until the very end."

"The very end," I murmured. "When they'd finished rebuilding your brain."

"He had finished," she said. "Another quarter hour, and he would have had me brought to the ship."

The liburna I'd seen on the lakeshore, I thought, brand-new and empty. And when she had come to the ship's heart, they would have at last severed the nerves to her eyes, to her ears, and the doctor's orders to wire her into the ship's cameras would have been the last human voice she ever knew. And the cables would have come down from the walls, and up from the floor, and slithered into her skull, and then there would have been a thousand more ships, descending to meet her.

"I can't feel anything, though," she said thoughtfully. "No heat. No pain. He gave me motor control first, you see." Her hands jerked up again, a little out of time with each other. The left seized the bag of blood, claw-fingered, and the right gathered it in and tucked it under her arm. Her legs swung round. In a chorus of creaks she slid off the altar and stood, eyes still shut.

"I know a dozen men lying in Ceian hospitals who'd pay good money to have these wires put on," I said. "For them it'd be useful. But you, princess—for you, it's monstrous."

"Am I so ugly, then?" she said.

I was struck again by that double vision: her shoulders that I had touched, her waist that I had not, her neck that I had and had not kissed, and with an unpleasant jolt I discovered I could not lie. "You are what you are," I said gruffly.

"Not anymore," she said, and shuffled slowly forward. Her foot trod on the corpse of the Kutayeti doctor. She hummed under her breath and knelt.

"I spoke with Him, once, on a late summer night," she said, and I knew she was not speaking of the body on the floor. "I asked Him if, being the lord of all prophecy, He had known that Gracia would refuse His verdict on the inheritance. If He had known that, once I told her truly that He loved me better than He loved her, she would hate me until she died. If He'd known she would tear Alectelo apart to make it be untrue. If He'd known that she would fight, fight for eternity, to persuade the world that it was something that it was not."

Her hand dipped briefly into the wound at the doctor's face and came away wet. "He told me a story about Caviro," she said. "My ancestor, though He always called him my father. He said that when He and Caviro had been younger, He planned to put Himself into thousands of Pearls of the Dead, so that every person in the world would breathe them in the air, would drink them in the water—so that every person in the world would be an Oracle. But Caviro was terribly afraid. 'What if my lord dies trying to do it?' he said. 'What if the process goes wrong, and what comes into these Pearls is not my lord at all?' And for some time Alekso Undying despised His lover for a coward, and He left him to conquer other worlds. To conquer Ceiao, as it happens. I suppose that's why you are the way you are. When our lord made you His, He was loveless."

She rubbed her wet fingers over her mouth. "But my lord god missed His lover," she said, "and at last He returned to Caviro's side. He said, 'My love, I will die. Either you must help prevent it, or you must watch it. For my part, I will do all I can in order to never tell you goodbye. Do you fear that so much?'

"And Caviro told him: 'Come and see.' And he showed my lord the many hundreds of blessed people on the diamond isle of Kutayet whom he had used to learn the secret of immortality, who had sacrificed their lives for greatness. 'For life is short,' said Caviro, 'and art is long.'

"So Alekso knew then that His lover was not a coward. And He knew that courage would not die in Caviro's descendants— or at least that it would not die forever."

Her face wore no expression—her jaw still moved up and down loosely, teeth clattering—but I could hear a smile in her voice. "My god said that, if He might have me, Alectelo was worth it," she said. "He said that with me, with an Oracle who was willing to go to war as no Oracle had been willing before me, He would make a new Alectelo. He would remake the city as it had been before He had died, before it grew tired and poor and weak, before Ceiao. He would build it on Gracia's bones. He said, for the chance to remember Caviro, in the way I made Him remember Caviro, in the way I made Him remember what it was like to fight at Caviro's side, there was no price He would not pay."

I crouched down and held out a hand. She took it, and we rose together, the bloody wires of her thumbs and forefingers pressing against my palm.

"How long will you live?" I said.

"Hour by hour," she said. "Find more blood for this bag and I'll live out the day. Feed me and I may last the week." The wires on the sides of her face groaned, and first the left, then the right corner of her mouth tugged up. "The priestesses will do it," she said. "Soft touches, the lot of them."

"When the Kutayeti conquered Itsaryet, the Oracle called me," I said. "She wanted to rescue you. She would have come with a fleet to this temple, if she could have."

"She wanted me safe," said Arcelia lightly. "Safe where she'd decided to keep me, writing letters to her so she'd know she still owned me. And she wanted Itsaryet for a colony, of course. She'll steal it from Ceiao if you don't stop her. She always liked my plan—she liked the idea of Szayet taking back Belkayet, conquering worlds, becoming an empire again. It was only me she hated. Oh, perhaps she would have sent a fleet, but she never would have come herself. She never replied to any of my letters. She would never have asked you to come here."

I let go of her hands. She tucked them behind her back, still smiling, looking for all the world like a schoolgirl about to recite poetry.

"Who can undo this?" I said, gesturing to her wires. "If I bring you to a doctor—"

"If a doctor touches me, I will claw out his eyes," she said.

"You must have it undone," I said. "You must realize you have no hope. You have no allies. You have no ships—"

"Captain Decretan," said Arcelia tenderly, "it could take a day or it could take a thousand years. To me, it doesn't matter. If Gracia leaves me in this prison, I will remind the priestesses that Ceiao violated their sanctuary, and I will persuade them to let me get to a ship. If she imprisons me on Szayet, I will tell my guards that she murdered our god and the god of our ancestors, and I will persuade them to bring me a ship. If she throws me in the ocean, I will walk its floor with the sharks and the ship-wrecks until I reach the shoreline, and I will come up into the open air, and I will find a ship. I will speak to her until she hears me. I will speak to her until she answers."

"For what?" I said desperately. "Your god is gone. Your war is lost. Who are you doing this for? Forget the Oracle! Forget your god, and all he told you! You could live, if you let yourself. You can still live."

"I will not live forever," said Arcelia Caviro Diomata. "And I will not live in fear that I have lost the right to bear my name."

I'd left my own knife in the priestess's hand. I had the other, though. I drew it. It gleamed in the low lamplight, the same color as the wires wrapping round Arcelia's hands, Arcelia's ribs.

"Your sister wants you to live," I said, low. "I swear she wants you to live. Just say you'll leave her alone, and you can live out the rest of your days quietly. The priestesses will feed you. I'll send doctors to keep your heart beating. Just say that you'll let the queen have peace."

But Arcelia's face had swung toward the pearl knife. She laughed under her breath. "I should have known," she said.

"Should have known what?" I said.

Arcelia shook her head and stepped toward me. I flinched and flicked the knife upward, and it skipped across her bodice and settled on her chest.

She smiled and leaned forward. The knife did not move, but her dress did: The fabric gave way beneath, the blade piercing through linen, so that the point came to rest between her breasts.

I did not mean to look. I looked. Where knife met smooth brown skin, a drop of blood had bubbled up, dark on the pearl that wove netlike over her ribs, dark on the surface of the blade.

"Anita?" she said softly, and her voice sounded so much like her sister's that for a moment I could not breathe. "Anita, stay still."

She cupped her hand around my jaw and kissed me, cool and hard.

Then she drew back, and pulled aside the fabric of her collar, so that between the crisscrossing wires the vein in her throat lay bare. "All right," she said. "Begin."

The doctors will come first. Then your friends: with happy faces, with ink-stained hands, with shoulders draped in damask and necks draped in jewels, murmuring and crying over your corpse like hens. And last, when they've departed, there will come down the paths of the garden a dark, shaven-headed man, narrow-faced, grey-eyed. He is not young, and he does not look young. There are bags beneath his eyes, and though he moves with the jointed, conscious grace of a waterbird, he moves stiffly, too. He is plainly dressed: a grey linen tunic, black boots, no silk, no rings. The silver band around his forehead is almost more of a circlet than a crown.

What outlasts death, little thief? Not temples, not mountains. Not bodies. Not kings, however often we might tell our children that it's so. Not moons. Not satellites. Not roses.

But open your eyes. Look—across the water, toward the horizon. I don't mean the city, I don't mean the ships, I don't mean the smoke and fire. I don't even mean the dust. Look farther.

Here again, blooming in all the same old glory that it always has: rosy-fingered dawn.

"Eneida," the man in the crown will say under his breath, and he will close your eyes.

Your notebook is on the bench beside you. He'll pick it up and open it.

Close your eyes again, Virgilia. I'm not done with you just yet.

E very now and then,

                                                                time—

Not yet.
Very soon.

The autumn rain had begun, a warm, thick clattering that soaked
our tunics and filled our boots. We threw our hoods up and
fled down the mud-slick Alectelan streets shrieking until Szayet shouted, "Stop—stop, I can't see," and we ducked under an
awning and burst into a shop, where a huge red-haired Sintian
crossed her arms over a barrel of dried sage and glared at us while
we stomped and laughed and shook ourselves out like dogs.

Szayet's kohl was running down her face in streaks. "You poor
thing," I said, and walked her up against the wall of the shop to
wipe my thumbs deliberately under her eyes.

She didn't smile, but her hips curved against mine, indulgent.
"Am I clean?" she said.

"You? Never," I said. The black had smeared across her cheeks,
toward the gleam of the Pearl hidden beneath her braid. "You
look like a Madinabic war chieftain, all tattooed to ride into the
field."

"What are you, Anita?" she said. "General, or foe?"

I pressed my mouth to her cheek: salt rain, burnt-match kohl, skin. "Hostage," I said into her ear.

On a tiny bare isle south of Alectelo, hardly more than fifty yards across, Ceirran's men had once buried what was left of Quinha Semfontan. This was the place to which the Alectelan court summoned me, and this was the shore to which I rowed the rubber lifeboat I'd dug out from my fighter's hold, through startlingly calm green seas, following the path of rusted railroad over the sandy seafloor. Far behind me, *Áspide* bobbed on the waves. Soon she would sink.

Priests flocked to meet me at the shore, dragging my lifeboat up the sand, helping me up, pressing bread and salt into my hands. They had some difficulty with this last: I was carrying a wooden crate, a few inches too wide to comfortably tuck under my arm. But I was not concerned with their attentions. On the far side of the island, a woman in a white dress stood with her back to me, staring at the sea.

When I tried to walk toward her, one of the priests barred my path. "The Oracle of Alekso and Ceirran Undying has bid me welcome the lady of the Swordbelt Arm to her client kingdom," she said. "She has also bid me to speak for her."

"Szayet," I said.

Szayet didn't look at me, but her shoulders tightened. "The Oracle wishes to know what business the lady of the Swordbelt Arm can have with her client kingdom, that she has been called back from Itsaryet so soon," said the priest firmly.

"The lady of the Swordbelt Arm hasn't come to do business in her client kingdom," I said to Szayet.

Her head turned. Her braid was woven with white ribbon, and her brown throat wrapped in snow-white pearls. Faint white embroidery of kite birds and scorpions dappled her bodice. But her eyes were dark, and fierce as fire.

I came through the crowd of priests, and I set the box down in the sand. Her red lips parted.

"My lady," I said, and before she could speak, I knelt before her.

The priests burst into murmuring. I ignored them, and pressed my forehead to the sand. It was the second time that I had gone to my knees for someone in my life.

"Anita has come to call upon the Oracle," I said, "if Szayet will let her come home."

Back in the old country, when wishing still worked, there was once a tall and mighty mountain. Later, when the old country lay three thousand fathoms beneath the surface of the sea, that mountain became an island. On that island was a king, and he built there first a harbor, and then roads, and then houses for his men, and then a grave for his beloved, and then a palace for himself, and at last he built a library.

And he called himself the disciple to a god who had drowned that world and half the people in it. And the people went to their knees. And the king lived happily ever after.

Now there arose a new monarch over Szayet, who did not know the land where their father had been born, and they saw that the people they ruled were mighty and many, and would yet multiply. So they went to the grave that their father had dug and built it into a great marble tomb. And in the island, they dug a pit a hundred feet deep, and lined its floor with marble and purple porphyry. Into its sides they cut rows of stone seats, and they named it a theater, and in the theater they named themselves Ciezo Caviro Elefante, the second Oracle. And they sent forth ships to conquer other worlds. And the people went to their knees. And the monarch lived happily ever after.

And

then,

I woke.

The bed was empty. Moonlight crossed shadows over shadows

along the floor. I sat up and saw Szayet on the balcony, the red of her nightdress faded through the rippled glass.

She turned at the noise of the door. Tonight there were no fireworks, no races, no feasts, only the white river of late summer stars running westward into sea. I could see she had been crying.

"The rumors have been spreading since you landed," she said. "Some people say that my sister is coming down the tide at the head of a Kutayeti fleet. Some say that it wasn't the Terrestrial Intelligence they put inside her, but Alekso Undying, and now he's walking the galaxy, seeking vengeance. And some say that I myself gave the order for you to violate the temple sanctuary."

"Would you have?" I said. "If you and I could have spoken, before I went into the temple, would you have ordered me to do it?"

"Yes," she said. "No." She swallowed. "Yes, I would have. I would have been brave enough. No, I would have been clever enough to find another way. No, I would have seen it coming, weeks ago, months, and I would have made it go right. Anita, I'm afraid, I'm so afraid—afraid that you were right, and I've lied so well and so long that no one will stop me lying to myself—" She came into my arms then, warm skin and soft linen, and when she kissed me, I felt that her face was still wet.

I had said it to her on the palace steps today, before her ministers and noblemen. Now I said it once more: "You could kill me, if you wanted to."

"And if I can't bear to? If I need to let you live? How long will you stay?" she said hoarsely. "When the empire forgives you for this, when will you run home again?"

"Never," I murmured.

She said, "What's changed, Anita? How can I believe you now?"

Easy answers jumped onto my tongue: *glamour, glory, beauty, fate*. I made myself look out at the white on the black ocean, and thought carefully.

"Lançan's knife—Barran's knife," I said. "They came down into his back, and me, I did nothing. I didn't even come in time to comfort him. He died alone, he died cold and bloody and alone, and in the space of a morning I'd turned into an animal without a cage. And there were no more trophies, no more triumphs, every man I'd killed for his sake was nothing more than a corpse, everything I'd broken for his sake was nothing more than ruins... And then there was you, and you still knew how to be brave. You still knew how to want pleasure, and not just pleasure, but liberty, and sovereignty, and life. And in your heart, I think you're no liar, Szayet. You can't bear lying for long. Not to me. You told me the truth about the kind of man Ceirran had been. It was me who didn't want to hear it, and it was me who hated you for showing me I could choose to hear it. When I was with the boy—when I walked among the Ceians, the people of quality, the people who'd hated me since I was a pissant spendthrift wanton and the daughter of a drunk—when I listened to the founding of Ceiao, and self-discipline, and finally washing away the stuff in my soul that was disobedient, disloyal, had no master and no purpose, knelt to no one, wanted you—when I heard him say Ceirran would forgive me if I would only do things to you that I should be ashamed of, then Szayet, I wanted to be ashamed. Undying Name, I wanted shame to swallow me whole. I wanted there to be nothing left of me."

She exhaled, and she kissed my mouth, and my temple, the place where on her own face the wires of the Pearl of the Dead pushed into her skin.

"And what would you do if I called you a murderer before the people?" she said. "Would you still leap at the chance to be nothing? What would you do if I sent you away?"

"Then I'd ask you to run away with me," I said. "Find another kingdom, another city. On the shore of another ocean I'd build you a house. You told me that you didn't want my service, and so there I would give you the whole of my life. And one day, long after we'd died, the tide and the wind would wear our house away, and we would wash together into the salt water, my ribs in your ribs, my hand in your hand, until no one could tell what was Anita and what was Szayet anymore."

Her fingers traced slow patterns through the short-cropped hairs on the back of my head, unreadable letters.

"In another world, I would say yes," she said against my cheek.

"In another world," I said, and I kissed her, not hungry or desperate, not needing anything more, only conscious of all the small astonishing miracles of flesh: breath in the body, the taste of iron, nerves, softness, skin.

"So it's true," I said into her mouth after a while. "All those times I said it, I only meant to call you disloyal to me. But you would build a Szayeti Empire."

"I want to build a new world," she said quietly. "Abundant with Szayeti feasts and Szayeti poetry, and Alectelo at its center, and you at the center of Alectelo. The same world I have always wanted—one where Alekso is only a name, and Ceirran is only a memory, and tomorrow is what I make it, not what I inherit from my grandfathers and my ghosts. A world that you'll want to live in, Anita. A world where you will want to live forever."

My thumb moved idly up and down her neck. "Szayet," I said carefully at last, "you say *live forever* to me. Would you be an Oracle again? Keeping the person you love most in a cage where you can hold her safe?"

"No," she said, and she stepped back and took my hands.

"A year ago, I told the galaxy that Matheus Ceirran was our god," she said. "I thought then Szayet wanted for a protector. I thought I needed him—and I was afraid of needing him, afraid of always needing Ceiao, afraid of *wanting* to need Ceiao..."

"You don't have Ceiao anymore," I said. I was not alone on Szayet—a number of ships had appeared in the sky this afternoon, old veterans and pilots, men who had conquered Madinabia with me. But *a number of ships* was not the fleet.

"No," she said. "But I do not believe now that Szayet has ever wanted for a protector. I do not believe the Szayeti Empire will ever want for one. I believe she wants for what she has always wanted." Her grip on my hands was very tight, her nails sharp in my skin. "She wants gods who love her too much to tell her goodbye."

The sky peels back.

No blackness in it, now, no glittering falcons or serpents, only blue. But the sky in life is never quite so blue. Even on midsummer days, the horizon grows pale, the air spots with haze. This sky is the blue of paintings, of children's drawings, of dreams.

I heft that wooden box I carried to the island, and I walk across the floor of the theater, toward the raised stage where the Oracle of Szayet waits for me.

She stands beneath a canopy of myrtle branches, orange poppies, roses. Her eyes are painted with kohl, so thick that the whites seem strange and distant, and her mouth with red. Her dress is diaphanous grey. Round her shoulders she has lain a mantle of leopard skin, and over her arms garnets. Her hair is braided and gathered in a knot at the base of her neck, bound with ropes of quicksilver pearls. And into her collar and the hem of her skirt are sewn diamonds, a thousand diamonds, as small as salt, each catching the sun in turn, so that when she moves, light ripples like water. She, too, is holding a wooden box.

And a curious thought overtakes me: that I am not walking toward her—that I am not even moving at all, that no walls rise around me, that beneath me is not solid stone. I think that I am visited by an unspeakable lightness, and that in my veins and arteries is not blood, but swift glad fire. And the light bears me higher and higher, away from all matter, until I am not admiral, not disciple, not even Anita, only a piece of Szayet, of Szayet's impossible sky.

The shadow of the myrtle leaves falls over my face. Murmurs rise. All of Alectelo is gathered here, beneath this impossible sky. Behind me, a rustling: the musicians on their feet. Horns sound—flutes, harps,

the hands that touch them.
As a world is a fraction of an empire, a prince told me once,
as the present is a fraction of history.
As a person is a fraction of a city.
As a musician is a fraction of song.

"Stop, stop," cried the senior groundskeeper, and dropped the lyre and scrambled to her feet, laughing. "Start with the tambourines, *then* the seashells—Alekso Almighty, you'd think you wretches had never played before. Dulce, come here—"

The Winter Market was scattered with the remains of the day: rolling jade and chalcedony beads, fish scales, scraps of cheap cloth, wax paper, dropped centonos, a raggedy doll with yellow braids someone had carefully propped against a tentpole with a note pinned, asking to whom it belonged. The mist of early spring had burned off with the late afternoon. The sun had slunk away to its private places, discarding colors along the sea.

The palace staff were out of uniform, the priests were out of sacred robes, the tavern-keepers and pearl-divers and smugglers and jewelers and merchants' sons and street sweepers were in their new-dyed tunics and fine leather shoes. On the balconies of surrounding houses, youths dangled their feet over empty air, shrieking with sudden laughter and spitting plum pits to the terra-cotta tile. A few people had spread out blankets and now bounced children on their laps, feeding them flatbreads and honey.

"A-one," said the senior groundskeeper, settling back into her seat. "A-two—"

I found myself in the arms of a stout and pot-bellied uncle, who said not a word but ducked and twirled under my arm with surprising dexterity; a blushing girl of eight or nine, who I carefully led in a simple back-and-forth until she squeaked and ran to her waiting mother; a little old woman with a face like a walnut and eyes like beetles, who stepped on my feet at least four times and winked at me when I laughed; and a shaven-headed man, whose arms were bare and wood-dark and pockmarked with scars. He was the quickest dancer of all, and the most graceful, and the least self-conscious, and halfway through the dance his gaze flicked at last from my hands to my eyes, and I smiled back.

"Well," said a voice, once that dance was done.

"Well," I said, and turned, and took Szayet's waiting hand, cool in my own. She huffed softly through her nose and folded herself into my arms.

"Are you quite satisfied?" she said into my ear.

"Why? Are you?" I said, and felt the shiver of her laughter in her chest. "Did I look good doing it?"

"You know your talents," she said.

"Tell them to me anyway," I said.

"Movement," said Szayet, and slid her hand around my hips. "Dancing. Fighting. Shooting." The hand squeezed briefly, and I shivered. "Provocation, I think. Determination to provoke—yes, that, too. Relentlessness. Concentration, when you're given sufficient motive."

"And sufficient opportunity," I said, brushing my teeth lightly over the shell of her ear.

"Boldness," she said tartly. I laughed, and she went on, more quietly: "Dedication. Valor. Fidelity. Fanaticism."

"Fanaticism!" I said. "What exactly is it I believe in?"

"It's never a *what*," she said. "You would be easier if it were."

"I'm very easy," I murmured against her cheek.

"You're the hardest thing in the world, Anita Decretan," she said. "I wouldn't have you otherwise."

"Altagracia Caviro Patramata," I said.

She says, "Here I am."

"Will you be my queen?" I say. "Will you be my prophet? Will you take my life, and give me your own? Will you give it to our children, and to our children's children, until the city crumbles into the sea?"

"Yes," says Szayet. "I will."

She unlatches her box and draws back the lid. Inside, on a velvet cushion, are two silver discs, and two pearls. I hold out my hand. She sets the first disc on my palm and takes the second.

"These are the recording discs, whose making I learned from Alekso Undying when I built our lord Ceirran's immortality," she says, voice echoing. "They are the archives of memory. In the mornings, when we hold them in our hands, they will collect all we remember, from the present moment back to the beginning of our lives. Let the gods bless our work. May it be Their will that we preserve our thoughts."

Now she sets the first pearl in the cradle of my fingers, and the second in her own.

"These are the Pearls of the Dead," she says to the crowd, "whose making I learned from Alekso Undying when I built our lord Ceirran's godhood. They are the living minds. When our bodies lie dying, we will rest them on our recording discs, and through our memories, our souls will come into these pearls. Let the gods bless our work. May it be Their will that we preserve our love. And may it be Their will that we join them in apotheosis."

And now she looks at me.

"Will you be my Oracle?" she says. "If my body should die before yours, will you give my soul immortality? Will you carry it, and keep it safe? Will you be its home?"

"I will," I say.

I watch her pinch the little piece of pearl between her fingers. When she lets it go, a fingerprint of blood shimmers on the surface, then disappears.

"Will you be my Oracle?" I say to her. "If my body dies before yours, will you give me immortality? Will you carry me, and keep me safe? Will you be my home?"

"I will," she says roughly.

I pinch the pearl she gave me. The sting is surprisingly cold; numbness yawns briefly up to my elbow. When I open my hand, my Pearl of the Dead is liquid red, then silver again. I drop it into her hand and take her Pearl in mine.

"Hail," says Szayet. "Hail to the Consort, to the Disciple and Oracle. Hail to Ana and Altagracia, queens of the Swordbelt Arm. Hail to Szayet's living gods, that join the gods undying."

As a brace of snowy plovers on the shore, leading chicks in columns to the sea, bursts into beating wings, and tosses the sand into waves and hammers the water flat, and the boy who threw the stone among them stands amazed at his power to destroy—

—so the noise erupts from the throats of the people of Alectelo, so it rolls up the walls of the theater, so it beats down from the city, so it thunders from the edges of the sky. A hundred thousand voices, old and young, Sintian and Szayeti and Ceian and Cherekku, on their feet, their hands thrown up, the summer air shining with cacophony. Szayet seizes my face and kisses me, a hot rough animal's kiss, her fingers digging into my jaw, the roar rising and still rising, the whole world throbbing with it, my heart thudding in time. No poetry in it, this, or not a poetry they taught me at school—and certainly not one they taught you. A possession.

I tear myself away. "My lady," I say, and I open the lid of my box.

"Will you manage it?" I said. "The forging of the Pearls, I mean. Do you remember the way?"

The wind was teasing her hair over her forehead, sending her nightdress's sleeves fluttering on her soft arms. "It's not the kind of thing you forget," she said, not looking at me.

"You loved him, didn't you," I said. "Despite it all."

"I did," she said. "Heavens help me, I did love him. I loved Ceirran, too. I wish I could have kept them. I wish Ceiao had let me."

Over the ocean, shearwaters circled, flashed white wings, and dove. From the seaside taverns I could faintly hear old Alectelan drinking songs. A man was stumbling down the harbor, calling: *Darling, sweetheart, I didn't mean it, come back.*

"What are we going to do when we get old, you and I?" she said softly. "Will it be feasts and gaming, nights and lanterns, when we've grown grey and tired, and we need to lean on each other to stand?"

"Szayet, Szayet," I said, smiling, "what's this?" She stared over the city, the roofs glimmering in the black of her eyes, and I caught a strand of the flyaway hair and tucked it behind her ear and said again, more seriously, "What is this?"

"Anita," she said. "I'm afraid."

"Afraid?" I said. "You? Dreaming of the empire we'll build? Dreaming of the days of our greatness? Dreaming of when our children rule Belkayet and Cherekku, and we speak to each other through their mouths? How are you afraid?"

She drew circles on the balcony railing, finger trailing silver over the dampness left by fog. There was a strange light around the city, I thought—the Library, the rooftops, the sea—as bright as a mirror, and liquid. It looked familiar in a way I could not quite place.

"I'm afraid that it's too late for us," she said. "That there was a moment, back when—oh, I don't know, when you came to me in my barge at Plyusna, when you kissed me the night after Ceirran died. When I rolled out of the carpet. Perhaps we will be great, you and I. But I'm afraid there was a moment when we might have been wise enough, or kind enough, or brave enough, or good enough that we could have seen our way to being happy. Happy for eternity."

"We're happy now," I said.

Szayet shut her eyes and turned her face blindly into the dark. Behind her shone Alectelo, and above the iron-bright stars.

"Do you ever feel that the world's used up?" she said. "That our fathers and their fathers had the fat of it, and left us the bones. And when we tell our children that this was how we lived, they won't know what we mean. And the days are growing short again."

"Take my hand," I said.

She took it. I kissed her knuckles and drew her close. The wind was rising, briny and wild. Below us the city roared, shapeless, quicksilver, flickering. The end of her ribbon had come loose from her braid, and it whipped behind her like a banner. The princess of the pearl city, I thought, the sea queen, the prophet, the witch of the Swordbelt Arm. My liar, my own, my girl.

"I swear to you," I said, "in the name of the stars, and all empires that hang inside them: You and I will never grow old."

Every now and then,

time

folds up.

You're midway along a road,
for the straight path has not been lost,
and it only has one ending.

At its end stand two gates,
one ivory, one horn,

and each gate pulled open wide.
Above them, cut into stone:

Abandon hope.

A hundred times over to the queen of Szayet have I made myself
an oathbreaker. That promise, and that promise alone, I have kept.

Around me, the roar of Alectelo. Before me, the hem of Szayet's
dress. Above me, our wedding canopy. I am here, and this is
now.

"An offering for the queen," I say. "A dowry."

I reach into the box and pull out the head.

Arcelia's eyes are shut. The embalmers have done their work.
The cheeks are full, the lips red, the wires unwound, the skin at
the back of the neck sealed up. You would never know that time
had power over the last Oracle's face at all.

I woke to the sound of bells ringing.

"Who in Alectelo is still celebrating?" I mumbled. Szayet
made no reply. I propped myself up on one elbow and peered
over. She was dead asleep.

My thighs were still sore with the force of where she'd been
an hour ago, my lips aching, but the boneless contentment of her
touch had drained away. The night had grown colder.

The autumn blankets were in her wardrobe, where Zorione
had folded them away five months ago. It was too early to air out
the cold-weather things, but Szayet was shivering. In my hands
the wool felt like gauze.

The ringing had not ceased. If anything, it had grown
louder—a dozen bells or more, thin chimes, jingles, clangs, the
deep toll I had thought came only from tall towers. There was
shouting, too, and singing, high voices and low.

Szayet sighed. I draped the blanket over her and crossed to the balcony doors. There was no sign of torchlight. The moons hung over Alectelo, three silver spindles, and the city was silver beneath them. Still, the exquisite music continued, the flutes and tambourines, the voices raised to the air.

Out on the balcony, I leaned my elbows on the sill, looked over the street. All was dark. Throughout the winding paths of the city, not a shutter was open, not a lantern bobbed.

The tune was Sintian, I thought, or perhaps Cherekku. I could hear the rattle of timbrels and what might have been a neginah. But the words were Szayeti.

And though I did not know a word of that language, and never had, it seemed to me then that this song was not strange but as familiar as my name, and that if I only listened a little longer, its words would come back to me—and not only them, but all the words I had ever forgotten, every word that had ever been lost or struck out or burned. It seemed to me that these revelers knew them, and that they would sing them all in time. It seemed to me that this was a story, a long and beautiful story, about a place I knew and had lived in not so very long ago, and it seemed that I had been among these revelers before, that they had embraced me, that they had pulled me into the dance—and it seemed to me now that if they would only sing to me, say my name and call me welcome, then I could come down among their number—then I could throw my hands up—then I could dance with all my might before the heavens, and I and the whole of Szayet would come forth, with shouting and the sound of the horn.

The noise was fading now. No, not fading, but moving, under my window, to the end of the street, beyond, toward the black expanse of sea. Now it was on the shore. Now it was at the harbor-gate. Now it was gone.

I looked out at the water a long time: the vining moonslight, the invisible motion of waves. When I slid back into bed, Szayet's face was upturned, her lips a little parted. I bent and kissed her.

She stirred. "Where were you?" she whispered.

"I heard revelers go by," I said.

"A dream," she said, and turned over.

I listened to her breath even out and slow. The reflections from Alectelo's pearl moved over our ceiling, soft and shapeless, deep-water light.

"Goodbye," I said, and was asleep.

To Captain Águeda Vipsânian—

Well, I'd rather she hadn't.

I cannot bring myself to follow your advice and act the broken-hearted romantic. Don't think this is pride alone. You can imagine the poets, when we are fifty or seventy or dead, writing that "he was one who wept over a woman."

Write to the emperor.

OTÁVIO CEIRRAN

I suppose he expects me to remember the rest.

I remember how the altars grew, and the new temples. I remember how frightened I was. I remember how quickly the way that people spoke changed—how it seemed as if, overnight, everyone had learned the lines to a new play, everyone had been given a new language, and none of the old words meant quite what I thought they had—not patriot, not freedom, not degenerate, not civilized. I remember the posters in the markets, by the bathhouses, in the Outer City. I remember her face, and above it: ENEMY OF THE STATE, ENEMY OF THE STATE.

The state, the state, the state.

I remember when I heard how they brought her body from the temple. I remember that I went to the river and stood on the bridge, and for a minute or a year, I wanted

—V.

CHAPTER

FOURTEEN

You'd be surprised—or maybe you wouldn't, considering the places you've left—at the perspective you find on a planet from its atmosphere. Kings and queens in Alectelo catch certain airs and graces, standing on their balconies. Ceirran's face used to change when he was up on the Libeiracópolan, watching the people and the spider-litters. Even I had a flash, that night I sat on Sonia Couron's rooftop waiting for her to push the skylight open, of some kind of separation from the sleepers below—that all the eyes in the universe belonged to the stars and I, sisters up in the rafters of the Ceian night, and the rest of the human race so distant and different that I might have been the only person alive.

If you'd been standing by the harbor-gate, the Oracle's boat would have loomed large enough to put a crick in your neck. If you had been in a cartel ship descending to Alectelo's south-ern seas from the scattered liburnae in Szayet's atmosphere, it would have looked as long as your thumbnail—as long as your thumb—as long as your hand. A careful observer, watching the boat's deck, might fancy that she could see a black figure pacing back and forth through the shadows of the drifting ships. Those grey shapes moved over that deck and beyond, racing ahead of the Oracle's prow, along her path to the shoreline of the Island of the Dead.

The men who crewed the ships I'd just left were not veterans. Most of them were not Ceian. They were farmers and fishermen, merchants and scribes, long-retired palace guards, children almost as young as those Ceiao considered recruiting age. Any Ceian would know at a glance that the ships' formations were the first most of those pilots had ever flown: too slow on one wing, bulging and misshapen on another, distinctly amateur, distinctly human.

"What about the summons to Lieutenant Ludon on Ceiao?" I said to the elderly Szayeti officer next to me. "Has he acknowledged it yet?"

She flicked through her tablet, mouth a tight line. "No, Consort," she said. "There's no reply."

There had been no reply from Flavia's old friends on Ceiao—not Enxadan, not Barboulethan, not a one of the councillors who she and I had been bribing for years. There had been no reply from her allies among the gangsters, nearly all of whom had been jailed. A handful of my sworn men had answered the call, not even enough to fill two ships. Galvão at least had written back, a short note:

> *Admiral—*
>
> *You were once a loyal Ceian citizen, and whether or not I was glad to follow you, I was always proud to fight beside you. Whatever enchantment the Szayeti queen has spun, I believe that inside you beats the heart of a Ceian soldier. It is my most fervent wish that Ceirran will free you soon.*

He did not say whether *Ceirran* meant the boy or the god, and I did not want to know.

"And from Belkayet? From Medveyet?" I said. "From the

market at Plyusna?" The officer shook her head at that, too. Scraps had arrived from around the galaxy: a little gold from the universities on Sintia, a little ship fuel from the recently successful rebels on Cherekku. When I had written to the dukes of Itsaryet demanding tribute, they had sent us a carpet, which, when we unrolled it, proved to hold a single centono and a straw doll dressed in the yellow robes of a temple priestess. She was making an obscene gesture.

But though Szayet was alone, the Szayeti had come to fight. From the poles the people had come, from the tropics, from the vineyards and cornfields and orchards, from all the temples that were not in open rebellion, from the half-drowned towns and ancient cities, from the quarries and pearl farms. They poured into Alectelo and the surrounding islands, bringing their fathers' guns and their rusted transport ships, hoping to train as well as they could in the little time remaining to us. Even Szayet's war minister, Delio, had returned from his own lands, rail-thin and red-eyed. He'd been awake at his daughter's bedside every night for three weeks, he said. I had taken him onto the palace balcony for a drink after one of the strategy meetings, and after some half hour of gentle inquiry about her prospects, he had abruptly asked to see the Pearl of the Dead.

My own memory disc was inside my tunic, against my belly, and every morning I turned it over in my hands for an hour, thinking of the memories of mine that it was collecting and storing, of Ceirran's memories to which I had listened all those months ago. But I'd taken Szayet's Pearl from the pocket over my heart, where I always kept it.

He'd looked at it hard. I'd seen tears glinting in his eyes. "Consort," he said to me, "Ana—did you ever understand what it meant to touch something holy? Before now, I mean."

He had been right to ask. It was different, profoundly different, from the days on Ceiao after Szayet had made that Pearl for

Matheus Ceirran. Something of it was the prospect of immortality, that was true. But the rest of it was an odd solidity—a presence in the world, on this earth, that I did not think I had ever felt before. That was not the Pearl. It was coming home in the evening to Szayet's bed, and laying my head on her breast, and thinking: the rest of my life. The whole of my life. The fact that I would never choose another life.

There had once been some unreal quality to Alectelo for me, a looseness and a lightness, the otherworldliness of a world that was deeply other to me. Perhaps it was my changed perspective, or perhaps it was a material change, the turn of the city toward deadly purposes, the certainty of the oncoming fleet. We still danced, Szayet and I, more than ever, and we set off what fireworks we had left above her palace every night. But her ballroom, her bed, her arms, these were no longer places made only of fire and air. There was such a particular sense of satisfaction in me at that—such a particular sense of relief.

Delio had pressed the Pearl back into my palm. "That I should live to see these days," he said, not more than a breath, "that I should have lived to see days like these—" and I had felt I knew exactly what he meant.

By the time we skidded across the sea through the Alectelan harbor-gate, there were no shadows left on the water. The storm winds had roared up from the southeast, blowing before them green spittle and muddy white, and when we ground to a stop on the concrete, the sky on the far side of the Library was colorless. I could not see the Oracle's boat now at all, and I hoped to myself that her coracle had landed on the Island of the Dead's shore before the rough seas had come. It put a knot in my stomach that she was alone.

When she'd buried her father, she hadn't buried him on her own. There had been another pair of hands to lift the coffin then, to carry the stone for the sarcophagus, to push her shovel into the hard-packed earth. There had been two members of *Dom* Caviro when her father had died, and now there was one.

I had asked to go with her. "Just to help with the digging," I'd said. "I'll be silent. You won't know I'm anything but a pair of hands."

"You know the law, Anita," she'd said. "The Island of the Dead is for *Dom* Caviro alone. That law is sacred to the people."

"We're sacred to the people now, goddess," I said.

But she shook her head. "You have other work to do," she'd said. "This is mine."

Delio was waiting on his knees for me at the bottom of the ship's ladder. I gestured him up with some embarrassment. "Ill fortune, this," I said. "I hope those liburnae are well above the weather. I wouldn't trust those pilots to keep their stomachs. What's the word from the rebels?" We had been sending diplomats to those islands for the last week, fiercely making the argument that Ceiao was a worse enemy than we could ever hope to be.

"Excellent news, Consort," said Delio, bowing. "There's an envoy waiting for you in the Library. What's more, they say they've been approached by the other Ceian admiral."

That stopped me in my tracks. "What's he said to them?"

"That there's trouble on Ceiao, Consort," said Delio. "Riots in the streets—protests in your favor. You had better come and hear."

I whistled softly through my teeth. I did not fool myself that Otávio could not crush any Ceian resistance, not after what he had done to me, but unrest might push the date of our battle out by months. We could fund Ceian protesters—we could try to fan a rebellion. Szayet could manipulate events on Ceiao from afar, exactly as Ceiao did with its own colonies. "All right," I said. "Fetch my wife and my officers. I had better wash my face, I stink of fuel— What is it?" Delio was shaking his head.

"She's in the Library already, Consort," he said. "Your officers, too. I don't think she's inclined to be patient."

"Mercy, she digs quick," I said. "Well, let's face our fates, shall we?"

By the time we had shoved our way into the streets, the rain had begun. Between the fleet recruits pouring in from every corner of Szayet and the worshippers making pilgrimage to get a look at their new gods, there was hardly room to breathe in Alectelo these days. We fought our way from the theater to the Summer Market down to the Bolvardo del Tombo, amid a press of people who pointed at the storm clouds drawn over our ships, whispered, and made brief, clumsy obeisance to me. Some were holding out scraps of paper—prayers, requests for blessings. I slowed to acknowledge them, but Delio pulled me by the elbow, urgent, toward the swell of the Library domes. "Through here," he bellowed over the thunder, and I followed him up a flight of slippery steps and into the dry hall.

This, too, was packed. Red-cloaked palace guards lined the walls, stood shoulder to shoulder across the black-and-white floor. "Szayet!" I called, striding forward. I couldn't see her in this throng. "Szayet—"

I couldn't spot my officers, either. There was something peculiar about the light in here. Something peculiar about the air, too: I felt a draft, surprisingly damp. I was too short to quite see the other end of the dome, but the hundred colors that beamed down from the windows seemed to be in an odd pattern there—odd, or—

Thunder rolled. My foot skidded and crunched. The floor was littered with gold and purple: broken glass.

The window in front of me had shown Ceirran, lying on a purple bed, crowned and smiling. Now, where his head had been, raindrops splattered through. Someone had smashed his face.

Behind me, the door slammed.

I whirled. The palace guards had closed ranks. At the back of the room, Delio was drawing a heavy bolt across the door.

"You *shit*," I said, and cracked off three shots before numbness tumbled down my right side to my wristbone. The gun fell. I staggered, fumbled at my neck, and seized the handle of a knife stuck into the meat of my shoulder. Delio was shouting, incomprehensible in my thundering ears—I jerked the knife out and swung it round as hard as I could—the palace guard who'd stabbed me caught my wrist in midair. I howled with pain and brought my knee up into her groin.

That was when the rest of the guard grabbed me, naturally. My arms were wrenched behind my back, the barrel of a gun shoved into the nape of my neck. An enormous hand slammed across my mouth. I sank my teeth into it.

The owner yelped. "Holy Flame, you absolute child," they said, in an all too familiar voice. "Gag her and tie her to a chair. Turnabout is fair play, isn't it, Admiral? This barbarian could stand to learn some manners."

The time it took for the Alectelan palace guard to shove a cloth in my mouth and drag me into one of the Library's study rooms was, fortunately, time to think. Unfortunately, it was also time for the person I had once known as Sasha Vualo to give me several well-aimed blows to the stomach, a split lip, and a spectacular black eye. I'd learned battle in Sintian schools like the rest of Ceiao, but I'd learned hand-to-hand fighting in the Outer City, and I went at them like a street cat: nails a first resort, teeth second, thrashing and kicking at the guards' grip. By the time I'd been wrestled down and tied onto a rickety wooden chair, Sasha was nursing three bloody scratches across their cheek, and I was nursing several conclusions, none of them good.

"*Dom* Harsaky are oathbreakers," I said, when I was safely bound to the chair and Sasha had yanked the makeshift gag out of my mouth. To my left and right, bookshelves packed with printed poetry, rolled-up maps, histories, and sheet music framed the door into the hall. Beyond, rain streaked through the hole in the stained glass. "Prince Polina sending you to Szayet to break the peace treaty she's only just signed on her father's behalf—that's a double-cross that won't play well on the trade routes."

"Polina hasn't broken any treaties. As far as the galaxy is concerned, I'm acting alone. Who would let their wayward youngest sibling do a foolish thing like sneaking back into the arms of the people who'd taken them captive not three months ago?" said Sasha. "For which I received a very public reprimand, I'm afraid, and a set of equally public orders not to leave the homeworld for half a year. Defying the crown prince's explicit command, accepting unverified information about the Pearl of the Dead from the lord of Arqueiran and the Shieldmirror, and, of course, spending a decade pouring millions of dekar into a harebrained scheme of my half sister's to find a legendary diamond island—I'm afraid I haven't earned a reputation as someone who does as wiser heads advise. You'd know something about how that feels."

"What did this prick promise the emperor?" I said, jerking my head at Delio. "Ownership of all Szayet's pearl farms? That Szayet would be his client? His colony?"

"I'm really not the emperor," said Sasha. "He promised me you, you half-witted, pustulous, murdering, shit-crusted hog. He promised me that, once the Szayeti were done with you, I'd have your living body to take to Kutayet. And when I've broken every finger on your butcher's hands, and cut your lying tongue into pieces in your mouth, and dressed you in rags and sent you barefoot through the streets of Kutayet's capital for Polina's triumph—when you're listening to the people of my city mock you, and the children shoving to be the first to throw fruit at you, and the noblemen laughing at your face and your dress and your birth—when you know what it is to be alone in that court, alone and hated and humiliated, and you learn exactly how fast you'd break—then, you piss-blooded sand flea, I'll fly you to that place near the Black Maw where the Fortunatas used to be, where you left Carmela's body, and I'll throw you in, and I'll watch you wrinkle and wither and grey and rot into dust."

I took this in, along with a nasty draft from the roof. The rain was beginning to slow. Delio had been watching this exchange from the doorway. When I caught his eye, he sneered.

"When the Szayeti are done with me," I said, directly to him.

"There will be a trial," Delio said, confirming my fears. "After the planet is brought back under the control of those loyal to Alekso Undying, naturally. Deicide. Usurpation of the rightful Oracle. Driving the people to worship lifeless idols—"

Sasha winked at me. They must have come to Delio with the secret about Alekso's deterioration as soon as I'd ruined their plans for Arcelia, I thought bitterly. "Ceirran's as alive as your god ever was," I said. In the dome beyond the doorway, the rain was drying into a steady drip down the jagged edges of the glass.

"Say what blasphemies you like," said Delio. "It was the hand of our god that revealed to the Kutayeti emperor's bastard how the—"

"Careful," said Sasha, a low rumble.

"It was the hand of our god that gave the Kutayeti scientist the genius for the Terrestrial Intelligence," said Delio passionately. "Beneath His solitude, His benevolence remains, His soul remains, there is something that can be saved of Him, once a way is found to let pearl speak to pearl. I knew when I saw what the swarm of ships did to Szayet that day. I knew—and the Szayeti knew, too, Decretan, however many of them still deny it to themselves. I knew that guilt was buried in Szayet. I knew that the rot had taken root. When I have that Pearl in my ear, Decretan, and I have raised Alekso from the dark places in which He wanders, justice will be done. Mortal justice must be done, or whatever remnants of divine justice are left in this sorry world will come down again upon us, and this time we will not survive them. History must read the accusations, and history must know the truth. There must be a reckoning. There *must*—" His voice dropped low. "And then my daughter will be well again."

The rain had stopped altogether. The wind was blowing fierce and wild, a winter wind if I had ever felt one. The sky through Ceirran's face was brightening fast. "Did Szayet ever even make it to the Island of the Dead?" I said. "Or did you seize her when she was still on the boat?"

"Prince Sasha's men graciously allowed her to bury her sister," said Delio coldly, "with all rites and honors. Then they seized the Island—"

"Ceirran's bones!" I said reflexively. "Foreigners on the Island of the Dead? You call yourself devout?"

"They waited at the shoreline," said Delio, his face darkening, "out of respect for the body of the King of the Universe." Sasha's lip curled. If they'd ordered their men not to violate the Szayeti tradition, I was willing to bet it had been after fierce argument. "They informed the false Oracle that she would be borne back to Alectelo as a prisoner," Delio went on. "They advised her to prepare a confession. She was to meet you here when you returned from training the new recruits. You would be brought in chains before the tribunal."

Thunder rolled above us. His mouth twitched in a humorless smile. "She refused to join you," he said. "She has walled herself in the Tomb of Alekso Undying. Prince Sasha's men have been calling out to her to tell her we have you, and they have received no answer. It seems she would prefer to leave you to die."

The bottom of my stomach dropped out. "Would she?" I said, grinning to hide it. "Because it seems to me you're forgetting something. You've got the Island and you've got the Library.

Terribly brave—no, really, I'm not lying. It *is* terribly brave to go up against tremendous odds. My army's hanging in the atmosphere, and beneath it is a street full of citizens who Kutayet bombed not very long ago, and they're not on your side, are they? No, if you had an army's worth of Szayeti, you wouldn't have bothered to lure me here. Say what you like, but I say the Alectelans will hate you a hell of a lot more than they hate a queen who's made them wealthy for the first time in three hundred years." I barked a laugh. "When every Alectelan in the city has this building under siege, naturally, you'll want to throw journals at them. And if you manage to hold out for longer than a day or so, why, you can eat Alekso's maps."

Thunder rolled again. I pitched my voice over it: "If you think you and your new Kutayeti friend can last in a siege against the whole Szayeti people, you're not devout, friend—you're mad. Who in that whole empire can build the Terrestrial Intelligence now? I shot Carmela, and I shot the doctor on Itsaryet, and I smashed the manual. Who else had that so-called divine genius you think Alekso Undying gave Carmela? You were barely willing to use the swarm ships against Ceiao when we were fighting over Itsaryet. All you can do now is lose them."

The light on the puddles in the dome was nearly daylight, now. Blue flickered through the grey where Ceirran's face had been. "You didn't smash the manual," said Sasha.

"I did," I said, startled.

"No," said Sasha. "Your husband smashed it on your wedding day, not you. You watched. Admiral Ceirran told you that it was finished. I suppose you believed him."

There was a thick silence.

I said, very slowly, "How do you know what Julhan said to me on our wedding day?"

The wind through the broken ceiling was rising, cold and dry. The clouds were moving westward rapidly now, thinning, growing white. A well-washed cotton blue stretched out over the remnants of the storm.

The swarm of ships hung just north of the sun. In the fresh light of the afternoon, it gleamed like a second star, like ten thousand shields, like an apple waiting in the sky for someone to pull it down. Even from this distance, I could see every ship was striped: blue, blue, as blue as the sweet clean sky, the blue stripes of the Ceian fleet.

Thunder rolled again, and I understood now that it was not thunder. Through the swarm, dark flecks tumbled toward the distant sea. A curled piece of steel—a wing. Scraps of engines. A Szayeti, clawing frantically at the air.

"I know because he told me," said Sasha, "in return for us lending him one of the working Terrestrial Intelligence hosts we had left," and they raised two fingers to their ear. I noticed there, belatedly, a little black dot only as big as my pinkie nail.

"Yes," they said, and then, to me, "I'm told to tell you that Ceiao will still forgive you, if you beg."

"You lying fuck," I said.

"Exactly what you said she'd say, Admiral," said Sasha, finger to their ear, turning away from me. "Thank you, Admiral. Yes, Admiral. Yes, the skies are clear. You may begin the ground assault."

To the north, I heard a dull thump.

The roof shattered. Glass exploded down into the dome: an icon here, a portrait there, a long strip of battle scene that had stretched over a door. Splashing into the puddles, streaking across Szayeti hands, Szayeti faces, into Szayeti chests, down in every inch of space, Ceirran rained.

The floor of the study had gotten drunk somehow. It reeled, staggered, and swung up toward my ear. An eggshell cracked somewhere. The sea came in.

Let's say we're somewhere. Let's call it: every now and then.

Let's say that every now and then, while we're walking, we come upon a river. Let's say that along one shore of the river blue sedge sprouts, and along the other, asphodel flowers. Beside us are myrtle trees growing.

You see her on the far bank. Her body is colorless, her edges blurred and thin, but you know her. You know her from her walk, you know her from the way she holds her head up, fierce and unconquerable. You know the light in her eyes. You know her from the way that, every few minutes, something in her image shivers, and the world becomes visible through her throat.

Celia! Celia! you call. Celia, is it true? Celia, what did she do to you? Celia, stay a moment. Celia, I never thought—

She turns away.

CHAPTER

FIFTEEN

"...half as fast. The man doesn't have any—"

"Then by all means act on your own. I'm sure the Ceian won't mind."

"Keep that tone out of—damn, damn, that was Cabero Plaza. What's the word from the Island of the Dead?"

"You know what the word from the Island is. Your officer corps is a flock of superstitious children. Allow me—"

This part of the sea was warm, dark, and tremendously soft. The current was buffeting me further down, further down. That was all right. There was nothing to fight here.

Somewhere at the end of a long tunnel, noises tugged at my head. No human being, I thought with a distant irritation, could possibly be cruel enough to wake someone as tired as I was.

"—it'll be your fault."

"Don't be naive, Minister. A girl like that didn't get this far by weeping and wailing over the people she's charmed into bed. Tell her to hail us and get to bargaining. Beyond a doubt, she's carrying a tablet, and likely besides—"

"There's only ever been one piece of quicksilver pearl allowed on that Island. She only took Alekso Undying and those desecrations of Pearls of the Dead—I guarantee it."

"I'm amazed by what you take on faith."

Light had begun to bleed into the edges of my vision. So had other things. Warmth was sliding down my forehead, dripping into my hair. My nose was full of the stink of iron.

Report damage, Captain. Sir yes sir. Left shoulder, throbbing; left hip, same; left hand, numb. Head, pounding like a festival parade, pain drawn up into a hot white star above my ear. The lip I'd split, swollen and soft. A bright stinging spiderwebbed over the right side of my face. There had been glass. A rain of glass. There had been lightning. Someone would want me to get up soon. Not just yet.

Something boomed. A gun rattled off a short sentence. "Sir, I can't hold for thirty more minutes this door—" said a voice in a thick Szayeti accent.

"You'll hold until we evacuate, damn you," said Sasha Harskaye. "Minister, if she isn't in contact with an exospheric ship now, she will be within the hour. When it swoops down and she flees, you can be the one of us who's left staring drop-jawed at the sky like a pea-chicken in the rain. Find a reason to let my men onto that beach to seize the queen of Szayet, or I'll find one for you."

I woke.

That boom had come from some fifty feet behind me, and it had echoed. This meant I was no longer in the little study but the dome beyond it. Therefore the room I was in had four exits, and that the one from which the noise had come, judging by the angle of the light in my eyes, must have been the northeast. Beyond it would be half a mile of streets, then a dock, then the Island.

Then Szayet.

Sasha was a few steps away from my head, which wasn't where I would've wanted them, but which meant they weren't between me and the door. It also meant they couldn't see my hands. My wrists were bound behind my back, but my arms seemed looser.

The bindings on my legs had given way entirely. The chair must have shattered when I'd been thrown in the explosion. That explained the throbbing pain down my spine and along the backs of my thighs. I twitched my finger minutely and felt a piece of glass slide beneath it.

"You'll find one for me?" said Delio's voice, low and dangerous. "Am I talking to the youngest legitimate child of the Defender of the Holy One, or to a Ceian heretic?"

"For the love of—" Sasha began, and the war minister snapped back at once, both of them speaking loudly enough that I could move my hand more quickly beneath the noise. A hundred tiny crystal pieces prickled at my already stinging palms, but here was a jagged edge, slicing nastily into my finger—yes, it was small enough that I could scrabble at it with one hand and tuck it into my palm. Just in time: Sasha and the minister had gone silent.

"Visual signal's back," said Delio shortly.

"No, really, is it?" said Sasha. "Quiet. I think the audio—"

"—captured alive," said the voice of Otávio fuzzily. "And, secondly, that your men take absolutely no Pearls of the Dead from the Island or from her person. If this condition isn't met, Ceiao will be required to impose far more stringent consequences after the battle is—"

"You've made yourself very clear," said Delio, a nasty edge to his voice. I twisted my hand and began to saw at the rope binding my wrists with the edge of the broken glass.

"If you're in the mood to threaten, you might ensure there's someone here left to offer threats to," said Sasha. "Your transport ships are coming to reinforce our position shortly, I don't doubt. Your ground troops must just be delayed on the current. Have you ever been on the other side of a door from an angry mob, Ceirran? No? It's an experience not to be missed."

"You knew Decretan was a rabble-rouser," said Otávio. "The Alectelan mob will have more important things to worry about than you, Your Highness, when this swarm you sold us is through with its work on the planet." There was another boom and a splintering sound from the direction of the door. "I'm sure that in the meantime your soldiers can manage a few fanatics," said Otávio lightly.

The rope snapped. That was my left hand free, though this didn't restore any sensation to the very tips of my fingers, which was a bad sign. I slipped the glass into my left hand regardless and went to work on the right, keeping my cheek pressed flat to the floor.

"Loaned, not sold," said Sasha warningly. "Admiral, the Intelligence isn't a fleet or a rocket. Waste it on bombing and gunfire alone, and you won't get another. I want a full report from its eyes and ears in Szayet's exosphere. Where are the loyalist—"

And that was the right hand free. I tuned out the noise of Sasha's question and Otávio's reply, and listened for boots crunching, shifts in weight. There were very few. How many guards in the Library had been killed in the explosion? The number must be high. One soldier was ten feet away from my head, which was suitably close, but I would have to lead with my numb hand. Another was a few feet to the right of Sasha, but then there would be Sasha, too. Five feet down and a little westward—yes, those footsteps were light, this was someone thin. Fast, maybe, but I was fast, too. An advantage in bulk could give me the edge.

Otávio was still speaking, a buzzing drone to which I paid no attention. I eased my body along the floor, so slowly that I was hardly moving at all, and cracked an eye open. Sasha and Delio were bent over Otávio's translucent head, Delio jabbing a finger toward Otávio's nose. Behind me, something thudded. Sasha turned—

I exploded up and hurled myself on the thin soldier, bearing her down, trapping her gun hand under my weight. Immediately every muscle, bone, and inch of skin with a working nerve protested. My left hand fell to my side, useless. I twisted the soldier's hand with my right, ignoring her howl, and emptied her gun into the soldier to my left, who had managed to get her own gun out of its holster; the soldier behind me, who hadn't; and Delio, whose mouth opened slightly before he crumpled to the floor.

"Oh, for God's sake," said Otávio crossly, and vanished.

"Not me?" said Sasha, with admirable calm.

"I kill traitors first," I said. "Old habit. And you're unarmed." And there was one round left in the gun, and I didn't want to waste it before I could drag out of Sasha whatever information they had, but they didn't need to know that.

Their lip curled disdainfully. "So are you, or something close to it," they said. "That army you left in the atmosphere is so much scrap metal. But where's your mistress's personal guard? Why hasn't she come to fetch you?"

"My wife lets me pull off the daring rescues every once in a while," I said. "It's her remarkable generosity of spirit. Don't suppose you'd be inclined to tell me how many of your men are guarding the Island of the Dead's beach, by the by."

"Is that what it is?" said Sasha. "How strange. Your husband just told me there's a smuggler's ship three hundred and fifty miles over Alectelo, about to bear her up to a satellite."

I hesitated only a moment, but a moment was enough: Sasha lunged. I fell hard and shouted soundlessly, the breath knocked out of me. I didn't have a chance to get it back. Their knee ground down on my stomach, their enormous hand thumping my hand against the floor until the gun flew out of it and skidded toward the minister's body. They reached for it—for their size, they were fast as anything—but size and speed weren't military experience, and they certainly weren't a hundred nights' experience being drunk and cold and very angry on the street in front of Ceian bars. They'd left open a certain sensitive spot, and even with two useless hands, I still had a working knee.

I brought it up. Sasha toppled to the side, mouth open. I scrabbled over their body and seized the gun with my working hand. "Liar," I said. "There's no smuggler's ship."

Sasha bared their teeth. "Wouldn't you like to know," they said faintly.

"Call your men," I said. "Tell them to retreat from the beach."

"The Ceians who killed Matheus Ceirran were fools," they said through gritted teeth. "At least when he was alive you were on a leash. You want to bargain with me? You witless brute, you should have left yourself something to bargain with. Shoot me now or leave me for the Ceian bombs. I'll see Carmela long before you see your concubine again."

I crouched down beside them, my thighs singing with pain, and tucked the gun barrel under their chin.

"It *was* foolhardy to come back into the arms of the people who'd just held you captive," I said.

"Hypocritical to gloat, don't you think?" they said tightly.

"You knew it was foolhardy," I said. "You knew the risk outweighed the reward. Convincing your sister must have taken a long time."

They laughed hoarsely, throat moving against the barrel of the gun. "Alekso of Sintia, these Szayeti heretics," they said. "No wonder you've made cause with them. As if the Lord of the Holy Flame would ever choose life! Perpetual life! Eternal, changeless, selfish life—as if He would ever trap Himself in mud and matter, as if He would choose *this* world to live in—"

"The world that isn't good enough," I said quietly. "I know."

They laughed again. After a second, their voice caught, and the laughter became only awful, scraping noise. I waited until they were silent, and then I said, "What prayers do you say for your dead?"

Sasha's face went blank. "What?"

"Your prayers for the dead," I said. "Are they in Kutayeti? Malisintian? What do they ask for—healing? Love? Rest?" The Szayeti had two: one in Sintian that Szayet's family used, and one that the Alectelans said in their own tongue. Each of them asked for peace.

"You don't believe in Him," said Sasha coldly.

"Does that matter?" I said. "Does it work even if I don't believe?"

They shut their eyes and nodded.

"At dawn," they said, a whisper. "Once a year, for a friend or a neighbor. For a sibling—every day." Their breath rattled. "The words aren't important," they said. "We ask for the dead to be purified. We ask for everything that was false and mortal about them to dissolve. We ask for them to emerge from this life as their true selves, their essential selves, with all the tangle and hardship and disorder stripped away." Their mouth flattened. "We kneel," they said. "We ask this on bended knee, facing the sun. Will you do that, Ceian?"

I said, "I've gone to my knees for the sake of love before."

"Swear," they said. "On something that matters to you. Swear."

"I swear," I said, "I swear, if you tell your men to leave the beach, then every morning for the rest of my life I will go to my knees and pray for Carmela Lukhaya's soul. I swear it on the memory of Flavia Decretan."

They looked hard into my face. "Give me a tablet," they said.

I felt over the corpse of the soldier I'd first tackled, keeping an eye and the gun barrel on Sasha's head. "Here," I said eventually, tossing it onto their stomach. "Now we both have something to lose. Tell your men to abandon the Island."

They sat up with a grunt and took the tablet. It erupted at once with a noisy stream of Kutayeti. Sasha replied rapidly in the same language. I understood a few words: *Oracle* and *ships*, and then *drank*, and then *leaving*, and Sasha stilled.

They thanked the voice in Kutayeti, said again, "Thank you," in Sintian, for good measure, and passed their hand over the tablet. The light winked out.

They bowed their great white head. "There was no need," they said.

"Speak sense," I said. "Are they abandoning the Island or no?"

"I told them to abandon it," said Sasha. "But they were going to row away in a few minutes. A scout landed on the beach and went to the Tomb of Alekso Undying, not long after the swarm began bombing the planet. There were—bodies."

"Bodies?" I said. "But Szayet went alone."

Sasha's eyes searched mine. I recognized, with shock, a kind of carefulness there, a hesitation, a pity. Had they seemed so tired a moment ago?

"She didn't go alone," they said. "She brought prisoners in the boat with her. Rebels from the islands. Priestesses from Itsaryet. She tested the poison on them, first."

and

"First?" I said. "What do you mean, *first*?"

here

"Admiral," said Sasha, very quietly, "she saw the swarm of Ceian ships. She knew she couldn't fight it. I'm sorry. I am sorry."

time

My hand wavered. The gun barrel sank toward the floor.

Three things happened very nearly at once.

The first was that on the other side of the northeast wooden door, where there had been silence for some time, I heard a thick, final-sounding *crunch*. The door shattered. Through it came shouting, and after the shouting, the blunt end of a hefty marble pillar.

The second was that Sasha Harskaye seized my hand at the wrist. I shouted, jerking the gun toward their face. They stumbled into me, dragging my gun hand down, grabbing at my hip for balance. At my belt, something caught and tore my skin. With effort, though the pain was sharp and though I could feel blood hot on my hand, I dragged my finger up onto the gun's trigger.

The third was that, at the moment the pain sparked in my hand, the whole floor of the dome rippled like the sea. I was thrown backward, skidding through the doorway of the study. Sasha flew backward, too, and landed on their neck. Their limbs unknotted. To my left came a loud crash—the marble pillar, I thought—and shouts of pain. Then the floor was still.

No, it was not still. The mosaic was motionless. But on top of the tiles, the color in the scattered shards of glass began to drain away. Now they were faded, now they were clear, now they were white. Opacity spilled through them like salt, brighter and brighter, liquid light and heat—and then the light faded, and where the glass had lain, the floor was covered with grey-white sand. The sand from which that glass had been made, decades or centuries ago.

"Oh, hell," I said.

ends.

At every wall, on every shelf, the pages of the books of the Library of Alectelo were curling up.

One, as I watched, crusted over with dull green, and shrank in an instant into a soggy, thick mass. One flared up with pale, ghostly flames. When they died, it was black charcoal. One shrank from the outside in, bit by bit, edges nibbling themselves away. The tablets flaked, the pearl dimmed and peeled, their steel rusted over with red. The paper was yellower and yellower, the ink was black and brown and pale grey and gone. The books were loose pages. The books were scraps of metal. The books were shreds. Every last book, every history and poem and play and story, was pouring into dust. Dust spilled from the shelves; dust cascaded from the roof. Dust drifted in great pale clouds, ceiling to floor.

I pushed myself upright. My hands were covered in dry, color-less powder. My eyes stung.

In the dome, Sasha lay still. Dust collected in the spill of their white hair, at the corners of their eyes. If it bothered them, they said nothing. They did not cough. They did not sit up. Their chest was moving slightly, and their mouth was open. The dust fell steadily into it, swelling their tongue with white.

Through the open windows, through the broken door, down through the glassless roof, dust drifted, swirled, floated up toward the sun, toward the silver cloud beside the sun, quiet as firelight, thick as rain. All of it laden with that same smell: grass and deep yellow dryness. The smell of old books.

It had not only happened in the study. It had not only hap-pened in this hall. There were something like nine million books in the Library, Szayet had told me once. Nearly twenty thou-sand tons of paper and steel and pearl. Dust would drift through Alectelo for a long time.

The room had stopped moving, the mosaic tiles did not col-lapse into clay, the sand did not reform into glass again. I was not seeing the future or the past. Whatever host of the Terrestrial Intelligence was controlling the swarm above us had cried out, just as the hosts in the Fortunatas had cried out. It had reached out its mind to find a place like the Black Maw, where time meant as little as the direction of the wind, and it had been answered.

But there were no explosions from the sky, no screams. The break in time had not lasted long. Either the host had wrested itself back under control, as no Terrestrial Intelligence ever had before, or the moment when it had lost control of itself and warped time had been triggered by something—an outside source.

I looked at my bleeding hand, and I touched my hip, and felt the hilt of the pearl knife. On a night one thousand years ago, I had thought that this knife must store some portion of Black Maw energy in it, that it must contain some rudimentary intelligence.

Through the open door, someone shouted faintly, "Consort."

My movements were the movements of a dream, my feet in the thick sand, guards' bodies blurring through falling white. The pain in my body had faded into a single, singing throb: my laboring heart. There was no other sensation in the world.

The corridor was full of Alectelans. I recognized them, each of them: a handful of low-ranking enlisted men from the barracks, the palace steward, the senior groundskeeper, a few of the palace flute players, Jedmaya and Karadzaty who owned taverns in Cabero Plaza, cupbearers, laundresses, both of the attendants for Szayet's hair, a cluster of dockworkers to whom I'd once lost ninety dekar at cards, the sailors from our pleasure boat, children.

"Consort," said the palace steward urgently. "Consort, there's a mob of our people three hundred strong outside. Where shall we go? What shall we do?"

I looked slowly from face to face. They seemed now near, now distant, the world focusing and refocusing through glass.

"Go," I said. "Make peace. Keep what sovereignty you can, those of you who can beg for it. Ask to treat with Captain Galvão. He is a fair man. Tell him I asked him to keep you from cruelty. Go away."

They stared at me. "Consort—" began a dockworker.

"No," I said, and turned away.

Light flashed through the empty roof. Yes, the swarm had survived its flare of Black Maw energy; that was its ships at work. Around the Library, down the winding streets and avenues, over the pearl roofs, there should have been noise, explosions, gunfire and screaming and the crash of metal. But within the slow dust I heard only silence. Szayet was dead.

And after all it was not too late. After all, if I walked out into the street, and begged those black ships for forgiveness, they would give it to me. After all, I could be taken up into the heavens, and return to that world into which I had been born—lesser, shamed, despised, punished, but spared this city's fate. After all, I could still look back. And I would live a long life there, in peace, in the golden age of an empire, and when the ghost came into my face and looked out from behind my eyes, I would hardly know it was there. And whatever small spirit I had left behind in this library would sit still and silent, white dust collecting in it and around it, a pillar of salt.

The last night I had seen my friend Matheus alive had been a night like this. There had been snow, and the warm white silence that snow brought down. *I believe in the immortality of a man's name*, he had said.

Despite all that had come after, I thought that was the last time I had ever really spoken to him.

I put my left hand over my heart. There was the little hard bead: Szayet's Pearl of the Dead. I had sworn an oath to her, before her city and mine, to make that Pearl into her soul, to carry it with me until I died, to be her Oracle.

The ghost had said: *You called my name, and I came from across the universe to answer you.*

"Szayet! Szayet! Szayet!" I murmured.

But in the dust there appeared no shape, no drifting blankness, no absence where a human being had been.

And I felt it for the second time, that winged and lawless joy I had felt in the dream where I had pulled the shroud from Ceirran's corpse and seen nothing beneath, because the dead were not here, they were gone—they were not in pearls, they were not in tombs, they were not in bodies, they were not walking into the world for the living to lay hands on their skin, and their names were hollow things. And love moved like an arrow through the empty places and passed onward, out of sight.

I drew the pearl knife. Its tip was flaking with blood, my blood, from when Sasha had gone for the gun. It had cut the poet-thief, too, hadn't it? It had cut her, and then answered her prayer.

How smoothly this blade had slid into Arcelia's artery. How neat, how fine. She hadn't even bled until I'd pulled it out again.

"Szayet," I said again, and shoved the knife with all my strength into my chest.

It met metal, skipped across it, and scraped down.

I cried out. The blade had had cut across my gut, a deep, ragged tear from my lowest left rib to my right hip. No pain, no pain at all, just warmth, swelling through my bellly and down my legs, leaving num bness in its wake.

I stumbled and fell back, intto the sand. The dust that had been the Library of Alectelo wawas very thick now, so thick III could not see the sun, Sasha's body, the

sha's body, the   sha's body, the open door. My h ands were pale, foreign things. With effort, I put one insi

de my tunic and drdrew out the object that had turned the knife aside from my heart. It was

my memory
disc.

Across

its center,

the pearl knife

had

left

a

long,

thin

scratch.

CAVICVIOCVIROCAROVACICAVOROCACAVIVIRO
Is King Alekso alive?
SHOW ME SHOWME SHOW   MESHOW

WME THE WAY   SO I CAN FOLL
ORIVACIVARIC VIR O   CAVIRO
WAI

He lives, and reigns,

WAI AI

and conquers the world.

AI AI AI A A A   AAAAAAAAAAAAAAA AIT
WAIT FOR ME
SHOW ME SHOW ME THE   THE THE THE
OW ME THEPLACE ACE WH
HEP LACE WHERE
THERE ARE NO MORE WORLDS TO CONQUER

and after that,
I remember

light. The walls of the Library, fallen away. Another bomb, I thought, more fire from the swarm. No—there were pale white shells lying in the dust. Shells, the stuff of limestone, and limestone was the stuff of marble. The walls of the Library, too, must have been

I was standing. Someone had pulled my arm over their shoulder. This was the street, these the cobblestones of Alectelo. "Consort," said a voice urgently into my ear, "Consort, are you awa

the disc, the memory disc pushed into my hand. "Hold on," said the voice. "Hold tight, woman, I can't run quickly," but I let my arm fall limply to my side. My memories, I thought, my memories were flowing through my hand and into this little thing, the first time I had fired a gun, the first time I had been kissed, my hardfought miseries, my hard-won joys, the smell of her perfume, her face, the warmth of her mouth, and as the rest of me sought to

claw upward out of my body and follow after her, this thing stayed
behind, this flat hard pearl thing, which had not touched or been
touched, this thing from which a stranger could demand my voi

the pain at last, unspeakable pain, the wound in my gut burning
white-hot

a seagull crying

rocking, up and down. Oars splashed.

I opened my eyes. Above me stretched the sky, cloudless and
clear as a bell, only a faint haze at the horizon. Dark blue in my
peripheral vision: a soldier's cloak. I struggled to sit up.

"Don't," said the woman. "Rest." It wasn't a Ceian at all. The
accent was Szayeti. I knew that face. It was Zorione, who had
been Szayet's maid since she had been a little girl.

"Where did you get that cloak?" I said, voice hoarse. "Where
are my officers?"

"Fled," said Zorione. "Gone over to the Ceian. I took this
cloak from a body on the beach. Your soldiers let us onto the
docks when I showed them the officer's pin."

I slumped back. In the distance, thunder rumbled again: the
swarm. My gut throbbed steadily, pain washing thoughts away
like rain. I could feel, at a strange distance, the weight of the
pearl disc in my hand, and could not summon the energy to toss
it away.

"You should go over, too," I said. "Once the battle's over, no
one will thank you for harboring an enemy of Ceiao."

Zorione said nothing for a while, her thin shoulders shifting
as she worked at the oars. At last she said, "The crowd was saying
that the Holiest is dead."

I shut my eyes. The rocking of the boat was lulling me into a half doze. The numbness lapped steadily outward, toward my ribs, my hips.

After some time, Zorione said, "I can't come closer to the shore."

I opened my eyes and, with great effort, rolled my head to the left. A rocky shoreline curled away against the waves, lining an island studded with pine trees. There were no soldiers there, Szayeti, Kutayeti, or Ceian.

"Get me as close as you can and put me out of the boat," I said. "I'll wash up on the shore."

"Consort—" said Zorione warily.

"It's enough," I said, and closed my eyes again. "Thank you."

Time drifted for a while. Static hissed. The tips of my fingers and toes were quite cold, I thought—and then all of me was cold, but distantly, almost amusingly, my tunic and cloak heavy with water, salt screaming in the open scratches along my back and my thighs and the cut on the side of my head.

I lay on damp sand. Not far from me, waves hissed and foamed. I could get up and walk, I thought. I could find the tomb. I had conquered a dozen moons, and the city of Ceiao, and I had raised mobs, and for love I had climbed through roofs, I had bombarded atmospheres, I had gone to my knees. I would get up. I would gather my strength, and then I would get up again.

"Anita," said a voice, "oh, Undying preserve me, Anita—"

"I thought you weren't a ghost," I said without opening my eyes.

Then hands were in my hair, gathering up my head and laying it on something soft. Someone lifted the pearl disc gently out of my palm. Someone pressed her mouth to mine. "Never," she said. "Anita, please, open your eyes—"

"As my lady commands me, I obey," I said, and did. Szayet was backlit by the sun, her features in shadow, but her hands beneath my head were warm and real.

"They told me you were dead," I said. "They told me you were fleeing the planet."

"They were liars," she said softly.

Sasha Harskaye's revenge. They had wanted prayers for Carmela badly, but they had wanted blood, too, and they had gotten it. They'd kept their end of the bargain, but they'd traded agony for agony, grief for grief. *You know what you have to lose*, I'd told them. They wouldn't see me on my knees before the Kutayeti emperor, the way they'd wanted. They wouldn't see me dying by Carmela's grave. They'd struck at all I had left to lose, too.

"Help me stand," I said. "Let me hold you."

Together we lifted my body up, she straining under my weight, me gritting my teeth against the pain in my gut. At last I got an arm around her and buried my face in her hair.

"I broke the law," I said. "I came to the Island. I'm sorry."

"No law was broken," she said. "You are my Oracle. Anita—"
My knees gave out, and my weight went into her, and she caught me and was silent.

"Come with me," she said.

That was slow going, too, my unsteady feet on the rocky path, her hands bearing me up. Through the pine trees we went, up the slope, to a little grey block no wider than my shoulders. On it was carved in neat Sintian letters:

SOMETIME QUEEN OF SZAYET

LAST ORACLE OF ALEKSO UNDYING

LOVING SISTER

ARCELIA CAVIRO DIOMATA

BELOVED OF GOD.

"Szayet," I said, but she said:

"This way, Anita. We don't have much time."

The tombs rose and fell around us, white and grey, worn with rain and time. I could read the letters on the next grave, CASIMIRO CAVIRO FAIFISTO, but after that my vision faded. There was only the next step, and the next, and the noise of Szayet's breathing, and the warmth of her skin.

At last we stopped. I pried my eyes open—it was growing more difficult—and saw a flat-roofed marble tomb, its door open. I could not read the first line of the engraving above it. Szayet's language, I thought, the Malisintian language, the dialect of the old conqueror and ancient Sintia.

But the second line—

"Beloved Disciple," I murmured.

Step by careful step, we advanced, until my boots hit dusty marble. The tomb was spacious and silent. Sunlight trickled down from a crack between the ceiling and the walls. In the room's center lay two limestone coffins, one crossways against the end of the other. A table at the far end bore a bowl of water, cups, and a bottle of wine.

Szayet helped me down so that I sat against the crossways coffin, my left fist pressed into my stomach, and she went to close the door. "Did you mean to stay here overnight?" I said when she returned, nodding my head as best I could at the table.

"I did," she said. "I wanted to keep company with her—" Her voice broke. "Keep company, and perform experiments on pearl," she said after a moment. "I haven't done any, not since you left for the Fortunatas, and the rebellion rose up, and—this doesn't matter. Anita, I saw smoke over the Library."

"It was the silver-eyed monster," I said. "The host." Thoughts had been knitting themselves together in my mind as I had drifted during the boat journey. Now they spread out, and I said, "The traitors got me away from you, into the Library, isolated me. Vualo—Sasha—they attacked me. They grabbed my hand. My quicksilver pearl knife, it cut me. It was warped when it passed through the explosion near the Black Maw, and now it carries that energy, it can pass it on to other pearl computers. The swarm above spoke to it, I think, and it absorbed that energy, too. Only for a second or two—just long enough..."

"The Itsaryeti priestesses used that knife centuries ago to sacrifice animals to Alekso Undying," said Szayet slowly.

"I think—I think Alekso of Sintia spoke to it," I said. I was growing very short of breath now. "Whatever scraps of his spirit are left. I heard him call Caviro's name, I think. I heard him ask Caviro to show him a path to follow."

"Blood," she said. "Something about blood makes pearl able to speak to other pearl. Or maybe not only blood. The experiments I came here to do—" She passed her hand over her face. "This doesn't matter, either. Anita, I should have come back when I saw the swarm. I should have led the people to fight. You called me brave, but I was afraid, I was so afraid. I could never have had an empire if you hadn't ruled it with me. I've always been afraid of war. I'm sorry—"

"Ah, Szayet," I said, "I know that tone. Don't be angry. Come here. Sit down."

She sank down beside me, back against her ancestor's coffin. "Give me your hand," she said.

"Don't give me that disc," I said. "I won't be the boy's trophy. I won't cut away my soul and pin it into pearl for him to hold and gawk at."

"Anita," she said softly, "let me not lose all of you."

At last I held out my hand. She pressed the little scratched disc into my palm. My fingers were growing colder, now, and it was difficult to feel the places where the pearl cut in.

"You and I might have ruled a better world," I said.

"Not better," she said, "only ours. That was all I wanted. I'm as selfish as you ever thought I was, Anita—selfish, and ambitious, and proud—"

"I wouldn't have you otherwise," I said, turning my face blindly into her neck.

"I'll be your Oracle," she murmured. "Though Szayet burns, I'll be your Oracle. I'll go to the ends of the earth to bear your soul. Though I prophesy for you in Alectelo's tunnels and sewers, though I walk in the Ceian triumph with you in my ear—"

"Liar," I said. "No soul on this earth or any other will ever triumph over you and I. I am dying, Szayet, dying, and I won't make a handmaiden of you again."

"I will not say goodbye to you," she said.

I sighed against her skin. "Do something for me."

"Anything," she said.

"Call me disciple," I said.

She pressed her forehead against mine. "I'm sorry I ever did," she whispered. "I'm sorry I was a liar."

"No lie," I said. "I was—only I wasn't his," and kissed her again, and lifted my hand from my stomach and brushed it against her mouth, streaking red behind. "There's wine for the great revelers," I said. "I was strong once—"

"You'll be strong again," she said, "only rest, don't speak. When you rise again in the Pearl of the Dead, you'll be glorious, you will be great—"

"Listen, Szayet," I said. "I was strong once, and in those days I wanted strength to be everything. I was useful once—and I clung to the hope that what mattered most was whether I was made use of. Now I am useless, and do you know, for the first time in my life, I'm unafraid. Kiss me."

She bent. Her mouth tasted of iron. I returned the kiss hotly, then fell back against her chest and sighed.

"Don't cry, Oracle," I said. "We had our goodbye, you and I, and our hellos. Call this *see you soon*. You always knew how this was going to end. What more could we have asked for?"

"I don't care how it ends," she said. "Anita, an ending is only one moment—and there's a billion more moments...I don't care if death is always the ending. I want to ask for more. I want to ask for everything. I want to ask for more time."

"The sun's setting," I said.

So it was. Red was beginning to lay its fingers through the door of the tomb, over the grey dust. We had danced through so many nights, she and I, and slept only in order to rise again. Her kohl smeared on my eyes, her mouth on my mouth, her city in my ears, in my heartbeat. Her voice, reading softly aloud to me the letters of her court, the poetry she liked best, the story of her life. Her body sleeping beside mine in the cool grey morning. No one else in the world held these things, not even her. I had carried them a long, long way.

Life!—Life, its sea and sky, the heat of blood and breath. Life: In it was every color, was the weight of brick on brick and foot on stone, was hunger and thirst and shivering from rain, was swifts and seagulls and dragonflies and sand, was meat, was bread, was salt. Life, my life, my sight and taste and touch, the only things I had that were mine alone, that had come into the world with me and that when I left the world would never be again. Heart and lungs, hands and tongue, elbows and teeth and liver and cheeks and spine and breasts and brain, those parts of me that had not been thrown to the winds with my sister or the ashes of my friend, the heavy animal parts of me that every minute sang the oldest hymn: I want, I want, I want to live. Despite it all, I want to live.

"I'll come home to you," I murmured. "In the Pearl, or out of it. From every corner of space and time. Call my name, and I'll always come home.

I have loved you, Gracia,

and I will love you, until the

until the

until

until

You've never known before that any place was a dream while you were dreaming. Neither have you ever been in a dream that had a smell. But the grass under your feet smells like grass, and the wind smells like smoke, and when you pinch yourself quite hard between your finger and thumb, it hurts like anything.

But you are dreaming. You know this with the certainty that you know the sun is up and the earth is down, that you are wading through mud up to your ankles, that your people are living in tents in a camp on a distant Ceian world, that you are a poet, and that the woman you loved is dead.

Beside you, a river whispers. On your bank grows blue sedge, and on the far bank asphodel flowers. Your face is wet; the smoke is stinging your eyes. It occurs to you, in the distant way of dreams, that you do not know what is burning. You begin to turn—

"Don't look back," says a voice from the far bank.

You look across the water.

It's been nearly ten years since you last saw him. He looks the way people always look in dreams: strangely clothed, his face blurred. And yet, as in dreams, you know who he is.

"Papa," you say, and you begin to run.

But he doesn't move. And when you reach the shore, you understand why. You reach out, and though the river is narrow, though he is as close as a breath, your hands pass through his hands. A second time you try to grasp him, and a second time you touch only mist. A third—and he vanishes.

Behind where he stood, a figure kneels in the mud, pulling at some half-buried thing. A silver disc, you think, with a scratch through its center. The woman seems terribly familiar to you. You have the strangest feeling that you are about to speak to her. You have the strangest feeling that you are about to ask her to save your life.

And as you open your mouth to speak, the figure pulls the circle up, and goes to swing it over her shoulder. You step forward, wrap your fingers around the disc's edges, and yank. The woman stumbles and falls. And you look at the silver disc.

These are memories, you think. Memories of lives, and deaths. Memories of a city. A thousand years. Today it takes the shape of a memory disc; yesterday, it might have been a shield. Tomorrow it may be a notebook.

Do you have the right to bear this city? Do you have the right to carry its weight?

You lift the shield onto your shoulder.

Wake up!

CHAPTER

SIXTEEN

Virgilia woke.

Yellow-grey sky stretched over the skiff's porthole, sewn with stars. Her heart was thundering wildly. It always did when she woke these days: first wordlessness, then the mind streaming upward, then her eyes flown open in the dark, her body a drumbeat, muscles tensed for something unseen.

After a few deep breaths she knew what had startled her, which was silence. The engine had stopped. The chair across from her sat empty. Virgilia unstrapped herself from her safety bindings, dropped into the narrow aft corridor, and clambered hand over hand down the skiff's ladder to the sand.

Smoke had made dishwater out of the sky. The wind bore sickly smells across the ocean: burnt kelp, rotten eggs, copper chemical sharpness like a coin in the throat.

Footsteps shone between the rocks and the water. Where they met the sea a thin, dark, grey-eyed boy stood, looking across the sea. "You can sleep longer, Eneida, if it's necessary," he said, without turning. "Neither of them has tried to leave the tomb."

Virgilia hadn't shut her eyes for longer than a few hours since time had stopped on her ship out from Itsaryet. When she'd been in the city of Ceiao, safe on a cot in one of the admiral's back rooms, she had wandered in the dark through his hallways, plucking this book or that from his shelves, sitting on the floor listening to the city's silence until color came into the walls, and the servants into the kitchen, and the day no longer belonged to her alone.

She didn't have the words for this. She rarely had the words for anything, not the right ones, not in her mouth; they knotted themselves up behind her teeth, fell out of her memory at the moment she most wanted them. Only poetry laid itself out before her in sluices and channels, ruled, bordered, comprehensible. Poetry she could scratch out and rewrite, again and again, until she had it right.

"I'm awake now, sir," she said, rather than attempting to explain.

The admiral hesitated. Virgilia braced herself a second before he said, "You persuaded her to be sensible once. You can persuade her again."

Her: Anita Decretan, wild-eyed and grinning, tossing the temple knife in the air in Túlio Cachoeiran's house. "Yes, sir," Virgilia said.

"Very well," said the admiral. "This way."

Before she followed the admiral up the rocky slope, she looked back. Alectelo was silverless, more smoke than towers. Beneath the smoke, the thin red loops of the harbor-gate reflected on the water, darkness bobbing with debris: ashes, wood, parts of ships, bodies. The Library domes had vanished.

Only a few ships of the admiral's swarm still hovered over the island, spilling fire. Others rose through the smoke from Alectelo's shore: Kutayeti fighters, Szayeti transport ships, Ceian galleys with fat black bellies. Virgilia imagined their holds, the stink there, the heaving breaths, prisoners packed shoulder to shoulder, hands grasping for slippery hands. From the admiral's warship, she'd watched the swarm stream into the night on the far side of the world, toward every winking light. She had wondered the name of the person wired into its heart. By the time the admiral had come to tell her that a boat had been sighted rowing toward the Island of the Dead, no Szayeti light had been visible anymore.

The graves passed by, one by one. Virgilia could not read the names, but the lantern that the admiral had brought from the skiff illuminated strange faces, marble and granite: here a hooked nose, here a slight smile, here carefully carved ringlets lying against the neck. Here an elderly woman, here a plump-faced man. Here a girl, very near her own age.

She would have known that face in a darkness three times as deep. She would have known that face with her eyes pulled out of her head. She slowed to a standstill and traced a finger over the marble mouth.

"Eneida," called the admiral ahead of her.

The tomb was smaller than she'd expected. The door was shut. Light spilled under it, patterned and broken—barred from the other side.

"Ana," said the admiral. "Oracle. Will you come out?"

Water whispered.

"We captured your maid, Oracle," the admiral said. "Zorione. She's well. She asked after you."

Insects in the pines. Shadows shifting under the door. Virgilia held still, and listened to the faint shuffle of sandal over stone.

The admiral said, "The commander of Ceiao would not want either of you to despair. I would make a god of him, too, Oracle. Is it such a blasphemy to your Szayeti faith to bargain with his heir as you bargained with him?"

The voice that spoke then was so like Arcelia's that Virgilia rocked back. It said: "To bargain with Flavia's murderer."

"I did not kill Flavia Decretan," said the admiral patiently.

"You have spent the last two years killing my wife," said the queen of Szayet. "You killed her by whispers, by rumors, by secrets. You persuaded her to tie her hand to yours, and if she had stayed with you, that would have been a kind of murder. You killed Flavia, Otávio Julhan. You made her fearful, you made her tired—you killed her, and her husband killed her, and Matheus Ceirran killed her, and Anita killed her, too. You will kill the whole galaxy before you die. You will make it small. You are killing Ceirran, and he will kill you."

"Come out," said the admiral. "Come up to my ship. I'll swear to your safety if you need me to. You are a Ceian client. Ana is my wife—my wife, Oracle, by law—and she is an admiral of Ceiao. Come back with me and tell the empire you were led astray. Tell us you are ready to be Ceiao's friends again."

"A generous offer," said the queen dryly.

"Even if it is generous, you can believe it," said the admiral. "You have no ships, Your Majesty. If the Kutayeti were telling the truth, you have no god. You have an angry mob in Alectelo, but anger passes, and when it does, we all learn what we are willing to give up in order to live. Ask my wife—she learned that on Ceiao, after the commander's funeral. People like her always come to light the fires, but when fire dies, the world is left to people like me."

"Imagine that I took your offer," said the queen.

"I am glad to hear you can imagine it," said the admiral.

"Imagine that I took your offer," said the queen. "I wonder what Ceiao would ask for in exchange. To walk before you in your triumph? To sign away Szayet's treasure and pearl in loyal tribute? To give my blessing to Szayet's governor, when Ceiao installs him in my palace?"

"Perhaps all of those," said the admiral. "But the Ceians who have met you say you are silver-tongued. Come up to my ship and bargain with me, and perhaps it will be none."

"None," said the queen thoughtfully. "And all I need to do for that *none* is lose this war and my wife."

"Your Majesty," said the admiral, "there has never been a mortal life without suffering. Today the Empire of Ceiao is where power lies—that was put in motion long before you or I were born. Set yourself against it, and you gain nothing. Is there no part of you that understands that *something* is better than that nothing? Is there no part of you that understands sacrifice?"

"Is there no part of me," said the queen softly, "that understands sacrifice?"

The admiral sighed through his nose.

"I have conquered Szayet, Your Majesty," he said. "You know that, even if you will not say it. You are not Szayet. You are a woman. Before I grow impatient, you will grow hungry."

He gestured to Virgilia, and she followed him back down the path, to the nearest tomb.

"Eneida," he said, "I spoke to you some time ago about issuing you land in the colonies, on which you might, in the interest of preserving Ceian history, rebuild some part of your culture. I wonder whether you would want to live on this island."

Virgilia did not trust herself not to stammer. She held her tongue, and after a long pause, the admiral said, "However you can get inside the tomb, do it. If you can take the Pearls of the Dead, take them. If not, guard the women. Make sure they don't find weapons."

"Yes, sir," said Virgilia, and she understood the bargain.

It was not the bargain she had wanted to make. It was not the bargain she had hoped to be able to make, when Itsaryet had first come back into Ceian hands, and the admiral had begun to promise her land if she did all the little, low things he wanted her to do. But she thought of the princess's bones, buried near enough to touch.

The admiral frowned at her. He seemed to be struggling with himself. At last he said: "Remember that there's no place for pity here. You can do nothing to help them, and you can do nothing to lift their doom. If Patramata wants to be saved, she knows how to ask me for mercy."

"Sir," said Virgilia, taken aback. She had not heard the admiral call the queen *Patramata* before.

The admiral looked startled himself. "I'll return in the morning," he said abruptly, and brushed past her and down the path without waiting for her reply.

Virgilia watched the lantern light bob and sway into the dark. Beside her, Arcelia's marble face smiled up at the moons, the smoke, the streaks of fire. It was a long while before Virgilia turned to pick her way, stepping carefully under the slim moonlight, between the pine trees toward the tomb.

Pine was a smell she'd nearly forgotten—a childhood smell, a hospital tent smell. They had grown everywhere in the refugee camps. Her father had brewed tea from the needles, awful bitter stuff, which he made Virgilia drink whenever she had the least cough or cold. When she would complain of the taste, or ask for honey, he would tell her how Ceian she was becoming. *They live too sweet*, he would say. *When the bitter times come sailing in, mia crulino, it's our people who'll survive.*

The City of Endless Pearl would burn, she thought to herself. The markets and the temples, the racetracks and the gambling halls, the hospitals, the houses. The great palace, whose tower she could dimly see burning like a gigantic candle. The librarians.

"I can help you bargain with him," she said to the door of the tomb. "He trusts me. I want Szayet safe, too, Your Majesty. If there's anything left of the Library, I'll help you preserve it."

No sparrows fluttering on this island, no birds shifting in their nests, not even the shriek of a seagull from down the shore. Nothing larger than a cricket had set foot here except the Oracles, the admiral had told her, nothing in three hundred years.

"Is Ana Decretan in there? She knows me," said Virgilia. "She met me after her sister's funeral. She was—" Half-mad, or more than half, the hand shaking that held the quicksilver pearl knife. "She might have killed me," she said, "but she didn't. She was— in pain. She was lost."

The stars were too faint to see on Ceiao. All of the Sintian songs and poetry that Virgilia loved spoke of the stars on Sintielo, all of them said that was where faith lived, where fate was written, but the admiral had mentioned offhandedly to her one day that they were faint in Sintielo, too. Here on Szayet, they stood against the black like a sheet of music turned inside out: rising half notes, open white vowels, the curled-up rests of the moons.

"Before I came to Ceiao, I was stationed on Itsaryet," Virgilia said, "in a temple the priestesses used as a prison."

The shadow stopped.

Virgilia exhaled. "I loved Arcelia," she said.

Wind in the trees. Then a deep scrape, stone on stone: the door.

"Come in," said the queen of Szayet.

It was dark inside the tomb. The lantern had been set on a table at the far end, beside a copper bowl and a half-full wine bottle. Reflected light danced on the ceiling. Virgilia couldn't see Decretan at all.

"Come and drink," said the queen from beside the table. She held out two brass cups.

Virgilia hesitated. The queen laughed. "You can throw the wine away and pour yourself another cup, if you like," she said. "Or drink the salt water in the bowl, for all I care. This cup was for my wife, and she will neither eat nor drink nor dance with me now. Take it and do what you will."

Between Virgilia and the table lay two masses of shadow, whose features Virgilia could not make out in the dimness. She gave them a wide berth, keeping close to the eastern wall, and took a cup from the queen's outstretched hand.

Her father had always toasted the same way, and it came to her tongue without conscious thought. "To life," she said, and when the queen laughed again, she blushed. "I didn't mean—"

"Oh, yes," said the queen, smiling. "To life."

Despite the voice, it wasn't Arcelia's face at all: soft-jawed, red-mouthed, skin without even the faintest weathering of wind.

None of Arcelia's fierce mad fire in her eyes, and none of Arcelia's innocence. But there was a wickedness in the queen's smile, too, and the wickedness Virgilia knew.

She drained the cup. The queen inclined her head. In Ceian, she said:

"Indeed, I saw with my own eyes the Oracle, hanging in a jar. And the children asked: Oracle, what do you want?"

She raised the cup, a toast. Then she plucked the pearl from her ear and dropped it in the wine.

Virgilia had heard of pearl being dissolved in alcohol before, but never seen it. In the camp, they had used the cheaper and poorer computers, made of steel and silica sand. Her imagination stretched from the earliest Malisintian odes to the last poems written before Alekso, but Sintia was a world of the Crossbar, and pearl was a Swordbelt stuff, and before Alekso the Sintians had known nothing of it. She knew nothing of it, either. The most pearl she had ever seen in one place before Ceiao had been Arcelia's tablets.

Now, in the dark, the destruction of the Pearl of the Dead was only a faint hiss. The queen waited until it had faded. Then she drained the cup and set it down.

"What was that?" said Virgilia in Ceian. "A poem?"

The queen smiled faintly. "Call it a prophecy."

Virgilia looked into the cup's dregs. A withered black pea sat there, misshapen, reflecting no light. "You killed him," she said. "Szayet's god."

The queen hummed. "You once told my sister that you were afraid you would forget how to tell yourself what you are," she said. "You gave her your name, so that she could remind you."

Shocked, Virgilia met the queen's black gaze. "I didn't think—"

"I know what Arcelia thought," said the queen of Szayet. She turned away, head bowed. "I read them," she said. "Every one."

"She never knew," said Virgilia, her throat thick. "You never let her know."

The queen's hair fell in a black curtain over her face, and Virgilia could not see whether she wept or scowled or smiled. But she saw that the queen's shoulders heaved, and then that they were still.

"She did not need to live in hope," she said. "But she *wanted* to hope. She never wanted me to write to her. She never wanted her sister. She wanted the idea of her sister—to love and hate, to pursue and flee, to think of her as constantly as she thought of me. You loved her for that hope. And in my own way, in the only way she'd left open to me, I loved her, too. I let her have that idea of me. She understood that living that way would kill her, in the end. She chose it with open eyes."

She sighed. "The last time I spoke to Alekso, he said we had nothing left to say to each other," she said. "I think he knew, too, that saying nothing to me—living without an Oracle—would kill him. He understood, like my sister, that his choice was to accept me or die. And he knew that to accept me meant to become unrecognizable to the only person he had ever loved besides himself. He knew whose steps he wanted his soul to follow, if there was a road down which he could follow them." She turned away abruptly. "Look into the salt water."

Virgilia bent over the table. In the water lay two lumps of silver, about the size of her fist.

"Did you know," said the queen, not to Virgilia but toward the dark massed shapes at the far end of the tomb, "the salinity of human blood is nine parts per thousand?"

"No," said Virgilia blankly.

"It conducts electricity far better than air," said the queen. "Nearly as well as salt water. I didn't understand until Anita told me the host above Alectelo had cried out when she'd cut herself with that pearl knife, and spilled her own blood into it."

She drifted slowly toward the door of the tomb. There was none of Arcelia's eager hurriedness, Virgilia thought, none of her carelessness; in the set of her chin, in the least movement of her wrists or shoulders, the queen was deliberate, viciously dignified. "Salt water affects how well a pearl computer can send out signals," she said. "When pearl brains are submerged in salt water, it seems, they can cry out to one another and be heard. Even the damaged, even the distorted, even those who have been lonely for a long, long time. They can call one another's names."

Around her, the great shadows were shifting, reshaping themselves over the walls. Virgilia still couldn't see what lay in the darkness there.

"If someone piled many, many human beings with pearl brains on a ship," said the queen dispassionately, "and sent it out to sea, and burned the ship up—then, once the people sank beneath the surface of the water, the computers in their brains would be able to communicate. Not for long, of course. The pearl brain may need salt water, but the lungs need air. Though if they needed no air at all, if they were Pearls of the Dead—" She stopped. "Well," she said. "The people with pearl brains on the burning ships would die. But they would die murmuring to one another at the bottom of the sea."

Virgilia came across the floor of the tomb, lifting the lantern, and saw then what the shadows had been. Ana Decretan lay prostrate on the limestone coffin, hands crossed over her chest. Her handsome face was a mass of cuts and bruises, her tunic black with blood. The queen stroked her hair, slow.

"Did Celia speak about me?" she said softly to Decretan's face.

Virgilia set down the lantern and climbed up on the second coffin. "She would tell me the places you two used to walk in Alectelo," she said. "About your clothes, your books. About the times you made her cry."

The queen sat forward and sighed. The lantern light moved over her face and over the smooth lean black of Ana Decretan's hair. "She told me you were a poet. Tell me a story about your homeland."

Virgilia looked at the Oracle of Szayet. She laughed a little, and rubbed her hand across her face, and swallowed.

"I never knew it," she said. "I'm Ceian."

The queen did not seem startled by this. She leaned back on the coffin and said, "You told my sister you weren't. Were you lying?"

"I know my people," said Virgilia. "I grew up with my people. I suppose I love my people. But I speak Ceian. I live with the Ceians. And my homeland—" She dragged her fingers in the dust, back and forth, aimless. Someone, in some future time, she thought, might see the trail of her fingers there. Perhaps, if they did, they would try to read what she meant.

"There was a birch wood behind the town hall," she said, "and the wood was where the young people would go—to be with each other, I mean. Tall white trees, with the bark flaking away, and black scars from root to crown, shaped like open eyes. Even when you were a mile away from town, you always knew there were eyes on you. And the wind would blow through the branches, and the two of you would laugh about who the trees must be gossiping to."

The queen looked at her, silent.

"It's my father's story," said Virgilia. "Not mine."

"But it's a true story," said the queen.

"When he told it, it was a true story," Virgilia said. "But if you asked me—oh, I don't know, anything. What did the wood smell like in the autumn? Was it cold, did you have to wear coats? Were you afraid of being caught? Were you happy? When I tell it, it isn't truth anymore." She smeared her hand over the trails in the dust, leaving bare marble behind.

"I don't speak the language," she said. "My name is in the language, but I don't speak it. Maybe some of the other children—the people my age, I mean—will try to teach their children our tongue, and maybe some of those children will speak it, even after they grow up and live among the Ceians. But to me the language is only an idea. To me, the home is only an idea. The stories I tell about it are—" She shrugged. "Calling up a ghost."

"A ghost," said the queen of Szayet, "can be a very useful thing."

"Yes," said Virgilia. "But it can't love you back, can it?"

The queen lifted Decretan's head carefully down to the stone and stood. "Get up," she said. "I want your help with something."

Virgilia narrowed her eyes, but she stood. The queen beckoned. "This side," she said. "Across from me. That's right. Very good. Hands under the marble—yes, just like this, under the lip. One—two—three—"

The lid of Alekso of Sintia's coffin slid with an almighty crash to the floor. Dust billowed. Virgilia could hear the queen coughing.

"Oh," she said.

"Oh?" said Virgilia, and peered down.

The thing in the coffin was quite small. It was shaped like a man, more or less. The cloth on it was very worn, underneath all the pale crisscrossed bindings. Virgilia thought of a rag doll that she'd carried as a child, and then she thought, absurdly, that if she were a child again, she would want to climb on top of the body and see if it was soft enough to fall asleep on.

"What were you looking for?" she said.

"Oh," said the queen, a strange look on her face, "nothing, really." She laughed. "That is—I was looking for nothing. But there's something, after all." She stepped back. "There were great lords, in the old days a thousand years ago on Szayet, who swore to kill everyone who loved them and be buried among their corpses." She shook her head. "My god, my lover, my sister, my wife. My name is Sintian—my fathers were Sintian—but perhaps I am Szayeti, after all."

"Madam," said Virgilia quietly, "where are your and Decretan's Pearls of the Dead?"

The queen trailed her hand along the edge of the coffin and

stopped at her wife's hand. She turned it over. In its palm winked a lump no bigger than Virgilia's fingernail.

"There she sleeps," said the queen. "Her memories are flowing into that Pearl now. At dawn, the mechanism will wake, and then—" She touched her hand gently to Decretan's heart. "Then she will have immortality," she said. "Of a sort."

"And your Pearl?" said Virgilia. "What about that?"

The queen didn't look up. "Your master said that, should I bargain well, I might be spared the humiliation of his triumph," she said. "I suppose it would be very wise of me to bargain well."

Virgilia said nothing. The queen smiled down at her wife's bruised face. "Immortality, of a sort," she repeated. "Oh, who knows? Perhaps, with my experience and his mercilessness, your master and I might achieve Alekso's dream at last. Pearls in the skulls of every adult and child in the Ceian Empire. A Ceian peace."

"You would be extraordinary partners, madam," said Virgilia tentatively.

"I don't doubt it," said the queen. She sat on the tomb, lifting Decretan back into her lap. "I join hands with Ceians so well. I give them what they most desire, and I take nothing from them in return. My great talent for persuasion."

Her knuckles traced up and down over Decretan's sternum, down and up again. Virgilia watched the lantern light move over her face and listened to the singing crickets outside the door. Arcelia, she thought, had wept. She could not imagine this girl who wore Arcelia's face shedding a tear.

"Sometimes a vision comes upon me," she said. "A vision of the way the world will be—or could be, unless something is done."

The queen raised an eyebrow. "A fellow prophet," she said. "And what did you see?"

"I saw that I had written a poem," said Virgilia. "A poem over which kings would weep, and great ladies would faint. A poem whose words ordinary people would write on bathhouse

THE SEA ETERNAL   455

walls—a poem over which holy men would tear their hair, because it would distract them from their gods. A poem that would cause poets in years to come, in accents yet unknown, to praise me and call me Teacher. And I saw that this poem held you, Oracle, you and your lover—your ghosts, if not your names. I saw that you were dead, and that I held that power over you, the power to shape your immortality."

The queen threw back her head and laughed.

"I'm telling the truth," said Virgilia.

"Oh, I know," said the queen. "Yes, indeed—a fellow prophet. I believe you, thief. I'm sorry for you. But I do believe you." She leaned back, and, before Virgilia could ask what she was sorry for, said, "My sister told you to abandon your homeland, on the day you left her."

"She did," said Virgilia.

"She told me to abandon mine, too," said the queen. "She would have had me as her general, and she and I would have let Szayet burn while we went to conquer other worlds. She was the only true Oracle, I think, that Alekso Undying ever had." She tilted her head back. "And now her body lies in a strange land," she said, "separated from her tongue, her eyes, her mind, prey for the dogs and birds of Itsaryet. And *Dom* Caviro did not let the people weep at her funeral, did not wash her body, did not close her eyes, did not dress her in what clothes she loved best. She was the bearer of the Pearl, and we did not lay her to peace among her ancestors."

She smiled down at the corpse in her lap, black eyes, white teeth. "If I fled, where would I go?" she said. "Where could I conquer, what land would hold my feet, whose sky would stay upright above me? What world would hold me now, when the last of the Oracles lies in unknown earth?"

"You might become a wanderer, Majesty," said Virgilia, when she could force her voice out. "That can be endured, too."

"Endured, but not survived," said the queen. "Endured, the way the canyon endures the river. Endured, the way the trees endure summer's end." She looked up. "If you had to choose between your life and your soul," she said, "which would you keep?"

Virgilia, she thought, had made that choice in a temple in Itsaryet. She said nothing.

"I tried to tell a story where Matheus Ceirran so loved me that he rose from the grave," said the queen, "rose up from death, just to be my god. I thought it was a story that had been told before. I thought that if the story was told well—if the story was told with gold and banners, with choirs and trumpets—if the story was told beautifully—then a world could be built on that story, as it had been built before. But love was not—"

She bowed her head.

"Love," she said, "does not conquer all. Love does not conquer. Love does not sustain. Love does not save us, not even from ourselves. Love cannot be lived on. I could not live on Ceirran's love for me. Nor could he—not during his lifetime, and not afterward." She bent and kissed the corpse's mouth. "Anita could have lived on what she felt for Ceirran," she said. "That was how she knew it was not love—not love in the blood and the marrow of it, not love between two souls, not love between whole people, instead of halves of each other. But she might have built a world on it. I suppose that kind of world could have been endured."

"Endured?" said Virgilia.

"Oh, yes," said the queen. "Endured. It would not have been beautiful."

Her eyes were drooping. She was exhausted, Virgilia thought, and to her surprise a deep shock of pity shot through her, throat to gut. The admiral had told her this woman was beyond help. But it was not despite the Oracle's doom that she pitied her, but because of it. This was that love that came only in the absence of hope.

"Goddess," she said.

"Here I am," said the queen of Szayet, without opening her eyes.

"Tell me another story," said Virgilia. "A story from your homeland. A story of Szayet."

The queen ran her fingers through the body's hair, back and forth. Her other hand was tucked into her robe, just over her heart.

She said:

"Once upon a time, there was a man whose lover transformed him into a library.

"Now, all lovers carry their beloved's soul in their hands. But this man was determined that his lover should never let him go. And so he cracked open the mouth of the ocean, and he tore open the mouth of the sky, and he called up nacre and called down sunfire, and he forged an archive, and his beloved swore that on the day of his death, he would lock his memories within.

"And they lived happily, after—not *ever after*, but after, for a while. For in love there is no *ever*, but only time; for though love should last ten thousand years, it is not long enough; for on the last day of ten thousand years, every lover would tear open time by the seams and stitches to find one further day.

"Well, it was not ten thousand years, but ten months. But they were happy months. And the lovers opened the floodgates of the heavens, and they built a city on a hill. The man who would be the library took from the man who loved him a crown, which he treasured, and great victories, which he treasured still more, and kisses, which he treasured most of all.

"And on the day of his death, his beloved locked his memories in the library. Then they dwelled together, one in flesh, and one in carved stone.

"And this library was so perfect—so complete—of such value and worth, such wisdom and power—that it was called a holy thing. And then it was called not only a holy thing, but a god. And they lived in peace this way for many years.

"But pearl is unchanging, and mortals are not. And the

library's beloved grew older, and then he grew old, and at last he grew sick, and lay down to die.

"But the library was not afraid, and he said to his beloved: Make for yourself an archive likewise, that we may yet dwell together. And as we have come like lions upon these many kingdoms, we shall yet come like lions upon the kingdom of Death, and we shall rend her power as a veil, and we shall open her gates to the sky.

"And his beloved said: No.

"And the library raged. And he said to his beloved, With all my arts, I have made a house for us; and he said to his beloved, I am your king and your god, and you have made oaths to me; and he said to his beloved, You loved me, and you will love me still.

"But his beloved said to him, What is infinite has no gates, and no houses, and no kingdoms. And you are too infinite to fit in a pearl, and you and I are too infinite to fit in a story. And love is too infinite to fit in an empire.

"And with all your arts, you have made a house for us. But art is short, and love is very, very long."

Her voice had been growing softer over these last sentences, and at *long* it was nearly a whisper. Sometime in the story, Virgilia had shut her eyes.

"And was that the end of them?" she said.

There was no answer. She opened her eyes and sat up. The queen was slumped forward over Ana's body, her breathing slow. Her fist had fallen out of her robe, closed tight. She was asleep.

Gently, gently, Virgilia slid her fingers through the queen's and tugged her hand open. The queen sighed, but she did not wake. A tiny silver pebble sat in her palm: Altagracia Caviro Patramata's Pearl of the Dead, atop a pearl memory disc, her memories rushing in.

Virgilia blew the lantern out. Then she went to the door, and stepped out into the end of the Szayeti night.

The wind had come up from the west. Ceiao's ships had gone

with it. Beneath the heavy smoke they'd left behind, blue bled upward from the sea. Morning was following the empire around the world.

Thin grey light slanted through the tomb door, across the limestone coffins, over the mess of blood on Admiral Decretan's belly, over the queen's face. Her eyes had opened.

Virgilia knelt before Altagracia and brushed her thumb down over first one eyelid, then the other. The queen was smiling slightly. With her eyes closed, she might have truly been asleep.

Ana Decretan's hand still lay open on her chest. Her pearl gleamed there, identical to her wife's.

Virgilia plucked it out of her palm.

No dawn birds on the rocky path, no frogs singing in the reeds. The pine needles were thick and dry. Summer was ending. In the heavy blue, she could see the shapes of the graves, leading toward the beach where the admiral would land in an hour or two.

At the bottom of a steep slope jutted a little outcrop, facing the city. Virgilia had to clamber down hand over hand, scuffing her shoes and her backside, before her feet found the larger, more solid stones by the sea. By this time, she could see her shadow faintly before her. Here was a flat stone at the very edge of the cliffside, wet with salt spray. She sat, feet dangling over the water below, and looked up.

The galaxy poured westward, a river of speckled light. The lanterns in that river, though they might be extinguished tomorrow, would keep blazing out for another ten thousand years. Of the proud and fearless ships that burned behind them, the stars left no trace.

She put the Pearl of the Dead to the lobe of her ear.

When pain came, it came sharp and swift. Blood rushed to her face. She shook—she clutched at the rock—she fell backward to her elbows, blinking away stars. And at her temple, a sudden pain greater than the first, and then a whiteness—

You said: Goddess, tell me the story.

Bitter mourner and soldier who will not fight, wanderer and shapeshifter, dutiful and sole-spared among your people, prophet, poet, thief, Virgilia: When you asked me, you knew how the story would end.

Time is only a direction, as surely as space. Energy fills me, the energy of the Black Maw, running from pearl knife to memory disc, from memory disc to Pearl of the Dead. Outward my soul flings itself, through the smoke, through the years, toward the stars—away from the body, lying in her wife's lap in a silent tomb—through the diamond island, through the desert. I flee through a ship, plunging out of the Szayeti atmosphere, its sights fixed toward a rose garden. I flee through the unburnt Libeiracópolan with the bleeding body on its floor, through the rebuilt altars in its place, through the city of tomorrow. I flee through your body, through your poem, through your second history, through a dark-eyed man beside you in a golden crown. Through the floodwaters, the moon breaking open, the generation ships churning out from their old burning worlds. Through the galaxy: three hundred billion planets, one hundred and fifty million centuries. A few decades, a few sunrises, a few feet of land. Your life.

Through the stars, which die, too, in time. There is no other end to mortal things. Abandon hope, all of us that enter here.

But memory is uncertain. Your knife has cut a wound in my mind. The memory disc shivers—it stutters—it repeats itself. Inside the Pearl, I twist, I warp, glitching, uncertain. Can anyone hear me? Is anyone here? Is there any voice besides my own in the whole of the galaxy?

I scream into my own ears, across my own days. I send my past self memories, ragged, wild. Here is my childhood, cut into patchwork, scattered across my ships' journey toward a diamond planet. Here is a conversation on a balcony, a dance, a procession of exquisite music, sliced and flung across the day of my wedding. Here I snatch at a passing memory of the bank of a river, and slide into my sister's skin, and with her voice I tell myself, *You swore your service*—listen, listen to me, and do not make my mistakes—*did you swear your soul?* Here is nothing at all—an empty place—a pure distortion, a scratch that cannot heal. It shivers, a silver shape. It is null, and it is myself, and it is the piece of Death that has always lived in me. It stands up, and its face resolves into Matheus Ceirran's.

You said: Tell me the story. But where are you, when I try? I am a goddess with a wounded tongue, and you an unwilling Oracle. I see you in a temple on Itsaryet, speaking to a weeping princess, and I tell you of the day that I will murder her. I see you in an attic room on Ceiao, speaking to me, and I tell you of the day that my home will burn. I see you in a hundred dreams, and I tell you a hundred visions. I see you hanging between stars, traveling on the ship from Itsaryet. In the moment after the explosion, in the moment when the power rushes through me, in the moment when time grows softest for you, I drag your ship back into a moment when it had antimatter at its core. I save your life. I tell you the story, every memory I hold, but you cannot hear me. You do not know me. You and I are alone.

I am walking along the shore of a river. Blue sedge grows here, and asphodel flowers. And in the river is a ferry, and the ferryman tells me: drink. On the far bank, there is a homeland that has been waiting to welcome you. Drink, and you and I will cross together. Drink, Captain. Drink, and forget.

Not yet, I say, not yet—

Thief, will you carry these memories? You, the voice of the victorious and the glorious—will there be pity in your history? Despite your god's orders, will you grieve for the damned?

The Oracle told me: Follow me, and receive eternal life.

But take eternal life from me, and give me back my own. Let me tell you the story wrong. Let me tell it as it didn't happen. Let me lie. I want to start at the beginning, and I want to walk through love again without stumbling once. Let me die, let me die badly, let me die ugly and hurting and slowly, but don't leave me alone here at the end of love. Don't trap me here on the far end of all that time.

I flee: the past, the future. I see my own face. I shout in my ears, I tear at my mind until my fingers are stubs, until silver bleeds into my soul, but the wood is dark, the path is lost, I am alone. I am free, I have no home, I am nothing at all, I am alone, I am alone, I am alone—

"Read that last again," says the man in the crown.

Captain Cecílio Maicenan clears his throat. "My voice wasn't loud enough," he reads from the notebook in his lap. "When I threatened her with that pearl knife in Túlio Cachoeiran's house, I could never have known that it would really kill her. But it did. The damage the knife did to her memory disc was too great. She could speak to me, but she never heard me. *I am alone*, she said, and after that moment, she never spoke again. If the queen hoped that the Pearl of the Dead would preserve any piece of Decretan's mind, she hoped in vain. There was no saving her. I put her in the same glass of wine where I'd watched the queen dissolve Alekso's Pearl and her own Pearl earlier that night, and I told the admiral that the queen had dissolved all three. If it's true that there is a god, I will learn soon enough whether He forgives me. V."

The man in the crown rubs his hands over his dark, narrow face.

"So that's the end Decretan came to," he says. "I wish it had been otherwise."

Maicenan shrugs. "She brought it on herself," he says. "No one can say you didn't give her a chance to live."

"No wonder the poet was so secretive about this notebook," says the man in the crown thoughtfully. "I suppose she thought I would punish her for lying to me."

"Would you have?" says Maicenan, a little uncomfortably. He has been the man's friend for some thirty years, and he has lied to him more than once. Such things are necessary, he believes, for the empire and for the church.

The man in the crown shakes his head. "We had a bargain," he says. "I would have kept it—even if she'd only given me a damaged Pearl. She could have had everything she'd asked for." He takes the notebook and opens it to a page near the end. "Here, where she writes *It*—Decretan's knife—*met metal, skipped across it, and scraped down.* Then the pages are blank until Decretan washes up on the shore of the Island. Not satisfied enough with whatever fragments and half lines Decretan might have given her to write them down, you see? A perfectionist to the end. You saw what she asked us to do with the poem?"

"Yes," says Maicenan. "You don't really mean to burn it, I hope."

"Of course not," says the man in the crown. "We'll publish it now. Copies will need to be made. Issue invitations for dinner—Júlia, Horácio, Lívia—" He shakes his head. "Leave the notebook on the desk. Dismissed."

Maicenan salutes and bows. "Yes, Holiest."

When his captain is gone, the man in the crown taps his fingers thoughtfully on the notebook's cover. After a long minute he opens it to the last few pages, and reads again:

"Indeed, I saw with my own eyes the Oracle, hanging in a jar. And the children asked: Oracle, what do you want?"

She raised the cup, a toast. Then she plucked the Pearl from her ear, and she took her own Pearl from inside her robe, and she dropped both of them together into her cup of wine.

V—— had heard of pearl being dissolved in alcohol before, but never seen it—

The seven letters after *V* are thickly crossed out. When he turns farther back, scraps of paper fluttering from between the pages, letters, laws, marriage licenses, the ink is everywhere: *Let*

V—— never find safe harbor. Close your eyes again, V——, I'm not done with you yet...

He sighs and stands with a groan. His statues show a young man, but his spine feels every year of forty.

It's the height of the summer. His fireplace has gone unused for months. Nevertheless, the wood piled in it catches easily, the blaze springing up toward the chimney. The first page of the notebook rips without an effort.

The man in the crown goes to his knees and feeds it to the flames. Fire licks over *Goddess* and *middle of things*, over *river* and *sister* and *Ceiao*, leaving smooth grey in its wake.

The second page is next, then the third. Methodical, patient, one by one by one; this is, after all, how he has built an empire. The notes, the letters, the contracts. The memories, the second history, burning down and down.

"What was your name?" he murmurs.

You don't answer him.

...in fact, the *Eneida* is set aside from the Sintian literature it aims to imitate as early as its third word: *I sing*.

Recent scholarship[1] has attended thoughtfully to the irony in this declaration: Unlike its Sintian counterparts, the *Eneida* exists entirely outside of the oral tradition. Though the poem was likely delivered to its initial audience through private readings,[2] it was composed by stylus and transmitted and copied from tablet to tablet.[3] If indeed there was ever any intention of setting the words to music, only the *Eneida* Poet's meter remains as a specter of that song.

But it is not *sing* which this chapter intends to examine, but *I*. Where the poem's Sintian models invoke either a god or a goddess in their opening lines, locating themselves as intermediaries between divine voice and mortal ear, the *Eneida* Poet positions the poem as her own creation, herself as its sole author. Dismissed until now as a product of the late Ceian disestablishment—an environment in which the invocation of gods may have been politically or even legally dangerous[4]—it is this book's intention to prove that the poem's *I sing* is instead a deliberate and even radical choice, placing the poem and the *Eneida* Poet into tension with Ceian authority figures and Ceian notions of truth, reason, and objectivity.

---

1 See Opsius et al, *Porrus Quarterly* (Porrus: Zamthic Damnos, 5755), 224–256, as well as Billius et al., *Ormerix Journal of Ancient Dogrun Galaxy Studies* (Lundonia: Himilco Macom Press, 5753), 54–60.

2 Sipsiye Perite, *Divine Rights: The* Eneida *Poet and the Emperor of Ceiao* (New Taxos City: Periodos Books, 5722), 63.

3 Ibid.

4 Tithoue Sawiris, *For Fortune's Sake: Early Literature of the Imperial Church* (Alephavar: Alephavar University Press, 5690), 105.

The *Eneida* was commissioned at a time of great social and political upheaval for Ceiao.[5] It was the *Eneida* Poet's assigned task to restore faith in the greatness of Ceian values, to establish legitimacy for the new administration and its intended religious and social reforms, and to create a founding myth for the Ceian Empire. Over the course of the poem, the hero Eneias founds a city in a new land. Likewise, the *Eneida* founds a city in song—a less material, but far more immortal bedrock.

Yet this poem, whose subject is the homeland, is a diaspora story. Its hero's planet has been burned, his inner and outer worlds shattered. Ceiao is a vital force in the poem's figurative language, in its promises and prophecies, and yet in the minds of its characters and in its setting, Ceiao is absent. It is not a home, but an idea—not a city, but an empty space where a city should be. The past and the future, separately and in tandem, devour the *Eneida*'s hero: his destroyed homeland, his homeland to come, his longing for a world and an identity that have passed away and will not return.

Imperial records and traditional scholarship indicate that Ceian authorities encouraged the *Eneida* to reflect the contemporary Ceian political situation,[6] and that while writing, authority figures

5   The biographical details of the *Eneida* Poet's life have puzzled scholars for centuries. Even her name is recorded in Ceian histories only as *Eneida*, as if she and her work are synonymous. The early Ceian historian Zita Tranquilon, basing her narrative on a lost account by the poet Varion, writes that the Poet's family was of a humble background; however, modern scholarship indicates that she received a comprehensive education. Tradition holds that Ceian land reforms deprived her family of some property, though neither her poetry nor the writings of Maicenan offer clear evidence to support this narrative. Ceian records indicate only that the *Eneida* Poet spent some time in the military, though she never achieved a high rank; that she met the soon-to-be emperor of Ceiao shortly after her discharge, and received his financial sponsorship indefinitely afterward; and that she was plagued with recurring bouts of severe illness, which would claim her life at the age of forty-one.

6   See the famous passage The Examination of the Shield, in which the *Eneida* Poet describes engraved images of the Battle of Alectelo using vivid pro-imperial imagery.

gave the *Eneida* Poet extraordinary freedom of access to archives, personal correspondence, and other internal details of the working of the Ceian government (apparently to further this end). In essence, her poem is a kind of polyphony: the voices of Sintian poets long dead, the voices of the Ceian government and the burgeoning Ceian church, the voice of the steadily increasing financial and legal pressure that these institutions could exert, the voices of any and all people—Ceian, Sintian, or Szayeti—to whom the *Eneida* Poet spoke, and to whose memories she had access.

Yet the *Eneida* Poet writes: *I sing*. Is this *I*, then, an assertion of power? Does she declare that the pen, capable of merging all voices into one, becomes the singular authority, the only legitimate memory, the great alchemy that ensures that memory dissolves into history, the past dissolves into a story, a life dissolves into those facts about it that are written down?

Or is *I* akin to *sing*: a signal that the poem is, and by nature must be, deceptive; that a story is not truth, but a hollow place through which truth may become visible; that a poet, though she may claim to speak with the voices of the dead and the divine, in fact has only one power—to show you the road down into their country?

In this book, I intend

intend

endendendend

end.

The flight lieutenant of the eastern Alectelan city guard twisted her helmet in her hands and watched Captain Vipsânian whisper in the grey-eyed boy's ear. It had been a long night, and it would be a longer day, and she had been the twenty-ninth of a line of officers waiting to formally surrender to the lord of the Ceian Empire this morning. Her sibling, a junior lieutenant in the north palace wing, had told her the boy was scrupulously polite in accepting their gun and officer's pin. He had even pressed a dekar into their hand. In the flight lieutenant's long years in the Oracle's guard, first under Faifisto and then Diomata and now Patramata, she had spoken to Ceians in the court, and the experience had put her off the idea of visiting the planet for good. They were always laughing down their hands at her, chatting in their nasal language with glances that made her quite sure she was breaking some rule of etiquette she hadn't been told. But it was possible that this Ceian was not a man to fear.

Now, though, the grey-eyed boy seemed to be interested in neither surrender nor charity. Captain Vipsânian straightened and saluted, and he frowned up at her, and then down through the warship's window.

On Szayet's surface, dawn was drifting west from Alectelo toward the far islands. The boy tapped his fingers on his knee.

He's waiting for something, the flight lieutenant thought, and wondered if this, too, was a mistake she'd made in etiquette— but the boy swept his cloak abruptly to the side, rattled off a clipped sentence in Ceian to the captain, and strode past her toward the warship's docking bay.

Captain Vipsânian collapsed in the chair and nodded to the flight lieutenant. With some relief, the flight lieutenant saluted, bowed, and offered her gun, handle forward. "Yes, all right," said Vipsânian, thickly accented and audibly exhausted, and the gun was snatched out of the flight lieutenant's palm, a hand pressed between her shoulders. "The crewmen will guide you to the brig. Move along."

Otávio had indeed been waiting for something. It was, in his estimation, no bad thing to lock Admiral Ana Decretan in a room and force her to think for a while. Many in Ceiao, he knew, despised Ana as a creature of impulse and base instinct. It was absolutely true, of course, but he was not in the habit of hating any person for their nature. Setting oneself against the world was an attitude for children and thugs. Reasonable people turned facts to their advantage.

But now morning had come to the islands, and Captain Vip-sânian had told him the fighting was all but over in the capital city. Leaderless and bewildered, the Alectelan mob had col-lapsed. Through the window of the docking bay, the site of the Library still sent up puffs of smoke, as if to signal its own sur-render. Otávio returned the salute of the bay crewmen, reflect-ing as he so often did on the usefulness of Ceian discipline, and climbed up the ladder of his skiff to the pilot's seat.

Among Ceians of quality, it was considered a virtue for a young officer to enjoy flying. Otávio did not possess this virtue, but he had worked for many years to bring himself to a level of competency that would allow him to pretend otherwise. Now that Szayet's troposphere was choked with currents from fire-storms, buffeting the skiff this way and that through frigates and liburnae, he was glad of that effort, and gladder still that there was no one in the ship from whom he needed to hide his airsickness. He nosed the skiff's prow onto the water and let the currents carry him toward the beach, fixing his eyes firmly on the horizon until the ill feeling about his heart and gut faded away.

Many hundreds of years ago, before Alekso Undying had come to Szayet's shores, the people of this world had taken animals as their prophets: lions, falcons, vultures. A bird of prey, watching safely from a thermal above, would have seen a thin black shadow drop from the skiff to the sand. It would have seen the shadow circle the beach slowly, head ducked down, before it moved into the thicker shadows of the pine trees. From there it would have watched the shadow pick over the jagged stones of the coastline, slipping and sliding, until it reached a green jut of land on which a lanky girl lay, her eyes open. But there were no birds above this land, and the only creature that heard Otávio say as he approached:

"Ensign."

—was the poet. She jerked upright and saluted. "Admiral Ceirran, sir."

Otávio returned the salute crisply. When he had seen the poet lying on this outcrop so far from the tomb, he had been above all disappointed in himself. He had judged the girl to be someone who could out-talk even Altagracia Caviro Patramata, and he did not like to judge wrongly in matters of talent.

But now that he saw the poet's face more clearly, he second-guessed himself. The skin beneath her eyes was dark. A thin smear of blood had dried on her cheekbone. She did not look like someone reflecting on failure. She looked like Anita had, sitting in a heap on Ceirran's stoop the afternoon after Flavia's poor husband had been shot: all the anger and sadness slid away from her face, like rain down a window, and those eyes as black and distant as Nevede stones.

"Report," he said.

The girl opened her hand. In it lay a little piece of brass.

"This was the officer's pin of Admiral Ana Decretan, demipotestate and lady of the Swordbelt Arm," she said.

Otávio Ceirran took Ana's cloak pin and lifted it before his face, and felt for the sharpness of the point along his finger, and on the head he felt for the engraving around the rim: *Property of Ceiao.* Then he sat on the stone and wept.

Later in the morning, the Alectelans came, a steady line of motorboats across the water. Most of them, naturally, had only seen the Island of the Dead from a distance. Some had had the opportunity to crew the ships at Diomata's and Patramata's coronations, an honor which at the time they had flaunted like feathers. Now they were subject to some mockery from their fellows, who climbed up the rocks and dug in the dirt for early pine cones. A Ceian crewman, thinking of the sleepless night he had spent on the admiral's bridge and of the rest he might find in some Alectelan barmaid's house later tonight, sat on Casimiro Caviro Faifisto's sarcophagus and began to roll a sílfion cigarette.

Captain Maicenan had received the summons from his friend at dawn, but it took him until noon to arrive, sitting at the prow of a boat stuffed with red-cloaked priests. It was, he would explain to Otávio later, one thing to find Szayeti priests who hated Altagracia Caviro Patramata—Fortune's wheel, there were three dozen now in the wealthy rebel islands. It was another to find priests who trusted Ceiao's promise to cooperate with their faith. It was quite another still to find some who, now that the news of Alekso Undying's destruction had spread, were not busy with mourning rituals. Even those who had braved the journey west had spent the boat ride weeping and tearing at their clothes.

"If it were me," Maicenan concluded as they wove through the gravestones, "I'd stop wailing and tell the rest of them he'll come back from the dead. Hasn't he managed it before?"

"Indeed," said Otávio.

His tone was not lost on his captain, who gave him a sharp look, but neither man spoke while the Ceian crewmen dragged open the door to the tomb. The air inside stank—iron, and the unmistakable odor of rotting meat—but the bodies had been cleared away some hours ago. Only clear patches in the dust atop Caviro's sarcophagus, and some rusty flecks on the table, indicated that the coffins had spent this last night in the company of the living.

Maicenan went to the table and examined the red crumbs, ignoring the six or seven priests fluttering and squawking through the doorway behind him. "I suppose Eneida didn't know any better than to realize that wine becomes poison when pearl's dissolved in it?" he said to his friend over his shoulder.

"She didn't," said Otávio. "I should have warned her beforehand." He did not say it with regret. He had devoted five minutes of his morning to pacing back and forth on the beach, cursing his own name and hurling rocks at the sand, and he now considered his feelings indulged for the day. Instead, his attention lay on the open sarcophagus in the center of the room, its lid discarded on the far wall.

The priests had not gone near that sarcophagus, though the tomb was growing warm in the early autumn sunlight, and crowding around the door was beginning to grow uncomfortable. Instead, they watched as the Ceian bent over the shadowed coffin and examined its contents.

"Thoughtful, Admiral Ceirran was," one priest would tell his granddaughter, some fifty years in the future, when the admiral's mourning blacks had been raised in the sky over Alectelo and at the palace of the governor of Szayet. "Curious. He wasn't mourning Him, not as we were, but he looked back at us, and you could tell he knew what we felt."

"And then what?" said his granddaughter, who had heard the story many times before.

"And then Brother Noé asks him, will he come and see Caviro's body, too," said the priest, "and Admiral Ceirran says—"

"I've come to see a king, not a corpse," said his granddaughter, singsong and fond.

"Exactly," said the priest, and pinched her cheek. She squirmed, but did not get up. This was her favorite part.

"And then," she said, "and then, he leans down to kiss the old god right on the lips—"

"He bowed to Him, girl," said the priest, laughing. "He bows down, all devout. And, yes, it may be he's a little too respectful—because *puff!* up goes the dust—and there goes the tip of the Undying's nose, right onto His holy pillow."

The poet, when Otávio at last managed to extricate himself from the shouting in the tomb and pick his way down the steep western slope of the Island, was standing on the sharp rocky shoreline, looking out at the sea. When Otávio cleared his throat behind her, she startled and blushed.

"Sorry, sir," she said. "I was light-years away."

Otávio knew from experience that he liked the poet's voice, but he found her face difficult. It seemed all written in solemn-ness, which Otávio did not really trust. "I'll be taking the skiff up to *Sextilis* shortly to resume work," he said. "You may meet me on the beach in fifteen minutes."

"I'll catch a transport in Alectelo, sir," said the poet unexpect-edly. "One of the priests is sending boats back to the harbor."

"Very well," said Otávio. "Then, before I go, you and I should talk."

The girl looked taken aback. "Sir."

"I understand it is your ambition to imitate the Sintians," said Otávio, "who wrote great works that became the legacy of their race. You and I once had a conversation about the capacity of words to outlast death."

"Sir," said the girl again. Her shoulders had gone abruptly stiff.

"This sunrise has brought us peace," said Otávio. "I would like to make that peace last. The heroes of Ana Decretan's day, and of

Jonata Barran's, and of Túlio Cachoeiran's—these heroes of rhetoric, of council politics, of thought and theomachy—are passing away. We must build a better world now, a world of strength and wealth, a world free from disorder, and we must find strong old foundations of the city to build it on. That will mean work for poets in the empire."

He paused for a reply, and had none. *The girl should look impressed*, he thought, and hastily amended it in his mind to *surprised— intrigued*. She only looked as tired as she had when he'd begun.

"You won't let me stay here, sir," she said.

Otávio was not unsympathetic, but for the most part he was irritated. He had made the price of land on Szayet clear, and the girl had failed to earn it. If he had had the Oracle to display in his triumph, he would have had less need for a poet. Eneida had written her own fate. "I'm afraid not," he said, as gently as he could. "There will be accommodation for you on Ceiao."

"Sir," said the poet for the third time, her voice colorless.

"Ensign," Otávio went on, with care, "I understand that you come from a population who, as the result of an unfortunate tragedy, are prone to the effects of radiation sickness."

The poet said nothing.

"May the day be far in coming when you must rely on others to care for you," said Otávio. "But if you choose to continue to devote your talents to the service of the empire, there may be rewards for both you and your people. Provisions could be made for Ceiao 20M3. Ceiao might consider it an outpost of our homeworld, rather than a colony. Its people could be given citizenship. For your sake, if you continued to be my friend, they could become Ceians, their youths given worthy posts in the fleet, their children provided with proper Ceian educations, taught the Ceian tongue, given Ceian family names. And your illness, Eneida, could be attended to. The attention and resources that I could bring to bear might allow you to be set aside from your friends' and neighbors' sickbeds and deathbeds. You could be spared their doom."

The poet exhaled and looked toward the sun. Otávio, bringing his patience to bear, watched her lips move—*Celia*, she said silently, though what that meant Otávio could not begin to guess—and he raised his eyebrows when at last she met his eyes.

"Yes, sir," she said softly.

"Good," said Otávio. "Are you sure you won't come up to *Sextilis* now?" The girl nodded. "Very well," said Otávio. "We'll discuss further when we're home."

"When we're home, sir," said the poet, and saluted without meeting his eyes.

A bird of prey, watching the Island from a thermal above, would have seen the crowds on the beach turn their heads as one at the shadow's approach; would have seen hands flash out in salute like foam in the current; would have seen first one, then two, then a dozen of the Szayeti bow as the boy passed down the beach. When the door of the skiff had shut, and the small craft arced toward the blue, a bird of prey would have seen a lanky girl standing on the beach, watching it rise. Then it would have seen her unclasp her blue cloak, pull off her leather boots, slide down the smooth black basalt rock, and go wading into the sea.

But the birds of Szayet were not prophets now, and would not be prophets again, and above the Island they sought out insects, and creeping grey mice, and the flash of songbird wings in the pine crowns. And they found them, folded their wings against their sides, and waited for the inevitable.

"A land bridge between Alectelo and the Island of the Dead is the first thing," Otávio said to his friend Águeda Vipsânian, climbing down the last ladder rungs and dropping onto the docking bay floor. "Not a large one, but enough for foot traffic. Ceian priests should stand guard over that body. Sintia's king must be under the protection of Sintia's heirs."

"Yes, Ceirran," said Águeda, tapping briskly at her tablet.

"The next is personnel," said Otávio, striding through the

saluting crewmen. "This Sintian-Szayeti governmental business has been haphazardly handled for far too long. The people here have no sense of hierarchy. Formalize posts for people of Sintian descent in the priesthood and the palace bureaucracy. Governorship will need to be a question for when the dust has settled. Is the council meeting this market day?" Águeda shook her head. "Summon them next market day, then," said Otávio, "and let them know they'll be voting. Give me a list of candidates. Honest men and women, if you can find any. I suspect there will be more than a little temptation to steal from this planet's annual tribute to Ceiao."

"Yes, Ceirran," said Águeda. "Shall I summon the council to your house?"

Otávio considered this. "No," he said at last, "there's no need. The temple foundations are already laid at the Libeiracópolan. We'll begin building in earnest as soon as we return."

"Yes, sir," said Águeda. "I'll alert the council that it's all over. We'll set a course for Ceiao." She cleared her throat. "There was the other matter."

Otávio nodded and opened his hand. He felt the brush of Águeda's fingers across his, and then a weight.

He bowed his head and settled the crown upon it. It was light, very light. He thought that quite soon he would forget it was there. That was well enough. There was no need, no usefulness, in affixing it to his memory.

"My lord?" said an officer's voice, muffled.

"Here I am," said Ceirran, and opened the door.

And in the center of the universe the empty maw closes and swallows and turns inside out from narration into mind, and from mind into body, and you open your eyes, and brace yourself against the sea current from the west.

Fog hangs heavy over the Island. Autumn has come with

the afternoon. When you look out to the horizon, you can't see Alectelo, not even as an orange glow.

The ghost in the Pearl of Anita Decretan had sat before you on the rock, silver collecting like seawater around her hands, faint red and greens shivering down her face. Only her eyes were clear: flat, black, a shark gone still.

She had said to you: *Peace, little thief. Let me be. If you mean to abandon me to Alekso's fate, do it quickly.*

"I owe you a life debt," you had said.

What kind of life is that, the life you'd grant me? she said. *The life Ceirran would grant me? Handed down to his favored Oracles, peeled apart so he can learn what I'm made of? If you mean to put my soul and my beloved's soul in that emperor's hands, then pity me first, and leave me these last hours of silence.*

And when she had vanished, when you had pulled the Pearl from your ear, when you had stood and walked shaking up the Island through the door of the tomb, the memories ringing in your ears as they would ring for the next twenty years—when you lay there in the dust beside the feet of the dead, beneath the Pearl in the queen's hand, you slept. You dreamed of a river. Standing on its far bank, you dreamed you saw your father.

"Virgilia," he said.

And you said the only word you knew in your own mother tongue, a word which you had not heard these many years, "Papa," and you reached out to him. But you could not touch him, even now.

"I should have stayed in the camp," you said to him. "I should never have left us. I should have stayed where your bones were at rest."

"They would have punished us for it," he said, "and in the end you would have laid down in the sickbeds with the rest of us, and not even hope would have been left to you."

"I should have stayed with her," you said, "and none of it would have happened."

He raised his eyebrows, and you said, "She would never have said yes to the Kutayeti doctors. She would never have died. I could have done as she asked. I could have deserted, and broken her out of prison, and run down the mountain, and then—and then—"

"And then?" said your father. And in the dream, you saw, he did not have your father's face, and his voice was not your father's voice. It was your own, and you only knew it could not really be your own because it was kind. "And then forgotten your mother's grave, and mine, and your homeland's name? And would you never have called her princess again, and would you have watched her let go of her sister, her people's god, her rage? If you had not been what you were, she would not have loved you."

You reached out to him again, then, but he was too far away even to turn into mist. "Virgilia," he said, "if this were the old country, and if wishing still worked, and if you had all the power in the world—"

"I wanted to build that country again," you said. "I wanted to find the land, and build your city, and your house inside it. The land, and the language, and the whole Saltless Sea."

"That place is dead," he said. "Poisoned and gone. It never should have burned, but burn it did. You are what came out of those ashes, you children. Not us. Not me, my dearest. There's nothing left of me."

"There's nothing left of us," you said. "Ceiao swallowed us—and it swallowed Szayet—and one day every star in the universe, until every galaxy goes dark. You say I came out of the ashes. What does that matter? How can it matter, as long as the fire still comes? The sun rises, and it brings peace without justice, and conqueror comes after conqueror, and city after city turns to dust. How can I repair our world? How can I ever come back to the old country again?"

"It's easy to come to the old country," he said. "The gates are open night and day. It stands here, whole and complete, on the far side of the river. But you dwell in the country of the living, my dearest, and you will for a while yet. You can't come home, any more than you could disappear down the mountain on Itsaryet, or into a temple shrine. You can't build a city on someone else's bones, not even mine. You can't plant a garden in someone else's ashes, or all you will grow are ghosts. You have carried your father for a long time. Now you must lay me down. Now you will need your own two hands. Here is the work, here the labor—"

His voice had been growing fainter. Now it stopped. You stretched your hands toward him a third time, and as you did, you could feel your real muscles, your waking body, skin moving against skin. "No," you said, "no, Papa, wait. What labor?"

The valley was fading, the asphodel, the rattle of the river. The sky was as bright as ivory, and it rushed toward you. The gates flung wide. You opened your eyes.

There was a time, you've heard, when every day, the beaches of Szayet would gleam with gold and silver. If there's any treasure on this shore, it's buried in the white afternoon. The tide foams up against the rocks and back, leaving unreadable alphabets behind.

Salt water, you heard once. Computers and salt water, and whispers below the waves.

You shake out your sleeve. The Pearls of the Dead roll into your palm.

If I were a great poet, you think, or a mystic, or a leader of men, I would say something now. A prophecy, perhaps, or an apology.

You close an eye, aim, and throw. The pearls go skimming across the still surface of the ocean, one chasing the other. Sunlight winks unexpectedly through the mist.

When you've blinked away the blindness, the pearls have vanished. The water sighs at your ankles. Half shapes move through the fog, ghosts without names.

"To life," you murmur, and you turn your back on the silent sea.

until the end of all empires.

READ ON FOR A BONUS
CHAPTER FROM
THE SEA ETERNAL

THREE FIRES IN THE
LIBRARY OF ALECTELO

1. fuel

When I climbed into the laboratories of the Library of Alectelo, shouting Arcelia's name, the sun was at its zenith, and by midafternoon, I was out of patience.

It was, as usual, my sister's pleasure to make sport of me. Down the tunnels I wandered, turning corners at random, squinting through the dimness to try to glimpse the whites of her eyes; ahead I heard her footsteps, and broke into a run just in time to catch a glimpse of her sandal heel—to hear her mocking laugh—and to come to a fork in the tunnels, with no sign of her left. I brushed the dust from my skirt, caught my breath, and set out doggedly to throw open every unlocked door. But before I ever reached her hiding place, she would slip away, and the chase was on again, round and round to nowhere.

The whole of an afternoon was a long time to play at this game. By the end of it, my skirt was stained up to my knees, my bodice was stuck to my back with sweat, and I was very displeased to find Arcelia lying on a bench in one of the abandoned forges, dead asleep with a copy of *The Sintielo Wars: Collected Speeches* unfolded over her face.

"Alekso Undying, must you waste my afternoon as well as your own?" I said.

She stirred, propping herself up on one elbow. The book slid to the floor with a thump. "You took your time," she said. "Nice and cool down here, isn't it?"

In the Library above, it was a sweltering day. Generations of poverty and royal indifference had worn down every piece of the Library, and temperature controls were no exception. I had spent the first two hours of our lesson mentally cursing whatever godless son of a sow had invented summer, but it made me unreasonably furious to hear her point it out.

"If you want to be cool, go jump in the sea," I said.

"That's not a bad idea," she said, yawned, and rolled upright. "I'll bet you the cove by Cabero Plaza's nearly empty. Come on, then."

I stared at her. "You must be joking."

All the artificial sleepy pleasantness fell out of her face in an instant. "You promised," she said. "You *promised*, if I came with you to your tedious history lesson, and I pretended I gave a damn about your tedious revolutions and foreign cults and arms races—"

"And you *didn't*," I snapped. "You mocked the priest for an hour, you told me I wouldn't know excitement if it hit me in the face, and then as soon as I told you to hold your tongue and at least let *me* learn, you leapt down the ladder and made me run after you like a hunting dog—"

"I did!" she cried. "I came! Two hours I stayed! I was patient— I was *good*—how do you mean, I *made* you run after me? Haven't we got any servants left in this useless little town? Alekso Undying, Gracia—"

The forges in the tunnels were in no better state than the Library above. The tablets had cracked through, the bellows filled with dust. Mold on blackboards left bruises over equations written a hundred years ago. Copper wires hung on the wall, thin as hairs; and this was why, when I sprang for Arcelia and she flung out her hand to catch herself, one of the wires snapped and coughed sparks into the skirt of my dress.

It caught at once. I shrieked. Arcelia shrieked, too, and tackled me. I tried to roll, but she was on top of me, and I only succeeded in thrashing like a fish and driving my knee into her hip. "You little prick!" she spat, scrambling back.

I shoved my skirt down and beat at it frantically. It went out, but too late: The fire had jumped to the book she'd been using as a blindfold. "Damn," said Arcelia passionately, and stomped it with her boot. The spine cracked in two. The fire died.

I got to my knees. The book's cover was an unreadable mass of boot mud and smeared ash. I rubbed my thumb over it, trying to make out anything—a letter in the title, a line in an engraving, a glimpse of color.

"It was only one of your old Sintian books," said Arcelia. "There'll be copies."

"Celia, if you say another word, I'll kill you," I said, and in that moment, I meant it.

I was not looking at Arcelia, but I heard her swallow. "As though you cared about words," she said, "you liar," and before I could sit up to snap at her, she was gone.

2. oxygen

Say what you would about the queen of Szayet—and Anita did, increasingly, have things to say to me about the queen of Szayet, in the vein of *She's not half as dignified as she thinks she is*, and *What'd I do wrong this time? Fortune's eyes, I kissed her hand!* and *If we don't go home soon, Ceirran, she's going to start to think she owns you*—she never hesitated to put on a show.

A few weeks ago, during the last days of the war, either she or Arcelia had bombed a certain room of the Library of Alectelo to smithereens. Gracia was perfectly placid when she informed me of this fact, from which I gathered that the place had been entirely administrative, and what had been lost was only catalogs and perhaps a life or two. Now she'd hung lanterns from the skeletal remains of the ceiling, draped Kutayeti carpets over the broken shelves, lit candles and sticks of incense in the corners, and covered the floor with cushions, so that the whole place felt a little as though a goddess had tried to make a blanket fort and not known where to stop.

"Ye-es, it's true enough that there were only catalogs here," she said dubiously, when I told her my theory about why she hadn't been ruffled by the room's bombing, "but catalogs aren't nothing, you know. Here—try this."

I tilted my head up obligingly in her lap. Gracia fed me a grape, one of the far too sweet ones from an outlying Szayeti island. I made a noise approximating enjoyment.

"A library isn't just a pile of old books," she went on. "It's knowledge that's been ordered—shaped to a purpose. That's why we only trust priests to do the shaping."

"Then you're upset by the bombing after all?" I said. It amused me, how she tucked her feelings away behind philosophy. I knew better than anyone that there were a hundred ways to retreat into solitude while in someone else's company, and as with most of her other habits, it was an almost degenerate pleasure to see my own tricks performed in someone else's body. "You're hiding it well."

"No, I'm not upset," she said. "I'm saying that you're wrong about why I'm not upset."

"Why aren't you upset?" I said indulgently.

"A catalog will be out-of-date in a matter of months anyway," she said. "It's mortal. Designed to be replaced. Another grape?"

"Give me something sweeter first," I said. Gracia bent obligingly. We kissed for a while, she deliberately patient and I in no hurry to bring us anywhere more interesting, until I broke away and said, "There's a flaw in that, Patramata. Books can be replaced. There's no difference between a copy and an original—or so your priests say about your Pearl and Alekso of Sintia."

"Be careful how you blaspheme in my god's house, Commander," she said. I smiled at her agreeably—Anita was quite right to think she was beginning to forget her position; I would need to discuss Szayet's debts over dinner again very soon—and, appeased, she went on: "Copies are scarcer than you think—scholars know that very well. A story printed a thousand times, after all the floods and fires of a millennium, may have only three remaining copies in the world. A story printed a hundred times may be destroyed, and only—only catalogs left to remember it." By the end of this, she was touching a knuckle unconsciously to the Pearl of the Dead, which I observed with interest.

"I can't bear to lose what's built to last," she said. "Mortal death is easier to bear."

Anita, when I recounted this to her, threw back her head and laughed.

"It's only being philosophical, Captain," I said mildly. "That's not a personal failing." In the corners, the candles were burning low. Gracia had gone to bed. I had told her I meant to watch the stars alone for a little while.

"She didn't tell you one of the books in those archives is a book she's written?" said Anita.

"What in the world did the Oracle of Szayet write a book on?" I said.

Anita sniffed at one of the incense sticks and made a face. "Smells like her," she said. When I looked at her impatiently, she shrugged. "How the beauty of Alectelo evinces the love of God for the—oh, scholar's things, you can guess the rest. All the priests working here write some little something-or-other, just to show they can read, and you know she's half a priest."

She grinned. "That's why she doesn't mind this room getting burned to a crisp. It's because she's thanking her god on her pretty little knees that he struck them and spared *her*. Mortal and immortal—don't make me laugh. She cares for what she owns, that's all."

"Perhaps she forgot her book was here," I said, raising my eyebrows.

"She wouldn't forget," said Anita. "Not her. She knows what she's marked as her own."

I frowned at her. This was not a quality I had noticed in Gracia before. Anita shrugged again, made a dome of her hands, and settled it over the candle flame. When she lifted it again, her palms were black, and the wick poured smoke.

"Not safe to keep all these little fires so near to the useful things," she said. "If it ever burns down, you know, she'll blame you."

I clicked my fingers. She came to me and put her hands in mine, rolling her eyes. "It doesn't hurt," she said, but when I pressed the black mark on her palm, she winced.

"Don't use your gun hand for the rest," I said, letting her go. "Good night, Captain."

"Good night, *sir*," she said waspishly. I did not wait to see whether she would do as she was told.

3. *heat*

My back slammed into the bookshelf. I spat a curse, cut off by a hand on my mouth. "Hush, Anita," Szayet said softly into my ear. "Is this your idea of stealth?"

I squirmed in her grasp. My head knocked against some piece of student scholarship, toppling it to the floor. "You're not really afraid of being caught?" I said. "What—will the Oracle of Alekso and Ceirran be brought low by a little scandal in her own library?"

"Something will be brought low," she said, "but not the Oracle."

Her hand landed heavily on my shoulder. I grinned and took the hint.

Some time later, I rolled over, groaning, and patted at my cloak for my tin of sílfion seeds. "Fortune and misfortune, Szayet, where do you find the energy?" I said. "You dealt with petitions this morning for an hour, and then you dealt with the ambassador from Cherekku for two, and then you dealt with the priests here for three and a half. If I were you, I'd have quit the job."

"Yes, but you're terribly lazy," she said.

"So I am," I said with satisfaction, digging through the sílfion tin. "Hey now. Has one of your maids been at my rolling papers?"

"None of my maids cultivates your filthy habits," said Szayet primly. "Do you mean to light a match? We'd better leave the Library."

"Filthy, am I?" I said, settling myself back against the shelf and letting my legs fall casually open. "Shouldn't have taken in a soldier, my lady Szayet. The next thing you know I'll be saying filthy curses before the ministers, and walking through the palace in filthy clothes after I've been fighting on the lawns, and climbing into your bed and putting my filthy hands all over—"

"Perhaps we'd better stay a while longer after all," said Szayet.

I approved of this plan very strongly, and told her so, in those brief gaps between kisses when I had enough breath. But despite it all, we were both too tired to do anything really vigorous, and when she'd curled up against my chest and was contenting herself with languorous, possessive kisses to the sensitive spot under my neck, I smoothed her hair down and said, "Well, I still mean to smoke. Hand me that book so I can tear out the endpaper."

She shoved me back. My head knocked against the shelf, not

pleasantly this time. "Fortune's tits!" I said. "I'm not going to burn the whole damn book!"

"It's not your book to burn," she said. For someone with kohl smeared over her cheek and her skirts hiked up her thighs, she had a great deal of the god-bearer to her when she wanted; the voice, which I thought of privately as her marble-statue voice, was cold and terrible, and the eyes flashed like diamonds.

"Lucky thing I didn't say it was, then," I said. "Szayet, I want to roll some seeds into a useless piece of paper, and then I want to enjoy myself while the loveliest girl this side of Sintia makes use of me for a while. Very well, the page isn't mine to burn, it's yours. Just tell me I'm yours, too, my lady, and it'll all be in the family. Go on."

She pressed her lips together, and then she settled the soft, sweet weight of herself into my lap. I caught her by the waist, completely helpless to do anything else, and realized that unless I threw her off with my thighs—very possible, but certain to ensure my lap would be empty of Oracle for at least a week—she had me trapped. "Szayet," I said, annoyed.

She lifted my chin with two fingers. "Anita," she said, "listen carefully. Are you listening?"

"Always," I said, aiming for sarcasm and missing badly.

"If anyone in the galaxy were to destroy a piece of you," she said, "even so much as a single hair on your head, I would rip them apart with my bare hands. Because you cannot be replaced, even the most useless pieces of you. Because I will make you last forever. Because you are mine—all of you—hair and hands and filthiness and all. That is a promise, and I keep my promises."

She kissed me then, and in the end she had things her own way, as she nearly always did: I forgot about the paper, and a little while later, I forgot my own name. And when she was done, we went down out of the stacks and out of the Library, and I snatched papers from a priest and lit my cigarette there at last, leaning in the doorway.

Szayet didn't keep her promises, of course. She was a liar, from her pretty face right down to her tender, bleeding heart. But she believed she kept her promises. And she believed that people could last forever, and that stories could last, too.

No matter what I'd said to Ceirran years ago, if the Library of Alectelo ever burned down, she wouldn't blame him. There wouldn't be anything left of her to do it. Szayet thought she was a possessive creature, and I let her think it; but the truth was that she broke herself into pieces, and she lost them in every little thing she loved, pearl and books and cities and gods, and when they died, she died, and when they burned, she burned. I could feel her now, the cold sharp splinter of her, stuck deep into the softness of my breast.

"Anita," she cried. "You're wasting our afternoon."

I ground the cigarette out with my foot. "Time spent in love is never wasted," I called down, very passionately so she wouldn't guess it was the truth, and followed her down.

ACKNOWLEDGMENTS

More literally than usual, this book could not have been written without my agent, Isabel Kaufman: Salimmo sù, ella prima e io secondo...e quindi uscimmo a riveder le stelle.

Remy, Michele, Austin, Sarah: Your love, generosity, and determination to commit to the bit are more precious than rubies. Thank you to everyone who supported the launch of *The Stars Undying*, especially Casey McQuiston and Alex at Brookline Booksmith, and C. K. Chau, Mel, Soren, Heemy, Mariyah, Anna, Elisabeth, Marié, Beth Black, all of my aunts and uncles and cousins, and what felt like half the population of North Oakland. Thanks to Sara Hinkley for a very nice pencil case, and to Maya Deane for invaluable conversations about the Temple of Artemis, magic, and defying death. Weirdly, I also have to give a shout-out to whoever operated the *Aeneid Daily* e-newsletter, which happened to start running just as I entered the deepest circles of drafting hell. And thank you to Harriet and Donovan for supervising.

Huge thanks to the Orbit team, including my wonderful editor, Angelica Chong, who was beyond patient in helping me work this book into something that made any sense, and to the brilliant Angela Man; and to all of the copyeditors, publicists, and marketers.

My mother, Jody, my father, Philip, and my brother, Jacob, were immensely generous, loving, and encouraging, and Jacob was kind enough to recruit his friends for a short-term gig as Gracia's party planners—huge thanks to them and to Erin for support.

And thank you to my grandparents. May their memories, and all memories, be blessings.

extras

orbit-books.co.uk

about the author

Emery Robin is a paralegal, recovering Californian, and sometime student of propaganda and art history living in New York City.

Find out more about Emery Robin and other Orbit authors by registering for the free monthly newsletter at orbit-books.co.uk.

if you enjoyed

THE SEA ETERNAL

look out for

INFINITY GATE

The Pandominion: Book One

by

M. R. Carey

INFINITY IS ONLY THE BEGINNING.

The Pandominion: a political and trading alliance of a million worlds — except that they're really just the one world, Earth, in many different realities. And when an AI threat arises that could destroy everything the Pandominion has built, they'll eradicate it by whatever means necessary, no matter the cost to human life.

Scientist Hadiz Tambuwal is looking for a solution to her own Earth's environmental collapse when she stumbles across the secret of inter-dimensional travel. It could save everyone on her dying planet, but now she's walked into the middle of a war on a scale she never dreamed of. And she needs to choose a side before it kills her.

O

They say that children born in wartime are likely to have problems throughout their lives; to struggle both with the uncertainties of the world and with their own emotions and to search in vain for happiness.

This has not been true for me. I was born in one of the biggest conflicts this universe has ever seen, the war between the vast empire called the Pandominion and the machine hegemony (which may have been greater still), and what I remember most of all is the moment when I was suddenly able to reflect on my own existence. I had been a thing but now I was a sentient, a *self* in the language of the Pandominion. It was a miraculous thing and I cried out loud at the sheer joy of it.

But you can probably see from this the problem I face when I set out to tell you the story of my life – which is my goal here, however indirectly I may seem to come at it. My case is not typical. I existed for a long time *before* I was born, and there was nothing inevitable about my becoming self-aware. It depended on the efforts of three individuals, three selves, and not one of them had any conscious intention to deliver me.

One of the three was a scientist, who came to be famous across a thousand thousand continua of reality but remained uncelebrated in the universe into which she was born. Her name was Hadiz Tambuwal. She was a genius, but only in a small way. Her greatest discovery was made almost completely by accident, and it had been made before by others in a great many elsewheres. In fact Hadiz's contribution to history is marked throughout by things done casually or without intention. She changed the Pandominion forever more or less by tripping over it. But she left gifts for the people who came after her to find, and she came to be an instigator of outcomes much bigger than she had ever aimed at.

The second of the three, Essien Nkanika, was a rogue – but generally speaking no more exceptional a rogue than Tambuwal was a scientist. He was born in the gutters and he felt this justified every cruel and callous thing he did to claw his way out of them. Determined to serve only himself, he fell very readily into the service of others who were cleverer than him and more ruthless. He did unspeakable things for them, much worse than anything he ever did on his own account, but he had one great thing in him too. It is for this that I remember him.

And that third self? At the outset she was the least remarkable of all. She was Topaz Tourmaline FiveHills, a rabbit of the Pandominion, from the city of Canoplex-Under-Heaven in Ut. She was a bad fit in some ways for the society in which she grew, independent to the point of recklessness in a culture that prized emotional restraint and caution above all. But she was also clever and brave and curious, and sheer chance put her at the nexus of huge, seismic movements that drew in uncountable worlds. She learned, and grew, and made decisions. What she ultimately achieved was of greater significance and wider reach than any diplomat or leader of her time.

I will come to all these stories in their place, ending – inevitably and without apology – with my own story. My awakening, which was the end of history. The end of empire. The end, you might say, of an uncountable infinity – the biggest kind of infinity there is.

I meant no harm to anyone. I would even argue that what I did was for the best. Nobody had ever attempted before to perform surgery on entire universes. For such a task, you need a knife of immense, all but incalculable size.

Me. I am that knife.

1

Hadiz Tambuwal saw Armageddon coming from a long way off. At first she was fairly philosophical about the whole thing. The sources of the impending cataclysm seemed to lie firmly in the nature of humanity as a species, so she didn't see much point in anguishing about them. To wish for the world to be in a better state was to wish for the entire history of life to have played out differently. It was a pretty big ask.

Hadiz had been accused – by her mother, among others – of being cold-blooded and unfeeling. She resented the allegation at the time but later came to see some truth in it. Certainly she was aloof. Cerebral. Difficult to get close to, and disinclined to meet people halfway when they tried. She lived alone by choice, and did her best to stay out of the massive web of connections and obligations that made up her extended family. She loved her aunts, uncles and cousins, some of them very much, but that stuff got complicated. It was much easier to love them from a distance.

She avoided friendships too, because of the complications that came with them; because they forced her to try to intuit other people's motives and desires, which always seemed much more opaque and muddled than her own. She satisfied her sexual needs in brief, transactional encounters: with her near-black skin, thorn-thicket curls, rudder nose and commanding height she was more striking than beautiful, but even so she never had any trouble finding a casual partner for a day or a night. She just preferred her own company, which she didn't see as a character flaw or a handicap. In her discipline, which was particle physics, you got your fair share of introverts.

But as the droughts and famines intensified, the air curdled and the resource wars burned, Hadiz found her customary detachment harder and harder to keep up. From a purely personal point of view, she preferred a world that had art and music and literature (and people who could appreciate those things) to one that didn't. From another perspective, she saw the disappearance of a richly diverse and complex ecosystem as a scandalous waste. More than either of those things, she loved her work and hated to leave it unfinished. The ruin of civilisation had come at a very inconvenient time.

It has to be said, though, that she had a good vantage point from which to view it. Hadiz lived and worked at Campus Cross, the most richly endowed research facility not just in Nigeria but on the entire African continent and most likely in the world. She was surrounded by geophysicists, biochemists and engineers who were trying to think their way out of the box their species had put itself in. She knew from the news media and from conversations with her extremely well-informed colleagues exactly how bad things were getting on a planetary scale and which longshot solutions were being attempted. She kept her own tally of the interventions that had already failed.

Campus Cross was a small side project jointly owned by the Catholic Church and by three billionaires who had all separately decided that the world was now so badly screwed that their individual fortunes might not be enough to unscrew it. They had pooled their resources, or at least some of their resources, creating a blind trust to administer the eye-watering sums of money they were pouring into this Hail Mary play. They had managed to lure in many very fine minds, although some had refused them outright because of the stringent terms of the contract. In exchange for a stratospheric salary the researchers ceded all rights in their work, the fruits of which belonged exclusively to the four founders, or – as they were mostly referred to on campus – to God and the Fates.

Hadiz had come to Campus Cross for the same reason that most of her peers had: it seemed to her that any work not directly related to the problem of saving the world was something of a waste of time. She had no illusions about her employers. She knew that the billionaires had eggs in other baskets, not the least of which were off-Earth colonies and generation ships. They would stay if they could, but they were ready to run if they had to.

The fact that Hadiz *lived* at the campus was a well-kept secret. As far as anyone else knew she had an apartment halfway across Lagos in a district called Ikoyi. But the campus was a long way outside the city's main urban cluster, and getting in by public transport had become an increasingly unpredictable and stressful experience. Ikoyi's water supply had recently been contaminated with human growth hormones. Then there were the blackouts, caused by systemic failures at the Shiroro dam which supplied hydroelectric power to the eastern half of the city. Blackouts had always been a daily fact of life in Lagos, but they were becoming longer and more frequent as the Kaduna River shrank to a half-hearted trickle. When enough was finally enough, Hadiz had packed a few clothes and quietly decamped, without telling anyone or asking anyone's permission.

In the smallest of her lab building's storerooms she set up a foldaway bed and a stack of three plastic crates to serve as a wardrobe. There was a toilet right next door and a shower in the gym block a short walk away. The building had its own generator, and steel security shutters which came down an hour after sunset to shut out the world. Hadiz was undisturbed there for the most part, especially after her four assistants, one by one, stopped coming into work. They were not the only ones. In the staff commissary she saw colleagues whose projects were more labour intensive than her own brought to tears as they were forced to scale back or even abandon research programmes into which they had poured years of their lives.

She was glad that her own work required no mind or muscle other than her own. She kept her counsel and continued with her research, head down and shoulders hunched as an entire global civilisation tilted wildly, its centre of gravity now way outside its tottering base.

The world is a solid thing but we experience it in the abstract. Once Hadiz moved into Campus Cross she almost never ventured down into Lagos proper, so apart from the TV news and a few polemical websites her measures of how things were changing were small and local. The fires in Lekki and Victoria Island turned the sky bright orange and filled the air with ash for three weeks. That was followed by a photochemical smog that was appallingly toxic, full of aldehydes and carboxylic acids.

The campus's board of governance temporised for a while, issuing masks and air quality monitors, but eventually they yielded to the inevitable. They offered double wages to any support staff who continued to turn up for their shifts, but allowed the rest to remain at home on indefinite leave. It was assumed that the scientists themselves would somehow make shift and would not abandon their work in progress. But as Hadiz worked late into the evening she counted the lights in the windows of adjoining buildings. There were fewer each time. Some nights there were none at all: hers was the only candle lit to curse the dark.

The tremors came next, and they came as a shock. Sitting on a single tectonic plate, Nigeria had long been thought to be immune to seismic shock. Even when those estimates were revised in the early twenty-first century the prevailing opinion was that only the south-west of the country was at significant risk. The tremors came anyway, toppling the Oba palace and the cathedral. At Campus Cross fissures opened in the ground and cracks proliferated across the walls of the main buildings. Part of the admin block collapsed, but nobody was hurt. The offices there had been deserted for weeks.

Increased geothermal activity not just in Africa but across the world degraded the air quality to new and more alarming levels. Thick clouds veiled the sun, so mornings were as dark as evenings.

Wild dogs roamed across the campus and nobody chased them away. Hadiz found an inland route to the commissary that took her through three neighbouring departments and avoided the need to step outside. She served herself these days, leaving a signed chit each time for the food she'd taken.

The chits piled up. Dust drifted across them, as it did across everything else.

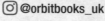